ACKNOWLEDGEMENTS

To Richard and my children, who are the
greatest adventures of my life.

To my parents and siblings, whose belief in me is the
foundation of this book, and all my life's work.

To my beta-readers: Richard, Chris, Mike, Shane, Lisa,
and Jason. Your ideas have made this novel stronger.

And to my editors: Mandi, Heather, and especially
Emma, for helping me bring this novel to life.

And to Helena, who believed in this novel from the first time
she heard about it and gave me the gift of her confidence.

CHAPTER 1

He liked to walk among the bodies in stasis. The translucent pinks and mahoganies of their skin in the half-light of the stasis chambers were a relief to his eyes after days spent in the angular, metallic body of the ship.

At first, after the ship had assigned Ethan to be Caretaker, he had sat on the floor of the corridor outside Aria's chamber and wept. He glanced at his wife now. Her distended belly stretched the fabric of the stasis suit, and he thought of the baby inside, also waiting for awakening. He wondered if it could hear the deep, rhythmic sounds of the ship. Closing his eyes for a moment, he listened to the whoosh of circulating air, the thrum of the stasis system, and, when he listened very closely, the almost imperceptible whir of the SL drive, propelling them farther and farther from home.

Opening his eyes again, he checked Aria's readouts. Everything still looked fine, and she was the last on his rounds. He didn't really need to make the rounds—the computer continuously monitored every vital sign on every passenger—but it gave him something to do during the long days of hurtling through space.

Ethan glanced down the row of stasis chambers. Upright silver capsules, each filled with stasis fluid and a human life. Aria's red hair floated gently in the clear fluid around her, waving with movements of the ship imperceptible to him. He felt the old ache gnawing at him—that need to touch her cheek, to pull her close to him. That had never gone away, even after five years of watching her through the glass. It was still strange to him, having her so close, being aware of everything about her, but still being so far away. He felt that he'd lived a lifetime since she'd closed her eyes. "Computer," he requested, "what is the status of passenger three nine nine nine?"

"Status normal, Mr. Bryant," the simulated voice answered. He had known that from the readouts, but he still liked hearing it. Laying his hand on the glass, he began to sing, softly at first, an old Earth lullaby:

"Soft the drowsy hours are creeping,
Hill and dale in slumber sleeping
I my loved ones' watch am keeping,
All through the night
While the weary world is sleeping
All through the night . . ."

He had taken up singing after about the third month. At first he just sang to his family as he sat in front of their chamber. As time passed, though, he started singing to all of them during his rounds. And he sang to himself in the Caretaker's hold or while he puttered around. He knew he wasn't good, but the sound of a human voice—even if it was his own—was a welcome change from the mechanical voice of the computer and the silence of the ship. Now, as he left Aria, he heard his voice dancing through the cavernous hold.

Ethan left Aria's passenger hold by way of the Caretaker's access door. The corridor directly in front of him lit up as the ship anticipated his journey back to the Caretaker's hold. The passageway was smooth and familiar, with matte silver paneling and black striping that could light up in different colors for help navigating through the ship. He'd once turned the whole ship orange, just to see if it helped alleviate the boredom. It had, for a while.

Despite the familiarity, though, Ethan sensed that something was different. He stopped, glancing around. The panels were the usual silver. The light was pale blue, like a summer sky. Everything in the corridor looked fine. Maybe it was a change in the sound of the ship. He closed his eyes to focus. Suddenly, he realized what it was: the air in the corridor was warm. In all the uninterrupted days on the ship, his living quarters had been maintained at a comfortable sixty-seven degrees Farenheit—the computer's determined perfect temperature for his body. This was the temperature at which he neither sweated nor shivered. Now, though, he felt slightly too warm, and he took several quick steps with the ever-growing feeling that something was wrong.

He walked cautiously, stepping across the six-inch thresholds and running his eyes up and down the corridor before spinning and instinctively heading back to the passenger holds. "Computer," he said as his steps quickened, "what is the status of the ship?"

"Status normal, Mr. Bryant," responded the mechanical voice.

"What is the temperature?"

"Temperature set at seventy-one degrees," the computer responded.

He stopped mid-stride and looked up, though he was no more likely to see the computer there than at his feet. He found that he usually spoke to the computer as if it were taller than him by about a head and standing somewhere to his right.

"Seventy-one? For five years you hold steady at sixty-seven and now you've shifted to seventy-one?"

"Please repeat the question." The computer's voice recognition software could understand the inflection of a question but not his meaning. He would need to restate it more directly.

"What's wrong with the ship?"

"All systems are functioning normally, Mr. Bryant."

"That can't be true! Nothing changes here without a reason." He ran a hand through his hair, pacing the width of the corridor. Changing his tactics, he tried a more specific question: "Computer, what system malfunctions could cause a temperature change?"

The computer rattled off a list of possibilities. It was long.

"Okay. What are the most likely malfunctions in that list?"

"Statistically, there have been far more heating system malfunctions and leaking seals."

"Computer, check the heating system and the seals. What is their status?"

There was a two-breath pause. "All systems are normal, Mr. Bryant."

Ethan swore. That couldn't be true. "I'll check them myself."

He headed for the life support room. Inside, he squinted at the system status panel. In all his trips here, he had never touched anything. Leaving his home planet and settling on Minea had promised to be a difficult experience, but nothing about it scared him as much as this ship. He was paralyzed by the knowledge that the equipment in this room made his existence on this ship possible. Back on Earth he had been a linguist, studying an alien language called Xardn. He'd never been skilled at mechanical tasks.

If he had been, he might have been sent to Minea earlier. The Colonization Committee had sent the experts first, of course. Astronauts and surveyors and planetary scientists to determine the feasibility of sending people to actually live there. After years of analysis, the first farmers and engineers had gone. They'd worked for a decade before the civilization had been ready enough to move in the builders and manufacturers.

And now the families were going. They were leaving their brick and lumber homes on Earth for the hundreds of cottages made from Minea's blue clay. The glossy brochures handed out in the malls and at parades on Earth for the last two years showed rows of neat blue houses with yards in front and gardens in back, free for families who were willing to colonize the new world.

Of course, they mostly needed people who could do things to build the fledgling society. Construction workers, cooks, laborers. Nobody needed a linguist whose specialty was a dead alien language. In fact, nobody really needed him on Earth, either. The linguistic community was busy consolidating all of Earth's languages into a single global language, and though the scraps and specks of Alien languages that had been uncovered in the quest for colonization were mildly intriguing, they weren't important and no serious academic would dedicate time to them. When he had mentioned at the university that he was applying for a spot in Minea, he had received good-natured but patronizing jibes. It was unlikely that the colonization committee would choose him when he had no real use on the new planet.

If he had stayed on Earth, he would have been forced by the university to abandon Xardn and shift his focus. The letter declining his last research proposal had been particularly stinging:

Dear Mr. Bryant,

Though we enjoyed reading your proposal, your request has been denied. The Xardn language, while important historically, holds little value for contemporary society and does not fit well with the University's current twin missions to support industry and colonization. We feel your considerable talents would be better utilized in the area of Standardized Earth Linguistics.

It was not the first time he'd run into the disdain his colleagues had for his work, but it was the most blatant dismissal of it. He'd decided to scrap the project, but Aria fought him.

"Ethan," she had said, "you can't quit your study. You have a gift for Xardn."

"You read the letter. You've heard the comments at parties. What I do isn't important, and no matter how much I love it, it will never be valued."

"Never is a strong word. Trends come and go, and I really believe that there will be a time when your knowledge of Xardn will be vital." He had looked for a trace of insincerity behind her eyes but found none. She really did believe in his work—in him. It was one of the moments when he had fallen in love with her even more.

Now, here on the ship, running his eyes over the readouts and trying to match them to the documents, he felt his uselessness acutely. His knowledge of Xardn did him no good as he searched. Fear pushed its way into his throat. The workings of this ship were a complete mystery to him, and though he had read about it extensively over the last five years, he still felt baffled and helpless in the face of it.

But then he remembered how Aria's eyes shone when he told her about his work. He wished he had her voice to tell him that everything would be okay, that he was strong enough to live his life without her and smart enough to solve this puzzle. Her belief in him then had gotten him through a lot of dark moments on the ship. He didn't know enough about the ship, but he did know a lot about Xardn. How could Xardn help him now?

Pushing his fear aside, he called up the readouts on the heating system. He requested some documentation from the computer about how things in there should look. As he studied them a Xardn symbol came into his mind:

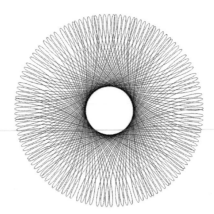

It was the symbol for number. That was something he could do. He took a deep breath and called up the status check directions for the heating system. He began to enter the sequences of numbers that would run the diagnostic checks manually. Though he didn't know how the ship worked, he had long comforted himself with his grasp of all the numbers that connected to his work as Caretaker. Because his life's work was language study, numbers made some sense to him. He found himself going over them now as his fingers ran across the entry pad. This was one of 15 ships that departed from Port 22. There were 4,000 passengers aboard the ship, split into 8 stasis groups of 500. Each stasis group had its own hold. Of the 4,000 passengers aboard the ship, nearly all of them were families except for a small contingent of soldiers, engineers, and doctors who were to be awakened in case of emergency.

Emergencies, like everything else, were determined by the ship. Ethan had realized early on that he and the ship differed greatly in their definition of an emergency.

Ethan and Aria were in Stasis Group 8. Because Aria was pregnant, they had been the last scheduled to enter stasis. Once the ship was en route, the passengers had been split into their stasis groups, and the process of preparing 4,000 people for nearly 53 years of hurtling through space had begun. It was an organized, mechanized process and was completed in less than 24 hours. Only Ethan and Aria were personally attended to. Because of Aria's delicate condition, McNeal, the Caretaker, had determined to put them in stasis personally.

Aria had squeezed Ethan's hand all the way to the sixth deck, where their stasis chambers awaited. He'd kissed her and stood for a moment with his hand on her abdomen until the baby kicked strong enough for him to feel it. Then he'd helped her into the chamber and stepped aside for McNeal to close the door.

Ethan had stood in front of the chamber as Aria's eyelids drooped. He made sure to be the last thing she saw before entering stasis. Once she was asleep, he watched the machine coat her hands, feet, and face—all exposed skin—with the waxy substance that would protect it from the stasis fluid for the next fifty-three years. It made her look porcelain, perfect, and as the chamber filled with fluid, he longed to hold her again. He'd been nearly mad to get to sleep himself before his longing for her grew any stronger.

McNeal had directed him to the final stasis chamber. Ethan had stepped into the chamber. He'd immediately turned around to lean back against the soft upright backing of the chamber. As he turned, he'd seen McNeal through the rounded glass door, slumped against the silver wall outside. Ethan had leaped out of the chamber and braced him up.

Three hours later, in the Caretaker's hold, McNeal had died. The computer assessed that he'd had an aneurysm. By the time his life signs faded completely, the rest of the crew was in stasis. Ethan was the only one left awake, and the computer assigned him to be Caretaker.

He'd had to take McNeal's body to the airlock himself. He'd had to watch as the last person he'd speak to for almost half a century spiraled out into the blackness of space.

Since then he'd read a couple thousand books, bested the computer at the first hundred levels of Chess, and slept through endless days and nights of sorrow. The days on the ship had passed in colors: pink morning light, pale blue days which faded to red sunsets and then to deep purple nights under the artificial lighting of the ship.

The heating system screen made a chiming noise, and Ethan read the instructions the computer had provided: "When manual diagnostic is complete, the following code should be visible on the screen: XRJT3496021r. If code differs, please check troubleshooting chart B in the Appendix."

He cross-checked the numbers and found that the code matched. The heating system was fine.

As he left the heating system room, he should have felt relieved. The discomfort continued to gnaw at him, though. "Computer, bring up the holoscreen." Immediately, it hovered before him, moving with him as he made his way back to the corridor where he had first noticed the temperature shift. "Give me a diagram of all critical seals."

There were three in this corridor, and he moved to the first, a thin white strip around an oblong window. Beyond it, he saw the broad, black nothingness of space, drawn through with pencil-thin strokes of color: the stars between home and Minea. He put his ear close to the window, closing his eyes and listening for a telltale hiss that would indicate atmosphere venting into the outer hull. Nothing.

He straightened and ran his fingers around the seal. A chill ran through him as he thought of how only these thin panels kept the vast darkness outside the ship at bay. Swiftly, he checked the other two seals in the corridor. He could find nothing wrong. But the air was definitely warmer, and he was desperate to find out why.

"Computer—" he started, and then abruptly stopped as a shadow played across the wall in the corridor in front of him. He stood still, frozen by the impossibility of the unexpected movement.

And then, there she was. A slender woman in a stasis suit, her black hair cropped to her jawline. She stopped, too, at the sight of him.

He would later remember the moment in slow motion, seeing her pause there in the corridor, watching her eyes widen as they found his. The pale blue lighting glanced off her hair and her shoulders, which were silver in the stasis suit.

They stood without moving for a long moment. Finally, she spoke.

"Hello," she said cautiously. "I'm Kaia."

Still he stared. He opened his mouth, then took two quick steps toward her. "Where did you come from?"

She smiled then. "I'm—I'm sorry," she stuttered, "I've just awakened. I'm not oriented yet."

"Awakened?" He was nearing panic now. "Why? Are there others awakening? I've got to stop it! We're still forty-eight years away! We'll never make it if they awaken now!" He turned his attention to the computer. "Computer? Computer!"

"Proceed, Mr. Bryant."

"How many have awakened?"

"One, Mr. Bryant."

"Only one?"

"Yes, Mr. Bryant. Passenger 3692, Kaia Raegan. Awakened on Day 2000 at 0836 as scheduled."

"What? As scheduled?" He turned back to the girl. "You were scheduled to awaken?"

At this, she looked shaken. "Could I see the Caretaker, please?"

"I am the Caretaker." His voice was sharp. It had been so long since he'd spoken to another human being. The girl looked scared. "I'm sorry," he started again. "I became the caretaker. I'm not trained for it. It was . . . an accident."

Her voice was shaky. "Where's McNeal?"

"He died. I wasn't in stasis yet, so the computer assigned me Caretaker. Hey—" He moved forward but couldn't catch her before she hit the floor. She was unconscious when he reached her.

CHAPTER 2

Ethan lifted the girl and took her to his cabin. He knew her now: 3692, Yaa Annan. She'd been in their stasis group and had shared the same hold as Aria, though her chamber was near the front of the hold and Aria's was near the back. She looked different now that there was nothing coating her skin and no stasis fluid between them. More vibrant, more alive.

Something didn't add up, though; she'd said her name was Kaia. A nickname, perhaps?

He laid her on the broad white couch and perched himself on the low chest in front of her. "Computer," he barked, "is she in stasis shock?" He remembered reading about the dangers of stasis in the legal disclaimers before the trip. One of the worst was a reaction to awakening which involved the body trying to compensate for the years of sleep. The heart rate increased, blood pressure skyrocketed, and the patient usually died of a massive coronary.

"No," the computer responded.

Ethan didn't wait for the computer to volunteer information like he had when he'd first started to talk to it. One could wait forever and it wouldn't provide answers to questions you didn't ask directly.

"What's wrong with her? Give me her vitals."

The computer rattled off a list of her vital signs. All were at the low range of normal. "She's sleeping, then?" Ethan asked.

"Yes."

"Will she wake up?"

"It appears she is doing so now."

Ethan glanced down. Indeed, the girl's eyelids were fluttering and she began to move her head back and forth. It was then that he noticed how bronzed her skin was. It shocked him to realize, very suddenly, that her body believed that the warm rays of Earth's sun had touched her only hours ago. For years he had shaved in the smooth steel mirror in the hold's lavatory and seen his skin grow more and more pale in spite of the artificial sun lamps in the hold. They may have stimulated his body to produce Vitamin D, but they didn't give him a tan.

As he looked at the smooth brown face, he felt in his chest an intense longing for Earth, for its sun and its breezes, for the taste of salt spray from its oceans, and for the sharp, sweet smell of a hot wildflower meadow from its summer mountains. It would be spring there now, he knew, and the last of winter's grip would be fading from the Western side of the North American continent. He thought of the horses Aria had loved that grazed across the street from their little brick house. This time of year they were shedding their winter coats and they were shaggy and short-legged, making them look more like toys than like the shining, powerful creatures of the summer. And then, in his mind's eye, he saw the little brick house they'd left behind, saw the rosebush and knew it would be unfurling its green leaves and pushing bright buds towards the crisp yellow spot in the sky.

She spoke and stopped his remembering. "I—I'm sorry," she said.

He glanced down into intense gray eyes. "Are you all right?"

"I think so." But she didn't stir more than to look away from him, up at the smooth, shining ceiling. "You said he . . . McNeal . . . he's dead?"

"Yes." He saw her wince at the answer. "You knew him?"

"McNeal and I—" Her voice grew softer. "David and I—" She kept her eyes on the ceiling—"were married the day before departure."

Ethan felt his eyebrows rise. He had read McNeal's biography several times. There was no mention of this girl.

She went on without looking at him, almost as if she were speaking to herself. "David and I met at a base party back on Earth. We went out a few times before things started to get serious. My father is General Reagan, head of the military detachment assigned to this ship. He's in stasis below. Once David was commissioned as a Caretaker, my father put a stop to our relationship. He didn't want me spending my life in a Caretaker's hold. As noble as the military makes the post sound, it is pretty much a life sentence."

She paused, glancing nervously at Ethan as if she had just remembered he was there. "I've never—I never thought I'd ever tell anyone this story." Her eyes were tight with sadness. "David and I didn't see each other for several months. Then two days before we left Earth I ran into him on base." She closed her eyes, remembering. "Seeing him then, I remembered that I loved him." She said it wistfully. "I talked him into this crazy scheme to marry me. The plan was that I'd go into stasis and wake up in time to spend our lives together. We paid off the girl who was supposed to come, the real Passenger 3692."

"Yaa Annan," Ethan said. Mystery solved.

Kaia bobbed her head slightly. "She said she'd been debating staying on Earth to get involved with the democracy movement anyway. We sneaked on board that night and used his access to set my awakening time differently from the others—2,000 days. As soon as I could safely break stasis. My father wouldn't know until we reached Minea, David and I would be together; I didn't see how it could go wrong. It seemed so romantic at the time." She lay very still, not looking at him, and then, all at once, she began to cry.

Ethan was shocked for a moment at the shift from her soft, clear voice to the ragged, splitting sobs. He simply looked at her, seeing for a moment his own face reflected in the glass door of Aria's stasis chamber those first few weeks. He watched, fascinated, as Kaia's eyelids closed and round, shining tears slid out from under them. Her chest heaved and her shoulders pitched as she lay on her back and cried. After a moment, she pulled her hands to her face and her cries were muffled.

It occurred to him that he hadn't heard another person's voice, their breathing, their small sounds, for five long years, and hearing it now was wonderful. Something deep in him remembered the response to human emotion, though, and he moved to sit beside her on the couch. He put his left hand clumsily on her shoulder.

She sat up and leaned into him, sobbing into his chest.

He patted her back awkwardly, his right arm still at his side. Her dark hair smelled like violets, and the stasis suit felt smooth and cool under his hand.

After several minutes, the sobs subsided. She drew away from him and wiped her face with the palms of her hands. Ethan drew away from her, moving back to perch on the trunk, looking at her with concern.

"I don't know your name," she said quietly.

"Ethan. Ethan Bryant."

She nodded, a small, stiff movement, and then stood shakily.

"Take it easy." Ethan stood and moved toward her. She pulled away from his outstretched hand.

"I—I need to be alone." Without another word, the girl left the hold, a gasping sob ringing in her wake.

Ethan moved to the door and watched her walk away, torn between the impulse to follow her and the desire to respect her wishes.

"Computer," he said quietly as she disappeared into a side corridor, "monitor Passenger 3692 and report to me if she is in danger."

The computer agreed and Ethan went back into the hold, shaking his head.

"Kaia?" he said aloud, the strangeness of the name bouncing back to him. He had long known passenger 3692 as Yaa Annan. The computer hadn't known about the switch, and Ethan only knew what the computer told him. In a way it was unsettling to realize that the computer on which everything depended could be mistaken.

Shifting to this new understanding of this passenger required some thought, too. He also had to think what to do next. She couldn't be put back in stasis for a minimum of fourteen days, and even then he'd have to be very sure she was ready. Stasis was a shock to the body, and he wasn't about to gamble with the life of one of his passengers. Not after keeping them alive this long.

At least they had a chamber to put her in. Because of the delicacy of the filters that cleaned the fluid, each stasis chamber could only be used once. Hers would be useless until the ship was refurbished at the spaceport above Minea. For once, Ethan was glad that his desperate attempts to put himself in stasis a few years ago had failed.

In fact, he was, for the first time, glad that all his plans to get out of being Caretaker had failed. He had tried everything: climbing in the chamber and initiating the stasis sequence, refusing to eat until the computer allowed him back into stasis, threatening, cajoling, coercing. None of it had worked. He couldn't stand the thought of being alone for the rest of his life.

His most selfish moment had come when he finally accepted he wasn't going back into stasis. He had not yet read about the 2,000-day stasis threshold and had resolved to awaken his wife so they could at least have some semblance of a life together on the ship. As he had held a hand over the key pad to enter the numbers, he had seen the baby move—slowly, sleepily—in her stomach and known that if he did this, that child would live its life in the sterile confines of the stasis ship. It would have its parents, of course, but no other human relationships until the day it reached Minea—middle aged, with all its youth wasted by his weakness. Ethan saw the child, recognized the great cost it would pay, and didn't care—punched the numbers anyway to welcome his wife back into his arms.

But that day, and every day since, the computer had thwarted his attempt, creating an emergency seal on the chamber that would not be broken until they reached Minea. His desperation to have her near had made her even more distant.

He shook his head to clear the image of his own weakness. "Computer, what is the status of Passenger 3692?"

"Status normal, Mr. Bryant."

"Where is she?"

"Passenger 3692 is travelling Corridor C."

Ethan tried to imagine her grief, tried to envision how it would feel to wake up to find that the person you loved was lost to you. A stab of regret, old and familiar, shot through him: Aria would feel that when she awoke. She would awake to find him changed, their future spent.

He paced, trying to think what to do next. Though he had a hundred questions for her, she needed time alone. He couldn't go after her, and he couldn't stay here doing nothing until she returned. The change had created too much turmoil for him to return to his usual routine.

He crossed the Caretaker's hold and stepped out into the corridor, heading for the passenger holds, where he had always found comfort. When he reached the access doors, Ethan found himself drawn to her stasis chamber. He entered the eighth hold and started down the long aisle. The closer he got, though, the slower he walked. He had so long seen the passengers in their chambers, so long comforted himself with their insulation and peacefulness, that the thought of an empty chamber disquieted him more than he'd expected.

As he neared the end of the row, he could see it. The curved glass front shone transparent where its neighbors shone pink. He stepped closer to it, placing his fingers on the handle.

He was surprised at how industrial it looked, how sterile. He raised a hand to the glass and traced the Xardn symbol for the adjective "empty":

Next to him, chamber 3693 had a warm organic glow, holding the life inside it. The girl's was stark and barren and cold. It chilled him to think of the delicate threshold between sealed and open, between sleeping and waking, between life and death.

It was a threshold he'd often considered over the last five years. Space was so cold, so unforgiving, and the thin walls of the ship were all that kept its vastness at bay. Sometimes, when he felt most acutely its indifferentness, when he was most missing the warm rays of the sun, he let himself remember when he'd met Aria.

He saw her first in a tawny field of ripe wheat. It stood shoulder-height, and Aria's red hair blowing in the wind above it drew his attention like a flag. He remembered stopping, watching her from the edge of the field. Deftly, she broke off the six-inch head of a wheat stalk. She rolled it between her hands quickly, and Ethan saw the chaff of it falling away. He was walking toward her before he knew what he was doing.

She turned a warm gaze to him as he approached. "Hi there," she said, "Thanks for being so careful walking through the stalks."

He nodded. "Could you tell me where the nearest hovercab stop is? I'm on my way to the university, but think I got off the train at the wrong station."

Her eyebrows drew together in concern. "You've come from the train station? That's miles back!"

"I know. I kept thinking I'd stumble onto a cab stop or a—a town, or something."

She laughed a little. "Instead you found a lot of nothing."

"I wouldn't say nothing." He'd started boldly but now he backpedaled. "I mean, these fields are amazing."

She brightened. "Thanks!" she said. "They're mine."

"Yours?"

"Yep. These are the field trials of a new strain of wheat I've been developing. You may not be able to tell, but this wheat has a third more protein than its parent crop."

"You're a crop geneticist?"

She nodded.

"Wow." Ethan knew too little about farming to say anything else.

She didn't seem to mind explaining. "I've isolated a molecular marker that has the potential to make wheat even more nutritionally complete! Do you know how many people could benefit from more protein in their diet?"

Ethan shook his head.

"Millions," she said, grinning. She turned her attention back to the wheat in her hands. Ethan looked and saw huge, round wheat kernels. She cupped her hand and held them carefully. Then she plucked a few up and popped them in her mouth. She offered some to him as she chewed.

Ethan took a few and chewed them.

"Feel how they're a little soft still?" she asked, swallowing.

Ethan nodded.

"That means they're not quite ready to harvest. You want them to crack when you bite them."

"They're delicious, though," Ethan said sincerely. Their rich, nutty flavor reminded him of the sweet dinner rolls his grandmother always baked.

"And because I've crossed them with a hardy strain, this high-protein variety will grow even in substandard soil."

Aria could make anything grow.

CHAPTER 3

When Ethan found his way back to the hold, he expected Kaia to be there. She wasn't. But something about the air had changed, and he suspected that she had been recently. "Computer, has Passenger 3692 been in the Caretaker's hold since I've been gone?"

"Yes, Mr. Bryant."

"Play the footage."

The holoscreen jumped to life and showed the girl entering cautiously and checking throughout the main room and in the bathroom to see if he was there. Then she crossed to the food-producing materializer and summoned a meal. She perched on the couch and wolfed it down hungrily before dropping the tableware into the recycler and beginning to search the room.

Ethan knew what she was looking for. Though she had been here hours ago, he found himself wanting to call out and direct her to it.

She found it, though, in one of the shelves behind the smooth silver wall panels. He was glad, after all, that he had kept it, though at the time he'd wondered if he was crossing a line taking it from a dead man.

He watched the recording until she left the caretaker's hold and then checked in on her location again. She seemed to have gravitated to a spot near the bow of the ship. He wanted to call up the holoscreen and make sure she was all right, but that seemed to be too much invasion of her privacy.

He waited for hours for her to come back. Ethan was used to the silence of the Caretaker's hold, but he felt it more acutely now that he'd heard another voice. He felt a loneliness and a fierce craving for her company that stood in stark contrast against the solitude of the last five years. He didn't know what he would say to her in her grief, but he wanted to see her again.

But she didn't come back. Not that day and not the next. He saw that she had activated materializers in various parts of the ship, so she at least had something to eat, but she didn't return to the Caretaker's hold.

* * *

Three days after her awakening, Ethan convinced himself that he should check on her. He called up the holoscreen and learned her location. He walked down the corridor and found her in an observation alcove: a small recessed part of the corridor that jutted out the side of the ship and offered a stunning view of the stars through its encompassing windows.

The girl was leaning against the window, her forehead resting against the dark of space outside. Her eyes were closed.

"Kaia?" He spoke her name softly, but she jumped anyway and whirled to face him.

"Why are you here?" she barked. The intensity of her voice surprised him. He took an involuntary step backward.

"I—I thought I'd check on you." He answered, stumbling. "Can I do anything for you?"

"I mean, why are you here on the ship? What was your assignment in the contingent? What contribution will you make on Minea?"

Ethan stumbled over his words again. "I'm a linguist."

Her eyes narrowed and she made a scoffing sound, turning back to the window. "There's nothing you can do for me." Her voice was scalding.

Ethan looked at her back, smooth in the stasis suit, aimed squarely at him and so effectively closing the door on further conversation. Her rejection of his concern was a shock. He turned and walked slowly back to the hold.

* * *

When, two days later, Ethan checked with the computer and found she was still in the same place, he decided it was time to stop waiting around for her to be his friend and get back to his routine. She was only going to be around for a couple of weeks, anyway. The rest of the trip would likely be even harder to bear if they became friends and he had to lose her, too.

He called up the ship's status reports and listened to information on all the major systems. Then he headed to the passenger hold to begin his rounds.

He turned the situation over in his mind as he checked each passenger, greeting them silently. It was strange to have another person there, awake and aware after all these years, and not be able to talk to her. And at some point they had to begin making plans to get her back into stasis.

He smiled as he came to passenger 0802. She was a young passenger. Her name was Solange, and her dark hair floated in the stasis fluid, framing her face.

She always had the hint of a smile on her features. He started to sing a little, hoping it would bring her a nice dream as she slumbered.

He sang softly at first and then more vigorously, enjoying the way his voice bounced around in the huge hold as he walked.

"What are you doing now?" The tone was caustic, accusatory. He spun to see Kaia, appearing as if from nowhere.

Ethan stumbled on his words. "I'm—I'm singing."

"What are you doing in the passenger hold?" She took a step towards him.

"Just checking the passengers." Ethan held his clipboard up, pointing to the list of names.

"Checking for what?"

Ethan felt defensive, and an edge crept into his voice. "Checking to make sure they're okay."

She scoffed again. "How would you even know that?"

Ethan started to speak, started to explain that he'd looked at them for over five years and would be able to tell if something was wrong. But the force of her gaze made the explanation die in his throat. He took a deep breath, steadying his nerves. "Kaia," he began carefully, "I know I'm not the kind of Caretaker that David was—"

Her eyes narrowed further. "Not even close. It's like you've had no training at all. Five years and you become this? You don't even act military anymore."

"Oh, I'm not." He answered quickly, seeing that she had assumed he was a military linguist.

"Not military at all? That's impossible. There's a whole contingent that could be awakened who'd have at least some idea of what was going on. Any one of them would make more sense than . . . than you."

Ethan let the insult slide. "Like I said, it was a mistake. I just happened to be awake when McNeal died. Because of the risk of breaking stasis so early, the computer calculated that the most reasonable thing to do was to assign me Caretaker rather than awakening anyone else. I tried to convince it that I wasn't trained. I said the same things you're saying now. But the computer assured me that the Caretaker's job is merely ornamental anyway." He snorted. "The computer has a high opinion of itself." There was a serious undertone in his voice when he added, "It runs everything around here."

"I know," Kaia said, her voice stronger. "I helped design this ship."

Ethan saw a way to shift the conversation away from his obvious inadequacies. "Really?" he asked. "I can't wait to pick your brain, then. I've gone crazy trying to think of ways to coerce the computer to do things."

Behind her sneer, there was the ghost of a smile on her face. "Oh, you can't coerce it. It will calculate the ideal solution to every problem and carry that through."

He saw the moment that the reality dawned on her: the recognition that given the circumstances, the computer would have acted exactly as he'd said. Her antagonism seemed to lessen slightly. She stepped back across the aisle, standing in front of Passenger 0831, a man named Waverly who had been a novelist back on Earth. She drew in a deep breath. Her eyelids fluttered closed for a split second. When she looked at him again she seemed to actually see him for the first time.

"It is an amazing machine. I'm sure that usually that programming is a great advantage," he said.

She nodded, keeping her piercing gray eyes on him.

Ethan tried to think of something light to talk about. "The only thing that isn't ideal is the food." He grimaced.

"What do you mean? There's a 3000 on board. The food should be spectacular." Kaia stood up straighter.

"I don't know, the food just materializes on the little square materializers," he realized suddenly how stupid he must sound. He had no idea what the squares were actually called. "Everything just tastes a little off." He shrugged. "Or, at least, it did at first. After five years eating the ship's cooking, Earth food would probably taste weird. Surely you've noticed it?"

Kaia's brow was furrowed. "I haven't exactly been relishing my meals. I couldn't even tell you what I ate these last few days." She looked away briefly and then focused on him again. "There's probably a nutrient lacking. Let's look it over."

This seemed to give her a purpose, and she turned fluidly away from him, her former shakiness gone. She started down the long walkway between the chambers. Ethan lengthened his own stride to catch up.

Kaia strode confidently through the corridors. Ethan was amazed at her ability to navigate these endless hallways. It had taken him nearly ten months to explore it all, and two years before he stopped asking for the holographic map that floated in front of him when he walked around.

He followed her quick steps until they stopped at the central control room.

"You'll have to access this one." Kaia said, tapping the big steel door.

"Access request two nine six nine," Ethan said. He heard the whine of the bioscan device above them, and the door slid soundlessly open.

The room inside was filled with aisles of matte black cabinets encasing the brain of the ship behind rows of blinking lights.. The room was considerably colder than the rest of the ship, and the roar of the fans discouraged conversation.

Kaia went straight to one of the many blinking panels and flipped down a control keypad. She typed in several sequences of numbers, then laughed.

"What is it?" Ethan shouted over the racket of the fans.

"It's set for David's British tastes!" She called back. "The food's fine; there's just not much seasoning." She laughed again and turned back to the keypad.

Ethan was impressed with her adeptness and the decisive way she worked the machinery. Her hands were small and delicate, yet they worked the keypad and the panels expertly. After a few minutes, she led the way out of the control room and back into the corridor, stopping next to one of the small square stations that had fed Ethan for five years.

"Try something now," she urged, the hint of excitement in her eyes.

"What?"

"Anything. Try anything you like."

"Computer," he said slowly, "give me a . . . bowl of chili."

Kaia smiled faintly. "I suspected you were from the American West."

Ethan took the bowl from the materializer and scooped a big spoonful into his mouth. He'd had the ship's chili before—it was uninspiring. Now, however, the spice of it hit his tongue and throat like acid. He coughed and sputtered, "Milk! Computer, milk!"

The computer hesitated. "More information is needed to process your request."

"*Cow's* milk!" Ethan gasped.

The materializer responded immediately and he gulped the thick, sweet drink.

"What did you do to it?" he asked as the flames in his throat died down.

"You're just not used to it. Try it for a few days, and we'll change it back if you still dislike the seasonings."

Ethan tossed the cup and the rest of the chili in its bowl into the recycler and scowled at her, wiping his streaming eyes. "You're smiling. You enjoy seeing a man swallow fire?"

"Very much," she said. "I haven't seen anything that funny in years."

There was a moment of genuine warmth between them. And then, like a curtain, he saw her grief descend upon her again. Her brows drew together. "I'm—I'm going to go. I hope the food tastes better to you now."

Ethan wiped his face hurriedly as he called to her retreating back. "Kaia, wait."

She stopped and looked back at him.

"I'm sorry that your plans got messed up. I'm sorry that you are going through this, and I'm sorry about David." She made a little gasping sob at the name.

He took a step toward her, moved by her raw emotion. "I know it's not going to change anything, but why don't you come back to the hold? At least you don't have to be alone. Come back there with me and we'll watch a movie. Get our minds off this whole mess."

She looked doubtful, but he could tell she was considering it. "I've already been back to the hold," she said, her right hand moving unconsciously to her left forefinger. He noticed, for the first time, that she was wearing a wide silver ring. David's ring. The one she'd found in the hold on the day she awakened. She spoke hesitantly. "How did you get this?"

Ethan shifted uncomfortably. "I—slipped it off his finger before—" he stopped and changed his words, "at the end." He rushed on, trying to explain an action that had barely made sense to him even when he was doing it. "You see, it was the only thing I saw that was really his own. I—I wanted something of his to make it to Minea. I thought maybe there could be a memorial service there, or, or at least something to show that there was once a man who sacrificed his life for the people on this ship. So they could, I guess, remember him."

He stopped talking. It seemed so heinous now, taking a dead man's wedding ring. Maybe he could have explained it better. She must think he was terribly callous.

But her soft voice broke into his thoughts. "Thank you, Ethan."

He looked up to see gratitude in her eyes. He nodded.

Without saying anything else, Kaia walked toward him, then past him, to the Caretaker's hold.

CHAPTER 4

He followed her. Even after all these years, the ship seemed to Ethan like a foreign country. He lived here, but he didn't understand it. A Xardn word described it best:

It meant stranger, outsider, and also, in some contexts, novice. The ship made him feel like all three.

He realized now that to Kaia it was like an old friend. He saw it in the way she ran her hands along the hallway as she walked, in the way she stopped periodically to pore over various panels, and the way her brow furrowed when she heard a squeak in the doors to the Caretaker's hold.

She seemed to have regained her composure by the time she slipped onto one end of the couch in the hold. Ethan sat on the other. She turned toward him, fixing him with her gaze. "What made you come, Ethan? Why did you want to go to Minea?"

She had a knack for directness. It was a question that Ethan himself had pondered often over the last five years. Still, all he could say was, "At first it was . . . adventure, I guess." He looked down. "I just always wanted to see what was out here. And then when the colonization program started, I thought it was my chance. When I applied, I never thought I'd have a chance because I was doubtful they needed a linguist to build a new society." He laughed a little bitterly. "They didn't even need my research in our old society. I was going to have to shift my focus to something that didn't interest me, and going to Minea became a whole lot more alluring. We were actually shocked when the acceptance letter came."

Kaia looked at him. "We?"

Ethan nodded slowly. "My wife and I. Aria. She's still in stasis."

"I didn't realize—" Kaia started. "I didn't realize you were married."

"Married and about to become a father. You wouldn't have known: my wedding ring is in the cargo hold in a little box with everything else we brought from Earth."

Kaia detected the bitterness in his voice. "You weren't expecting to end up hurtling through space all by yourself, were you?"

Ethan shrugged. "Life is full of surprises." He stood suddenly and walked across the room. "When I first realized that I'd spend my whole life here, I tried to think of it as noble—watching over all of them. The truth is, I'm afraid, that the ship doesn't need me. It runs everything all by itself. Their nourishment, temperature—even navigating to Minea—is all automatic. Even if I could do something, I wouldn't know what to do. As I said, I'm a linguist."

He was pacing, walking a line he had walked nearly every day for more than five years. He had often wondered if the smooth steel floor here would be worn by the end of the voyage. He had a feeling—a fear—that it would not. That nothing on the ship would be any different for his spending his life here.

Kaia watched him, seeming to note his agitation. "The ship's not that complicated. I could teach you about it if you want." When he glanced at her, her gray eyes were fixed on his. "It might make you feel more . . . useful."

"Maybe," he said, "but I thought you just knew about the computer."

"I'm a comprehensive engineer," she said, a hint of pride in her voice. "I know everything on board these ships. I've worked on every system."

Ethan was encouraged. "I'd love to learn more about it. But I warn you, I'm not much of a mechanic."

"I'm sure you could pick it up. Languages have complex structure and work in specific ways. So do the various systems of the ship. In a lot of ways, language is mathematical and so is engineering. So you could say that both our fields started at the same place. What language is your specialty?"

Ethan felt calmer back on familiar ground. He stopped pacing as he answered. "Xardn."

Kaia narrowed her eyes at him. "Are you making that up? I've never heard of it."

He saw that she was teasing him. It made him smile. "Maybe you don't know everything after all," he retorted. "It's a dead alien language."

"A language of dead aliens or a dead language of aliens?"

"Both."

It struck Ethan how nice it was, talking to someone—a real human being—again. Communicating with her was so different from his conversations with the computer. He realized he liked the hesitation in her speech. The way she stopped to think before she spoke. He leaned on the back of the couch as he told her so.

Her expression was puzzled. "You mean I sound like I'm unsure. Like I don't really know what I'm talking about."

"Yes." He saw her expression switch to annoyance and spoke quickly. "Sometimes. I mean that your logic is not always precise, your phrasing is sometimes awkward—"

She was actually mad now. "Well, I'm no linguist, but I take great pride in being very logical and articulate. It's possible that five years of stasis has fogged my brain, but I'm generally very—"

"No, no, Kaia, don't be mad. I just mean that you're not a machine. It's so nice to talk to someone besides the computer. I like the *humanness* of our conversation." He paused to see that he'd assuaged her feelings. "I even like that you get mad. I once tried to make the computer mad. I just ended up feeling like an idiot."

She was smiling now, no doubt enjoying the thought of him insulting the computer. "I suppose I see what you mean."

He went on. "There are a lot of things that I never thought about before I was isolated from all of humanity. We're a pretty complex species. I never really realized it until I spent five years with the computer."

"What else have you discovered about us?" She pulled her knees up to her chest and looked at him intently.

"Well, We're unpredictable, of course. Emotional. Irrational. Much funnier than machines." He shifted from his leaning position and sat back down on the couch. "Because all I know of the computer is a disembodied voice, I've thought a lot about body language. I remember days back on Earth when I'd come home from work and Aria would come out onto the porch. I knew before I even got out of the hovercab when she was happy or upset, whether she'd had a good day or a bad one. I have no idea how to read the computer's analysis or motivations. And the computer doesn't pick up on stuff like that from me, either. I laid on the couch for three days straight once, despondent, and it never asked how I was or what was wrong. I asked it later, and it said that my vital signs were normal, so no action was required."

"That sounds like most men's idea of the perfect companion. Never hassling them about how they feel. Never expecting to give a rundown of the day." She smiled.

"You'd think. It is interesting, though, how the computer's indifference affected me. I found for a while that having no one concerned about me in the least made me pretty reckless. I tried prying into the wiring to see what was there. I tried to get outside a time or two. Then gradually I became the opposite; I became hyper-concerned about myself. I guess I figured that since no one else was going to look out for me, I better do it."

"Makes sense," Kaia said, shifting on the couch.

"I ran the disinfecting sequences six times every day here in the caretaker's hold. I worked out four or five hours a day. I had the computer calculate to the gram what nutrients I needed and ate only foods that satisfied those nutrients. All kinds of neurotic behavior." He laughed. "It was exhausting, though, and I was eventually too lazy to keep up all that effort. It makes me wonder, though, how the situation would affect different people." He leaned forward. "Hey, there's a question I've wondered about: how do they train someone to be a caretaker? How do you prepare someone to be alone for years and years?"

A faraway look crept into Kaia's eyes. Ethan knew she was thinking about McNeal. He felt sorry he had asked.

After a long pause she spoke: "It's called isolation training. David compared it to solitary confinement. Every group of recruits has a bit different experience. He said that for him it started one night near the end of his summer training. They held a big party for all the caretaker candidates. Gradually during the evening they were called out one at a time. He was taken through a maze of corridors with doors along them. He heard the music and laughter of the people at the party getting further and further away, until all he could hear was the buzzing of the lights above and the sound of feet on the floor. They finally opened one of the doors and asked him to wait in a small room. Nobody ever came back for him. He eventually tried the door and found it locked. He said that for all the months he was there, he kept hearing the sound of that party fading behind him."

Ethan thought how similar his own experience had been. Suddenly taken away from the joy and anticipation of his life and secluded here. He knew those echoes.

"Eventually, when the recruits get hungry enough they figure out how to run the 3000 and produce food. When they get cagey enough they learn how to summon the exercise equipment. They learn, through all those processes, how to deal with the computer and how to get what they want from it. They also learn," she paused and looked at him, "how to be alone. They have no idea how long they'll be left there. It could be months or years. Most can't handle it. After weeks or months they crack. Those who don't break down go on to the next stages of training. That's when they learn the practical skills needed to be Caretaker—the mechanics of the ship and how to navigate should a disaster happen, stuff like that."

"That would have been helpful," Ethan mused. "So, what makes the difference? Why do most crack and so very few make it through? What is it?"

Kaia looked away. "David said he thought it was . . . motivation."

"Internal motivation? The 'I can do it no matter what' military variety?"

"Maybe. For some. For others it's making someone proud or, as you said, belief in the nobility of the position."

"I don't think that's true of me. Why didn't I crack?"

"I should think that would be easy enough to see."

Ethan shrugged at her.

"Your family, Ethan. You have a very personal investment in the role of Caretaker. You had to hold together and be sure they make it to Minea."

By the time she finished her sentence, Ethan's mind had filled with the image of Aria, as it had so many times over the last five years. Her red-gold hair, pale skin, and the few freckles across her nose came to him in sharp detail. When he looked back at the small, dark form on the couch, there were tears in his eyes. He felt that was happening a lot lately. Something about reintroducing a human into his life had reignited emotions that he'd had no use for when he was alone with the computer. It was strange, feeling things so deeply now.

"You're right, of course," he said, clearing his throat. "I couldn't have let them down. I . . . can't let them down. Or, at least, that's how I feel. But logically, they probably would make it there anyway. Seriously, Kaia, I do *nothing* on this ship. Why is there a Caretaker anyway?"

She blinked. "You don't know? The Persephone? You didn't watch the footage?"

Ethan shook his head. "There's a lot of footage in the library," he said defensively.

"The Persephone was one of the first ships we sent out. It was an early colony ship with about 600 people on it. It was the third ship on which everyone was in stasis. The other two had been sent to the colony on Copernicus and arrived without any problems."

Kaia shifted again and he noticed how her slim form folded neatly into the corner of the couch. Her lips seemed a little dry as she spoke, and he remembered that she would need special attention to hydration for the first few days after stasis. He stood and walked over to the materializer to get her a cold drink of water.

She raised her eyebrows as he walked away but went on with her story. "About two thirds of the way to Copernicus, something went wrong. The control center on Earth saw the malfunction but was completely powerless to fix it. They determined that a tiny fan had lost power in the central control room, one wire disconnected. If someone had been on board, a quick solder would have fixed it. Instead, as the panel heated, it caused catastrophic failures in the system—" Kaia paused, surprised, as he handed her the water, and she smiled at him before she took a sip.

"Drink it all," he instructed. "You've got to be careful not to get dehydrated."

She smiled again, finishing the glass, and set it on the chest to her left. "Thanks. I didn't realize it, but I needed that."

He sat back down, and she continued.

"The affected panels controlled the circulation of the stasis fluid. The people at the control center watched the footage weeks later, when it made it back to Earth, and had to watch as one after another of the passengers received contaminated fluid and died in stasis. The whole ship was lost. When it landed, every passenger aboard was dead." As she said the last word, Ethan saw a look of pain shoot through her eyes. She closed them, and the delicate muscles around her mouth trembled. Keeping her eyes closed, she was quiet for several long seconds before she spoke in a wavering voice, "One person on board, awake, could have repaired the fan and saved all those people. One Caretaker."

Ethan nodded. The story scared him. He thought of all his passengers, all that fluid being circulated and recirculated every day, the temperature control system that kept them from freezing or boiling, the delicate mixture of substances that kept them sleeping, dreaming of their new home. Such a complicated system, and yet, he knew that if something went wrong, the computer could use him, guide him, to repair it and get them safely to Minea.

"I do want you to teach me about the ship," he said suddenly, the passengers' faces still swirling in his mind. "Not just for something to do, but so that I'll know what to do if something goes wrong. I want to know about all the systems. Will you show me?"

Kaia nodded. "So the Caretaker needs a caretaker?" She smiled a weak smile.

Ethan smiled, too. "Looks like it."

CHAPTER 5

The lights in the Caretaker's hold had dimmed, and Ethan sat on one end of the wide leather couch, gazing at Kaia on the other.

Her eyelids were drooping. Ethan knew he should suggest that she get some sleep, but he couldn't bring himself to end their conversation. Part of him—a very silly part—was afraid that she wouldn't be there when he woke up, was afraid that this whole marvelous conversation was a dream.

"I'm sorry," she said as she yawned for the third time.

"Don't be. You must be exhausted."

She laughed, a sound like crystal glasses clinking together. "Exhausted from sleeping for five years."

He couldn't stop another question from slipping out. "What was it like? Stasis?"

Kaia's brows furrowed. "It wasn't like sleeping, exactly. It was . . . I remember feeling very, very heavy. Like I couldn't move because there were lead blankets covering me. Sometimes I felt like I should wake up, like I had something to do, but as soon as I tried to think what it was, I slipped back into unconsciousness."

"Did you—" He hesitated. "Did you dream?"

"Yes. I dreamed sometimes. Sometimes it was just darkness." Kaia shivered involuntarily.

"It was bad?"

"Awful. I don't ever want to do it again. I thought I'd just fall asleep and then wake up after five years. I guess they can shut the body down but not the brain. I dreamed . . . a lot . . . about David. I felt the anticipation of seeing him again, and this urgency to find him, even when I was unconscious. Five years of longing is—" She stopped. "But then, you know about that."

Ethan felt his stomach twist. Felt the pain that had been ever-present these last five years flood over him again. He swallowed and nodded.

They sat in awkward silence for a few moments, both full of their own loss. From her gray eyes, a few tears escaped. Her small shoulders drew in as she crossed her arms, hugging herself. Suddenly he was overwhelmed with a desire to pull her close and comfort her. The power of it brought his breath up short. He looked away and then stood up and walked a few paces across the oblong room, leaving her with her sorrow.

"We should get to sleep," he said, when he thought his voice was strong enough. "You take the couch. I'll sleep back here." He looked up. "Computer, the massage table, please."

A panel in the ceiling slid open noiselessly, and a long, narrow table descended. "Do you prefer Swedish or Shiatsu, Mr. Bryant?" the computer asked.

"Neither. I only require the table. I will be sleeping here."

"The couch is more suitable for sleeping, Mr. Bryant."

"The couch, computer, is occupied." Ethan shot a weak smile at Kaia.

"The surface area of the couch is well able to handle the mass of two persons of your dimensions," the computer continued.

"That will be all," Ethan said decisively.

The computer fell into silence.

Ethan sat on the edge of the table, facing Kaia. She had curled onto the couch, her knees tucked up to her stomach, her arms still crossed. She looked so frail. He felt awkward and sorry that nothing he could say would heal her anguish.

"You can take a blanket out of the chest there, if you want. The temperature should be perfect, but sometimes a blanket is nice. Makes it feel a little more like home."

"Thanks," Kaia said softly as the lights shut off.

Ethan lay down on his back. The familiar silence of the ship was broken by her muffled sobs.

* * *

The daylight cycle of the ship initiated too soon, and Ethan felt sleep slipping away as the room grew lighter. "Computer," he mumbled, "postpone daylight for one hour."

The room darkened again and he rolled over, pulling the pillow farther under his jaw. His thoughts glided back towards dreams, but a small sound from the other side of the hold jarred him back to consciousness. There were never unexpected noises here.

He squinted through the darkness and saw Kaia slip into the bathroom. The door slid closed behind her. He remembered, with a flash of happiness, that there was someone else in the hold. He sat up, swinging his legs over the edge of the table. There was no going back to sleep now.

He felt the solid floor beneath him, but so many changes after years of monotony made everything feel a little surreal. The comfortable sounds of the ship, the brush of the circulated air on his skin, the dull gleam of the walls, and the bulky shapes of the few pieces of furniture all hummed with new energy now that someone else was sharing the space.

The computer sensed that he was awake and brought up the lights.

Ethan crossed to the materializer and ordered some orange juice, which he drank while trying not to be too impatient.

"Computer," he said, "when Kaia comes out, provide two plates of buttermilk pancakes, butter, and syrup; Dutch bacon; and eggs over-easy. And two glasses of cow's milk." She must be hungry, Ethan thought. He certainly was after their long day yesterday.

"Confirmed, Mr. Bryant," said the computer.

Ethan called up his exercise program as a diversion. A panel slid back in the floor and he stepped onto the pressure-sensitive, moveable pad. The program initiated and he bowed to his opponent: Bruce Lee, a kung fu master from the twenty-first century. The first few blocks were easy—warm-up, really. But soon Lee was whirling and ducking in front of him, and Ethan felt his breath coming hard as he tried to keep up. He broke into a sweat and felt the room cool to compensate. He focused on the simulation, turning as his opponent circled around him, lashing out when he saw the slightest chance to land a blow.

When the bathroom door slid open, it took him a moment to pull his mind back from the workout. Kaia came out and stood watching him. He turned to toss her a wave. While his attention was diverted, holographic Bruce Lee delivered a virtual roundhouse kick.

"Knock out," declared the program. Kung fu music played. "Workout complete." The main lights came up in the hold, and Ethan saw that Kaia was trying to suppress a smile.

"How many years have you had to perfect your fighting style?" She ran a hand through her damp hair.

"Not enough, apparently." Ethan shrugged.

"Your meal is ready," the computer reminded him. He glanced over to see his order steaming on the materializer.

Kaia brightened. "I'm starving." She crossed to scoop the trays up and carry them to the low trunk in front of the couch.

Ethan had barely reached the couch, and she had already begun eating. She glanced up at him as she put another bite in her mouth and closed her eyes. "Delicious," she said.

"Delicious" in Xardn flashed in Ethan's mind:

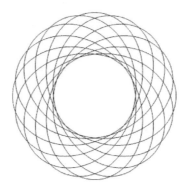

It always looked a little like a donut to him.

Ethan was glad she was eating. It seemed important, considering her recent loss and that she was still recovering from 2,000 days in stasis.

"This is my favorite breakfast," he said, "but the stewed fava beans run a close second."

She glanced up at him, wrinkling her nose slightly. "You chose well—" she began, but the computer cut her off.

"Day 2007 report."

Ethan instinctively quieted and listened.

The computer went on, "Passenger status, Hold One: normal. Passenger status, Hold Two: normal. Passenger status, Hold Three: normal . . ." The computer continued through the remaining passenger holds, the major equipment, and the ship's systems. It finished up, "Calendar items: Ethan Bryant's birthday."

Ethan's eyes widened. He glanced at Kaia. She was looking at him in surprise.

"Your birthday?" she asked incredulously.

He nodded. "I forgot. There's been a lot going on." He smiled sheepishly, but there was a disquiet rising in him. He remembered now.

She smiled at him. "Happy Birthday, Ethan!" She ordered two cupcakes from the materializer. She was grinning as she set one in front of him and started to sing.

He tried to smile. But suddenly the joy was gone from the day.

Kaia noticed and stopped her song. "What's wrong, Ethan?"

He started and then stopped. How to explain? "It's just . . . I'm thirty."

Kaia scoffed. "That's not so old."

"No, I know. But I planned on a very different birthday. I was going to be on Minea. My son would have been five. I would have been *living*." He felt his voice break a little on the last word.

He couldn't stand to sit there. He stood and strode to the wall and then turned and walked to the opposite wall. A bitterness grew in his throat. His words spilled out. "This isn't how it's supposed to be, Kaia. This isn't how I'm supposed to spend my life. Alone. Doing nothing. I know it can't be any other way, but every time I think about the five years I've spent in this hold, every time I think about the forty-eight in front of me, I just—"

Ethan slammed a fist into the wall. The pain of it shooting through his knuckles and the small bones on the back of his hand was both a release and an admonition to calm down. He took a deep breath and leaned against the cool steel. "I just feel so cheated." It felt good to say it aloud.

The hold was quiet. When he finally glanced at Kaia, her eyes were on his. The depth of understanding in them made him immediately grateful to her.

"You know what I mean," he said, softly. It was nice to be able to say how he felt, nice to have someone to hear him, to listen, to *know*.

Her voice was gentle when she responded. "I'm sorry, Ethan. About all of it. I know this isn't the life you chose."

He tried to smile, surprised at how deeply glad he was for her company.

Kaia looked at him for a long moment. A new connection passed between them—an appreciation. Suddenly, Kaia fidgeted and dropped her gaze.

"You said last night that you wished you knew more about the ship. Do you still want to learn?" she said, standing to take her breakfast dishes to the recycler.

Ethan felt weary. He felt drained and a little sorry for himself. But he wanted to be with her, to forget his birthday and all the bitter disappointments of the last five years.

"Yes. Show me."

* * *

It felt wonderful to finally have something to do, something to learn. Ethan spent the day exploring the ship with Kaia, who turned out to be a conscientious teacher. She answered all his questions and had been meticulous in covering all the different systems of the ship. She prepared little tests for him, like turning the artificial gravity on and off and reprogramming the computer to recognize her by her name instead of by her passenger number.

In the faint early light, he opened his eyes with the anticipation he remembered from Christmas mornings. He hadn't felt this way since his childhood. He rolled onto his side and looked across the hold. The blanket on the couch was tossed back, and the room was empty. This only heightened his anticipation.

"Computer," he said, "where is Kaia?"

"Level Three, Mr. Bryant, in the cooling room."

Ethan headed out of the hold.

When the door to the cooling room slid soundlessly open, all Ethan could see of Kaia was her legs. The rest of her was inside the silver paneling about halfway up the wall. He cleared his throat.

"Good morning, sleepyhead," she said without coming out. Her voice sounded more melodic than he remembered it.

"Up early burrowing in the walls, eh?" He leaned against the panel she was in.

"Just checking out the cooling system. Having the stasis fluid at the proper temperature is fairly important to our passengers."

At that, Ethan remembered her story about the Persephone. He felt a pang of anxiety as Aria's sleeping form flashed through his mind. "Is everything okay?"

"Everything looks great," she replied. "Back on Earth, though, we were having some trouble with these bearings. They would wear unevenly and cause fluid to leak from the cooling system, which would then result in the system overheating . . ." Her voice trailed off, and she sat up, pulling her shoulders and head out of the wall. "It looks like we solved it, though. I see no evidence of wear."

She sat in the wall, smiling and dangling her feet. She had a smudge of grease on her left cheekbone. Ethan couldn't help but think she looked childlike.

"So," she said, "Ready for another engineering lesson?"

He looked at her with mock seriousness. "I'm telling you again: I failed physics."

She sighed and shook her head. "I'll try to make it simple. Come here." She waved him over as she leaned back inside the wall. "Look up there. See those tanks? That's where the stasis fluid started out when it was first pumped onto the ship in the docking station back on Earth."

Ethan looked up and tried to focus. He spent the next hour leaning beside her into the wall, asking questions about what he saw there. Then they moved out of the wall and started on the equipment in the cooling room itself.

* * *

As they found their way back to the hold that evening, Kaia said, "Well, you know what I do. Tell me about this dead alien language you know so much about."

"Xardn?" Ethan shrugged. "What would you like to know? Etymology? Vocabulary? History?"

"Yes." Kaia smiled up at him.

He was still adjusting to his responsibility to respond to her facial expressions. He had gone so long without any reason to communicate that way. But this time he remembered and smiled back.

He thought about Xardn, his life's work. "Well, let's start with a little history. We know that there is life out there, but it's mostly beyond our reach. We have bits and pieces of civilizations: a few tools found on Zenepha, some symbols scratched into the rocks of Thelonius, an object here, a painting there, enough to know something about the others who are out there. But we had never found anything significant until about fifty years ago, when we were looking for planets to colonize, and something led a simple cartographer— Zhang Hai—into a cave on a planet called HD 126c where he made the most important linguistic discovery since the Rosetta Stone. The entire cave was filled with records chronicling the rise and fall of the Klaryt civilization. From those records, we were able to decipher Xardn.

"We found that it's historically written and spoken in the Circinus galaxy. As the primary inhabitants of that galaxy, the Klaryt civilization, colonized other galaxies, Xardn grew in use. It became the intergalactic language of commerce, science, religion, and academia. This went on until the Klaryt empire became too huge to control anymore. It fragmented, and Xardn was incorporated into local, cultural languages. We recognize it in the bits of other languages we have, like Trapzn, Ikastn, Chardch—"

He glanced up, suddenly aware that he was getting too technical. "Anyway, many alien languages come from Xardn, and we've connected it to most of the fragments of alien languages we've discovered. However, the records detailed that after the fall of the Klaryts to the Aolians, Xardn fell into disfavor. The Aolians were a brutal race and punished severely anyone foolish enough to use Xardn. That, it is speculated, is when the spoken language died."

She was nodding, taking in the information hungrily.

"We don't really know how it was spoken, though we have guessed at it. The real study lies in the written language. That's all we really have to go on."

"Show me," she said as they reached the door to the hold. "Say something in Xardn."

Ethan smiled. "Mnradak."

Her eyes shone. "I like the way it sounds. What does it mean?"

"It means the generic object. Something. You asked me to say 'something' in Xardn."

She swatted him playfully on the arm. "You knew what I meant!"

"Okay, how about this: grnathrak minscn scth?" He raised his eyebrows expectantly.

"It's a question? You want me to respond?"

"Yes or no."

"Well, I have no idea what you said! Maybe you're asking if I want to run around the ship five times! How do I know what to answer?"

"I asked if you're hungry."

"Then the answer is yes."

"No," he said, "the answer is rnmak. Rnmak is the positive reply."

"Rnmak? Are you making all this up? That sounds weird."

"I told you that the spoken language is just our best guess. I could only vouch for anything I *wrote* to you."

"Well, then, write "yes" and I'll see if it looks like rnmak to me."

"It won't."

"Let's just see."

Ethan rolled his eyes, something he hadn't done in a long time. He stood and walked to the shelves where he kept the few things that were important to him and retrieved a leather-bound book and a brown case a little smaller than the journal. He returned to the couch, and then opened the book to a blank page. Next, he opened the case, revealing his glyphtol, the instrument he used to write Xardn. It was not much larger than a pen, fitted with a series of interlocking wheels. He slid his fingers down the center shaft. It was made with smooth wood and shining metal and had the precision of a surgical tool and the style of a fine musical instrument. He squinted at the small dials near the top of the glyphtol, set them to particular numbers, and then scrawled:

Kaia looked at him. "Are you kidding?" she asked. "That looks nothing like re—ran— whatever you said 'yes' was."

"I told you it wouldn't. You just had to see for yourself." Ethan liked the feeling of knowing something she didn't.

"All right. Let's pretend that that circle does mean yes. How do you get that pronunciation from it?"

"Good question. The symbol is like our letters. There is nothing about the word 'chair' that looks like a chair. We just accept that those symbols stand for the objects and concepts in our world. As for pronunciation, we could go into the whole system, or I could just tell you that we have extrapolated the pronunciation of each symbol from the various pieces of Circinic languages. Based on the remnants of Xardn left in those languages, we can guess at how these things were originally pronounced. But nobody claims that we're absolutely sure."

Kaia looked thoughtful. "So do the symbols correlate to our letters?"

"More to our words. Yes, no, names of animals, people, gods, places, emotions, experiences. They seem to have corresponding symbols. Up until recently, Xenolinguists have spent most of their time cataloguing the words we can decipher from the texts we've found. But that's mostly done now." It felt wonderful to talk about his work again. "The exciting thing about studying Xardn right now is that the real discoveries have yet to be made."

"What was your research?" she asked.

Ethan brightened. "Well," he said, "when my project got shut down I was just about to reveal that I've discovered patterns in the language that everyone has insisted was completely random."

"Wow," she said. "What kind of patterns?"

"Visual patterns—patterns you can see and use to categorize Xardn symbols into the basic parts of language: nouns, verbs, adjectives, all those."

"And no one has seen these patterns yet?"

"They've had their hands full with translation." He sketched another symbol.

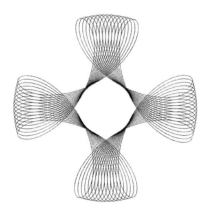

"What's that?" She leaned close to him and ran a finger lightly over the curves on the paper.

"It's the symbol for water. Pop quiz: what part of speech is the word 'water'?"

"A . . . noun?"

Ethan nodded. "It's a trick question, really, because in our language it can be either a noun or a verb. But in Xardn it's only a noun, and this is the noun: water." He tapped the symbol. "And I've discovered that nouns in Xardn have certain characteristics in common."

"What are they? So I can tell when I see a noun."

"Nouns have cusps or curves on the outside edge instead of a perfect circle. They're made with multiple rotations of the glyphtol, so you see lots of lines instead of just a few, and they are symmetrical across the y axis."

Kaia was nodding. "Okay. I can see two of those. I'm still a little unclear on the rotations."

Ethan sketched again.

"Here's a comparison. This is 'brave.' It's created exactly like 'water,' but only a single rotation of the glyphtol. See the difference?"

Kaia's eyes were shining. "I do!" She looked at the page again. "So, what does a sentence look like?"

"That's a little trickier." Ethan sketched again:

Kaia watched the wheels turn as he spun the instrument to inscribe the paper with symbols.

He looked at her. "Any guesses?"

"Well, that one looks kind of like yes, but not really."

"Let's start with the important stuff." Ethan traced the first symbol. "This is the pronoun used for anyone that is not the self: 'you,' essentially." He skipped the second symbol and his finger moved to the third. "This is 'eat' or 'ate' or 'will eat' depending on the time marker—we'll get to that in a minute." He touched the symbol below it. "This is the symbol for the self: 'me' or 'I.' And that time marker I told you about? This one—" He pointed to the last symbol on the second line. "This one happens to be "now." So, can you translate it?"

"You're going to eat me now?" Kaia said doubtfully. "That does sound like an alien language."

Ethan laughed. "Oh, yeah. Prepositions. This symbol—" he pointed to the symbol he had skipped—"is the preposition 'with'. 'You with me.'"

Her eyes lit up. "Oh. Okay, then." She traced the symbols as she spoke: "Will you . . . eat . . . WITH me now?" She immediately looked at him for confirmation. He smiled.

"Perfect! And you even got the interrogative form! Nicely done! Literally, it says: 'You with me eat now?' In translation, I'd probably say, 'Will you have dinner with me?'"

"Absolutely." Kaia said. Ethan set the glyphtol back in its case and offered her his hand. Though he didn't want to, he let go once she was on her feet.

"That's amazing!" she said as they crossed the hold. "What's for dinner?"

"Whatever the materializer can whip up," he said.

She grimaced. "You can't keep calling it that."

"Why not?"

"Because it sounds dumb. It's like calling a refrigerator a 'coldifier.' That's just a made-up word. The 3000 is an Atomic Assembly Unit."

"Now, see, that's why nobody can talk to you people."

"Us people?" She looked at him with raised eyebrows.

"Engineers, tech people in general. You use so much jargon that your language becomes impractical. Nobody is going to walk into an electronics hub and say, 'Pardon me, but do you have the latest Universal Electronics Atomic Assembly Unit?' No couch potato husband is going to call out, 'Hey Baby Doll, grab me a cold one from the Atomic Assembly Unit.' No child is going to gaze up at his mommy and say, 'I wan' a tweet fum da Atomic Assembly Unit.' No—"

"Okay, you can call it whatever you want! Just stop giving me examples!"

"But do you see my point? It's an impractical name. It's too long and too technical for everyday communication. You can't tell me that when you were assembling the ship you said, 'I need to order an—'"

"I said no more examples!" She threw her hands over her ears and started to hum.

Ethan couldn't help but grin. "Okay. No more examples." He pretended to zip his mouth.

They stood staring at each other. Slowly, she lowered her hands. "Can we eat now?"

Ethan gestured at his mouth, mumbled, and then threw his hands up.

"Oh, that's right. The linguist's lips are zipped." She considered a moment. "This could be nice. A little peace and quiet in the hold for a change . . ."

"Mmree mmrrmrng," he said.

"And maybe if you weren't always talking, you would learn a thing or two as well. Like the fact that 'we people' already thought of the little linguistic problem that you were so concerned about, and we shortened the name ourselves. In the trade we call it an AAU. So there. Short, succinct, descriptive, and intelligent-sounding."

"Mmmnhnmgnt hmng," he repeated.

"So there. Maybe I'll just leave your lips zipped." She looked up at him with a hint of a smile. "But, then again . . . the computer isn't that fun to talk to . . . and I don't know all I want to know about this Xardn business . . . and he does occasionally make a good point. I guess I'll unzip his lips and see if he can keep his engineer-bashing under control."

She leaned close to him, reached up, and drew her fingers across his lips. At her touch, his smile froze and the playfulness disappeared from his eyes. Her touch was like fire. Her fingertips lingered at the corner of his mouth for a heartbeat, two, before she pulled her hand back and turned toward the AAU.

Her voice was shaky when she said, "Computer, preprogrammed meal seventeen." A tray appeared. On it was a juicy hamburger, fries, and a chocolate shake.

Ethan was jarred out of his frozen state. "What? Preprogrammed meals? I had no idea! I've been spending five minutes every meal explaining to the computer what I want, how much of it, how I want it cooked! How many are there?"

Kaia spoke over her shoulder. "About 6,000."

"6,000? I could have eaten a different meal every time and not gone through them all!"

"Some of them you wouldn't like much."

His eyes narrowed. "Like what?"

"Hmmm. Like meal number forty six thirty: Supu. It's a Tanzanian dish—like a stew—made with goat lungs, heart, and liver and cow stomach, intestines, and tongue. If you're really lucky, you might also get some of the goat heads, cow hooves, and cow tails in your bowl." She couldn't help but shoot a wrinkle-nosed face at him.

"Why don't they just say goat and cow stew? It sounds like all the parts are in there."

"All but the meat."

"Okay. You're right. I wouldn't like that much. How do you know its number? Have you requested it often?"

"We had to read through them all. The really weird ones kind of stick with you."

"What else?"

"I'm not going over every disgusting dish in the galaxy. Especially right now, when I'm starving and my burger's getting cold."

"Okay. But we're revisiting this topic." Ethan stepped up to the AAU. "Is there a preprogrammed number for a shrimp dinner?"

"Sixty-three. It comes with—"

"No, don't tell me! After five years, I could use a surprise. Computer, preprogrammed meal sixty-three." Ethan grinned as a tray appeared with coconut shrimp, scampi, butterflied shrimp, broccoli, garlic mashed potatoes, and cola on it. "Fantastic!"

They sat on the couch, trays on the low chest in front of them, and ate in silence for a few minutes. He wondered if he'd ever get used to sharing a meal with someone again. The comfort of it always surprised him.

He glanced up at Kaia, wondering if she'd been as shaken as he a moment ago. He spoke to chase the thought from his mind: "So, what else could I have this AAU whip up?"

"Anything you like."

"Really? Anything? Like new clothes?" He was a bit tired of the caretaker's uniforms, all a little too big, that he'd been wearing.

She laughed. "No, not *anything*. I should have said, anything you want to eat."

He was a bit disappointed. "Just food?"

"Hey, that's quite an amazing feat: just food. Do you have any idea how complex it is to reassemble organic material?"

"No. But I have some idea of how complex it is to not make you mad."

She glared at him and then caved into a smile. "I'm not mad."

"I know. But you sure are fun to tease."

"That's what David used to say, too." Her eyes dropped and she pushed some food around on her plate.

Ethan looked at her. "How are you doing, Kaia?"

"I'm fine." She sounded stronger than her face looked. "I'm fine. It's fine. It's not like he's really gone."

Ethan shot her a puzzled look.

"Well, you know." Her cheeks colored slightly. "I was thinking, there could be a way, maybe, if his system was just shocked by the aneurysm, maybe you thought he was dead, but he wasn't really. Maybe he's in a kind of stasis . . ."

Ethan swallowed hard, all the flavor gone from his meal. Her irrationality surprised him.

She rushed on. "It's okay. We can talk about it later. I just was thinking about it."

CHAPTER 6

Kaia had been awake for ten days, and they were now up to the second deck. This was where the engines were, and the days passed with amazing speed as Kaia explained the engines, the artificial gravity system, and how the Castovian uranium that powered the ship eliminated the need for huge fuel tanks. In the evenings, they sat on the wide couch in the Caretaker's hold and studied Xardn. He had explained most of the basics of grammar and she could recognize about fifteen symbols.

"Pop Quiz!" he announced as they left the fourth engine room.

"Urrgh! Now?" She rolled her eyes playfully.

"Now. Computer, display the symbols I entered earlier."

"This is premeditated? I thought you just wanted to get out of seeing the nav room."

"That too. But I put these—" Ethan waved his hand at the symbols floating in front of them. "—in earlier to see if you're retaining any of the content we've discussed."

"All right. Let's get it overwith." Kaia pointed at the first symbol.

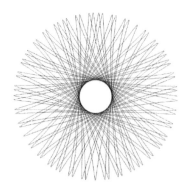

"Space," she said.

"Home."

"Power."

Ethan clapped. "Very nice! I picked the hard ones."

"No way. Those are easy because the others don't look like them. It's the pointy nouns that confuse me. So many of them look alike. You know, like those two sun ones."

"Ah, fintrk and samalt. Computer, show fintrk and samalt." Two symbols appeared in front of them.

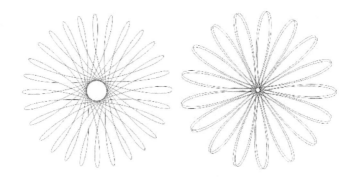

"Do you remember which one is which?"

"I know one is death and one is joy." She studied them. "How can 'death' and 'joy' look so similar? They aren't related concepts at all!"

"So all words that mean similar things should look similar?"

"It would be nice, yes."

"I told you, the symbols of any language are somewhat arbitrary."

"Well, at least in our language, they *sound* like what they mean."

Ethan raised his eyebrows, slightly amused. "Oh, do they?"

"Yes!" She was getting worked up now. "Death," she said, her voice low and ominous. Then, making her voice high and light, "Joy." She repeated the two words.

Ethan was laughing.

"Don't laugh. See, death sounds scarier than joy."

"Only because you know what it means."

"Words in any decent language sound different when they mean different things. You should be able to decipher some meaning from the sound." She stomped her foot lightly for emphasis.

"Okay, let's say that's true. Computer, give me manual control of the holoscreen and give me a keyboard."

A keyboard appeared, projected in the air like the symbols, but slightly lower so as to be within easy reach. He raised his hand and swept fintrk and samalt to the side, then typed quickly, tapping at the air where the keys hovered. As he typed the letters, different symbols appeared for him to choose from. When he saw the symbols he wanted, he simply tapped at them on the holoscreen.

"Do you think these two symbols—'limnar' and 'sandala'—look alike?"

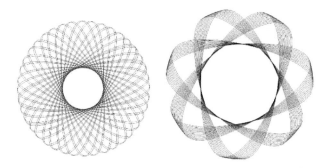

She squinted. "Not particularly. I could tell them apart."

Ethan contained a smile. "Okay. Limnar refers to a bunch of baby farm animals, kind of like Earth's pigs. Sandala is used to refer to a great ruler, a king. Do you think they should sound alike?"

"Of course not."

He grinned "And yet, in your own language, the words for those two entities are indistinguishable to the ear!" He typed quickly and two images appeared in front of them. The first showed several baby pigs snuggled up together. The second showed the golden bust of Tutankhamen. "Farrow: a litter of pigs. And pharaoh: a great leader or king, particularly Egyptian! The two words sound alike, but represent completely different concepts. You only think 'death' and 'joy' are so different because you know their meanings. There really is very little about the symbols themselves that *look* like the word. Another example: ferry and fairy. One's a big, clunky ship, the other a dainty mystical being. They sound the same, but they mean different things. Other words look the same but have multiple meanings. Think of the English word B-O-W. It can mean the front of a ship, a weapon that shoots arrows, a gesture of respect, a big frilly decoration . . ."

Kaia was glaring at him, and he knew he had convinced her. "You really are a geek, you know," she growled. "A language geek."

"I know." Ethan smiled at her, rubbed his hand in the air to erase the two pictures, and slid the original symbols back to the center of the hallway. "Okay. Which one is death and which one is joy?"

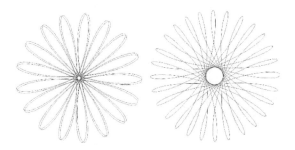

Kaia deliberated, then pointed to the first one. "Death," she said, then, pointing to the other. "Joy."

Ethan's eyebrows drew together. "You are getting better," he said begrudgingly.

Kaia smiled broadly. "I knew it! I remembered because I pictured joy as an explosion, so it had more . . . what are they called?"

"Cusps. Points."

"Right! I'm going to get this language yet." Kaia looked at the symbols again, smiling proudly. "*Now* are you ready for your lesson on the stasis system?"

Ethan sighed. "I guess. Computer, eliminate the holoscreen." The symbols and keyboard disappeared.

CHAPTER 7

Day twelve. Two days until they reached the threshold. Ethan's body tensed involuntarily as the thought crossed his mind. He pushed it away and rose from the massage table as silently as he could. It was early and still dark in the Caretaker's hold. Carefully, he retrieved his satchel and slipped out of the hold into the hallway. He held the satchel in front of him so it wouldn't bump the doorway as he slipped through. Inside was his journal and the little wooden case that accompanied it. Once the heavy door slid closed behind him, he walked several paces down the hall and sat on the floor.

Opening the book in front of him, he leafed through it from the beginning. Over the years he had become an avid journal writer. There were pages of writing: descriptions of the ship, his loneliness, and Aria. There were large and small sketches of her everywhere, of her sleeping face, her relaxed hands, and strands of her hair drifting in the stasis fluid. There were short poems—some that rhymed and some that didn't—about their life on Earth together and about his impressions of hurtling through space alone. He got to the last page of writing, where he'd scrawled the Xardn symbols for Kaia, and paused.

The thought came again. It was nearly time to put her back in stasis. His stomach knotted at the thought. How could he let her go? How could he willingly forego her companionship? Since she'd awakened, he'd come to crave their easy friendship.

Shaking his head, he tried to process it all. He wanted to write, wanted to record the miraculous happenings of the last few days and gain some perspective on the tangle of feelings he was having, but he paused thinking about Aria finding the journal somewhere decades hence. He knew his affection for Kaia would be hard for anyone to understand unless they'd spent years in isolation as he had. He couldn't hurt Aria, couldn't take the chance that after he was dead she'd find the journal and think he'd loved her any less than he did.

And then he realized the solution. So clear and so easy. He could write in Xardn. He opened the glyphtol case and removed the instrument from it. He began to write:

* * *

When the artificial lights came up, Ethan realized he'd fallen asleep in the hallway. His head was tipped back against the wall and tilted toward his left shoulder. The glyphtol had slipped down to rest on the floor beside him. His journal lay in his lap, the open pages covered with complex curves. He raised his head to see Kaia crouched beside him, peering at the symbols.

"This is 'I', right?" she asked, then, "And 'light?'" He glanced down at the journal as she continued. "Is this 'woman'? I love the puzzle of it." Ethan moved his hand reflexively to cover the pages. Then he closed it and reached for the wooden case in which to place his glyphtol. Slipping his stuff into the satchel, he stood and carried it back to the hold. He avoided meeting Kaia's eyes. As he placed the items on the shelf, he finally spoke. "How about some breakfast?"

They got their trays and sat facing each other. "What's up today?" He knew that Kaia would have some interesting adventure planned. They had been through most of the ship, and although much of it was still a mystery to him, he was beginning to feel more oriented and more confident. He had found her to be a good teacher, making the details of the systems accessible through her explanations.

"Today?" She smiled over at him. "A surprise."

"It's not the waste water recycler, is it? Because that's not a surprise as much as a shock. I explored it a couple of years in. Do you have any idea what we're drinking here?" He tapped his glass of orange juice.

"Hey! Don't knock it. That thing took forever to perfect. And do you know who had to taste all the glasses of orange juice that led up to that one?"

"Don't tell me it was you."

"Well . . ." She hesitated, and he could see that she didn't want to lose ground in the argument. "Okay, it wasn't me, but it *was* some poor engineer who had to taste all the not-so-recycled waste water attempts. Show a little respect for the many brave taste buds who sacrificed to keep you happy and healthy for fifty-some years."

Ethan gave her a wry look. "So it's not the recycler, then?"

"No. It's a surprise. Not even a fully mechanical one, so you should enjoy it."

"I admit it. You've got me curious now."

She smiled mischievously. "Finish your orange juice, then, and we'll get going."

"I think I've lost my appetite. All that stuff about waste water." He crossed and discarded his tray. He heard her speak but missed what she said. When he turned around, Kaia was across the hold, sitting on the floor close to the wall beside the door. She had procured a set of shining silver tools from the in-wall shelves and was using them to remove a venting panel. He walked to her and crouched beside her.

Ethan watched her hands as she worked. They were small hands, delicate, covered with that smooth brown skin. They were agile, able, and sure as she adjusted the bolts holding the panel on. Kaia's hands didn't look as if they had enough strength to turn the wrench, but still the bolts loosened. She moved to the last bolt. His eyes moved up her arm to her turned head, traced her jawline, and saw how her teeth were set. She was putting more effort into the bolts than she wanted to let on. He moved closer.

"Here. I can help." He put his hand over hers on the handle of the wrench. She pulled hers back and rubbed them together as he finished loosening. The panel fell off with a crash. She grinned at him.

"Come on!" In a second, only her calves and feet were sticking out of the shaft. Seconds more and she had completely disappeared.

"Kaia!" he called, "you've got to be kidding! I'm not going to fit in there!"

He heard her speak. She was already a good distance down the shaft, but he thought she said, "Don't be a baby." He growled and stuck his head and shoulders into the darkness.

He caught up to her quickly, and the two crawled single-file through the long dark shaft. "My elbows aren't made for this kind of thing," Ethan complained, taking a moment to rest on his stomach as he watched the soles of her stasis shoes disappear in front of him.

She stopped a few yards ahead. "I promise you, this will be worth it!" She could move through the shaft on her hands and knees pretty easily. He was too tall, though, and had spent the last ten minutes army-crawling and scootching along with his toes.

"Nothing could be worth this. Do we have to come out this way, too?"

"Of course. If there was an easier way, I'd take you there first."

"I'm not sure you would . . ."

"All right, enough complaining. Let's get moving. You're going to love it. Anyway, you should get used to this. There's all kinds of great stuff you haven't seen on this ship yet, and these shafts are the only way to get to it!" Her voice echoed ahead of her down the shaft and he missed the last few words. Groaning, he propped himself up on his elbows and followed her.

Ethan looked up to see Kaia removing the bolts from another vent panel. She had her fingers laced through the grate so that when the last bolt came off, the panel didn't fall. She held it awkwardly in front of her as she pulled herself out of the opening. She reached up with her free hand as she swung her feet out of the shaft. He heard her feet hit metal, and then, as he reached the opening, he heard her voice.

"You're not afraid of heights, are you?" she asked.

As he pulled his torso out of the shaft, Ethan saw that she was standing on a catwalk above an enormous room. He had to grab a pipe above the shaft in order to swing himself out and onto the catwalk. As he landed on it, he looked out over the expanse.

They were above one of the stasis holds. The pink-lighted stasis chambers of their passengers reached off into the distance twenty feet below them. Like strings of pearls, the chambers glowed in the half-light of the hold. Their human cargo shone pale within them, held in delicate suspension.

Ethan couldn't speak. He'd never before seen so many of his charges at once, never quite grasped the volume of humanity he was guarding. He walked carefully along the catwalk, trailing his fingers along the handrail, gazing at the rows upon rows of men and women and children below him. When he reached the wall at the end of the catwalk, he turned around slowly and walked the length of it again. Finally he stopped as he caught sight of the last, empty chamber and his eyes moved to the one next to it.

There she was. Even from this distance, and even with the strange angle, he knew Aria. The shape of her, the way the light shone on her hair. His right hand gripped the rail, and his left reached involuntarily toward her. In his mind, he saw her smiling, saw her turning to look at him, saw her wide eyes as he closed the door of the chamber. He felt her soft hair on his cheek, felt her playful kisses, felt the last touch of her hand. He heard her laugh, heard her speak his name, and heard her soft, even breathing as the fluid began to fill her chamber. His breath caught in his chest and he raised his left hand to wipe away a sudden stinging at his eyes. He stepped back and looked up at Kaia. She was standing at the same place he'd left her, gazing absently down the rows.

He managed two words. "She's . . . there." He pointed down the last row. Kaia came to him, standing against the rail and peering into the distance.

"Your wife." She smiled up at him with a depth of sadness that brought the sting back to his eyes. He nodded.

"The last chamber." Then, amending, " . . . that has . . . someone in it."

"I see her red hair," she said. "And the baby."

He swallowed hard, nodding again. "She'd laugh that we can see her belly from here. She . . . thought it was huge. She joked that she was afraid she'd pick up a satellite on this trip because of her gravitational pull . . ." His voice cracked and he stopped, feeling guilty for sharing their private joke and missing her even more with every word he spoke. Kaia smiled.

"She's funny, then?"

He nodded. "Very. She . . . she always makes everyone laugh. I was the . . . serious one."

"The straight man."

Ethan finally looked at Kaia directly. "That's what she always said, too. 'Every great comedian has to have a brilliant straight man.'"

"Sounds like you were a good team."

"Yeah." Ethan was coming out of it. His reason was kicking back in and his openness shutting down. He looked across the cavernous room. "So many of them."

"Holy cow, yeah. I never imagined it, even when I saw all the chambers. I couldn't fathom this many people in them!" She walked quickly down the catwalk. "It's incredible."

Ethan followed her.

"I'm getting my bearings, though."

"Oh yeah?"

"Yeah. This is alpha-theta row. If you look, you can see our oldest passenger about thirteen chambers down, on the left. He's fifty-two."

Kaia looked at him quizzically. "Fifty-two? That's not so old. I thought they were accepting people on Minea up to seventy-five if they were in good health. Seems like we'd at least have some people in their sixties, doesn't it? Out of all these people?"

Ethan shrugged. "I just know he's our oldest. And I'm catching up fast. We won't even be halfway there before I take the title."

Kaia's brow was furrowed. "Weird. Who else do you know?"

"Well, some of the more interesting passengers are clustered over in that far corner. You can't see them, but there are three families with twelve kids apiece."

Kaia raised her eyebrows. "Wow. Bet it was fun getting that group into stasis."

Ethan smiled. "I'll bet."

They looked around for a while more. Suddenly, Kaia's face brightened. "Hey! Do you know where my dad is?"

Ethan thought. "What was his name?"

"Reagan. Phillip Reagan."

"I remember the name. I think he's somewhere near the beginning, on beta or epsilon row in Hold One. But the door's way up there—" He pointed toward another corner. Kaia squinted in that direction and then headed back for the hatch.

"Let's go down!" she called over her shoulder. "I want to find him!"

Characteristically, she was gone before Ethan could say anything.

He looked back over his shoulder towards Aria's chamber. "I'll come see you soon," he said quietly. Then he climbed into the shaft.

Ethan could hear Kaia scuffling down the tunnel in front of him. "Wait up!" he called, knowing he'd never find his way back through the right turns. He heard her pause. When he caught up, they continued on in what Ethan felt sure was a different set of turns than they'd taken before.

"Are we going a different way?"

"Yeah. We're getting closer to the first passenger hold. No reason to go back to the caretaker's hold first."

"You're like a mouse in here. I think you know these back ways better than you know the main passages."

"I spent enough time in them. I ought to know them."

"Where are we now?"

"We're over the navigation rooms," she said. "Here's the main nav room." She crawled a few more lengths. "Here's the secondary nav room."

"How can you tell where they begin and end?"

"Listen. As you go over the rooms, you'll hear the hollowness under you. Air whooshing right below you. The bigger the whoosh, the bigger the room. When you reach the walls, there's a solid sound; the whoosh of air is deadened. See, the secondary room here is smaller. Next we'll go over the hall, which is a *huge* empty sound, but only lasts for a dozen feet or so . . ."

"We should try *walking* in the huge empty space next time—" Ethan nearly ran into Kaia before he realized she had stopped. "What—"

"Shhhh," she said, tilting her head to the side. "Back up."

"Are you kidding? I can't—"

"Ethan, BACK UP! I need to listen to something." There was a puzzled edge in her voice.

He braced his elbows on the floor of the shaft and pushed backwards, using his knees for extra traction. Going backward was definitely harder than going forward. He thought about grumbling, but Kaia moved backward with such ease that his pride wouldn't let her know how hard it was for him.

They backed up about twenty feet, and then Ethan rested on his stomach while Kaia crawled forward and backward, cocking her head at different angles as she crawled. Every time he tried to ask her what she was doing, she shushed him and hissed, "I'm listening!" Finally, she said, "Huh."

"What?"

"Well . . ." she said slowly, "something's strange here. I can't figure it out, but it *sounds* like there's a weird little room here, like a closet, in the secondary nav room."

"Maybe there is."

"But there isn't. None of these ships have one. There's no reason for one. Why would there be one here?"

He wondered if she'd been in the shaft a little too long. He'd tried listening, and he couldn't hear a difference between being over a room and being over a wall. "Maybe you're not hearing it right."

She made an annoyed sound.

"I just mean, well . . . it's been five years, you know . . ."

"Not for me. I was crawling through these tunnels a couple of weeks ago. This ship is different."

"Okay. You know, my knees are killing me."

Kaia's tone changed. "I'm sorry, Ethan. Let's get you out of here." She started to crawl forward again. "You'll like this next bit."

They'd crawled another ten minutes when Kaia said brightly, "There we go!"

Ethan glanced up and saw that the shaft widened ahead. He also saw that the bottom dropped out. "You have a way of dealing with that gaping hole, I assume."

Kaia laughed as she reached the hole. "Of course." With agile grace, she reached up, swung her legs around, and dropped them into the hole in one fluid motion. For a moment, Ethan thought she was suspended in midair, but as he approached he saw a perpendicular shaft extending above and below this one. Inside it, along the wall, was a ladder.

"Tricky," he said as she laughed and began to descend. "What does a ship like this need with secret passageways?"

"Not secret passageways. Just maintenance access. How do you think they put one of these things together?"

After twenty more minutes of climbing through the shafts, they emerged through a vent panel in the lower deck hallway. Ethan stood up and stretched his arms and back. "Not my favorite way to get around the ship."

"Effective, though, huh?" Kaia's voice was still slightly distracted. He could tell that she was thinking of the unexpected room they'd gone over.

They crossed the hall to the main door of the passenger hold. Kaia stepped aside so Ethan could open the door. He stepped up, barked the access code, and then stood still to be scanned. The door slid open, and they stepped inside.

The shadowy, cavernous room yawned around them. The bulkheads at the end of each row of stasis chambers stretched away on either side of them. In front of them the bulkhead read $\Theta\lambda$.

"Theta lambda." Ethan said. "We're near the middle. Computer, give us the coordinates to Phillip Reagan's chamber."

"Passenger one sixteen Phillip Reagan—is in Epsilon twenty-six," the computer responded.

Kaia hesitated.

"What, you don't know how to get to Epsilon?" he teased.

"Actually, I don't. The chamber labels went on with the finishing. Long after my step in the ship-building process was over."

Ethan grinned. "Finally," he said, "something for me to teach *you* about the ship! This way." Ethan turned to the right and headed confidently past the bulkheads. "See, the rows are marked with the letters of the Greek alphabet. Once they've gone through the whole alphabet, they go to two letter designations: Alpha alpha, Alpha beta, Alpha gamma, Alpha delta, Beta alpha, Beta beta, Beta gamma, Beta delta. Then, you can count from the front chamber, which starts at one here in the front, to get to the right chamber."

They passed several more bulkheads before finding Epsilon row.

"He should be down here." As they passed the upright chambers, with their sleeping cargo standing inside them, Ethan pointed out the numbers on the engraved plates below each clear door. "We're looking for twenty-six."

Kaia was practically running down the row in front of him, ignoring the numbers as she looked eagerly at each face. Ethan saw the number twenty-six and called her back.

"Here, Kaia. Here's twenty-six."

She turned and came back quickly. When her eyes fell upon the man in stasis, though, her face fell.

"What is it?"

"Ethan," she said with a tiny shake of her head, "that's not my father."

Ethan looked at the man. "Well, they look . . . a little different in the fluid . . ."

"Ethan." Her voice was shaking. "Ethan, my father is fifty-five years old, big, strong . . ." her voice trailed off as they both looked at the small pale man in the chamber. "They can't look *that* different."

"Computer," Ethan said, "give us the coordinates for Phillip Reagan."

"Passenger 116—Phillip Reagan—is in Epsilon twenty-six."

Ethan checked either side of the chamber. "Is this chamber labeled wrong?"

"The chamber is correctly labeled, Mr. Bryant."

"Then where is Reagan?"

"Phillip Reagan is in Epsilon twenty-six," the computer said.

Kaia was pale. "No, he's not. That is not my father."

The computer didn't respond, but Ethan saw her trembling and stepped over to her. "It's probably just a mistake in the roster." He tried to sound comforting. "Maybe he was boarded in the wrong order. Look around. He's probably in this guy's chamber here somewhere."

This seemed to encourage her and she set off down the row again. Ethan turned to inspect the passengers toward the other end of the row. Suddenly he heard her call out.

"Ethan!"

Ethan hurried off toward the sound of her voice. He found her near the end of the long row.

"What is it?"

"Something's wrong. I mean—" Her voice faltered. "This is supposed to be the ship's military contingent . . . they should all be here in the same area . . . " she waved her hand down the row. Ethan gave the passengers a closer look and immediately saw the problem. The people on this row were all like Passenger 116: young, thin, pale. Some of them looked to be little older than children.

"They don't look very military."

"Somewhere here should have been my dad's lifetime friend and his lieutenant, Case Jenkins. When I asked where he was, the computer directed me to this man." Kaia tapped the glass of a stasis chamber holding a seventeen- or eighteen-year-old kid. "Do you think—" She hesitated. "Could they all have been mislabeled?" Her eyes showed deep doubt at the proposition.

"Maybe. Let's look some more. I'll go over one row and you keep looking around here." Kaia nodded and let him leave. When he was out of earshot, Ethan spoke quietly, "Computer, bring up the holoscreen." Immediately, it hovered before him. "Show me a picture of General Phillip Reagan."

The picture of the blonde man in Epsilon twenty-six hovered in front of him.

"Cross-check that photo," Ethan said.

"The passenger pictured *is* General Phillip Reagan," the computer said with finality.

Kaia's voice startled Ethan from behind. "Ethan, something is going on." He turned to see her staring, wide-eyed and shaking, at the floating image. "Someone has removed the entire military contingent from this ship. We are defenseless."

Ethan shook his head slowly. "But Kaia, that doesn't make sense. Who would do that? Why?"

He looked into her eyes and saw suspicion. "Perhaps you can tell me, Mr. Bryant."

He took a step toward her. "Kaia—"

She stepped back. "Stay there. I want to know what is going on. Right now. Where is my father?"

"I have no idea where your father is. The computer seems to think he's in Epsilon twenty-six."

"He's not."

"So you said." Ethan's eyebrows drew together. "Kaia, I don't know what's going on any more than you do."

"I didn't think of it before," she said, shaking her head quickly, "but your story is pretty suspicious."

Ethan could tell she was growing agitated. "Kaia—"

"Very convenient," she went on, "that David keeled over just as you were supposed to go into stasis." She looked him in the eye, and the acidic tone he remembered from their first few encounters had returned. "You killed him, didn't you?"

The words hit Ethan. "Kaia—I've never killed anyone."

"Prove it," she said, fury burning in her gaze as she walked back and forth across the end of the row.

"I—I can't, Kaia. You'll just have to trust me."

"Sure. Trust you. Like everyone else here trusted you. Why would you want to hijack a passenger ship?"

"Kaia—"

The metallic sound of the computer's voice rang through the room. "I'm detecting elevated heart rates and adrenaline levels, Mr. Bryant."

"Not now, computer." Ethan didn't take his eyes off Kaia. "Listen—"

"I WON'T listen! You killed David, and now I find out probably my father, too! You took my whole future!" Her eyes widened. "And I'm probably next."

Ethan reached toward her, his eyes pleading, but she lashed out, knocking his arm aside. She spun and ran away from him down the aisle. Before he could stop himself, Ethan was running after her. The grays and pinks of the chambers blurred in his peripheral vision. He saw her turn, dart up the central aisle, and then veer right down another row. She was fast. He pushed himself.

When he reached the center of the row, she was already rounding the other end of it, heading right. Just as she moved out of his view, Ethan heard a small cry. When he reached the end of the row, he saw her on the floor fifteen feet ahead, clutching her ankle, her face a mask of pain. He sprinted to her.

"Kaia, are you okay?"

As he leaned down, she pushed him savagely away, catching him off balance. "Leave me alone! Murderer!"

He fell back against the bulkhead and slid to the floor. When he looked up, the holoscreen had suddenly appeared in the air in front of Kaia. She sat transfixed as she watched the surveillance video of David McNeal helping Ethan into the stasis chamber.

The broad-shouldered blonde soldier swung the door of the chamber wide for Ethan. "Last but not least," McNeal said. His voice was deep and musical.

Onscreen, Ethan was still standing in front of Aria's chamber, one hand on the glass. "She'll be okay?"

"She'll be just fine." McNeal gazed at Aria's sleeping form and then put a hand on Ethan's shoulder. "It's scary to see them so still, huh?"

"I just—" Ethan swallowed. "I can't imagine the next half-century without her."

A shadow passed across McNeal's face. "Yeah. It's hard to be apart, even for a little while." Then, regaining his military persona, said, "But once we get you in the chamber, it won't feel like long at all. Just a real good night's sleep. C'mon. You're aging as we speak."

They both laughed weakly, then Ethan allowed himself to be directed to the chamber. As he stepped inside and began to turn around, McNeal convulsed once, horribly, then slumped against the big steel and glass door.

Watching, Kaia covered her eyes briefly, and then looked back up.

On the screen, Ethan was moving a shoulder under McNeal's arm, supporting him.

"McNeal! McNeal, what's wrong?"

When the Caretaker spoke, the words were slurred and strained. "I'm . . . I can't . . ." His free hand went to his head.

"What should I do?"

"The ... hold." McNeal mumbled, "computer ... holoscreen map ... to the ... Caretaker's hold." The map appeared, and the two on the screen moved painfully through the shining silver halls, the surveillance cameras tracking them seamlessly from passenger hold to hall, deck to deck, until they reached the wide couch in the Caretaker's hold. Ethan helped McNeal onto the couch, where the big soldier lay breathing heavily. The tape sped up, showing McNeal's still form and Ethan moving about the hold, trying to make the ill man more comfortable, then stopped as Ethan sat on the low table beside the couch during the last moments of David McNeal's life.

The soldier stirred slightly and opened his eyes. "You ..." he whispered, "protect ... them ... until ... " In his eyes burned the frantic need to communicate and the frustration of being unable to.

"You're going to be all right," Ethan said. "Just rest. You'll feel better soon."

McNeal shook his head, almost imperceptibly. "Not ... better. Every ... everything ... wrong ... I'll ... miss her ... waking ..." Then he shuddered and was gone. The onscreen Ethan closed McNeal's eyes and wept.

On the floor of the passenger hold, as the holoscreen faded, Kaia wept, too. She held her ankle with her right hand and covered her face with her left. Her shoulders shook.

Ethan moved carefully to her. When he was beside her on the floor, he reached across her shoulders and gathered her to his chest. He rested his chin on her head. Tears slipped down his own cheeks as he felt her clutch his shirt and tremble against him. He held her a long time.

As her tears subsided, she curled tighter into his embrace. "I'm sorry, Ethan," she said quietly.

"I know."

"He was right. Everything's wrong. We should be ... together."

Ethan nodded against the top of her head.

"I miss him so ... deeply," she mumbled into Ethan's chest. "I thought we'd have so much time to be together. I was actually a little worried about spending our whole lives only seeing each other. I worried we'd tire of each other. Now ... now I wish we'd gotten the chance to tire of each other. I can't believe I'll never see him again ... never hear him say my name ..."

Ethan's embrace tightened as she spoke. Waves of his own loneliness and longing washed over him. They fell into silence then and sat breathing together.

When she finally shifted away from him, she winced and took a sharp breath. She reached down for her ankle.

"Are you all right?"

"It's just a sprain."

"Let's get you back to the hold." Ethan stood and carefully helped her to her feet. They made their way through the passenger hold and up to the Caretaker's hold. As they walked, Ethan suddenly felt Kaia's shoulders shaking again.

"Does it hurt?" he asked.

She nodded.

"Is that why you're crying?"

She shook her head, no.

"David?"

Kaia nodded again. "I was just thinking how . . . you came this same way with him . . . then. I wish I'd been here for him."

Ethan thought for a few steps and then said, "I never understood that last thing he said. In fact, I'd forgotten it until today. He didn't want to miss you. Didn't want you to wake up without him. I'm sorry I didn't remember it so I could have told you earlier."

Kaia shrugged. "At least you remembered the surveillance footage and called up the holoscreen."

Ethan stopped walking. "I didn't." His brow furrowed as he tried to recall the moments after Kaia had fled.

"You didn't?"

"No. It just . . . it came up on its own. Computer?" He switched to the commanding voice he usually used to speak to the computer.

"Yes, Mr. Bryant."

"Did you project the holoscreen without being commanded to do so?"

"Yes, Mr. Bryant."

Kaia raised her eyebrows.

"It's never done that before," he said. "Computer, why did you project the holoscreen?"

"As I mentioned, Mr. Bryant, your heart rate and adrenaline levels were elevated to dangerous levels. The conflict between you and Ms. Reagan seemed to center around a misunderstanding over the incident in the surveillance log from Day 1, so I deduced that reviewing the scene may help alleviate the tension and bring your heart rate and adrenaline level back into an acceptable range."

"Thank you, computer. It seems to have worked." Ethan glanced down at Kaia again.

"Creepy," she said under her breath.

Ethan said nothing, unconcerned about the computer's actions as her tears subsided.

As they walked on, he felt an almost fierce protectiveness about this girl. There hadn't been a moment, day or night, since she awakened that she wasn't in his thoughts. It had been so long since anyone had held such fascination for him. And they had not been this close to each other since he'd first carried her to the caretaker's hold when she'd fainted. Since then he'd come to know her, had seen her laugh and shared some of her pain. He'd been impressed by her expertise and intelligence and had seen her both vulnerable and strong. Feeling her arm around his waist, feeling the way she leaned into him as they walked, filled him with excitement and apprehension.

"You shouldn't walk on that," he said sternly.

"I'll be fine. I sprain it pretty often. It's weak from an old virtual gaming injury." As she glanced up at him, he saw her wince as she stepped, and in one fluid motion, he leaned down and scooped her into his arms.

In spite of the day's tensions, she laughed in surprise. "Ethan! Put me down."

"No." She fit in his arms nicely, but he had to adjust his balance. "Quit squirming or I'm gonna drop you," he said.

She settled down grudgingly. Her arm around his neck, she stroked his hair. "You'd never get away with this sloppy of a haircut in the military."

He felt a little self-conscious and growled, "Give me a break. I do it myself."

"What?"

"Sure. Who else is going to cut my hair?"

"Ummm. The computer."

"*Oh*, no. We tried that. Lasers shot out at random angles. I stopped it before it vaporized my brain. I shave with an old-fashioned razor and I cut my own hair."

Kaia was giggling. "Vaporized your brain?"

Ethan walked faster, a little embarrassed. "It's certainly a possibility."

"A grooming laser is an attenuated laser. It couldn't even singe you. It's calibrated to only affect hair. Five years you've been living in the dark ages? Using a straightedge? Where did you even find such an antique?"

"I brought it along. It was my grandfather's. Eversharp, clean cutting, works great."

Kaia shook her head. "You're an interesting man, Ethan Bryant."

They'd reached the elevator, and he asked for her help. "Wanna push the buttons?"

She reached out, poking the key sequence for the caretaker's hold. Ethan felt the muscles in her back twist as she reached. He liked the feeling of her in his arms. As she settled back, he couldn't help but hold her a little tighter. Her arms tightened around his neck, too. As he felt it, his eyes darted down to hers. She was looking up at him with a new light in her eyes. He looked away hurriedly.

When they reached the hold, Kaia did something unexpected. As Ethan set her down on the couch, she reached up and kissed him quickly on the cheek. "Thank you, Ethan. That would have been a painful trip back here on my own."

He straightened and then smiled down at her. "You're welcome. Let's see what we can do with that ankle. Computer, assess this injury."

"It is a musculoskeletal injury commonly known as an ankle sprain," said the computer.

"Get the AutoMed, please, computer."

"Repair of the ligaments is possible using the Automatic Medical Assistant, however, it cannot be used on a patient until fourteen days after awakening from stasis. You will need to use the manual medical kit provided in cabinet B25."

Ethan looked up as one of the small doors on the back wall slid open. He crossed to it and retrieved a white steel case that was heavier than it looked. Ethan opened it and took out a polymer wrap and a cold pack.

"Okay. Let's take a look at that ankle." Ethan sat on the chest and lifted Kaia's calf, placing the ankle in his lap. He saw her wince as he moved it. It was swollen and bruised. "I'm sorry. I'll try not to hurt it too much."

He slipped her stasis shoe off and ran his fingers over the swollen ankle, positioning it on the wrap and gently pulling the soft, stretchy material around it. He hated hurting her but was impressed by how she gritted her teeth and let him work.

"Don't look so grim," she said teasingly.

He noticed that he was gritting his own teeth, his empathy for her pain transferring to his jaw. He consciously relaxed, shot her a weak smile, and then looked back down at the wrap. When he was done, he put the cold pack around her ankle and eased her leg back onto the couch.

"Okay," she said once it was settled. "Your turn."

Ethan looked at her quizzically.

"Go get your old-fashioned razor. I'm going to give you a decent haircut."

"No way. You've got to rest."

"You can sit right here, and I'll be able to reach." She pointed to the floor in front of the couch. "I need something to do, and I have to pay you back for all this medical care."

Ethan saw in her eyes that there would be no argument. He stood and went to the bathroom, where he found his razor and a comb. He brought them back to her.

Sitting on the floor in front of her, he couldn't see what she was doing. His only sensory information came from her touch. He felt her fingers in his hair, on his shoulders, and on the back of his neck. Sometimes she laid a hand against his cheek to have him turn a little to the right or left. The feel of her touch overwhelmed him, and he closed his eyes and held his breath until the wave of desire subsided. By then she was really cutting, and he focused on watching his dark hair fall around him. It had been longer than he realized since his last haircut. He felt the comb, her fingers, and the cold blade moving over his scalp and found himself again fighting the sensation of her hands sliding over his skin. Too soon it was over.

"Go check it out," she said lightly, though he thought he detected a slight breathlessness in her voice, too.

Ethan avoided her eyes as he took the tools from her and then walked back into the bathroom as the computer disintegrated the cut hairs and swept the particles away for recycling. In the mirror he saw that she'd done an expert job. It was clean and even, a much better look than he'd had for years. He told her so as he walked back to the couch. "It looks fantastic. You've got a second career there." She smiled up at him as he stepped in front of her.

"I used to cut my dad's hair all the time. He didn't like paying for a haircut when it would just grow back in a couple weeks." At the end of her sentence, Kaia's voice cracked in a yawn.

"You must be exhausted. Why don't you take a nap?" he asked. "I've got a few things to do, and then I'll be back to get you some dinner."

Reluctantly, she nodded. "Okay." He lifted her ankle as she lay back on the couch, and then he turned and strode toward the door. Glancing back, he saw her curled on the wide leather seat. Her eyes were already closed. He walked back toward her, opened the chest in front of the sofa and pulled out the blanket inside. Gently, he spread it over her, tucking it carefully around her shoulders. Her eyes fluttered open.

"You really are a Caretaker."

He smiled. "Sleep well," he said, and he left the room.

Out in the hall, Ethan leaned against the smooth wall. Though she seemed to be doing better and though their last hour had been light, Ethan couldn't forget the look in Kaia's eyes as she watched the footage of that first day on the ship, full of the pain of David's death. Somehow, there had to be a way to help her grieve.

"Computer," he asked, "I need a photograph of David McNeal." The image floated in front of him almost instantaneously. "No, I need a hard copy. A printed version."

"Yes, Mr. Bryant. One is printing now in the Primary Navigation Room."

Ethan turned and headed there, a plan forming in his mind.

CHAPTER 8

Ethan knew something of the pain that Kaia was going through. He remembered the night he'd sent McNeal's body into space. He'd stood at the interior airlock door a little longer than was reasonable, staring at the still form. When he had finally pushed the button and opened the airlock, Ethan remembered the hot tears on his face. That almost ethereal moment had stayed with him all the years since. The way McNeal had risen and drifted, spinning gently as space took him, had eased the grief inside Ethan somehow. It had seemed a noble and good way to go.

He wanted Kaia to experience something like that. Watching the footage of McNeal's last moments had made Ethan acutely aware that Kaia needed to say goodbye. And so he spent the night scrounging for items to make a frame for David's picture. When he was done, the framed photograph was rough but adequate. He took the elevator down to the bottom floor and left the photo near the airlock.

He went back upstairs just as square faces of the clocks above each bulkhead read 0800. The door slid open soundlessly, and he walked into the hold to see Kaia sitting on the couch weeping. She raised her head, startled, and tried to cover her swollen eyes.

"I didn't expect you back yet," she said.

Ethan sat next to her. "You were supposed to sleep."

"I did," she protested, "for a while. I just—" She had stopped trying to control her sobs and her voice came out strained. "I can't stop seeing his face at the end. I just can't get it out of my head."

Ethan nodded. "I know. It was hard for me to watch it again, too."

"I don't know what to do, Ethan. I don't know—" she bent over, her shoulders shaking.

Ethan began to reconsider his plan. He was no psychologist. What if this just caused her more pain?

"I just want to see him like I remember him . . ." She trailed off, looking pleadingly up at Ethan.

"Can I take you somewhere?" Ethan asked, almost before he knew what he was saying.

She nodded slightly and he stood and lifted her into his arms. As he carried her to the elevator, Kaia covered her face with her hands and cried.

Neither of them spoke on the way to the bottom deck. Once there, he carried her out and stood her in front of the interior airlock door. She leaned on the wall for support, and he reached down and picked up the photo, offering it to her as he stood.

Kaia's eyes widened. "Where did you get this?" she said softly, running her fingers over the image of McNeal's broad smile.

"The—uh, computer called it up. It's McNeal's official ID photo."

For the first time, she smiled weakly. Her eyes lingered on the picture. "He replaced the official one, then. This is cropped from one of our wedding photos." She looked up at Ethan. "You made the frame?"

He nodded. "It's not much, just what I could find around here—"

"Actually, it's really fitting," she said softly. "He would have liked to be surrounded by the ship." Her eyes met Ethan's. "Why didn't you just bring it to me in the hold?"

The question took Ethan by surprise, and he felt immediately embarrassed at the morbidity of his earlier plan. Of course he should have just made her a keepsake, not an effigy. His eyes darted involuntarily to the airlock.

He saw his reflection in the window. His jaw was dark with scruff, and his newly-cut hair was unkempt from the night awake. He pushed the image aside and tried desperately to think of an answer for her.

But it was too late. She was looking around with understanding dawning in her eyes. "Oh," she said, very softly.

Her knuckles had whitened. She was clutching the frame furiously, her eyes taking in the image hungrily.

Ethan looked down, ashamed to admit what he'd made the photo for.

After a long time, she spoke again. "You think I should . . ." She glanced at the airlock.

"I don't know, Kaia. I wasn't really thinking. I just—"

She stopped him, "No, I see what you were trying to do." She looked again at the photo. "We could have . . . a memorial service, or something."

Ethan nodded but still didn't look at her. "Only if you want to."

She stood quietly for a long time, so long that Ethan moved away from her, down the corridor, back toward the elevator. He leaned against the wall and stayed quiet until he heard her voice again.

"Ethan," she said, her voice a little stronger, "will you help me?"

He went back to her, aware of the brightness of the corridor, the darkness of space outside the exterior windows of the airlock. He caught her eye as he stepped up to the interior door. "Are you sure?"

She nodded, swallowing hard and fighting more tears.

Ethan had to use a manual keypad for the airlock in addition to the verbal code and bioscan required on the rest of the ship. He went through the usual routine and punched the code into the panel. The interior door slid open. Ethan held Kaia's arm as she limped in, clutching the photograph. She set it on the floor in the back of the airlock.

Ethan was conscious of the sound of the engines, the hiss of the atmosphere venting in and out of the room, and his own breathing. Then he heard her voice, barely a whisper.

"I meant what I said in our vows, David. 'Our love for each other spans earth and beyond, from time to timeless.' I'll miss you and all the adventures we were going to have together." She stood quietly, then reached up to the shoulder of her stasis suit and grasped the patch with the ship's insignia and her passenger number on it. She tore it from her stasis suit, then bent and slid it under a gap in the frame. "Passenger three six nine two loves you, David McNeal, and wherever you are, a part of her will always be with you."

She reached a hand toward him, and he helped her out of the airlock. The door slid closed behind them and she stood at the window of the interior door. She nodded, and Ethan entered the code that opened the exterior vents above the airlock. Slowly, the airlock atmosphere began to be replaced by the great nothingness outside. At first nothing happened, but then the photo rose gently. The exterior door opened, and the photo floated, spinning out into the blackness, propelled the last of the escaping atmosphere in the room.

Ethan realized she was repeating the same words she'd said before—"earth and beyond, from time to timeless"—over and over again. He saw tears slipping down the cheeks of her reflection in the window and felt his own returning.

Long after the speck of David's image had disappeared, they were still standing motionless. Kaia's tears had dried when she held out a hand to him and weakly slumped into his arms. Ethan carried her back to the Caretaker's hold, again making the journey in silence. He laid her down, covered her with the blanket, and left.

Just before the door closed, he heard her say, "Thank you."

He nodded and made his way to the passenger's hold. He walked along the first aisle, trailing his fingers along the convex fronts of the chambers. These were the living, and he needed to be with them now. Finally he stopped in front of one of the upright cylindrical chambers and stood face to face with Eli Santos, a middle-aged wood carver. Eli's family surrounded him as he slept peacefully. Ethan found a spark of hope growing within him. It wouldn't be long for Eli. None of these horrors existed where he was. Eli would wake up with the same enthusiasm for life on Minea that he had gone to sleep with back on Earth, oblivious to McNeal's and Kaia's and even Ethan's own pain.

Somehow, that made him feel better. Loss and longing were not all there was to life. There was more, and if Eli could experience all that good, then all these sacrifices would be worth it.

Ethan walked on through the holds for hours, thoughts tumbling through his mind. Something was still bothering him. Kaia had insisted that McNeal had been murdered. Who would murder a Caretaker? It wasn't a coveted job. And why? What would one possibly gain by doing away with someone whose life was already, for all practical purposes, done away with? And how? McNeal was on one of the most extensively inaccessible crafts known to man, in part because of its sheer size, in part because of the high security surrounding passenger ships. Ethan found McNeal's murder unlikely, but something about it nagged at him still.

He crossed through several of the smaller bulkheads and finally looked up. The clock above him read 15:59. He had spent nearly the whole day here. He needed now to check on Kaia.

CHAPTER 9

Three days later, Ethan carried a tall glass of pomegranate juice to Kaia on the couch. Her grey eyes shone up at him as she took it. She seemed much more at peace with David's death, and Ethan was relieved that his plan hadn't backfired as badly as he'd been afraid it would.

"I love this stuff!" she said, taking a long drink.

"I'm picking that up. That's your third glass today."

"Well, if you didn't bring them to me, I wouldn't drink so many."

He nodded. She was right. He found himself constantly on the lookout for things that might make her more comfortable, that she might enjoy. There was something thrilling about being with someone whose every need wasn't filled by the computer.

"How's the ankle?"

"Still pretty painful." She tried to flex her foot and winced. "But I think it's less swollen."

He sat beside her on the couch and pulled her feet into his lap, laying a gentle hand over the polymer wrap. "An old injury, you said?"

"Yeah. I used to be quite the virtual gamer. My mom died when I was young, and my dad was always involved at the base, so I entertained myself a lot. I actually went to the world championship of Drezen's Colony Wars."

"What? You're a pro athlete, too?"

"Not really. Have you ever played?"

"I wasn't much for any of the virtual games. I couldn't keep my equilibrium in the sphere. I was always falling down and throwing up when I got out."

She made a face. "Not the most popular guy at the parties, then?"

"Never."

"Well, it was a variation on a classic game: capture the flag. You played that,

I'll bet."

"Sure. I had lots of cousins. We mostly played that and baseball."

"Drezen's Colony is like that, but it's much more intense. You're in the sphere, you start out in the first few rounds with a basic commando model. You have to charge in, avoid capture, and get the Drezen insignia, which is the key to unlock the next level. After the basic rounds, the playing field can be anything: underwater, in space, whatever, and you have a really limited amount of time to find and capture the insignia. I blacked out many a time before I could navigate the first vacuum level."

"Whoa. Sounds intense."

"It is. There's a lightning level where you get shocked repeatedly throughout the game. There's a cliff level where you're essentially falling the entire time and you have to catch onto ledges to look for the insignia."

"And I couldn't even keep my lunch in the virtual racecar games."

She laughed. "But I wasn't very good."

"You went to the world championships."

"But I bombed out in the third advanced level."

"That's not so bad."

"There were 200 advanced levels."

He glanced away sheepishly. "Oh. Well, then . . ."

She hit his shoulder. "You're not supposed to agree."

"Sorry." He glanced at her just in time to see the end of a yawn. He stood and reached to take her glass. "You'd better get some rest."

"You need some, too. You're worn out." Kaia put her hand on his arm and let it trail down to his hand. His eyes found hers and he saw the invitation in them.

"I'm—I'm not sleepy," he said, but he didn't pull his hand away. His voice was quieter than before.

"Just take a catnap with me."

She didn't let go of his hand, and he found himself moving beside her onto the couch. Ethan laid back, and she curled against him. The couch was roomy, soft, and cool. She felt warm against his side. He felt her shift and move her hand onto his chest. He reached up and held it. Soon he felt her breathing evenly. His own eyes closed, and for the first time in five years, he slept without dreaming.

CHAPTER 10

When Ethan woke in the early hours of day 2021, he was lying on his side with Kaia in his arms. She was breathing softly into his neck, and he closed his eyes again, feeling the feather touch of it. She stirred slightly, and Ethan shifted his right arm out from under her. He slid carefully off the couch, leaving her there as he stepped into the hall. He stood catching his breath, images of her dancing in his mind. Already he longed to go back to her, to hold her until she woke up, but he didn't dare, knowing that he wouldn't be able to let her go if she looked up at him with those soft gray eyes. He willed his legs to move and walked alone down to the passenger hold.

He maneuvered among the rows until he stood in front of Aria's chamber. Her red-gold hair shone in the half-light. She was so still, so perfect. Her face was gentle and kind. He could see the smile lines next to her eyes, the slight creases framing her mouth. How often he'd kissed them. He always liked the feel of her smiling under his kisses.

Her body, round and smooth, looked delicious through the glass. Her legs, long and strong, and her feet seemed impossibly relaxed for her upright position. He longed to slide his hand over her belly, pull himself close to her, and sleep with her in his arms. He didn't care if they never woke up.

He sat on the floor in front of her chamber and then lay back with his head on his arms. He closed his eyes. The winds of Earth seemed to ruffle his hair. The smell of a hot mountain meadow and the bitter wildflowers that grew there seemed to fill his nostrils. He remembered lying with Aria on a mountaintop a year before they'd boarded this ship. They'd been backpacking for a week, camping beside streams and lake mountains, tasting the world before they left it. They'd stopped in a meadow that hot afternoon, shrugging their packs off and crumpling to the warm earth. He remembered rolling his head to the side to look at Aria, lying beside him. A crown of wildflowers poked up around her hair. The green leaves entangled themselves around her, making it look as if she was growing out of the meadow herself. She'd looked over and smiled at him, and he'd felt the pull of his heart, that old feeling of contentment beyond what he could express in any of the languages he knew.

They had lain in the meadow all afternoon, talking about the possibility of a trip to the stars. Their application was in, but Ethan sensed in Aria a hesitation.

"I'm not sure you want to go," he'd said carefully, afraid to belie his own yearning for the trip.

Aria didn't answer. She sat up and reached to cup a vibrant tangerine-colored flower in her hand, gently bending it toward him. "It's a California Poppy," she said, running a gentle finger over the curves of its fragile petals.

Ethan had peered at it closely, seeing, for the first time, its exquisite delicacy. He wondered briefly how many of them he had trampled, how many he was laying on. He sat up.

She went on, still gazing at the flower. "Its scientific name is Eschscholzia californica. When the Spanish explorers first saw it, they named it 'cup of gold.' It's pollinated by beetles as well as bees. It has four petals, and they're shaped like fans . . ." She paused. "I could tell you all that even if I wasn't looking at it right now." Her eyes met his. "And I could tell you more than you'd find in a wildflower handbook. I could tell you about the California Poppy's small genome and its short life cycle, how it changes quickly when new elements are introduced, and how it is perfect for studying plant metabolism and plant morphogenesis. I used it when I was making my wheat more drought-resistant and again when I taught my wheat to pull protein more efficiently from the soil." She looked at him pleadingly and gently released the flower.

He took her hand. "Aria, you're amazing. I—" He'd searched for the right words. "You'll be such an asset to the colony. You know more about plants than anyone I've ever met."

"Earth plants, Ethan." She returned his gaze with an annoyance in her eyes. When she spoke again, there was an intensity in Aria's voice. "I know these plants at a molecular level, Ethan. I know them. I know their soil. I know what blights threaten them, what viruses attack them. I feel like, somehow, they are mine. And leaving them is . . ." She let go of his hand and brushed at the tears on her cheeks. "Leaving them is like . . . leaving part of myself."

They were quiet a long time before she spoke again. "Ethan, this is not just another Earth. This is a completely new planet in a new solar system. It's not going to be the same. The plants there will be aliens to me in every sense of the word. I'll be starting my entire career over, rebuilding every piece of knowledge. It will be like trying to learn to walk again. And who knows if anything I know about soils or genes or proteins will be useful there?"

Ethan felt then, for the first time, how truly unknown Minea was. Beyond the glossy photographs and the buzz on the evening news, he knew very little of what awaited them there.

She moved close and took his hand in hers. "You're the only reason I would even consider it," she said. "The only person I would leave this and go to the stars with. But I still need some time to know if I can give it all up." She kissed him.

He could almost feel her lips now as he opened his eyes and looked up at her. He wished he could talk to her, tell her how much he missed her and how sorry he was that he had taken them from their home.

They hadn't mentioned the trip again for several weeks. He saw now that during those weeks, she'd been grieving the loss of her research and her home. He had tried rescinding the application, but it was already being processed. He'd tried reassuring her that they could stay, that he would not ask of her such a sacrifice, but she'd already started saying goodbye.

Their acceptance to the Minea colony came three days after the rejection of his proposal by the project review board at the university, and she had told him that evening that they would go. Aria had denied that her decision was influenced by the prospect of his having to abandon Xardn, but he knew that she was as loyal to his life's work was as she was to her own. She would not let it be taken from her when he could continue it on Minea without interference. "Besides," she said with as much enthusiasm as she could muster, "maybe I'll find a new challenge there, too."

It was that gift that came back to him every time he reached for Kaia, every time he found his eyes lingering on her dark hair, her shining eyes. He couldn't bear the thought of Aria's sacrifice culminating in his betrayal. But the years stretched before him, and he wasn't sure he could fight this feeling forever. There was only one way to stay true to Aria. Though her stasis dreams still haunted her, he would have to convince Kaia to go back into stasis. His unused chamber shone dull and empty beside Aria. If he could talk Kaia into using it, the chamber could sustain her until she made it to Minea. Once there, she could start a new life, and Ethan, an old man, could look his wife in the eyes when she awoke and tell her he'd always been true to her trust.

* * *

He stayed away from the Caretaker's hold all that day, making the rounds of his passengers, standing on the observation deck gazing out at the infinite blackness of space, and tinkering with some of the climate control adjustments that Kaia had shown him. In his mind, he talked through several possible conversations where he would convince Kaia to go back into stasis. He looked critically over his behavior since Kaia had woken up. Out here, in the shining halls of the ship, he could only just remember the way he'd felt when he'd looked at Kaia these last few days. He was sure that his reactions had been due to his being taken off guard. He felt he could quell his desire for her if he was strict with himself. He'd had friends who were women before. There was no need to fear being with her. He went back to the hold with new resolve to avoid any more close contact.

She was awake reading a book when he came in, and she smiled at him from the couch. "Out and about?" she asked.

Ethan was surprised after his sternness with himself that his heart still thrilled to see her there. He nodded and walked over to the AAU.

"Did you do anything interesting? Blow up any part of the ship?"

He felt awkward as he carried his tray of food over to the chest. "Surprisingly, no. What are you hungry for?"

"Fried chicken. Meal three four two."

"That was quick."

"I've been thinking about it all afternoon. I'm starving!"

"Didn't you get any lunch?" He felt a pang of regret for having stayed away all day.

"Oh, yeah. I hobbled over there. But it wasn't worth it for an afternoon snack. So I just waited for dinner." He brought her tray over and situated it on her lap.

"I'm sorry. I was just checking things out around the ship."

"It's okay." She glanced at him from the corner of her eye.

He pretended not to notice and very carefully stayed at his end of the couch. The two ate in silence. That night, Ethan summoned the massage table early and pretended to be asleep long before the artificial lights went out.

CHAPTER 11

Three days later, Ethan and Kaia sat on the couch with a bucket of popcorn between them, watching an action movie called *Platinum Heart*. Her ankle was wrapped, propped up on the chest by the couch and well on its way to healing. She'd stayed off it, watching movies and reading while Ethan stayed out in the ship, coming back only at lunch and in the evenings. Finally, she'd suggested they watch a movie together.

This was one of the newest flicks in the computer's databanks, having been released just days before they'd left Earth. Ethan had seen it before, but she hadn't. The story was set in a time where platinum was the only currency. The main character was a soldier in love with an android girl. He had to rescue her from rebels who were trying to get her platinum heart in order to buy their ship back and escape the horrors of their post-apocalyptic society.

When the popcorn ran out, somewhere around the time that the android girl got kidnapped, Ethan picked up the bucket and leaned over to set it on the floor by his feet. When he sat back up, Kaia had scooted over beside him. She leaned slightly into him. The pleasure of having her there swept over him. He willed himself to shift away but found the pull of being close to her too strong to overcome.. When things on the screen started exploding, Kaia grasped Ethan's arm tensely. They both watched as the action scenes played out in the middle of the movie, but during the lull that preceded the final fight, Kaia's head drooped onto his shoulder and he realized she was asleep.

Her vulnerability prevented him from moving her. He took a deep breath. There was no harm in her resting there, and the strain of avoiding any contact with her over the last few days was beginning to take its toll on him. Involuntarily, he leaned his cheek onto her hair and his own eyes closed.

The hold was dark when he awakened. His head was resting on Kaia's soft hair. She was still sleeping on his shoulder, her arms curled around his bicep.

Her breathing was gentle and even. He could see just the tip of her nose and her lips below it. He reached up and moved her bangs out of his line of vision. As he did so, she awakened and tilted her head back to look up at him.

"How did it end?" she asked sleepily.

"Happily, of course." His voice was huskier than he expected it to be.

Her arms tightened around his. Her sleepy gray eyes held him. He found himself leaning down to her. Without hesitation, he kissed her, a soft, careful kiss. She responded, kissing him back with more passion than he expected. He moved his hand up to her cheek, pulling her closer. As he let his defenses down, their kisses came like rain. He closed his eyes, inhaling her violet scent. His affection for her mingled with the ecstasy of having physical contact after so long, and he kissed her lips, her cheeks, her jaw, her neck. Her fingers were again entwined in his hair, and he was completely surrounded by her.

As his lips touched her collarbone, Aria's green eyes suddenly flashed in his mind. His lips found Kaia's and he kissed her wildly, hungrily, feeling for a moment the two combined in his soul. Even as he kissed her, though, his fingertips were finding their way gently across her cheek, to her lips, caressing them as he pulled away, willing his arms to release her. He saw the confusion in her eyes as he sat back, his fingers still on her lips. He closed his eyes briefly to block out the confusion he saw playing across her face.

"Oh, Kaia, Kaia, I—"

Her eyes searched his face.

"I can't." His voice was gentle. "I can't." He breathed deeply. "I can't."

He saw his words hurt her. Saw the pain ricochet across her face. Suddenly, she slid close to him again, tucking her head under his chin as she wrapped her arms around his torso. She held him tight and said nothing.

He let his hand go up to her hair and rest there. When she let go, he stood and walked to the AAU. "A cola, please." He drank the cold liquid and turned back to see Kaia slipping on her stasis shoes.

"Kaia, I—"

"Ethan." She was still as breathless as he was, and she avoided his eyes. "Let's just—go for a walk."

"Okay." Getting out of there seemed like a great idea. "Do you think you can make it?" His eyes darted to her ankle.

"It . . . feels fine today. Probably be good to stretch it a little." He felt the pain behind her false cheerfulness and longed to cross the room and take her in his arms again, to finish what they'd started. She was already at the door of the hold, though, on her way into the hall. Ethan took several large, quick steps and caught up to her.

They walked down the hall in silence, not touching each other. "Ethan," she finally said. "I—I'm in love with you."

Ethan didn't say anything.

"I know it's awful. David's only been gone . . ." She trailed off. "But I feel it so strongly. And, I think—I think you feel something, too."

They kept walking.

"I'm not asking you to—" She hesitated. "I just want you to think realistically about what lies ahead of us on this ship. If we're going to be here for almost five decades—" Again she stumbled on her words. "Do you really think we can go on—that we can just live here together all our lives, feeling the way that we do, without . . . Just think about it, okay?"

He looked at her then, and nodded.

"Kaia, I—I've been thinking about it since the moment I saw you. I think about it all the time." She brightened slightly, so he hurried on. "I . . . I'd have to really *love* someone—"

"You don't love me?" She was characteristically direct.

He was tempted to tell her how he felt, in all its complexity. But he knew that it would take away his only reason not to hold her, to be hers. He also knew he couldn't, knew that his soul belonged to the woman frozen in time below them, and to give himself to Kaia would mean the ultimate betrayal. So he looked away from Kaia and shook his head quickly.

"Ethan, that's not true. You—I felt it. I've felt it since you first touched me."

He walked faster, fighting the urge to take her in his arms. He couldn't let it go on any longer. If he hurt her now, she'd hurt less later, and maybe the plan for her that he had formed in his mind—putting her back into stasis in his unused chamber—would work. She'd been planning on living her life out with David in this empty ship. She'd never leave him here alone if he was in love with her.

"Kaia," he said, with an edge in his voice. "I haven't seen anyone—I haven't touched a woman—for five years. I couldn't help wanting . . . you. Wanting is not . . . it's not . . . the same . . . the same as love." He glanced swiftly and saw her fallen look from the corner of his eye.

Her breath came quickly. "Oh," was all she said.

They walked in silence, wandering aimlessly and awkwardly together.

When Ethan dared look up, he saw that they'd found their way to the cargo hold at the bottom of the ship.

"Do you want to check out the cargo hold?" He tried to keep his tone neutral.

She only nodded, biting her lip, still avoiding his eyes.

Ethan gave the code and the big door slid open to reveal another cavernous room. Smooth white plastic shelving stood in front of them. The shelves held round-cornered boxes containing all that the passengers were allowed to bring from Earth. Each box was branded with the passenger's number.

"Wow," Kaia said, momentarily forgetting the tension between them.

Ethan grabbed the new subject readily. "It's impressive, huh?"

"I've never seen them with the boxes in them. Just the bare, open shelves. It's awesome. 4,000 people's whole lives packed up in this single room." She began walking down the rows, reading the numbers.

Ethan followed her, watching her walk.

"Here it is! Here's mine!" She reached for the second shelf, where her passenger number was branded on a box like all the others. She took it out of its depression on the shelf and opened it. On top was a photograph of Kaia and David McNeal. He was in his dress uniform, and Kaia was wearing a bright blue dress. They were looking at each other, not the camera, and as Kaia ran her fingers across the photo, Ethan felt a wave of discomfort, as if he were intruding. She set it aside and began to take out other things. He turned and continued down the row to find his own box.

Number 4,000 was his. He pulled it out and set it on the floor, where he crouched beside it and started sifting through his memories of Earth. On top were his baseball glove and ball from his childhood. He knew that Minea had manufacturing facilities, but he doubted that baseball equipment was a top priority to the new civilization. He thought of how he'd planned to play ball with his own son, and how that was no longer in his future. Next, he found some small gifts from his parents and grandparents: a silver watch, a book of scripture, a set of paints. There was a gap where his glyphtol and the razor had been stowed before he had taken them out years ago. There were some love notes from Aria, worn with the past five years of reading them over and over. Now, he pushed them aside a little guiltily and dug under them for his wedding ring. Finding it in the bottom corner of the box, he slipped it onto his finger and felt its heft. It reminded him of the first few months of his marriage, when the band was new and strange and he awoke in the mornings wondering what it was. He put the top back on the box and replaced it on the bottom shelf. Next he reached for the box above it: 3,999.

She had brought a sheaf of her own wheat from Earth. She had brought dirt from their backyard and a dried rose from their front yard. Her wedding ring was in there, a sapphire with filigree around it, and the first ultrasonic pictures of their baby. He ran his finger over its alien form on the page, traced its beanlike shape, and felt a pang of sadness that the child wouldn't know him. He gently replaced it.

He heard Kaia's footsteps and slipped the lid back on Aria's box.

"Ethan," she said excitedly, "I think I know how to find my dad."

He raised his eyebrows. "Okay."

Kaia held up a picture of a stern-faced man. "We can have the computer scan this and match it with the passenger list."

Ethan nodded, trying to hide the discomfort he felt at seeing the picture. "Good idea."

She handed it to him. "You're better with the computer."

Ethan made the necessary commands and they watched the screen as passenger faces flashed across it too fast for them to register.

"No match found." The computer's announcement confirmed Ethan's suspicion. The same words flashed on the screen.

Kaia looked frantically at Ethan. "That can't be!" she said desperately. "He's on this ship. He is the ranking officer on this ship!"

Ethan nodded, disquiet filling his chest. "Okay, wait. Maybe the picture is just hard to match—maybe the angle's wrong or something. We'll try this. Computer," he said, "show any *possible* matches to the picture. Anyone who has even a sixty percent match."

The faces flashed again.

"That will get anyone with almost any characteristic similar to your father's. That'll find him, or he's not on this ship." They waited a few seconds, and then several screens of faces appeared down the row. They began to search through the faces and names. As they determined that General Reagan was not on one screen, they walked through it and assessed the next. At the end of the last screen, Kaia's lip trembled.

"Ethan, he's not here. He's not on this ship." Suddenly, she stood and headed to the passenger hold. "I'll look myself."

Ethan followed, a growing dread filling him. He had never seen General Reagan on this ship, not under any name.

It took hours, but they looked at every passenger. Kaia's father was not on the ship. As they reached the last stasis chamber, standing open beside Aria's peaceful form, Kaia's hopeful expression fell, and her tear-filled eyes found Ethan's.

He took her hand. "Maybe there was a change of plans at the last. Maybe he was transferred to another ship."

"But don't you know what this means?" Kaia began to weep. "It means I'll never see him again."

Ethan saw his chance. "Kaia," he said softly, stroking her hand. "It doesn't have to mean that."

She looked up at him, questioning, and he turned toward the empty chamber, hurrying on, "You could meet him on Minea. I'm sure he just got placed on another ship for some reason. If you went back into stasis—"

Her eyes darkened. "No!"

"Kaia, don't be silly. You could use my chamber and—"

She wasn't crying anymore. "And leave you alone here? All alone for the rest of your life? I won't do it." She grasped his hands. "I know what these years have been like for you. Don't ever ask me to do that again. I told you, Ethan, I love you. I'm not leaving you to hurtle through space alone!"

He was desperate. "Kaia, you can't waste the rest of your life just because I'm doomed to waste mine!"

She shook her head stubbornly.

"There won't be anything between us," he said frantically, holding up his left hand. The band glinted as he gestured toward the sleeping form of his wife. "Don't stay awake hoping—"

Kaia cut him off by dropping his hands, turning sharply and walking away from him, down the long corridor of chambers and out the door of the hold.

He followed her into the cargo hold. "Kaia!"

She was standing in the center of the aisle. "I won't do it, Ethan. Don't ever bring it up again."

He saw the set of her jaw, the fire in her eyes, and knew that there was no convincing her right now. He clenched his teeth and breathed hard through his nose. The two faced each other in the aisle, shiny white boxes on either side. After several tense seconds, Kaia turned again and walked up the aisle, more slowly this time. Ethan saw her limping slightly and jogged to catch up.

When he spoke again, his voice was controlled. "Kaia, I won't give up the idea."

She glared at him. "And I won't change my mind."

"But for now," he asked, trying to keep his voice cold, "how's your ankle?"

"It's fine."

They had reached her box, still open in the center of the row. Its contents were spread around it. She moved down smoothly and began to pick up her earthly treasures.

Ethan saw several pictures of her as a dark-haired child, an awkward teen, and as the woman who stood before him now. He saw some small trinkets and some jewelry. As she moved a silk handkerchief, something else caught his eye.

"Is that a weapon?" He was incredulous. Passengers were forbidden to bring weapons aboard the ships, though the military detail had weapons stowed in a separate part of the cargo hold.

Kaia blushed. "It's just a simple energy pistol," she said, scooping it into the box hurriedly.

"You're quite the rebel, Kaia Reagan. Sneaking aboard, awakening early, packing heat." He couldn't help smiling a little.

"You don't understand. It's sentimental." She put the lid back on the box and lifted the whole thing back to its indentation on the shelf.

Ethan raised his eyebrows. "Sentimental?" He was teasing her now.

She was still slightly flustered. "My dad gave it to me when I was a kid, okay? I used to do target practice with it. He'd take me out and we'd shoot bits of garbage with it." Her tone turned sad. "It was the only thing we did together. He was gone a lot to the colonies. He . . . I liked being with him."

Ethan saw that he'd struck a nerve and backtracked to make it up. "I know what you mean. It was baseball with my dad and me. I brought my glove from Earth, too."

Her melancholy look disappeared, and they started to walk back to the door of the hold. "It's worth more to me now that I know he's not here. I'm glad I smuggled it on board."

CHAPTER 12

Ethan and Kaia settled into an uneasy peace. He continued teaching her about Xardn, and she kept showing him around the ship. They didn't talk about the future, and though she still reached for him, Ethan never touched her intentionally.

"Your turn," Ethan said.

"All right! This way!" Kaia impulsively grabbed Ethan's hand and towed him down the broad hall. He felt the tingling he'd begun to anticipate when she touched him. Her skin was soft and her hand small and cool around his. The sleek walls of the hallway slipped by, and he was both relieved and disappointed when they reached the door to the navigation room and she let go.

"Access request three five five eight," Ethan said, and the door slid open noiselessly.

They walked into the navigation room. It was cooler in here, both because the space was bigger and because the ship compensated for the heat generated by the navigation equipment. It was a cavernous room. All but one wall were lined with banks of computers and control panels. They blinked bright yellows and greens as the ship steered its way through the stars. The other wall was made entirely of windows. Outside, the vastness of space stretched away from them, its bright stars and cloudy nebulae hanging suspended outside the great windows. For a moment, both were quiet as they took in the view of slanted stars through the huge banks of windows.

"I forget how fast we're moving," Ethan said quietly.

"It is a little disorienting," Kaia admitted.

"And dazzling." Ethan walked forward toward the windows until the room dropped from his periphery and all he could see was the vastness of space surrounding him. "It's like flying."

"Yeah. Wow."

Suddenly Ethan remembered standing on the observation deck with Aria. He could almost feel her heartbeat against his shoulder blade as she stood behind him, her arms around his waist. He stared out at the stars and remembered feeling the baby kick at his side through Aria's belly. Ethan breathed deeply, fighting the tears that had welled up in his eyes. He could almost see the Earth retreating, a dot of life in the midst of all that blackness. Now his eyes picked out a new dot.

Both he and Kaia spoke at the same time. "Hey."

He stopped and pointed.

"I know," she said. "I see it! Is it a planet?"

"Computer, enhance the image of that object." As he spoke, a large part of the window transformed to a zooming screen and seemed to draw the object closer. Slightly more detail was apparent.

"It looks like Earth," he said. "It has to be a planet."

"It's still really far away," she said. "But, Ethan, we don't pass any habitable planets on the way to Minea. Otherwise, they would have done the trip in two stages like they did on the journey to Salris Alpha. It can't be livable."

Ethan was quiet, squinting at the screen. "Computer, what planet is that?"

"Beta Alora," the computer answered.

Ethan thought. He had studied the route in the ship's computer many times. He remembered the names of several suns that they would pass, but the name of the planet didn't seem familiar. "Computer, what system are we in?"

"Sardon Major," the computer replied.

"I don't remember that one," Ethan said, "but we pass so many on this trip. Computer, what type of system is Sardon Major?"

"It is a triple star system."

Ethan wracked his brain, trying to remember anything about this system.

"It would be neat to pass a planet like Earth," Kaia said.

Ethan nodded. Something was bothering him, but he wasn't certain what it was. Every time he came to the navigation room, he felt disoriented. Even after studying the maps, he couldn't bend his mind around the vastness outside, around the distance that lay between where they were and where they were going.

He tore his eyes from the screen and paced to the center of the empty room. "Computer, produce the dimensional star map." A huge black globe appeared, hovering in the air. Ethan walked through the solid-looking side of the sphere and stood in the middle. The inside had the same view as he had seen out the window. "Computer, plane out fifty light-years." His view swooped back, making him stagger and close his eyes. "Computer, adjust for my equilibrium." When he opened his eyes again, the computer had skipped ahead to his desired perspective.

Kaia poked her head in the sphere near a star cluster to his left. "What the heck is this?" she said.

"You don't know about the dimensional map?"

"I'm mostly a hardware girl." She stepped the rest of the way in, standing near him and craning her neck to look around. "Wow. How'd you figure this out?"

"Lots of trial and error." Ethan pointed to the little silver ship in front of them. "There we are."

"Now *that* I recognize."

Ethan grew quiet again as he looked at the little ship. "Computer, generate a course estimation." A red beam of light shot through the sphere, showing where the ship had been and where it was headed.

"No," Ethan said with horror, "that can't be right."

The line ended at Beta Alora.

CHAPTER 13

"Computer," Ethan barked, a panic rising in him, "what is the destination of this ship?"

"The planet Minea, Mr. Bryant."

"Computer, make course corrections for Minea immediately."

The even voice of the computer came again. "No corrections are necessary, Mr. Bryant."

"Computer, why are we going to Beta Alora?"

"Beta Alora is not on our route, Mr. Bryant."

"The course estimation shows that we are headed directly for Beta Alora. Why?" Ethan was exasperated, and his voice came out higher-pitched than usual.

The computer was silent.

"It's processing," Ethan told Kaia.

After thirty seconds of tense silence, the computer spoke again. "Error: Irreconcilable information. Dimensional map temporarily disabled." The sphere disappeared from around them and the computer offered no more information.

Ethan looked at Kaia. "What would cause that?"

She shrugged. "It sounds like a glitch in the program, but we could look at the nav system and see if it has any obvious problems." She walked through a sliding door into the secondary nav room. This smaller room was lined floor to ceiling with computer banks, monitors, panels, and cabinets. Kaia walked confidently to a cabinet near the bank of computers against the right wall. "Computer," she said, "unlock the crack kit."

The computer responded quickly. "The request requires an authorization code."

Ethan thought through the list in his mind. Maybe the tools code would work. It had gotten him into toolboxes in other rooms. "Authorization code five six three two," he said firmly.

The lock on the cabinet clicked, and Kaia opened the door to reveal a large black case. She pulled it out and opened it, revealing various shiny tools in neat rows. Ethan marveled as she selected a few of them and then moved along the wall of computers.

"What did you call that tool set?" he asked her.

He saw her smile in profile. "We call it a crack kit. It has some particular tools that help you get into sealed systems like this one. See, this nav system was never meant to be accessed. It was designed to run all navigational functions of the ship completely independent of human interference. Now—" She fitted the tool she holding into a slot. "—we're going to interfere with it." She twisted the tool, torquing the levers inside, and the panel loosened. She moved to repeat the motion. "You have to have a special set of tools to loosen these 'unloosenable' panels. There's a set on every ship. Most engineers can't stand the thought of being without a good crack kit in time of need. This one is a particularly nice one. Nicer than the one I had at home."

The panel sprang open with a final twist and left a gaping hole crisscrossed with wires and glowing cables. She started to inspect them.

Ethan moved over to her and looked over her shoulder. "What do they do?"

"Well, these—" She ran her fingers along a bundle of multicolored iridescent wires. "—are the relays within the nav system. They connect various types of hardware with the main nav system. These—" She pointed out some basic grey cables. "—go to the monitors, these to the cameras outside, these to the sensors, these to the various parts of the hull, and this one . . ." She pointed out the largest of the glowing cables, back behind the rest. ". . . connects the nav system to the main computer."

"Do you see anything weird?" Ethan had no idea how it should look.

Kaia shook her head. "Honestly, it's all set to specs. I don't see a single hookup out of place." She left the open panel and began to prowl along the bank of computers. Ethan studied the jungle of cables, amazed at its complexity.

"Ethan, something's been bothering me," Kaia said, as she crouched down and ran her hands over the wall beneath a monitor.

"Yeah?" He was still peering at the cables.

"Do you remember that weird closet we heard in the shafts?"

"I remember you heard something."

"It should be right here. Behind this wall."

"Well, then, we should be able to see it on the map, right?"

Kaia nodded.

"Computer, bring up the map of this room." The map hovered in front of him, making him think of those first few months on the ship. "So, we're here. In the secondary nav room."

"Computer," Kaia said, "show the layout of this deck." The floor plan for the entire deck appeared. The primary and secondary nav rooms were in place. On the other side of the wall in front of them, the map showed the hallway. No third room was shown.

"Nothing's there, Kaia."

"Something's there, Ethan."

He shifted uncomfortably, glancing from the map to her determined face and back again. "You're sure there's another room?"

Kaia shot him an annoyed look. "I'm sure, Ethan. I thought maybe there would be a door or an access, but there's not. It's sealed up."

He nodded, waiting for her to go on.

"I think we should try to get in there, find out what it is. It's too weird that it exists at all. I've worked on fifty-six of these ships, and I've never seen it before."

"Okay. I don't have any other plans today." He tried to lighten the mood, but the sinister feeling he'd been getting throughout the last few days persisted behind his levity. "What do we do?"

"Well, I think we should take off several of these panels and see if any of them are open in the back. They shouldn't be, but it's a good place to start. Grab the other tool that looks like this." She held up the one in her hand. "It's slightly bigger, but it should still work fine. These panels seem to be sized somewhere between the two anyway. Crack all the panels that don't have visible equipment: monitors, keyboards, readouts, any blank panel."

Ethan was a little nervous. "It won't mess it up any worse?"

She shook her head. "Not if you don't unplug anything. Just open the panels and the system doesn't know the difference."

"Okay." Ethan grabbed the other tool and went to work at one end of the wall. Kaia started at the other. Every panel opened to reveal wires, plugs, equipment, and a shining silver solid wall behind it. They were sweating when they met in the middle. Behind them a stretch of panel doors hung open and several yawning holes of various sizes made the wall look like an abandoned house.

Ethan looked over at Kaia. She was pink-cheeked and exhausted. "How about we eat something?" he suggested.

She nodded.

He gestured toward the wall. "Will this be okay until we get back?"

She nodded again. "It'll be okay."

They made their way back to the hold, ate a huge lunch, and then headed back to the nav room. They were almost there when Kaia stopped in the hallway and put an ear to the wall. Her palms were spread against the silver surface, and she looked somehow stronger to Ethan.

He brushed the wall with his fingertips.

"It's in there, Ethan. I know it. I can hear the space."

"I believe you."

She slid her hand along the wall. "There's no way in here. These walls are structural, thick and reinforced on the inside."

They proceeded to the secondary nav room. It was slightly warmer inside now that the panels were all open.

"Ethan," Kaia said carefully. "I want to do something. I'm not sure if it's a good idea or not."

He felt tense. "What?"

"Well, I really really want to see what's in that room. I want to crack it open."

"How? I didn't see any more panels, just a solid wall."

"Yeah . . . We'd have to . . . cut through the wall." She went on quickly. "We could use an attenuated laser. I could make it so it would only cut through the wall, not through anything important. I . . ."

Ethan's brow was furrowed. "Is it dangerous to the passengers?"

She looked away. "A little. If we somehow cut through a cable . . . it could leave us without navigation."

"Drifting in space?"

"We could navigate manually," she said quickly and then reconsidered. "Maybe. It would be tricky."

"Navigate manually for forty-eight more years? And never make a miscalculation? We could end up missing Minea and drifting forever."

"But we could just be really, really careful cutting the panel."

"How reliable is the attenuated laser? Really?"

"Very reliable. And this is a thin wall." She knocked on it, cocking her head to listen to the sound. "Almost a partition, a false wall. It's thin and solid. There's no room inside it for ductwork or anything else important. I can guarantee I won't cut through anything in it or on this side. I just don't know what is on the other side."

"What else could be there?"

"Worst-case scenario? Life support systems."

"It could kill us?"

"Well, if for some reason that closet has extra life-support systems, or climate controlling, or . . . there are hundreds of systems on this ship, and I suppose theoretically any of them could have been put in there for some reason. So, if I messed up some of those, yeah, it could be bad."

"Why don't we cut in through the shafts?"

Her eyes widened. "No way. Everything important runs alongside the shafts."

"Kaia, going in any way seems pretty dangerous. Why risk it at all?" Ethan began pacing around the room.

"Honestly?" she said. "Maybe it's just my curiosity. I can't stand not knowing what's in there. But there are also a lot of weird things going on on this ship. Out-of-the-ordinary things. And the colonization of Minea is, as far as I've seen, a completely uniform and ordinary thing. It makes me nervous. Anything could be in there . . ." She paused, hesitating. "And, Ethan, I'm wondering something else."

He looked at her, a question in his eyes.

"It's far-fetched, but not impossible. What if . . . what if they decided to hide the military contingent for some reason? What if they wanted them inaccessible?"

"You're hoping your dad is in there?" He tried to keep the doubt out of his voice.

She was defensive. "It's not impossible. He's supposed to be on this ship. He's not in his chamber. There's this weird room . . ." Her voice trailed off. "It could be."

Ethan nodded. He tried to picture Aria's chamber behind this wall. What would he do to get to her? "We can try. If . . . if we're really careful."

Kaia smiled. "I thought I was going to have to come down and do it while you were asleep."

Ethan sensed that she was only half-joking.

He swallowed the acid taste of fear in his throat. "What's next, then?"

"Well, I've got to set up the laser. I'll need your grooming laser. We'll have to go back to the hold."

"Should we just leave this . . . mess?" Ethan was surprised how much it bothered him to see the room in disarray. Perhaps the last five years of absolute order and predictability were affecting him.

"It'll be fine for a few days. It shouldn't take me long to tinker with the laser. Anyway, I'll have to have access to all those cables eventually so I can tune the laser not to affect them." She was already walking into the primary nav room, and Ethan followed.

As they crossed, he shot one more look out the big windows. The bright dot of Beta Alora sent a feeling of dread through him. He turned and headed for the hold.

Once there, Ethan began to feel unnecessary. Kaia took over from the minute she stepped into the room. "Command the computer to give you a haircut," she said.

"I just got a haircut."

"The computer doesn't care. It will trim the millimeters that your hair has grown in the past few days. I need to see the actual laser. There are three designs of grooming laser installed on these ships. I need to see which one this is. That will affect where it originates from, how portable it is, and how easily I can modify it."

Ethan could see she was determined. "Okay." He crossed to the bathroom and stood in front of the mirror. "Computer, I need a haircut."

Kaia watched through the open door as the laser immediately shot out of a panel next to the door behind him.

Ethan stood frozen, terrified to move, even as he saw the hair falling. Finally, he blurted stiffly, "Millimeters?!"

Kaia stifled a giggle. "I'm sorry. I realized too late that it would be set for David's preferences since you've never reset it. Ethan, it can't hurt you. Move a little. You'll see. It's only capable of cutting your hair."

He stayed still.

"Ethan," she crooned, "turn your head to look at me. I promise it won't hurt you. This is the great genious of an attenuated laser. It resonates at just the right frequency to cut through the material it's designed for. It's not even a laser in the traditional sense—it's much more sophisticated." Her voice was gentle, inviting. "Come on. Turn your head. It will make you feel better about our whole plan. Look at me . . ."

He turned slowly, stiffly, and saw from the corner of his eye how the laser shifted, following his movements. He felt the laser still ruffling his hair slightly. "Hey," he said cautiously. "It didn't vaporize my brain."

He had now turned all the way around to face her. His eyes darted to the panel from which the laser was shooting.

Kaia laughed her smooth, bubbling laugh. "Of course not. It's tuned to only affect the hairs on your head. It won't cut your clothes, your flesh, your bones. It's harmless to the tissues."

He turned back around abruptly. "It still makes me nervous."

She laughed again. "No, not now." She turned back to the laser. "Hmmm. Okay. It's the ICT 160. Great. I can do it."

"It's the right one?"

"Yeah. It won't be as easy to modify as the Tracer, but it's definitely easier than the other option, the ICT 140."

The laser suddenly ceased.

"Looks nice," she said.

He grunted. "Did you see everything you needed to? If not, maybe we could just go for the bald look. It wouldn't be much different."

She smiled and ruffled her hand across the cropped hair. "Thanks for letting me check it out. You've earned a piece of pie. Go have one while I get this thing out of the wall."

He scowled at her as he edged past on his way to the AAU. She moved to the panel, and he heard her digging in her tool kit as he ordered his pie.

* * *

She had the laser out within the hour. Ethan watched an old Earth movie as she cracked open the laser and started her modifications. He heard her mumbling about various lengths of specific wire, certain bits of hardware, or tools with complex-sounding names. When he glanced back late in the evening, he saw that she was working on a box connected by wires to a long steel tube. The tube was tapered at the end like a giant pencil. He recognized the taper as the part of the laser that poked out of the wall while he was getting his hair cut. The box was laid open like an oyster, and Kaia was holding it on her crossed legs, using impossibly tiny tweezers to remove and replace small bits inside the box. She finished what she was doing as he was watching.

Looking up, she said, "Let's test it."

"I don't have any more hair to cut," he said bitterly.

"Oh, no. It's not a grooming laser anymore. It would slice right through you now. Let's see what it does on the titanium."

She laid the box carefully on the floor and sprang up, retrieving from the bathroom the small panel that had concealed the laser in the wall. She set it against one leg of the massage table.

"Okay. You might want to stay back a little."

Ethan crouched down on the couch further.

Kaia pointed the tapered end of the steel tube at the propped-up panel and flipped a switch in the open box. A beam shot out, boring an instantaneous hole through the titanium panel and into the floor behind it. As she moved to turn it off, the beam moved, slicing the panel, the leg of the massage table, and the floor behind it. She quickly turned it off as the pieces of the panel fell to the floor and the table tipped crazily to the side. "Whew. Well, that seems to have worked." She laid the tube down, carefully pointing it at the empty back wall of the hold.

Ethan crossed cautiously to the table and picked up the sliced-off piece of the leg from the floor. He held it up between them. "Seems to?"

"Okay, I may have the intensity turned up a little . . . too much."

"Maybe."

Kaia sat back down and fiddled with the settings in the box.

Ethan put down the severed leg and looked at the clean edges of the titanium panel, sliced partway across. He shivered, running his other hand over his freshly-cut hair. "If you don't need me, I'm going for a walk." He crossed the hold and got his journal and glyphtol. Then he backed toward the door.

"Okay. I'll page you when I get it working."

Ethan crossed into the hall. He felt helpless again, like something was happening to him that he couldn't stop and didn't understand. The gleaming ship stretched before him, and he took the elevator to the observation deck.

The passengers had spent time here waiting to be put into stasis, so it had a much more communal feel than the rest of the ship. Here there were comfortable chairs and sofas, placed in various positions to take advantage of the 360 degree view of the stars. There were several AAUs and several bathrooms. He found his favorite chair, the one very nearly in the center of the deck. If he sat just right, he couldn't see the silver walls behind him at all, only the transparent bubble that looked into the universe. He stretched out and lost himself in the stripes that were stars around him.

He opened his journal and the case for the glyphtol. He started writing quickly in Xardn. He poured onto the paper his feelings for Kaia: his awe at her engineering abilities, his appreciation of her wit, and his intense desire for her. He'd been fighting them, but they hadn't subsided, and her words came back to him. He knew he couldn't spend the next five decades pretending he didn't feel anything. It felt good to write about it, to admit it. If he wanted to remain true to Aria, he could never let Kaia know how he felt. He scrawled for hours, writing all he'd thought about her over the happenings of the last several days. Finally, he had written all he could about this fascinating, funny woman who'd awakened and walked into his lonely life. It was liberating to have let it out, and he set the journal and glyphtol aside with a sense of peace and confidence. Then he found his way back to the hold.

"Holy cow!" he said as he walked in.

Kaia was asleep on the floor beside the laser. She awoke when she heard his voice. "What?" she asked sleepily.

"What? What? You've turned this place into some kind of arts and crafts project." The broad walls were carved with intricate designs: her initials, his initials, and pictures.

"I had to test it, Ethan," she said irritably as she stood up.

"On the walls?"

"Where else? The Caretaker's hold has the most free walls of anywhere in the whole ship. Anyway, I didn't just burn random holes. I think it's kind of nice." She was moving a little stiffly from her nap on the floor.

Looking at it, Ethan had to nod. "Okay, so it's not so bad. It is kind of nice to have a change." He ran his fingers over one of the pictures. It was a tree on a hill. "Actually, you are quite artistic."

"Thank you. I think I've got it down, finally. I'll have to finish calibrating it when I get to the nav room because there are some cables in there that aren't found anywhere else on the ship. But it's pretty close to done. Watch this." Before he could stop her, Kaia had pointed the laser at the couch. She flipped it on and before his eyes he watched the beam shoot through the couch and through the chest, where she carved a little bird in the floor in front of the movie screen. The couch and chest were untouched.

"That's crazy!" he said. "I can't believe it works."

"It's just physics. The laser is set to only vaporize the titanium molecules. It doesn't affect the others—" Her sentence ended in a colossal yawn.

"You're beat. You should get some rest."

Kaia nodded. Then a shadow crossed her face as she glanced at the massage table, still careening off on one corner. "I'm sorry about your bed. You can have the couch. I'll sleep down here." She pointed to the floor.

"You know what? I just remembered the observation deck. There's plenty of room for me up there. I hadn't been up there in so long that I'd forgotten how amenable it was. I'll sleep up there."

"Oh, that's not fair, to run you out of your hold."

"You're limping again, and you're exhausted. I'm not making you go all the way there."

She started to protest again.

"No argument. I'll go up there for tonight. We'll talk more about it later." He was already leaving. "Maybe we'll trade off." He stopped and turned around on the other side of the door. "And Kaia?" She looked at him. "No more art. Get some sleep, Picasso."

He saw her smiling as the door closed.

On his way up he evaluated what he'd told her. It was true. In the last nine days, he'd never once considered the observation deck, though it was a perfectly suitable place to sleep. He realized with chagrin that he hadn't wanted to leave the close quarters of the Caretaker's hold. He also admitted to himself that he didn't want to leave now, but he kept walking.

CHAPTER 14

Ethan opened his eyes to a dazzling array of stars. He lay still, watching the nearest stars, visible as stripes against the sky, and letting his eyes roam to the soft spots of light further out. He was amazed anew at the rainbow of colors he saw outside the windows of the observation deck. Large golden suns shone at various distances from the ship, and smaller stars winked red, blue, purple, and white. The vastness of the galaxies both thrilled and scared him. He finally rose and grabbed a glass of milk from the AAU.

"Computer," he said, "where is Kaia?"

"Passenger three six nine two is in the secondary navigation room, Mr. Bryant."

"Already?" Ethan exclaimed, wolfing a quick breakfast before heading down to meet Kaia.

She was leaning inside one of the panels they'd cracked open yesterday. He noticed that she'd exchanged her stasis suit for a pair of engineer's coveralls.

"New outfit?"

"Yeah. I had the computer find them for me. They were stashed in one of the miscellaneous compartments. I needed something with more pockets. Stasis suits weren't designed for this sort of work." As he approached, he took a closer look at the open panel. The cables inside had been carefully moved aside and attached by small clips to the inside of the wall. He watched as she secured a small cable inside a clip and then turned to him triumphantly.

"I tuned the laser to avoid any cables in this room. I also adjusted the cutting depth to the exact millimeter of the walls. It should be ready as soon as I make a big enough space to cut here."

When she had clipped all the cables and wires back, she stood up, shaking the cramps out of her muscles. She looked at Ethan, standing against the wall a few feet away. "Ready to give it a try?"

"What's the phrase?" he said. "Ready as I'll ever be?"

She smiled. "I know you're nervous. I am too. I'll try to be very careful." She crossed the floor and picked up the laser and its now-closed control box.

Ethan looked closer at the laser. There were several rings that made up the tapered end. Notches in the rings seemed to indicate intensity. Small ports and connections studded the topmost ring, and the very end of the point was an open, perfect circle. Kaia held it in the crook of her arm and moved back to the panel.

On the other side of the control box, wires extended out to an energy port beside the door. She had altered the hardwire and made it easy to connect to the port. Ethan was impressed with her skills.

She sat on the floor, bracing the laser against her shoulder and sighting down it like a rifle. "Here we go, Ethan," she mumbled.

The beam shot out, and Ethan held his breath as she moved it slowly in a simple square. One of the bundles of cables drooped slightly into the path of the laser, but before he could warn her she'd already passed over them and they remained unhurt. She completed the square, and the section of titanium fell forward, clattering to the floor. She held the laser steady and switched it off, leaving the rest of the wall untouched.

Ethan breathed again as they both moved forward eagerly to peer into the hole. Wires and cables laced the hole on the other side and he felt a slight disappointment to see the back of another panel just past the cables.

"It's okay," Kaia said, reaching for her crack kit. "I expected that there might be more paneling. I'll have it off in a second." She slipped into the hole and slid her small hand up into the darkness on the other side of the wall she'd just cut. Ethan heard her prying at the panel and then heard it give way and pop open. She spread the wires and slipped through.

He was right behind her.

They emerged into a much smaller room than the one they'd left, but otherwise it looked very similar. The walls were lined with monitors, control panels, and readouts. The two looked at the wall they'd just come through. A star map monitor tracked the ship's progress through space. A readout beside it gave coordinates. They moved around the room, looking carefully at the various monitors. All were identical to those in the secondary navigation room until they reached the wall opposite the one they'd come through. Here things changed dramatically. Keyboards on this side were infinitely more complex.

Ethan ran his fingers over the keys in wonder, centimeters above actually touching them. "It's a Xardn keypad."

"Xardn? Are you sure?"

"Yes. It's the only hardware one I've ever seen outside of a university. Almost every computer has one buried in its memory banks, but no one ever uses them." His eyes moved up to the monitor. Several lines of numbers and single letters filled the screen. He stared at it for a long moment and then muttered, "Impossible." Moving closer to the screen, he said, "That can't be."

Kaia looked at the jumble of characters on the screen. "What is it, Ethan? What are those?"

He turned slowly to her. "I'm not sure, but . . . I think they might be the parametric equations for Xardn symbols," he said. "Computer, show the holoscreen."

Nothing happened.

"Computer," he barked, low on patience.

Still, there was no response.

Kaia said quietly, "Ethan, it can't hear you. The computer can't hear you here."

He looked at her skeptically. "Kaia, the computer is omnipresent. It can hear you anywhere."

She shook her head. "Call it again then."

He tried several times, from various places in the room. "How can that be?"

"This room must be shielded from the computer for some reason. I've never seen anything like it. I don't even know how you'd do it. It raises a thousand questions. What is this room for? Why is it hidden even from the computer? What are these machines controlling?"

Ethan turned back to the screen, slightly shaken by the absence of an entity he'd come to feel was everywhere. "I think we need to decipher these equations. Maybe then we can find some answers."

The screen scrolled through a dizzying array of letters and numbers. It moved quickly, obviously never intended for people to watch.

$$x(\Theta)=((135\text{-}315)\cos(\Theta)+(\text{-}98)\cos(((135\text{-}315)/315)\Theta), y(\Theta)=(135\text{-}315)\sin(\Theta)\text{-}(98)\sin(((135\text{-}315)/315)\Theta)); x(\Theta)=((78\text{-}117)\cos(\Theta)+(32)\cos(((78\text{-}117)/117)\Theta), y(\Theta)=(78\text{-}117)\sin(\Theta)\text{-}(32)\sin(((78\text{-}117)/117)\Theta))); x(\Theta)=(76\text{-}243)\cos(\Theta)+(115)\cos(((76\text{-}243)/243)\Theta), y(\Theta)=(76\text{-}243)\sin(\Theta)\text{-}(\text{-}115)\sin(((76\text{-}243)/243)\Theta); x(\Theta)=(53\text{-}124)\cos(\Theta)+(205)\cos(((53\text{-}124)/124)\Theta), y(\Theta)=(53\text{-}124)\sin(\Theta)\text{-}(\text{-}$$

$205)\sin(((53-124)/124)\Theta)$; $x(\Theta)=(118-124)\cos(\Theta)+(205)\cos(((118-124)/124)\Theta)$, $y(\Theta)=(118-124)\sin(\Theta)-(-205)\sin(((118-124)/124)\Theta)$; $x(\Theta)=(111-222)\cos(\Theta)+(205)\cos(((111-222)/222)\Theta)$, $y(\Theta)=(111-222)\sin(\Theta)-(-205)\sin(((111-222)/222)\Theta)$; $x(\Theta)=(113-210)\cos(\Theta)+(150)\cos(((113-210)/210)\Theta)$, $y(\Theta)=(113-210)\sin(\Theta)-(150)\sin(((113-210)/210)\Theta)$; $x(\Theta)=(78-210)\cos(\Theta)+(151)\cos(((78-210)/210)\Theta)$, $y(\Theta)=(78-210)\sin(\Theta)-(151)\sin(((78-210)/210)\Theta)$

Ethan stepped closer to the screen, mumbling under his breath. "One-thirty-five . . . cosine . . . theta . . . equals . . . that could be 'yesterday.' No, I think more specific . . . but it's a date of some kind. This one—" He traced the equations as they moved up the screen. "I've only seen that in verbs, but it seems surrounded by . . . no, that can't be right . . ." Finally, he turned from the screen in frustration.

"I can't keep up with it. Just when I get a handle on the part of speech, it's moved to another equation. I can't concentrate on one long enough to decipher it. And most of them I don't know by heart anyway. I need a readout that I can freeze, and I need my glyphtol to plot the symbols. It's impossible this way." He headed for the hole in the wall.

"Where are you going?"

"I'm going for my journal and my glyphtol. Maybe if I can record some of the equations I can decipher them." He was down and gone through the hole before she could protest.

Ethan returned quickly, reaching through the hole and setting his instruments in the room ahead of him. He crawled through after them and then stood in front of the screen. Taking a laser pen and opening his journal, he began writing as fast as he could. The equations appeared on the surface of the paper, letter after letter, number after number. His eyes darted from the paper to the screen and back, capturing one line at a time. As he struggled to keep up, he realized with chagrin how easy this would be if the computer could record the readout and freeze it. He couldn't dwell on the thought, however, because he had already missed several numbers and letters by letting himself get distracted

He had two pages of notes by the time his hand cramped up badly enough that he had to stop. He seemed to start breathing again and he looked up at Kaia.

"Did you get it?" she said carefully.

"As much as I could of it. I know I missed a lot. And it's still scrolling. I don't know how much good this bit will do us. But we'll see." He took out the glyphtol.

"Are you okay?" Kaia asked suddenly.

"Sure. Why?"

"You look a little pale . . . paler than usual, I mean."

Ethan looked at her. "I'm a little dizzy," he said. "I've never read anything so quickly."

"Sit down."

He followed her advice and then bent over his journal.

"I'm starved," she said as he began to work. "I'm going to get some food to bring back here."

He nodded, and she slipped out the hole in the wall.

CHAPTER 15

Ethan worked feverishly. He flipped from the page with his scrawlings to a blank page, where he carefully found his starting places and drew the figures. He didn't bother stacking them, just drew them in straight lines, left to right, across the page. It was complex work, and as the symbols slowly appeared on the paper, he knew that there was a risk that he'd written a number wrong or forgotten a negative sign. Wherever he'd made such mistakes, the symbols would turn out wrong.

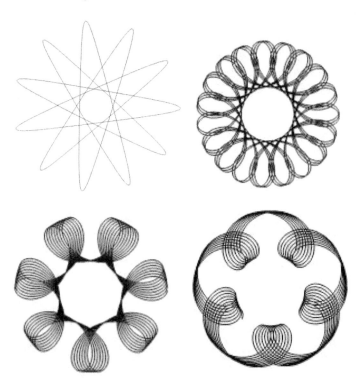

As the symbols appeared, Ethan tried to do a progressive translation. Many of them were new to him. He had to approximate their meanings based on other symbols he knew. By the time Kaia came back, he had translated most of the equations into symbols and many of the symbols into words. It was, seemingly, a list of parts and items on the ship. Chairs, assembly units, engine parts—the list ticked on from the top deck down. This bit was on the third deck, where the Caretaker's hold was located.

Kaia looked over the list. "Hmmm. I guess it's just the ship's manifest."

"Seems like it."

"It's odd, though."

Ethan nodded. "It almost raises more questions than it answers: why is it hidden back here? Why is it streaming? And most importantly, why is it written in a language that only a handful of people in the world can read?"

"It is strange."

"I think we need to see more of it." He stood, turning toward the screen again. To his surprise, he staggered slightly. "I'll jot down some more."

Kaia was suddenly at his elbow. She put a hand on his arm. "First, I think you need a break. You've been in here for hours."

Ethan raised his eyebrows. "Really?"

"Really. It's 2 AM. Come get some sleep." She pulled him gently toward the exit.

"Actually, I *am* really tired." He followed her without argument, bringing the journal and the wooden case carrying his writing instruments with him.

"I've turned off the day and night cycle," Kaia said, as she helped him stagger to the the couch nearest the door on the observation deck. "Sleep as long as you can." She was still standing quietly beside the couch as he fell asleep.

He slept a long time. The curves of the Xardn language ran through his dreams. He chased them as he slept, trying to capture their meaning and the reason for their existence on this ship. He slept through the next day and night. When he awakened, it was mid-morning and thirty-two hours had passed. He ate a huge breakfast, drank three glasses of orange juice, and took a hot shower.

"Computer," he said, as he dried his hair, "where is Kaia?"

"Passenger three six nine two is in the secondary navigation room."

Ethan made his way there. Kaia was not in the room, but when he stuck his head through the hole in the wall, he found her inside the closet. "You fooled the computer," he said as he wriggled through.

"What?"

"It thinks you're in the secondary nav room."

"Well, according to its schematics, I am."

"It really doesn't recognize that there's a wall here and a whole lot of extra computer equipment?"

"Not from what I can gather. It still knows we're here; it just thinks that this is part of the secondary nav room. I have decided we should call this the "Tertiary Navigation Room" between us so we can keep them straight." Kaia turned back to the bank of computers. Ethan noticed for the first time that she was manipulating a slender glowing cable that was connected to an open panel in the bank of computers. His eyes followed it back to where it connected to a small computer terminal at her feet.

"Keeping yourself busy while I slept, I see?" He crouched down to get a closer look at the terminal. It was a small squarish box covered on the topside with knobs, switches, and buttons.

"This," she said, tapping the cable, "is going to make your life easier. You should thank me."

"Thank you," Ethan said exaggeratedly. "What is it?"

"Oh, just your standard DR6320."

"Of course . . ." Ethan waited.

"Okay, okay," she laughed. "It's a holographic storage module. Primative, as I scavenged the main bits from one of the AAUs." She pointed to the screen with its scrolling data. "In a few more minutes, anything that has ever been on this screen, or the module that's feeding it, will be in this little box. All you'll have to do is plug this cable into the screen in the hold and you'll have the data at your fingertips. You can pause it, go back, go forward, enlarge it, whatever you want. Of course, you can also feed it directly into the ship's main computer and have the translation done in a matter of seconds." Her eyes sparkled at him.

"Wow. Kaia, you're an engineering marvel."

"I knew that all those extra courses would pay off someday."

"You took extra courses?"

"Three every semester. I didn't want to miss anything. Of course, I probably learned more from taking apart every mechanical thing I could get my hands on. I've done that all my life. Way before coursework." She checked the colored lights on the box. "When the purple one lights up, the copy is complete. Then you can take it back to the hold if you want."

"You're not coming with me?"

"I have another mystery to solve," she said, moving back to the open panel and pointing inside. "I've got to find out where this comm cable goes. It appears that this information is being communicated somewhere. That's weird because the ship's manifest should be a static document, available for access, but not of importance or interest to anyone other than the Caretaker. Unless there's other info on this system, I can't see why this cable is here. I'm going to track where it goes. If it's linked into the other computer, that's one thing, but this kind of cable is usually used to send information out to other systems outside the ship, which makes no sense."

Ethan was only half-listening. He was itching to get the Xardn information into the ship's computer. When he saw the purple light, he couldn't help interrupting her. "Looks like it's done."

She double-checked and then reached up and unplugged it, coiling the cable, scooping up the terminal, and handing it to him in one fluid motion. "I'm off to track down this cable. I'll check on you in a while."

He was back to the hold in a heartbeat. He found the input port on the screen and plugged the box into it. A list of equations appeared. "Computer," he said, "please translate the information on the main hold screen."

The computer was quiet, scanning. "Information not found."

"What?"

"Information not found, Mr. Bryant."

"Computer, the information is clearly visible on the main screen."

"The screen is blank, Mr. Bryant."

Ethan felt the old exasperation rising in him. It was impossible to argue with the computer. It would simply restate its position over and over. It obviously didn't see the information which was so plain to him, and he didn't want to leave the puzzle any longer.

"Computer, do you recognize the external module attached to the main hold screen's input?"

"Yes, Mr. Bryant."

"Please translate the information available on that module and make it available via the holoscreen."

The computer was quiet. "Information not found."

"The module is full of information!"

"The module is blank, Mr. Bryant, except for ghost images of the food prepared by Atomic Assembly Unit number six."

"That will be all, computer." Ethan realized that he'd have to get started on the information the old-fashioned way. Maybe Kaia could do something about the computer when she got back from her quest.

Ethan sighed and crossed to the shelf where he kept his glyphtol and his journal. He retrieved the instruments and began his work.

The screen read:

$$x(\Theta)=(75\text{-}125)cos(\Theta)+(44)cos(((75\text{-}125)/125)\Theta), \ y(\Theta)=(75\text{-}125)sin(\Theta)\text{-}(\text{-}44)sin(((75\text{-}125)/125)\Theta);$$
$$x(\Theta)=(39\text{-}120)cos(\Theta)+(44)cos(((39\text{-}120)/120)\Theta), \ y(\Theta)=(39\text{-}120)sin(\Theta)\text{-}(\text{-}44)sin(((39\text{-}120)/120)\Theta);$$
$$x(\Theta)=(75\text{-}134)cos(\Theta)+(98)cos(((75\text{-}134)/134)\Theta), \ y(\Theta)=(75\text{-}134)sin(\Theta)\text{-}(\text{-}98)sin(((75\text{-}134)/134)\Theta);$$
$$x(\Theta)=(50\text{-}201)cos(\Theta)+(100)cos(((50\text{-}201)/201)\Theta), \ y(\Theta)=(50\text{-}201)sin(\Theta)\text{-}(100)sin(((50\text{-}201)/201)\Theta);$$
$$x(\Theta)=(230\text{-}50)cos(\Theta)+(50)cos(((230\text{-}50)/50)\Theta), \ y(\Theta)=(230\text{-}50)sin(\Theta)\text{-}(\text{-}50)sin(((230\text{-}50)/50)\Theta)$$

Ethan started with the first equation and worked out the symbols:

He jotted down the translations: "Navigational Coordinates," then went on to the next equation, which yielded three symbols.

And the translation: "List of Items."

"This must be a main menu," he mumbled to himself as he worked out the next several symbols. They translated to "List of Human Cargo" and "Treaty Documents." He paused as he looked at the "Treaty Documents" folder. It was different than the others, embedded later and by someone who knew little about the coding of this system, maybe an intern from the United Earth Government. He didn't think the Treaty Documents would hold much interest because he'd read the whole history of the purchase of Minea and the many peace and trade treaties with various alien powers. No one had really been interested in Minea or its surrounding galaxy, deeming it too small or claiming the atmosphere was unsuited for their various physiological needs. Though humanoids found it charming, most of the rest of the universe found it quaint but useless.

Right now he was most interested in where the ship was going, so he decided to investigate the Navigational Coordinates folder first. It took him a few minutes to figure out how to use the dials and buttons on the computer terminal to navigate through the menu and choose what he wanted. Once he was into the folder, he spent several hours deciphering the equations into various dates and coordinates for the ship's travel.

He was just finishing charting the ship's trajectory when Kaia came into the hold, looking exhausted. But her eyes burned as he looked up at her. They both began to speak excitedly at the same time.

"Kaia, I just plotted—"

"Ethan, I followed—"

"You go ahead," they both said.

Ethan started again while Kaia stayed quiet. "According to these coordinates, we've been off course for months!"

"About 5 months, I'm guessing."

"Exactly! How did you know?"

"Because an FTL tracking beacon was activated in the external comms center on Day 1755 of the voyage. It's been receiving navigational information from somewhere and transmitting that information to the tertiary nav room ever since."

"What?" Ethan's breath was coming quickly now. "FTL tracking beacon?"

"Yes. That comm cable I found led me straight to it. There's a good chance that it's overriding the system and taking us to Beta Alora. And Ethan . . . it's way too advanced to be ours."

Ethan was on his feet. "We've got to cut that cable!"

Kaia laid a hand on his arm. "We can't, Ethan. Not until we find out what that beacon is doing there and what its override capabilities are. Cutting it may fry the whole nav system. Or it may be booby-trapped to do something worse."

"Worse?"

"Someone took a lot of care to hide this. It's wired into several key systems, and I'm not sure why. If we mess with it, it's not impossible that the whole ship could be disabled."

Ethan sank back on to the couch. "How do we find out how it got there?"

"I'm not sure, but I suspect that the information is in that box." Kaia gestured to the computer terminal, with its oddly cheery flashing lights. "What does the computer make of the information?"

"Nothing."

"Nothing?"

"The computer can't find any info on the module. It says the module is blank."

Kaia looked at the screen, where the equations were still prominently displayed. "We could just have it read from the screen. It would take a while, but—"

"It can't see that information, either." Ethan interrupted. "It thinks the screen is blank."

"What?"

"Computer, please translate the information on the main hold screen," Ethan said, in order to prove his point.

"Information not found."

"Please report what you detect on the main hold screen."

"The screen is blank, Mr. Bryant."

Kaia was looking at the screen in fascination. "Wow. Either it's electronically shielded information or the computer itself is programmed not to see it. Electronic shielding *is* virtually invisible to computer systems. But that's very, very complex programming. Nearly impossible, in fact."

"It sees the module, even what was on the module before you wiped it clean, but none of the new information."

Kaia's eyebrows drew together. "What are we going to do, then?"

"I guess I'll just keep translating it manually. I may make some mistakes, but I think I can get the gist of it."

"How long will it take?"

"Well, I don't think I can translate everything, but if I'm selective, I should be able to get a good chunk of it done in a week. I'll aim for the important stuff. Like the Navigational Coordinates, that sort of thing. Maybe the ship's manifest will have something about this homing beacon. Maybe a clue as to where it came from or why it activated so suddenly." He gazed across the hold. "If we can find out about it, maybe we can trace what its connected to and find out how to shut it off."

Kaia looked doubtful. "That's an awful lot of information, Ethan. You'll have to sleep. You'll have to eat."

"I will." Ethan shifted uncomfortably. "But, Kaia, I have to try. It would drive me crazy to just sit around here and watch us drift closer and closer to a planet we're not supposed to go to." He swallowed. "I keep thinking about the dimensional map. I keep thinking that we can't be more than a few weeks away from Beta Alora. I want to know what we're in for before we get there. Maybe, like you said, some emergency protocol was activated somehow, and the ship is responding by taking us to the nearest planet. If we can find out what that protocol is, we can determine if it's valid or not. If it's not, maybe we can steer the ship back on course before any more time is lost. But we can only do that if we find out quickly enough. Once we've reached the planet, I don't know how hard it will be to get back on course. They'd have to have a spaceport for us to dock . . ."

Kaia interjected. "If we wanted to start again once we were docked, we'd have to initiate the propulsion sequences . . ."

Ethan nodded. "And—" He paused. "I don't know if I *can* get us started again manually. The real Caretaker would have had that kind of training, but I—I don't. I'd rather get us back on course without having to use the manual navigation system."

She saw the burden of 4,000 souls in his eyes. "Okay. Get to work, then. I'll get us some supper."

Ethan shot her a weak smile and turned back to the journal.

CHAPTER 16

For the next several days, Ethan lived on the couch. He would eat his meals while walking around the hold, stretching his legs. As soon as the food was gone, he was back at the journal. The ship's manifest ticked on, item after item. He worked steadily but only uncovered the most basic of information. When he reached the list of items in the cargo hold, he learned quickly to identify the symbol for "container," used to designate each passenger's box, and skipped translating the contents of each. That information was found on the ship's main computer in English, so retranslating it seemed a waste of time.

Upon realizing that the main computer also had a manifest, Ethan would take a break from translating occasionally and cross-check his translation with the ship's main computer. On the sixth day he finally found a rather glaring difference in the two records.

"Kaia," he said, startling her from her own work. She was refitting the laser razor to be more compact and portable so that she could take it through the shafts. Her plan was to open all the panels along the length of the comms cable she'd found to see what else, if anything, it was linked into. "Come look at this."

She crossed to the couch and gazed down at his journal, which was filled with curves and symbols almost beautiful in their complexity. He had abandoned flipping back and forth in the book and had developed a new system in which he read the equation from the screen, wrote the symbol in the journal, and then typed his translation into the holoscreen using the hovering keyboard. This made it much easier to cross-check with the computer, as he had a second holoscreen displaying the ship's manifest next to the one he was working on.

"I found a discrepancy," he said, pointing to the two screens. "The ship's main computer has listed a whole section in the cargo hold full of weapons for the military contingent."

"The *nonexistent* military contingent," Kaia corrected him.

"Well, according to the new manifest from the tertiary nav computer, the contingent also has *nonexistent* weapons."

Kaia squinted at the screens and saw that the section where the weapons were listed on the main computer was omitted on the translated version.

"The weapons aren't even mentioned."

"That raises a pretty significant question," Kaia said, looking him in the eye.

"Right. Which of the two manifests is correct? Are the weapons here or are they not here?"

"I guess I've got another excursion." Kaia was already headed for the door. She turned back to him. "You should come. It's time for your break anyway."

Ethan nodded. "Okay. I need to get out for a minute."

Six days of intensive translating had made him stiff and achy. Perhaps a quick trip to the hold would work out some of the cramps in his muscles. He noticed the stretch in his body as he lengthened his strides down the long silver hall. He saw, from the corner of his eye, how Kaia had to take quick steps to keep up with him. Suppressing a smile, he started to take exaggeratedly longer strides. She nearly broke into a jog. He kept at it until she was almost running to keep up. Then he broke into a headlong run toward the elevator. He heard her burst of laughter and then her pounding feet, surprisingly close to him. He pushed harder, but she was right on his heels when he barreled into the elevator and slammed into the back wall. She slammed into him, and he turned and caught her in his arms, laughing. Their breath was coming hard, and he felt her ribs rising and falling against his. Involuntarily, he pulled her closer to him, tickling her playfully. She squirmed as his grip tightened.

"Don't—" she gasped, "tickle me! I can't breathe!" Her voice was high and light, and he laughed.

"I won!" he said, still tickling.

"Okay! You won! But that's just because you've been saving up all your energy sitting on the couch." She twisted out of his grip and hit the button for the cargo hold.

As the elevator began to move, they leaned side by side against the wall, still laughing and catching their breath.

"Computer," Ethan said, as the elevator stopped, "project the map, please."

The map appeared in front of them.

"Direct me to the weapons storage."

A pulsing yellow line appeared on the map and they followed it through the hold. At the back, a huge door separated a walled-off compartment from the rest of the hold.

The door remained shut as they approached. "Computer, access code eight eight eight four," Ethan commanded.

"Access denied," replied the computer. The door remained shut.

"What do you mean, 'access denied?'" Ethan barked.

"Your access to the weapons storage is denied, Mr. Bryant," the computer explained with its customary circular logic.

"Wrong access code," Ethan said, glancing at Kaia. "I'll try the red code. That gets me into anything. Computer, access code vermillion four six." Ethan opened his eyes wide in anticipation of the retinal scan that usually came along with that code.

It didn't come.

"Access denied," the computer responded again.

"Computer! What code do I need to access this storage hold?"

"You'll need the military clearance code in addition to the Caretaker's red code, Mr. Bryant."

Kaia nodded. "That's right. I forgot. The ranking ship's officer also has a code. Both are needed to open this door."

"But we have no ranking officer," Ethan said. He realized too late how this statement might affect Kaia. "Sorry," he said quickly.

"It's okay." She tried to smile at him. "It's true. I don't know where we could find that code."

"Looks like this may be one mystery we can't solve," he said.

"Unless . . ." Kaia reached into the pocket of her coveralls. She produced a small, tapered tube. The new, improved laser razor. She looked at him her eyes full of anticipation. "It's still calibrated for the exact thickness of the titanium walls."

"How will it affect an entire arsenal of highly volatile weaponry?" he asked, though he wasn't nearly as nervous as he had been about cutting through the walls near the navigation system. "Could you just cut the lock?"

"Too destructive. The door wouldn't close again, so it would be flapping open for the rest of the journey. I was thinking we'd just make a little hole here. If we need to, I can solder it back closed later. That also keeps us well away from anything explosive."

He could tell she was itching to try it, and the closer he got to the unknown planet, the more he wanted reassurance that they had the ability to deal with any unforeseen hostile situations.

He gestured toward the door. "Okay. Crack it."

She moved forward and carefully aimed near the bottom of the door. The laser was silent as it sliced a round-cornered hole just large enough for them to get through. The piece fell inward with a crash as the last corner was cut.

CHAPTER 17

The room was dark and cool as they moved through the opening. The automatic lights didn't turn on until they stood up. The room was big, but not as dramatically big as others on the ship. It was maybe three times the size of the Caretaker's hold, with large shelves holding giant metal boxes. In contrast to everything else on the ship, which looked new and shining, the boxes looked as if they'd been knocked about a lot. They'd also experienced some heat; random scorch marks marred the boxes.

Ethan immediately sensed that Kaia was disturbed. "What is it?"

"These should all be big glass-fronted weapons lockers. We should be seeing the whole arsenal of particle guns and mini-bombs and . . ." She walked to one of the boxes, laying her hand against its tarnished surface.

"The whole room has been modified to hold these." She ran her fingers over the side of the box. Ethan walked up to stand beside her and noticed an incredibly complex locking mechanism holding the box closed. It was a sort of keypad, but the buttons were arranged in oddly diagonal rows and had strange markings on them.

"What are the chances of cutting into one of these?"

Kaia shook her head. "Too risky. I have no idea what they're made of or what they contain. Could be explosive or—" He saw her shiver. "Organic."

"Organic? Alive?"

Kaia nodded. "Who knows? I couldn't cut through them without knowing what's inside."

Ethan knew she was right. "Well, then, a mystery within a mystery. Could it be possible that the weapons are in these boxes? Maybe they tried a new shipping technique with this ship?"

"Possible," Kaia said doubtfully. Then she glanced at Ethan with fearful eyes. "But, Ethan, look at the locks. They're not—" She hesitated and put a slightly trembling hand up to the keypad. It was immediately obvious that her hand would not fit comfortably on the keys.

"Not made for humans," he finished.

Hearing him say it chilled both of them.

Kaia dropped her hand and turned away from the box. "Maybe there's some diplomatic reason that we're transporting alien cargo. Or maybe the boxes contain gifts for the human race."

"Maybe."

Kaia's face brightened. "But, Ethan, if the contents were dangerous, they would never have made it on board. I mean, there are really strict regulations about what's allowed on passenger transport ships."

"Right." He tried to sound convinced.

"No, really—you can't get dangerous items even close to the spaceport. Much less on the ships—"

"Dangerous items like energy pistols?" He looked her in the eye.

Kaia stopped, taking that in. "Okay. That's a good point. But a little energy pistol is a lot easier to sneak on board than forty huge crates."

He shrugged. "Depends on your connections, I guess." Turning back toward the door, he continued. "Anyway, there's nothing we can do about it right now. I should get back to work on the data upstairs. At least now we know that the Tertiary Nav system's manifest is more correct than the main ship's computer. Unless the alien boxes are, for some reason, filled with human weapons, there are no weapons on board."

"Except my energy pistol."

"Except," he conceded, "your energy pistol."

As they slipped back through the hole in the door, Ethan remembered the modified grooming laser. "Hey," he said as he reached down to help Kaia up after she came through, "nice work with that laser, by the way."

She beamed. "I am pretty proud of it. It seems to be working well. I gave it a portable power source, so it's much more useful now."

"Should you need to slice through any more walls in the ship."

"You never know."

"Well, just don't get too excited with it."

They finally made it back to the hold, and Ethan grabbed a steak and fries before settling back to his work again. He went back to the manifest and checked out the cargo hold. This time when he looked at it, he noticed something new. At the end of the cargo manifest were several equations he'd skipped, thinking they were passenger box contents. Perhaps translating them would solve the mystery of what was in the big tarnished boxes. His excitement was quelled quickly, though, when he graphed them and realized that the symbols were not familiar to him at all. He was almost sure they weren't pure Xardn. Rather, they looked like some of the modified symbols found in the branch languages. He felt sure that they held some clue, but for now he was out of ideas on how to determine their meanings.

Frustrated, Ethan navigated back to the main menu. He'd sorted through as many of the Navigational Coordinates as he could stand, and now he felt out of leads in the List of Items.

He expected no surprises in the List of Human Cargo, but he liked the idea of finding Aria's name in Xardn, so he entered the list and skipped to the last column of equations. The last passenger he assumed was himself, so he quickly jotted down the equations for the second-to-last passenger on the list and began charting it with the glyphtol. He wrote the symbols:

To his disappointment, it simply read *Human, Female, 24 Spaces of time, Pregnant*. Her actual name wasn't on the roster at all. In fact, none of the passengers' names were there. The roster simply listed the characteristics of each. As Ethan scanned through the columns of descriptions, something about the equations began to puzzle him. Quickly, he sketched the symbol for the word *passenger* on the open page of his journal.

Then, carefully, he counted the cusps and did some calculations. The result were the parametric equations:

$$x(\Theta)=(53-124)cos(\Theta)+(205)cos(((53-124)/124)\Theta),$$
$$y(\Theta)=(53-124)sin(\Theta)-(-205)sin(((53-124)/124)\Theta)$$

He cross-checked it with the symbol before every passenger description. It was a different equation. He reached for the glyphtol and began to chart, a tightness growing in his chest. Kaia, fiddling with a bundle of wires on the other end of the couch, glanced up and noticed his new intensity.

"Find a clue?" she asked lightly.

His voice was anxious as he answered, "Maybe."

Sensing his anxiety, Kaia went back to her work, waiting. Seconds passed as Ethan moved the glyphtol over the paper, the laser burning its path. He slid the instrument to the side and looked at the remaining symbol in horror.

Seeing his expression, Kaia was suddenly at his side. "What does it mean, Ethan?"

He answered in a trembling voice. "It means 'those who were taken in conquest.'" He looked up. "Slaves."

"What?"

"On this list, the people on this ship are all designated by the term 'Slave' and then their number. This line lists Aria as 'Slave three nine nine nine,' and then lists her species, gender, age, and the fact that she's pregnant. It's like a bill of sale."

Kaia was shaking her head. "But, Ethan, that makes no sense."

He was switching the levers on the data box. With trembling fingers, he opened the "Treaty Documents" folder on the screen in front of him. He entered the first folder. As the equations appeared, he reached for his writing instruments and began to chart the symbols.

The Treaty of Peace
between
the Human Race
of
Earth, the Milky Way Galaxy,
and
Colonies Established Thereby
and
the Aloran Race

of Beta Alora, Sardon Major,
and
Colonies Established Thereby
respecting
the Colonization and Occupation
of
the Planet Minea
and the
Cessation of Aggressive Actions Thereon
signed at Theta Tersica: Universal Date Q3165
Beta Aloran Date Sansquit 13
Earth Date December 16, 2206

In an effort to establish peace and tranquility among the Human and Aloran Races, and by the authority of the leaders of the same, the Human and Aloran Races agree to the following terms:

The Aloran Race, recognizing the sovereignty of the Human Race on the surface of the Planet Minea, and on its moons, satellites, suns, and planets of its system, consents to allow the aforementioned Human Race to dwell there in peace and security, with no threats of aggression nor acts of aggression toward said Race until the natural end of the aforementioned system or until such time as said Human Race deems to leave the Planet Minea.

The Human Race, recognizing the superior military and technological forces of the Aloran Race, consents, in exchange for sovereignty on the surface of the Planet Minea, and on its moons, satellites, suns, and planets of its system, and in exchange for dwelling on said planet with no threats of aggression nor acts of aggression from said Aloran Race until the natural end of the aforementioned system or until such time as said Human Race deems to leave the Planet Minea, to provide said Aloran Race with 4,000 healthy humans, detailed in the appendix at the end of this document.

In light of the vastly superior military and technological forces of the Aloran Race, and in an effort to promote peace in the Universe, in the case that the Aloran Race violates in any regard the provisions of this treaty, it shall be recognized that said Aloran Race has committed an act of hostility disruptive to the security of the civilizations of the Universe and is subject to reprisal from the Universal Council of Peace in the form of planetary annihilation.

In light of the still-developing Human Race, its attempts at leaving its home planet and finding its way into the Universe, and in an effort to nurture said attempts by this and all newly-colonizing civilizations, in the case that the Human Race violates in any regard the provisions of this treaty, it shall be recognized that said Human Race has failed to uphold honorably its treatises and is subject to reprisal from the Universal Council of Peace in the form of disallowing further colonization or interstellar trade for the space of three Universal Spaces of Time.

Ethan was trembling violently when he finished writing out the translation. Kaia was silent, her gray eyes wide.

"We're on . . ." Ethan's voice cracked. " . . . a slave ship.

CHAPTER 18

Ethan manipulated the switches and buttons on the data recorder. The silence hung heavily as he maneuvered the screen back to the "Treaty Documents" menu. Once there, he feverishly jotted down the equations and painstakingly charted and translated their symbols. The resulting menu read:

"Treaty"

"History of Human/Aloran Treaty"

"Negotiation of Treaty Terms"

"Official Apologies"

"Future of Minean Civilization"

Ethan switched to "History of Human/Aloran Treaty." Instead of the usual stream of equations, a video screen appeared, showing images of the stark white interior of the first colonization ship sent to Minea.

Captain Arthur Flynn, the first man on Minea, appeared on the screen. "Base Twelve, Base Twelve, do you read me?" he said to the screen.

A disembodied voice answered. "Base Twelve here. Report, Flynn."

"Colonization efforts on schedule. Agriculture is fully established. Engineering is complete. We are ready for the shipments of builders due to arrive over the next few weeks."

"We will prepare the manufacturing ships. They will be en route within the year," said the voice of Base Twelve.

"Thank you, sir."

"Thank you for the report. Please return to your duties."

"Yes, sir." Flynn hesitated and then added in a rush, "Sir, there is one more thing."

"A problem, Flynn?" The voice of Base Twelve was impatient and annoyed.

"Not yet, sir." Flynn waited. He shifted his gaze nervously.

"Well, Flynn, get on with it! What is it?"

"Sir, unidentifiable ships have been observing the surface of the planet."

"What? What ships?"

"As I said, they match none we have on record."

"Flynn! You're wasting my time. Find out who they are, get me that information, and I will get the diplomatic team on the task of drawing up a treaty with them. This is standard procedure, man."

Flynn's eyes flared, "Sir, with all due respect, this is not standard. The ships have abducted nearly twenty of my men."

"Abducted?" The voice scoffed. "Impossible. There are strict interstellar laws about removing other species without consent of their home planet. No civilization within a hundred light-years would dare 'abduct' your men. It's a big planet, Flynn. I'm sure they're around somewhere."

"Sir, the men were dissolved, vaporized. A lot of people saw it."

"Probably gas vents in the planet's surface. I'm telling you, no species would dare. Find me the name of your aliens, and I'll get the ships out of your atmosphere. Will you feel better then?"

Flynn was angry. "Yes, sir." The transmission cut out. The screen went black. A second passed, then a much more haggard Flynn appeared again. The date on the bottom showed that three years had passed since the earlier transmission.

"Base Twelve, do you read?"

"Go ahead, Flynn. What is the situation with the alien race?"

"We've learned who they are. They are from Beta Alora. It's a long way from here. They're kind of a pirating race, going around collecting what they want from various new colonies. They're a Class 15 civilization, so they have incredibly advanced weaponry and technology. I don't see any way to beat them, sir."

"What is recommended by the Universal Alliance?"

"We met with them this morning. They have advised us to meet with the Alorans and work out a peace treaty. Apparently, this has been successful in the past. The Alorans are interested in seeming reputable, so they will get what they want through peaceful means if necessary."

"And what *do* they want, Flynn?"

"I don't know, sir. Could be the planet, could be resources, I don't know."

"How do we meet with them?" the voice asked.

"The Universal Alliance will arrange the meeting if we are willing. They recommended designating a cabinet to work through the terms of the treaty."

"Tell them to set it up. I'll get the cabinet together. We need to get this taken care of ASAP. We have Passenger Ships en route."

"Yes, sir."

"Base Twelve out." The screen went blank again.

As the next clip came up, Ethan glanced over. Kaia was curled in a tight ball on the end of the couch. He knew she must be exhausted. Neither of them had slept since long before their trip to the weapons hold, and that must have been at least a day ago.

He looked back at the screen. A title screen reading "Treaty Cabinet Meeting" was just fading. Next, the screen was filled with the image of six people, five men and one woman, around a table. Ethan immediately recognized the broad face of Phillip Reagan.

Kaia drew in a sharp breath and sat up, leaning forward on the couch, eyes trained on her father. The rest of the cabinet was identifiable only by their uniforms. Three military members, including Reagan, the President of the Earth Alliance, and two, including the woman, from the Department of Alien Relations.

The voice of Base Twelve from the earlier transmissions belonged to Syd Allexis, a general in the Earth Defense Force. He was obviously the head of the cabinet as he began the first meeting by introducing the members and explaining the situation.

"People, you don't know why you're here, but I thank you for coming. The very fate of the human race may hang on the decisions we make here today. First, let me introduce you to each other. We'll start with General Phillip Reagan, with whom I've worked many years in the Earth Defense Force. Next to him is Himura Akio, of the Earth Offensive Force." He nodded toward each as he said their names. "We all know President Khouri, and these two are Hoxna Kelty and McKendra Thrush, joining us from the Department of Alien Relations."

Allexis sat still and upright in his chair, his hands folded on the table in front of him, his holographic rank insignia flashing light back toward the camera. "There is no easy way to start this," he said authoritatively. "We have a serious situation on Minea. A very serious situation. The colony is well-established. Everything is on track. We have farmers, scientists, builders, manufacturers, and military leaders there. Our passenger ships are set to leave very soon. In fact, Phillip here is set to be on one of those ships." Reagan nodded. "But a conflict has arisen on the surface of the planet. An alien race called the Alorans have occupied many of our cities. They have come in and are threatening to take possession of the entire planet, including the 80,000 people we have there already."

Every eye in the room was trained on Allexis. "We have been able to secure diplomatic assistance in dealing with these marauders. That is why we've brought you all here, taking the risks of rapid space travel, to reach an agreement with the Alorans."

The President of the Earth Alliance spoke up. "And just where, Allexis, is 'here?' We've been shuttled around in windowless transports for two weeks. We have no idea where we are."

"I'm sorry about that, Mr. President. Unfortunately, we couldn't take the risk of anyone knowing who was involved in these negotiations. You may be glad of that before this is all over." His voice was flinty and impatient. "You are, now, on the planet Theta Tersica. It is about halfway between Minea and Earth. It is about 600,000 lightyears from Beta Alora. Theta Tersica is a neutral planet, used often for these kinds of negotiations."

"How long will we be here?" Kelty asked.

"I don't know. Our hope is that we can reach an agreement with the Alorans before our passenger ships leave next month."

Reagan spoke up. "Why wasn't this taken care of during the initial purchase of Minea? Eighty other treaties were signed before we even set foot on the planet. Why didn't we deal with these Alorans then?"

Allexis spoke again. "Beta Alora is galaxies away from Minea. It has no claim on the planet, nor on the system. Our original negotiating team would not have even seen them, much less found it necessary to approach them about rights to the planet."

"Then why are we even dealing with them? If we own the planet, where is the Universal Alliance? This should be their problem."

"The Universal Alliance assists in negotiations, and they enforce interstellar law to a certain extent, but I've not yet briefed you on a significant detail: the Alorans are a Class 15 civilization."

The indignant group around the table stilled momentarily.

Allexis went on, "There are only maybe forty civilizations in all of known space that would have any chance at all of winning a conflict with them. Most of the Alliance wouldn't be able to enforce sanctions even if they wanted to get involved. The Alorans have historically been a peaceful, advanced civilization. Only in the last 1,000 years have they become aggressive towards younger civilizations like ours. They seem to be taking advantage of the colonizing civilizations, raiding colonies and threatening to annihilate them, but they are easily pacified through negotiations. Once what they want is discovered, they take it and leave, never actually doing any serious damage."

"So you think they're bluffing?"

"Oh, no, they're not bluffing. They're just using their obvious advantages to 'encourage' civilizations to give up things that they otherwise wouldn't. Things that the Alorans can't get any other way."

"What kinds of things?" Reagan asked guardedly.

At this, Allexis shifted almost imperceptibly. "Well, they've taken cultural artifacts: books, folk art, music. And they've negotiated for minerals and animals from the colonies' home planets. They wanted things that were unique, that the Alorans, with all their advanced technology and weaponry, couldn't manufacture for themselves."

"What, do they have a huge museum they put all of this in?"

"No one knows what they do with it. Their home planet is so spectacularly shielded that no one goes in or comes out without several levels of security clearance. It's unscannable, even by the most sophisticated of equipment."

"Why don't the other Class 15 civilizations do something about them?" asked Himura, speaking up for the first time.

Kelty caught Allexis' eye.

"Let's let our DAR folks field that question," Allexis said.

"Class 15 civilizations are incredibly complex," Kelty said, almost excitedly. "They have a very hands-off approach. They have evolved so far beyond the realm of other civilizations that they could very easily destroy all of organic life indefinitely. They see themselves as observers of other civilizations. They refuse to interfere with conflicts because if they joined forces with nearly anyone, they would make it impossible to beat that civilization. The Alorans are something of an anomaly. The other Class 15s view them sort of like a misbehaving younger sibling. They are disapproving, but indulgent. They will not interfere, as the ramifications of causing conflict between the Class 15 civilizations themselves are beyond imagination."

"What happens if they go back on the terms of the treaty?"

"First of all, history leads us to believe that they won't. Once they've 'collected' their treasure from a civilization, they've never seemed to pay them any more attention. None of the other civilizations on record have ever been reapproached."

"Well, it seems a straightforward enough decision," the president said decisively. "Let's give them what they want and get back home. I've got a planet to run."

Allexis stiffened. His jaw tightened. "Mr. President, this decision is anything but straightforward. Please, with all due respect, wait until you've heard the proposal before you agree to it." There was a bitter edge in his voice.

The president, obviously offended, snapped back, "Well, then, quit playing games, Allexis. Give us all the information. What do the bugs want?" His publicity team would have been horrified by his use of the crude term for Aliens.

Ethan sat tensed on the edge of the couch, his fingernails digging into his palms. He wanted to turn it off, to erase the drive, to go back to not knowing what was coming next. But he kept watching because part of him wanted to hear them actually say it.

Allexis, for the first time, looked at the table. His voice was quiet, unsure. "They want people."

The next few seconds of footage seemed to be in slow motion. Himura and Thrush looked confused, Reagan swore explosively, and Kelty nodded sagely, as if it were no surprise to him.

There was no change in the president's expression. "How many?" he asked in a low voice.

Reagan was on his feet. "How many? What kind of a question is that? What does that matter? Absolutely not!" He circled the table.

"Settle down, Phillip," Allexis growled under his breath.

"Settle down? Are you really considering this? Did you really bring us here to discuss selling people? If that's what you want, you've picked the wrong delegate, Syd. I won't go for it."

Thrush spoke up. "I don't know, but it seems he might be right. There has to be another way."

Kelty was shaking his bespectacled head. "No, no, no," he mumbled, "you don't know the Alorans. I've studied some of their history. They want what they want. Of course they want people. Of all the species they've encountered so far, they've never seen anything like our little Class 3 civilization. I'm sure they find us quite cute and quite amusing. But we're relatively intelligent and hardy in comparison with many others. They may have a collector's interest in us, or they may have work that needs doing that humans are particularly suited for. They love what they don't have. It's perfectly understandable that they would want some human specimens. Perfectly understandable." He looked around the table, nodding.

The president spoke again. "Allexis. I asked you *how many*?"

Allexis' voice was flat when he spoke again. "They started out at 50,000. We've talked them down to 4,000."

"4,000?" Himura's voice was doubtful. "Why were they satisfied with so few?"

"We were surprised, too." Allexis's voice lowered and he choked out the next few words. "After negotiations, they settled on a suitable number for a breeding colony." Avoiding their eyes and the curses from Reagan, he said, "If you'll look at the screens in the table in front of you, you'll see the document they've sent us with their demands. It has been translated for your convenience."

As the group read, curses and horrified comments bounced around the table.

"4,000?"

"*Breeding colony?*"

"Of high-quality genetic material?"

Reagan, still standing as he leaned over the table to read, slammed his fist on the table. "This is despicable. It's wrong. We find another way."

Allexis spoke. "Phillip, there is no other way."

"There's always another way."

"Phillip, we've had extensive negotiations already. We've brought the number down from 50,000 to 4,000—only one ship's worth. We've secured a commitment that if we . . . do this, the people on Minea now will be safe and those on their way there will be guaranteed a planet unthreatened by these pirates."

"Pull the people on Minea. Get them home, turn the other ships around, and leave the forsaken rock to rot." Reagan was pacing again.

"We can't. We don't have the resources to get them out of there in time."

"What about RST? Bring them back the same way you got us here."

"Don't be a fool, Reagan. It's way too risky with that many people. Too many variables. Besides, we only have enough RST ships to transport a fraction of the people we have there already. You need to face the fact that without this treaty, the Alorans will simply take the people already on Minea anyway. This way, at least we minimize the damage."

"Minea isn't worth this. *Colonization* isn't worth 4,000 *human* lives." Reagan was looking at the table, his hands open, pleading.

"Don't be so quick to judge that," the president said quietly, but firmly. Every face turned to him. "That's right—there's more complexity to this than any of you know. That's why I'm here, isn't it, Allexis? To spill the top-secret information that these bugs have already vaporized people on Minea? To destroy your carefully publicized picture of Minea as a safe, happy haven?"

He punched some codes into his computer. "Look at your screens now. What you're watching is footage of an attack on Minea—an attack that officially never happened—when these bugs disintegrated an entire squadron of our most advanced defense ships. And now, on the screen, you'll see something worse." The delegates looked back up at him in horror, one by one, excepting Reagan and Allexis, who both continued to stare at the table in front of them. "That's right. That is the same Aloran ship above Earth. They've been here. They have nearly instantaneous travel capabilities."

Allexis spoke again. "If we don't give them what they're asking for—" He looked the delegates in the eyes. "They'll take what they want and possibly destroy Earth. If we don't sacrifice 4,000, the Alorans have assured us that there will be no humans left." After a pause, he added, "One way or another."

It was obvious that the people around the table were coming to accept the inevitability of the decision. Except Reagan, of course. He began to speak again, in that explosive voice, but Allexis interrupted him in a quiet, measured tone.

"What about Kaia, Phillip?" Reagan went quiet and his eyes grew wider. "Do you want your only child vaporized? Do you want her life cut short? If we do this, everything goes on the same. We continue colonizing Minea. You can take Kaia there with you. You can see her raise your grandchildren on a beautiful, lush, *safe* new world."

Reagan was still. He sank into his chair and put his head in his hands. His voice was muffled as he said, "Can't we fight?"

Allexis spoke again in the same subdued tone. "We tried. They are too advanced. Even the Universal Alliance can't promise protection."

"We can send them in families," the president said, in a falsely hopeful tone. "They will stay together and go as ambassadors of the human race to a planet where no human has ever set foot." He stood, straightening the wrinkles out of his suit with his palms as he did so. As he spoke, he made large, sweeping motions with his hands, as if he was painting. "Think of it! Humanity in close contact with a Class 15 civilization. Why, we could leap ahead in the civilization development cycle. Should they learn some of the secrets of such a civilization, there is no reason that they couldn't leave whenever they wanted to. They could come to Minea on ships of such speed that they may beat people leaving today! They could bring us new technologies, new weapons. These 4,000 could be the greatest heroes the human race has ever known!" He finished with both arms raised and spread open, taking in the whole room.

A small sound was heard in the silence that he left. McKendra Thrush was weeping. Kelty was shaking his head. "That's unlikely. This type of a civilization would be ready for any escape attempts. No, no, we need to understand, if we do this—"

"They'll be the property of the Alorans," Thrush said through her tears. "Somewhere in the universe, humanity will be in bondage . . . forever."

The president switched his tactic. "If that's true," his arms stayed still at his sides, "then the sacrifice they make for the rest of humanity will still make them heroes."

"And you plan to recognize them as such? Have a big ribbon-cutting ceremony when the slave ship leaves its port?" Reagan's bitterness was unrestrained.

The president turned on him. "Pull yourself together, Reagan. You've been in battle before. You've made these sorts of decisions. Which men do you send to the front lines, knowing full well that they won't come back? Which do you put in the office, where they'll never see a day of action? You buy and sell your men every day." He turned and walked stiffly back and forth at the end of the table. "This will, of course, have to remain classified. Few beyond this room will know of the decision or its implementation."

"So the decision has been made, then?" Reagan raised his head and looked around the table.

"The facts are on the table," the president said. "We know the proposal, and we know its implications, either way. It's time we call the vote, Allexis."

Allexis shifted uncomfortably but nodded. "Yes, sir." He looked around the table, sorrow in his eyes. "I'd trade this assignment for any bloody battle on any field in the galaxy," he said softly. Then, "It is proposed that we meet the Aloran terms of peace by trading 4,000 human souls for the sovereignty of the planet Minea, and for the safety of our home planet, Earth. How do you vote on this proposal?" He looked at the president first.

"I vote in favor," said the president. Allexis nodded and then looked at

Hoxna Kelty.

"I also vote in favor," said Kelty, shaking his head again. Then he looked around the table. "Don't you see, it's the only way."

McKendra Thrush, still weeping, gave her vote in favor.

Himura spoke quietly. "I don't like it, but I . . . for the greater good . . . " he looked up and nodded. "In favor," he said quietly.

Phillip Reagan paused and then looked back at Allexis. "I'm sorry. I know the fate of the planet seems to hang on it. I know that you say there is no other way. I know that I may be consigning myself and everyone I love to an awful fate, but I can't. I've spent my whole life fighting for freedom and peace on Earth. I can't sell people into slavery. I—I won't. I vote against."

Allexis nodded, his own eyes shining with tears. "I wish I had your conviction, Phillip. I admire your courage. But I don't see any other way. I vote in favor." He closed his eyes for a split second and then looked around the table with dry eyes and a returned military manner. "The proposal passes by a majority. We will accept the terms of the Alorans' proposal. You may return to your quarters while I inform the Alliance and proof the final treaty. We will meet again to sign the treaty and settle the final terms. Please consider the following: How will we decide who is sent to Beta Alora? What resources will be needed to ensure the secrecy of the mission? You will receive a bulletin when it is time to meet again. All efforts will be made to expedite this process and get you home as soon as possible. Thank you for your service. You are all dismissed."

Six doors opened in the oval room, one behind each chair. The delegates stood and each entered a separate hallway leading to their chambers. The screen went dark again.

Ethan looked over and saw Kaia. She sat frozen, fists clenched. Tears were streaming down her face. He switched the box off and the screen faded, leaving them in the hold's half-light.

"Now I know why he didn't want me to marry David. He knew. He knew that David's ship was going to Beta Alora. He knew David would be a slave." There was anger and pain in her voice, and then her eyes grew wide. "Oh, Ethan, you don't think he knew . . ." She shook her head, as if it were too horrible to say. "That David would be . . . murdered?" She was trembling.

"No, no, Kaia." Ethan moved to her and put his arms around her. "He tried to stop it. There was nothing he could do." An idea dawned on Ethan. "And I see it now. Your father embedded the treaty documents, probably hoping

David would find them in time to turn the ship."

There was bitterness in Kaia's voice. "But then David was murdered. Not by you, maybe not even by my father, but murdered. He would have known within hours that the ship was off course. He would have overridden the computer before the ship even—" She saw the guilt in Ethan's eyes. "I'm sorry. It's not your fault either . . ." Sudden anger flared in her and she slammed her fist on the couch. "My father could have told me. I could have warned David. I could have stopped this whole thing . . ."

"You can't take that kind of responsibility for this. This was decided long before even your father knew about it."

"It can't have been the only way." She wiped her arm across her eyes, leaning against him.

Ethan was silent. Waves of disbelief and fear washed over him. He was thrust back to the long, dark days after McNeal died. Everything he'd come to expect was washed away in light of these new revelations. There would be no forty-eight years aging in space, but there would also be no blue cottage for Aria and the baby, no future of blue skies and clean air for them. He would be reunited with Aria in a few days time, but they would be subject to the whims of this new, brutal alien race. The thought of Aria's delicate wrists in shackles, of their child being born under the yoke of bondage, made something inside him snap.

He stood and walked purposefully to the door.

"We can't change their decision," he said sternly. "Earth's government wouldn't fight for these people. But I was charged with protecting them, and I will fight for them now." He turned and strode out of the hold.

Kaia caught up with him halfway down the hall. "Where are we going?" she asked, stepping quickly.

"To the nav room. I need to know how much time we have before we land on Beta Alora, how much time we have to pull this ship off its course and point it toward Minea."

When the door to the Primary Navigation Room opened, Ethan and Kaia both stopped short. The huge observation windows were filled with the red planet Beta Alora. The ship was moving down through the atmosphere already.

"It's too late," Kaia said.

Ethan's jaw tightened as he walked to the window. Around them, the air was foggy and translucent. Below them, on the surface, they saw the beginnings of pinkish mountains and deep umber valleys. Spots of water reflected the pale red sky back at them.

"Ethan, we'll be on the surface in hours. We must have been locked into a tractor beam that accelerated our descent. We don't have time to switch to manual navigation. Anyway, even if we did, we couldn't get out of this tractor beam."

"We'll have to come up with a new idea, then. Once we've landed, we've got to get back off the planet before the aliens board."

Kaia shrugged. "Ethan, this ship was built in space. It doesn't have the power or the equipment to take off from a planet." He saw a dullness in her eyes which he'd never seen before. "Anyway, they said the planet was fantastically shielded."

"Kaia!" Ethan whirled on her. "You're ready to give up? Just throw in the towel and commit yourself to slavery?"

"Ethan." Her eyes shifted. "What if they're right? I mean, we're talking about all of humanity. What if we did get away and . . . and they came for *everyone*?"

He paused. "There has to be way to fight them."

"Sometimes you run out of choices, and you just have to accept your fate." Her voice was weary.

"My fate?" He shook his head. "This isn't about me, Kaia. Or even about you. Even if I accepted it as 'my fate,' does that give me the right to give up and turn this whole shipful of people—of *families*, Kaia—over to these Alorans? These people went to sleep expecting to wake up on Minea. I'm the Caretaker, and I'm going to do everything I can to make sure they do."

It was then, as Ethan and Kaia stood facing each other, with the scarlet clouds billowing just outside the window behind them, that they heard the voices.

CHAPTER 19

Ethan and Kaia's eyes locked, seeking confirmation of what they thought they'd heard. They both looked back toward the door to the navigation room. Rough, low-pitched sounds were coming from the hallway on the other side.

"Someone's here," Kaia hissed. "They're not speaking our language, either."

"The Alorans must have come to check things out early," Ethan said softly, slipping an arm around her and pulling her over to the wall.

"How did they get on? The computer announced no ship docking."

"I have no idea. But they're here now. And they're headed this way." He looked puzzled. "Why can we hear them? The doors are closed."

"They must speak on a different frequency, one that travels through titanium like our voices travel through water. And it sounds as if they talk significantly louder than we do too." She cringed closer to Ethan.

"We've got to get out of here." Ethan's eyes scanned the room. There was no good place to hide.

Suddenly, he felt Kaia pulling him by the arm toward the Secondary Navigation Room. Once inside, she pointed to the one panel she'd left open after closing up the computer banks. They slipped through the hole into the Tertiary Navigation Room and she pulled the panel closed behind them. Carefully, she unclipped the wires inside the panel, letting them fall back like a curtain over the hole, and used the clips to secure the loose piece of wall. In front of it, she released the wires on her side of the hole and closed the panel, setting it into the grooves that held it, but not securing it.

Ethan listened carefully to the sounds from the hallway on the other side of the wall. Recognition came to him and he looked up in surprise. "Kaia," he whispered. "They're speaking Xardn!"

She looked at him.

"Yes," he said softly, "yes. I hear it. It is . . . different, slightly, than we speak it. It sounds like a strong accent, but it *is* Xardn." A hope began to grow in Ethan. Perhaps, if he could communicate with them, he had a chance of finding a way to negotiate with them.

They listened again. Kaia caught his eye and held up four fingers, raising her eyebrows in a question.

He nodded. It did sound like there were four of them. They had reached the Primary Navigation Room, and as their voices intensified, Ethan realized they were in the Secondary Navigation Room. He stepped softly toward the computer bank and pressed his ear against a panel.

A gruff voice was speaking in Xardn. Ethan caught most of the sentence. "No humans appear to be left aboard. Perhaps the human military did away with the Caretaker as we proposed."

Another one spoke. "If they were wise, they took our advice."

"Have they fulfilled the terms of the agreement?"

"It appears that they have. There are 4,000 slaves aboard. They are in stasis below."

"I think it wise to keep them that way until after they are distributed to the buyers," said another one.

"I agree. There is less complexity that way."

"Are the slaves suitable examples of the species?"

"Come see for yourselves."

There were grunts of agreement, and the voices and thumping feet moved out of the nav rooms, back into the hall. The silence of the ship returned.

Kaia looked at Ethan with wide eyes. "What are we going to do?" she asked in a tiny voice.

"We need to see what we're dealing with. Maybe we could somehow gain the advantage here on the ship and use these four for leverage."

"We take them hostage?" Kaia looked doubtful.

"Well, we've got to try something. I'm not huddling here in this little room to see my family 'distributed' to Aloran buyers. We've got to get out of here and get a look at them."

He saw that she was looking above him, her eyes focused on some point above his head. A panel had been removed in the ceiling and the shafts stretched away on either side of the hole it left.

He held out his hand. Kaia took it and he boosted her up into the shaft. She leaned down and gave him a hand up. When his shoulders were through, she sat back and he grabbed onto her knees to wiggle himself in the rest of the way.

They moved as quietly as possible in the shafts. She led the way, and they came to the overlook above the passenger hold without incident. As they slipped out onto the high walkway, they immediately laid down on their bellies, freezing as they heard the door at the far end of the room open. The voices of the Alorans got louder as they approached.

Suddenly, the creatures came into view. Ethan drew in a sharp breath.

They were taller than humans, perhaps an average of about eight feet tall. Their heads were even with the fans in the tops of the stasis chambers. Though they had two thick legs and walked upright, the broad plates of dark armor covering their bodies reminded Ethan of Earth's scorpions. They moved with remarkable grace for creatures of such bulk. At the ends of their two plated arms were powerful appendages—a combination of digits and claws, like complex crab's claws. One was substantially bigger than the other and had two barbed pincers. The other smaller claw was a combination of claw and hand, with individual plated digits almost delicate in their intricacy.

In the light from the chambers, Ethan could see that each creature was a different muted color: blue, maroon, orange, and purple.

His stomach turned as the creatures walked down the row of passengers, stopping to ogle them and tap on the glass. He dared not move enough to see Kaia's reaction, but her ragged breathing beside him indicated that she was upset at the scene too.

"They appear to be healthy specimens," said the largest of the creatures, whose armor shone dully blue. He ran a clinking claw along the fronts of the stasis chambers as he walked. "And young enough for breeding, certainly."

"I think they'd make very interesting pets," said another, a maroon creature with a hint of malice in his voice.

The dark blue creature chided him. "Their buyers will decide what they are to be used for. You are to make sure they arrive at the auction in exactly this condition. Understood?"

The maroon Aloran grunted.

They had reached the end of the row and now wandered along the center aisle. To Ethan's horror, they were heading toward Aria's chamber. He felt Kaia's firm arm across his back and realized that he had started to rise. He pressed closer to the metal grating of the walkway, trembling with the effort of keeping still.

Just as the creatures reached Aria's row, the ship gave a sudden slight jolt.

"Ahhh. We've landed," said the dark blue creature. "We'll have only a few minutes, then, to finish our observations. We'll be needed at the arena to prepare."

"Nakthre, look at this." The maroon creature was standing with his claw on Aria's stasis chamber. "This one is deformed."

The blue creature, apparently Nakthre, approached and peered at her. "It has some sort of growth. Possibly still healthy. A minor removal procedure should—" The creature whirled, peering up into the darkness, directly toward where Ethan and Kaia were cowering. The big, sloped head inclined slightly, as if listening. "Hmmm," it growled, turning deliberately back to the chamber. "It is a female, isn't it? Perhaps . . . perhaps it has young."

"Inside it? Wouldn't the young devour the female?" the maroon creature was obviously disgusted.

"They are a . . ." Nakthre looked pointedly back toward the walkway. " . . . fascinating species. The plates on his face moved slightly, in a gruesome imitation of a smile. "I look forward to studying them more closely."

The others glanced in the direction Nakthre was gazing. Finally, the smallest Aloran, the one with a deep purple shell, growled, "Should we be going, Nakthre? Before we're summoned?"

Nakthre spoke slowly. "Yes, yes. We will go now." His voice raised in volume until it rang through the hold, shaking the walls. "We will return soon enough." He looked at his companions.

Ethan watched the plates over the creatures' eyes slide closed. Then his own eyes widened as he saw them become transparent and disappear altogether. The hold was eerily silent.

He and Kaia lay still a long time before they dared slip back into the shafts and find their way back to the Tertiary Navigation Room. Once there, they collapsed onto the floor. The smooth, clean lines of the ship spun around Ethan as he lay looking up at the ceiling. The creatures would be impossible to beat, considering their obvious physical advantages alone. Their advanced technology added another layer of difficulty. He closed his eyes.

"What are we going to do, Kaia?" His voice was a whisper.

"I don't know. They're so powerful. So impenetrable. We're on their home planet. I don't see any way out."

"Me neither. They're completely armored. We don't even have the most basic density vests. We don't have any weapons—"

"Wait, Ethan. Wait." Kaia sat up. "No, I *do* have a density vest. I wore one when I came on board. And we do have a weapon. My energy pistol is in the cargo hold." Her eyes were sparkling. "Ethan, David had a vest, too! There should be two density vests onboard somewhere. We've got to find them."

Ethan sat up, a thought coming to him. "I know where they are." He looked at her. "The trunk in the Caretaker's hold. McNeal must have wanted to keep them close."

"Of course," Kaia said softly. "He wanted something of mine. He had me infuse it with my violet perfume so that it would smell like me."

"We've got to get to them." Ethan was already pulling the panel open. "And get back here before they re-materialize onboard. We've got to have some protection. And we've got to get the energy pistol—we've got to arm ourselves as much as we can."

They carefully worked their way through the wires, pulling each panel closed behind them.

Kaia checked over the panels, making sure there were no signs of disturbance. "We can't take the chance that they'll find our hiding place."

They ran down the hall, but the headlong rush of yesterday was gone, replaced by careful scuttling, running close to the wall, trying to stay as small as possible. They found their way to the boxes in the cargo hold and retrieved Kaia's pistol. Ethan slipped it in his pocket as she replaced her box. Then they headed to the Caretaker's hold.

Ethan turned away as Kaia put her vest on under her clothes, not wasting time going into the bathroom to change. Ethan put his own vest on, keeping his eyes focused on the couch. He secured the pistol in the holster inside his vest.

Glancing back at the couch, he swore. "My journal's gone! I left it here on the couch with the data recorder!"

"They've been here, then." Kaia was already headed toward the door.

"Don't you see? They'll know we're on board. I wrote about it in that journal. They'll know—"

Ethan's panicked voice faded as he saw the air in the hold shimmering between them. Before he could blink, three of the four Alorans stood between them. Ethan felt an immediate weight come over him. It forced him to the ground. It felt like the time he'd shattered his knee and had to be anesthetized for the surgery. But this time, instead of just his legs, he felt the weight in his whole body. His thoughts moved quickly, but his body was immobilized. Beyond the aliens, he glimpsed Kaia falling as well.

Nakthre's rumbling voice filled Ethan's head. "Yes. We know." He walked forward, eying Ethan as he did so. "You are the human male called E-than Bryant?" The stresses fell wrong on his name.

With great effort, Ethan nodded. It felt like he'd been buried beneath bags of sand.

"And you understand my words?"

Ethan wondered if he had given away something he shouldn't have but nodded again.

"Fascinating. This is not the language of your home planet, though?"

Ethan shook his head, trembling with the effort. Nakthre tipped his head slightly, and the weight fell off Ethan's shoulders. He still could not stand, but he could move his head and neck freely now.

"You can speak to me then? In my language? Please, do so now."

Ethan heard a small cry from Kaia. She sounded as if she were being crushed.

Ethan put the sentence together in his mind, trying to copy their accents. "Take the weight from the girl," he said in Xardn.

The other creatures made growls that seemed to show their amusement. It was a disturbing kind of laughter, and it grated on Ethan.

His eyes flashed. "You're crushing her!"

Nakthre inclined his head slightly over his shoulder, in Kaia's direction. Her strangled sounds stopped. Ethan could hear her catching her breath.

"You do know the Language of the Ancients, though you speak it poorly. How is it that you know this language?"

Nakthre had moved closer. Ethan weighed his odds of being able to pull the pistol out of his pocket and fire on the creature. Moving his frozen arm half that far would be like lifting a hovercar over his head. He'd never be able to do it quickly enough. He would probably make things much, much worse, and possibly lose the only advantage they had at this point.

Nakthre was still waiting for an answer.

"It was my field of study on Earth. We learned it from ancient documents gathered from across the galaxy and traded to Earth several hundred years ago."

"Fascinating. This will be of interest to the heads of state. We will take you to them."

CHAPTER 20

Before he knew what was happening, Ethan felt himself growing lighter and lighter until he couldn't feel his body around him at all. With a sickening feeling, he realized that the creatures were more powerful than he had guessed. They could control matter. He was being transported. Ethan was acutely aware of the presence of the creatures and of Kaia's presence in a soft darkness through which they seemed to be moving. His mind seemed to be moving, anyway. In a few seconds, he felt himself growing heavier again until he found himself in the same crouched position, the strange weight on his body restored. He was looking down at a smoky, clear surface below, where other creatures walked. He blinked as the creatures below him seemed to overlap and merge as they moved. Squinting, he realized that he was looking down through a transparent gray building, the floors below visible as far as he could see.

He turned his head and saw Kaia beside him, also crouched and immobilized. "Are you okay?" he asked her in English.

"I think so." She seemed unable to move her head, staring down fixedly through the transparent floor. As he began to speak again to her, a deep rumbling filled the room, so loud that his ears began to buzz. Ethan raised his head to see a tarnished, dark yellow creature seated on a raised throne in front of them.

The creature began to speak in Xardn. "Well done, Nakthre!" it cried in a harsh, grating voice. "You have brought two excellent specimens to illustrate the stock at this day's auction! The crowd will clamor for such appealing creatures."

Ethan decided the creature thought that he couldn't understand him rather than was trying to intimidate him.

The yellow creature stood and descended to where they were, walking around them, his plated eyes appraising them. "Yes," he said, entangling the digits of the smaller claw in Kaia's short hair. "Very appealing." He ran the claw down her spine, and Ethan saw her flinch.

"Don't touch her!" he shouted in English.

The creatures around them laughed. Ethan realized that there must be many of them in the room, many more than he could see from his position.

"Defensive behavior. Are they a pair, then?" the yellow one asked, amused. He continued to stroke Kaia's hair and back.

"That is unclear. I've brought them to you because they were not in stasis. They were living, awake, in the ship." He gestured with his smaller claw toward Ethan. "This one can speak the Language of the Ancients."

The yellow creature paused, leaving a claw lingering on the small of Kaia's back. "Is that so? How is this possible?"

Nakthre related what Ethan had told him.

"This is surprising." The yellow creature left Kaia and walked over to Ethan. Speaking in Xardn, he said, "Welcome! You will soon see more of our magnificent planet! I am Traxoram, ruler of Beta Alora. I wish for you to demonstrate your ability to speak our language," he commanded.

"Leave the girl alone," Ethan growled in Xardn.

Traxoram's face brightened. He clicked the digits of one claw together with pleasure, almost as if in applause. "A valiant attempt. Well done, for such an undeveloped tongue. You'll bring a nice price, with such a unique quality. Tell me, human male, is this delicious creature your mate?" He nodded toward Kaia.

Ethan was silent. Saying that she was not might make them feel as if she were up for grabs. Saying that she was might bring on more torment for her if the Alorans wanted to see his "defensive behavior."

"Ruler," the small Aloran stepped forward from the crowd and into Ethan's line of vision. "We found a record written by this human male. He is called E-than Bry-ant." The creature handed Traxoram Ethan's journal. Traxoram took it and opened to a page near the front. He gave it a cursory glance and then flipped through the pages until the symbols in the last few pages of writing stopped him. He opened the journal wide, tipping it toward Ethan.

"You wrote this?" he asked, indicating the page full of Xardn symbols.

"Yes," Ethan said in Xardn.

Traxoram peered into the book, his smaller claw rising to hover over the page. Ethan's mouth dropped open as he watched the delicate digits begin to trace the symbols. The digits rotated in their sockets in perfect circles, tracing over the complex shapes. Though Ethan was still stiff with fear, part of his brain lit up with excitement as he realized what a breakthrough this was in the study of Xardn. It had always been assumed that the Xardn civilization had written their documents with the use of equipment similar to the glyphtol. He had never heard it proposed that the Xardns had had these sorts of orbiting digits.

His mind was pulled from the discovery by the grotesque laughing of Traxoram.

"Oh, yes. It appears that the two are paired." And amidst his laughter, Traxoram began to read:

It's been so long since I felt anything but duty and despair. Her intelligence, her sweetness, the way she moves, makes me crazy. I want to be with her all the time. I would stay up talking to her and looking at her all night if I could. I find little opportunities to touch her—to brush her hand when we're walking, to steady her arm as she steps over the doorjambs. Though I never thought I could love anyone again, I think I'm falling in love with Kaia.

Traxoram was still laughing. His laughter encouraged the others around him to join in. Soon the room reverberated with the grating sound.

Ethan's cheeks burned with humiliation.

"He's written it in the Language of the Ancients." Traxoram held the journal up for the room to see. "Only such a primitive creature would use a language older than time to describe the most fleeting and ridiculous of emotions."

Ethan's head snapped up. He spoke angrily in Xardn. "Your species doesn't know this emotion? This 'ridiculous' emotion?"

Traxoram looked down at his captive. "My brothers and I—" He waved his large, clawed hand at the crowd in the room— "have evolved beyond such trivialities. We know what brings progress. This 'love' you speak of brings only distraction and weakness. Many a civilization has fallen to the lusts of the body, my young friend. Many a creature has died on a battlefield sown by false affections."

"Then let us go!" Ethan cried, looking the creature in his flinty eyes. "What use have you for such primitive, weak creatures? You, in all your might and power?"

"What use, indeed?" Traxoram said, almost as if he were purring. "Shall we show them, my brothers?"

A deafening roar went up.

Suddenly, Ethan felt the weight fall off his body. Freed, he shot up, seeing Kaia doing the same.

Finally able to turn his head, he whirled around to see that hundreds of the creatures surrounded them, roaring and jeering.

"Come, my pets, now that you are freed of your fetters. Walk with me."

Ethan and Kaia followed cautiously, holding onto one another. Ethan felt light. Each step had extra bounce. He wondered if there was some kind of difference in gravity, or whether it was simply due to the absence of the extra weight.

The transparent walls made travel through the huge building disorienting. Rooms layered upon rooms, doorways stretched to infinity. The huge crowd jostled behind them.

Ethan felt a blast of cool, clear air and realized that they had walked directly out onto a balcony of sorts. A pale red cityscape stretched around them, and Ethan felt dizzy looking down at the vast distance to the ground below them. The dizziness suddenly merged with the peculiar feeling of lightness that told Ethan they were transporting again. Again he was surrounded with the darkness. Again the presence of Kaia and the others was obvious to him. This time, with so many intelligences sharing the darkness, their overwhelming presence was almost painful, like being in an overcrowded elevator. It was a relief to feel his body again around him.

As he came to consciousness, a cold awareness dawned on him. Kaia gasped beside him as she, too, realized what they were looking at.

CHAPTER 21

A vast suburban landscape stretched before them, perfect in every detail except for one. All of the houses, like every other building they'd seen so far, were made of smoky, transparent glass. The town was an exact replica of the settlement on Minea except for that detail.

Traxoram turned to them. "You see? We have created for you a very hospitable habitat."

"So you just plan to keep us here and watch us live out our lives? Like pets?" Ethan asked.

Traxoram's voice was menacing when he spoke again. "I grow weary of your demanding. I grow tired of your hostility. You have no idea how easy it would be for me to completely do away with you. If you had any idea, you would cower at my feet. If you weren't so valuable, I would show you how insignificant you and your entire species are. You are not pets to us. Oh, no . . . pets are kept for pleasure only. They amuse, delight, entertain. We have thousands of species kept for that purpose. We have a rather more . . . lucrative interest in humans." His features contorted into a mask of concentration. "I would use the word . . . livestock. Kept not for pleasure, but for profit."

Traxoram walked down a small slope leading to the nearest street between the houses. Ethan and Kaia were compelled to follow by the press of the crowd behind them. The swarm moved down the street, stopping in front of one of the little houses.

Traxoram gestured to Ethan and Kaia. "Enter. Enter the domicile. See how carefully it has been constructed for your pleasure."

Ethan and Kaia walked carefully toward the front door, holding hands. He tried the clear knob and the door swung inward. Walking in, he was overwhelmed with a sense of surrealism. The walls were right, the distances gauged correctly, but the transparency made him feel disoriented and vulnerable. When the door closed behind them, the sounds of the crowd died and he and Kaia were left in silence. She pulled him by the hand down the hallway that stretched in front of them. They entered a bedroom, where the familiar furniture had the same transparent quality as the walls.

Kaia, still holding Ethan's hand, sat cautiously on the edge of the bed. "It's soft," she said with surprise.

Ethan reached down past her and ran his hand across the smooth coverlet. He pressed his palm into the yielding surface of the mattress, then stood straight again.

Kaia leaned her cheek against his arm. "Oh, Ethan, it's all so strange."

"Did they hurt you back there?" he asked, staring through the walls at the distorted but still visible mass of creatures outside. Though Traxoram's attention remained on the little cottage, the others were conversing with each other, seemingly excited about the humans inside.

"Yes, at first. On the ship. But after that, it was just difficult to breathe."

"I'm sorry I couldn't stop them."

"But you did! I don't think we would have made it this far if you couldn't speak to them."

Ethan shrugged. "We need a plan."

"What plan? Ethan, we don't know where the ship is, and if we did, we wouldn't be able to beat their matter control techniques. If we could, we wouldn't get the ship out of the planet's shielding . . ." Kaia's voice trailed off. Her shoulders were slumped. "And even if we did get away, they'd just come and get us from Minea, anyway." She looked up at him. "I know it's a terrible thing to say, but I've always faced facts, and, well, what *would* it be like to live here? Would it be unbearable?"

Ethan pulled his hand from her grip and walked to the wall facing the Alorans. He leaned across a dresser and put his hands against the wall. "Look at them, Kaia." He glanced over his shoulder to see her raise her head and stare complacently past him. "See them watching us? Do you see them?" Ethan struck his fists against the solid wall, shouting, "They'll always be there! They'll watch us every moment!" He saw the creatures laughing at his anger, and it made him frantic.

"Kaia." He turned and strode over to her. "Kaia! We can't live like this! What if I were to hold you? What if I took you in my arms right now?" She looked up into his eyes and he reached down and pulled her roughly to him. He stared frantically into her eyes. "Kaia." His breath caught. "Kaia, they're there. They're watching me. They see you in my arms. It would never be just you and me. Every detail of our lives would be scrutinized, publicized . . ."

Suddenly, Kaia crumpled against him, the terror creeping into her eyes told Ethan she was again under the influence of their captors' shackles.

He held her to him, scooping her into his arms and sinking onto the edge of the bed. He sat stroking her hair. "Can you talk?" he asked her.

Her wild eyes answered his question.

"It's okay. It's okay. I'm sorry, Kaia."

"We have the power to do with you what we wish. Do not forget this." Traxoram's voice was in the room though the Aloran still stood out in the street. The creature's false congeniality had returned. "Now. We can't have you wearing yourselves out before the auction this afternoon. You must rest. Our buyers must see two perfect specimens. We will release the female if you will please find comfort in the accommodations we have prepared for you. Eat, sleep, refresh yourselves. We will return for you very soon." Traxoram and his entourage disappeared.

Ethan felt Kaia's limp body tighten and curl against him. She began to weep.

His arms tensed around her, pulling her into his chest. He buried his face in her hair and felt tears making tracks down his own cheeks. This was nothing he'd ever expected. How did he end up on an alien planet, holding a girl he should never have come to love, facing a future in which he'd be a captive? It occurred to him that he was very, very tired. He couldn't remember the last time he'd slept, and it seemed a lifetime since he'd shared a meal with Kaia in the Caretaker's hold.

As he and Kaia clung to each other, their weariness overcame them, and they lay down as one on the soft coverlet and slept. When Ethan's consciousness returned, it came slowly. He smelled steak cooking, felt the softness of the sleeping woman beside him, and thought he was home. As he opened his eyes, the transparent room seemed part of the dream until his memory of the creatures came back. He looked down at Kaia, her face still smoothed with sleep, and closed his eyes again, trying to recapture the fleeting feeling of security.

It was to no avail. The impossibility of their situation weighed him down almost as tangibly as the Alorans' shackle technique had earlier. His stomach growled, and he rolled gently away from Kaia.

She reached for him and mumbled.

He looked at her for a long moment, willing her to stay in the safety of her sleep, and then walked out into the hall.

The scent led him to the kitchen, where the table was heaped with steaming food, all of it familiar: ham, mashed potatoes, curry, fruit, hummus, rice, many of his favorite meals. Figuring that the Alorans wouldn't bring them this far just to poison them now, Ethan filled a transparent plate and ate.

It tasted good, though he hated to admit it. The seasonings were right, every dish was at its correct temperature, and the textures were perfect. He was reaching for a plate of yams when a scratching sound over his right shoulder made him spin in his chair. A flash of movement caught his eye, and he half-rose before he saw it again and froze. Beneath the cabinet next to the back door, a pair of eyes was watching him. They were small, about the size of house mice back on Earth. In a second, they had blinked away and were gone.

Ethan relaxed somewhat and settled back into his chair. Even alien worlds had pests, apparently. He reached for a golden loaf of bread and tore a chunk off, tasting the hot yeasty flavor. He was less surprised when he heard the scratching sound again, and he turned his head just slightly to see it scurrying along the edge of the floor. It darted under the table and he watched through the smoky tabletop as it deftly climbed the table leg and slipped onto the table.

It was only about a foot away. Ethan held out a hand and the little creature moved closer. It was something like a cross between a mouse and a tiny armadillo, with iridescent scales on its back and tail that looked almost insectlike. It approached cautiously and then stopped and watched Ethan.

Slowly, Ethan picked up a crumb of the bread he'd been eating and held it out to the little creature. At this proximity he could see its eyes: golden and catlike with vertical pupils, they focused on the crumb, and the creature rushed forward and snatched it.

It ate desperately. Ethan grabbed another piece of bread and laid it beside the little creature. As it began to devour the morsel, Ethan reached for apple slices, a hunk of cheese, and several nuts, laying them all beside the little creature. It ate until the pile of food was gone and then looked up at Ethan. Was it his imagination that it seemed grateful?

"You're welcome," he said, surprised at his own voice. "There's more where that came from." He gestured at the table.

"What is it?" Kaia's voice was quiet behind him.

"I don't know. An alien mouse, I guess."

At that, the little creature froze, looked at the two of them, and slipped down off the table and away under the cabinet.

"Nice to see that not all aliens are hostile, though," Ethan said as he loaded his plate with a second helping.

"That smells delicious," she said, wiping the sleep from her eyes.

His mouth was full, but he nodded and gestured toward an empty plate. She sat and ate, though rather more conservatively.

"Ethan," she said without looking at him.

He glanced up at her. Her eyes locked with his, and he put down his half-raised fork.

"I'm sorry about what I said earlier. I—I don't want to stay here, either."

He smiled grimly. "I know, Kaia."

"It's just—" She hesitated. "I don't know what we can do. I don't know how to get out of here. I don't even think it's possible. But I have to admit that I *want* to. I don't want you to think I want to stay here. I want to get back to the ship, to someday see Minea. Just like you do."

"We'll think of something." Ethan walked to the wall, looking out. "How do you feel?"

"I feel fine."

"Rested?"

"Yes. Very."

"Me, too. Maybe we can do a little exploring before they come back for us."

Kaia finished quickly, and the two of them ventured out into the street. Ethan hadn't noticed it before, but the climate was perfect. A cool breeze blew across the little town, and tall, clear trees, more opaque than the rest of the town, provided shade.

"I have to admit it's pleasant," Ethan said.

"Fresh air feels strange," Kaia said softly.

"Yeah. It's been so long since I've been outside." He looked up to watch the clouds again. Above the clouds, between them and the suns, a soft smokiness could be detected. "Wait. Kaia." He stopped, squinting at the sky. "We're not, actually."

"Not what, actually?"

"Not outside." He pointed up.

"A giant dome, over the whole city."

"A giant cage," he corrected.

They continued down the street, slightly more wary now. Every house was the same. Every yard had the same two trees in front and three trees in back.

Every street had the same number of identical houses. They walked and walked and eventually came to the end of one street.

Ethan walked to the clear wall at the end of the street. He peered out into the vast cityscape beyond. On the other side of the wall was an enormous building in which Alorans went busily about, walking, talking in groups, and working on various machines.

"It looks like an office building," he said. Kaia was beside him now.

"Or a laboratory," she said. "They seem to be recording something from those machines on these lower floors."

"Could be." Ethan looked up at the huge, solid wall. "At any rate, it doesn't look like we have an exit here."

They heard a whining noise behind them and turned from the wall in time to see two Alorans materialize behind them. Without explanation, the creatures shackled them and began transport.

CHAPTER 22

They were standing in a cold, clear room. Only a few Alorans were scattered throughout the room, concentrating on various screens and panels of strangely-shaped buttons, switches, and knobs. Ethan immediately recognized the tawny yellow plates of Traxoram. The ruler stood in the center of the room, next to a transparent silver cylinder. Traxoram turned to the creature nearest him, whose plating shone the color of a bruise. Its eyes, surveying the little party of four beings who had materialized so suddenly, were penetrating and gleaming. It stepped closer to them and evaluated Ethan and Kaia as Traxoram spoke.

"We will begin with these two specimens."

The new creature registered surprise. "My Ruler, I did not realize we would begin so soon. Mustn't we wait for the auction?"

"Fortune has smiled upon us and given us these two in advance. Should the upgrades you've been bragging about prove as revolutionary as you have claimed, perhaps we will not need more experimentation."

"But, Ruler, the contest—"

"Perhaps the contest will be over before we have need of the other humans."

"Would that not make many Alorans—"

"Angry? Their anger is not your concern. You should be more wary of my anger." Traxoram was pacing now. "If I unlock the secrets of civilization class advancement, I have no need of other Alorans! I have no interest, Klactalar, in sharing my throne if such an extreme can be avoided."

The creature took the chiding with a bowed head and rushed to speak once Traxoram was finished. "Of course, my Ruler. You have all rights to the throne. The accelerator is ready for testing."

Traxoram nodded once. "Very well. Begin with the male. He will be the more hardy of the two."

Klactalar moved to Ethan and then looked to Traxoram for reassurance. "This one?"

Traxoram growled. "Did you even bother to review the materials I sent you?"

Klactalar dropped his head again. "Yes, my Ruler."

Traxoram dropped the matter. "Oh, get on with it." He was pacing again. The other creatures had moved closer, making a half-circle around Ethan and Kaia. They studied them with great interest.

Klactalar reached for Ethan, seizing his upper arm roughly with the larger of his claws. He began to drag him toward the cylinder.

"Wait!" Ethan cried, in Xardn. "Wait! What are you doing?"

At his words, Klactalar's claw dropped to his side and he whirled, staring at Ethan. The entire room had frozen. Traxoram laughed.

"Ah, yes. I forgot to mention that this one has an interesting talent." He looked around the room. "It is no matter. You must continue with the experiment. Time is of the essence!"

"My Ruler, does this not suggest further investigation—"

Klactalar cringed as a deep growl emitted from the ruler.

"You will not question me! You will begin the advancement process or you will die!"

Klactalar reached again for Ethan, but his claw stopped before he touched flesh. He turned timidly to Traxoram and, with a pleading tone in his voice, said, "May I . . . at least . . . follow second-level protocols? This would ease my mind in case . . ."

Traxoram nodded impatiently. "Yes, yes, treat them as second-level specimens if you must. Just *get on with it*!"

"Oh, thank you, thank you . . ." Klactalar bowed to Traxoram and then turned back to Ethan, speaking slowly but distinctly. "You will forgive my earlier lack of manners. I was not prepared for this level of sophistication in your species. I will attempt to make this procedure as . . . comfortable . . ." He looked away quickly. ". . . as possible."

Klactalar held a claw out in front of him. Atop it materialized several layers of folded white material.

"You will please follow me to the changing room," he said.

Ethan was led to a sliding clear panel behind which was a small closet. He shot a look back to Kaia as he noted that all the walls were the same transparent material. It seemed pointless to him to have a privacy chamber for changing when the walls were clear, but he went inside nonetheless.

"You will please put this on. We do not know what substances might be found in the weaving of your native clothes, and we do not know how those substances might react to the acceleration process, so we must ask you to wear this sterile robe." Klactalar handed him the folded clothes and the door slid closed.

Ethan had the distinct impression that had he not spoken up when he did, he'd now be standing in the silver cylinder naked.

Ethan looked through the walls at the rooms surrounding him. They seemed to be laboratories, with various Alorans working around different kinds of machines. In the laboratory next door he saw two of the huge, scorched boxes that he and Kaia had discovered in the weapons storage hold on the ship.

Ethan watched, fascinated, as one of the big creatures stepped up and poised a claw over one of the strange diagonal keypads he remembered. The creature's claw worked deftly, punching in a code that immediately opened the lock. Ethan felt a growing anxiety as the lid was raised and other creatures stepped up to remove its contents.

He didn't realize he was holding his breath as he watched. Inside the box were clear containers of water. Inside the containers were preserved saltwater fish, sea animals, and coral. More containers held uneven rounded rocks that took him a moment to recognize. As he gazed at them, though, their lumpy exterior took him back to an undersea expedition he'd gone on and gave them away as manganese nodules: formations found on the bottoms of Earth's oceans.

So the boxes contained other species and elements from Earth? A quick glance at the items being removed from the other box confirmed his hypothesis. That one held sand, preserved animals, plants, and minerals from Earth's deserts. The Alorans were exploring everything about the little green planet.

He started to breathe again and realized he'd been watching far too long. But the Alorans didn't pay him any attention. Though the Alorans in the room he'd just left kept a watchful eye on his closet, none of the Alorans in the other rooms seemed to notice or care that he was there.

It was then that he remembered the energy pistol concealed in his vest. How was it that the Alorans had failed to detect it? In fact, he realized, they hadn't even checked him or Kaia for weapons. Now, though, as Ethan slipped his shirt and vest over his head in one fluid motion, he held the lump that was the pistol in place and dropped the whole pile on the floor nonchalantly. None of the creatures seemed to notice anything unusual, and as he pulled the long white robe over his head, he slipped his trousers off and added them to the pile. When he had finished, he waited for the door to open. When it didn't, he reached up and knocked on it lightly.

Klactalar stepped to the door and opened it without touching it. He motioned toward the cylinder, and Ethan walked over to it, catching Kaia's eye as he did. He stopped a few feet before he reached it and turned to Traxoram.

In the most polite form of Xardn that he could put together, he asked, "Ruler, what is the purpose of this experiment?"

Traxoram looked at him, measuring him. "You will enter the chamber, human."

Ethan didn't move. "Yes, but may I please understand what will happen to me inside?"

Traxoram laughed. "Your primitive brain would rupture long before you understood the smallest part of what will happen to you. Our technologies, our knowledge, has taken eons to acquire and eons to decode. You are not prepared in any way for such an understanding."

Ethan stood his ground. "Please attempt to tell me."

"Such impudence! Such a waste of time!" Traxoram rapidly opened and closed his large, barbed claw, but he relented. "I must say, your peculiar ability to speak our language has intrigued me. It is possible that your species is even more capable of adaptation than we had previously predicted. Or that you are a unique anomaly. We shall see."

He then gestured to the chamber. "It has long been known that civilization class advancement is an evolution. It is, essentially, a resequencing of genetic material in response to environmental triggers. When an aquatic planet begins to dry up, the gills of the species that live there transform into lungs. Mental and emotional transformations take place during the process, as well. As civilizations advance beyond mere physical beings, they seem to develop the genetic markers that make possible the control of matter, suggesting that mental advancement is also an evolution. Species that evolve far enough also gain control of emotional responses, allowing them to make decisions based on logic, which gives them yet another advantage in the competitions between species. We have advanced to the point which further improvement is considered impossible. There are physical laws that restrict us from evolving further. Or so it is thought."

Traxoram seemed to smile that grim smile again. "Other Class 15 civilizations have given up the study of class advancement. They seem to accept that they will not evolve any further. This means that all Class 15 civilizations, including ourselves, have reached an impasse. There is no more competition for territory, knowledge, or dominion between us. There is no more *striving*. My brothers and I are not satisfied with this. We believe that further advancement is possible. We have devoted vast ages to the exploration of this possibility. Your species is amazingly adaptable. Though you may not realize it, you have advanced through the civilization classes more quickly than any species yet known. We have studied your current genetic material, and it holds more promise than we had hoped. In this chamber, we are prepared to attempt a modification of this genetic material, an *enhancement* of it. By so doing, we can isolate the triggers and the markers essential for class advancement. Once we have done so, we can apply the knowledge to our own species, making it possible to advance to realms of civilizations never imagined."

Traxoram peered at Ethan with an amused look on his face. Ethan could tell he was not expected to understand what the creature had explained.

"Will the genetic material not naturally evolve? In such a great civilization as yours, surely—"

Traxoram cut him off. "This takes several generations, many spaces of time, and very specific conditions. My brothers and I will be here for a long time, but perhaps not long enough to see such advancement. We are not satisfied, like others, to believe that these things must be left to nature or to chance . . . we wish to experience class advancement for ourselves."

"But what about—"

"Enough!" Traxoram thundered. "I told you you had no hope of understanding. You know it well enough. Now you are simply stalling. The tests will begin now." Traxoram waved his hand and several of the Alorans took a step toward Ethan. He held up his hands in surrender and stepped into the chamber.

It was spacious enough when he first entered, but once he was inside, a panel slid across the opening and the chamber resized itself to fit snugly around him from head to toe. A cool breeze began to circulate through the chamber.

Ethan looked out through the smoky silver and fixed his eyes on Kaia. Hers were wide and brimming with tears. She had, at some point that he hadn't noticed, changed into one of the white robes herself, and he saw, through the walls of the closet, her engineering coveralls piled atop his own clothes. He found her face again and tried to smile at her. This seemed to make her cry harder. He tried to raise his hand to the side of the chamber, but found that he was immobilized.

Ethan became slowly aware of a light green mist filling the chamber. It tasted clean and cool as he breathed it in, and his body felt very relaxed. In spite of the cool breeze still blowing, Ethan began to feel a warmth. It occurred to him that it was not an exterior warmth. The surface of his skin still felt cool, but within him the heat was growing. At first, he felt as if he'd just had a hot bowl of soup, but then the interior warmth spread down his legs and arms. It was as if his bones were heating up. Within seconds, he felt the heat throughout his body. A few more seconds, and it was no longer a pleasant vague sensation. Rather, it felt like hot needles were penetrating every cell of his body.

He tried to move away from the pain, but he couldn't. It intensified. He felt himself trembling and then shaking violently. The chamber filled with intense green light, and he realized that it was shooting out of his pores. A wailing filled the chamber as he faded into unconsciousness.

* * *

Shadowy figures materialized around him. He was lying on his back, floating, he realized, about waist-high to the creatures surrounding him. It seemed to him that they were speaking from a vast distance away.

" . . . obvious progress at a cellular level . . ."

" . . . modifications were successful . . ."

" . . . undetermined amount of advancement."

At that point, the creature he recognized as Traxoram barked impatiently, "Well, what about the brain? Has the procedure brought about the desired cortical development?"

"We are not yet sure. It may take some—"

Traxoram thundered, "What are you waiting for? Split the creature's skull and check for proof of advancement!"

"Ruler, the specimen may not yet have reached the stage of advancement allowing him to regenerate. If he has not, the procedure you recommend may kill him."

"So? We have *thousands* more! Get on with it. I must know if this procedure works!"

"Ruler, I must protest again. If the procedure worked at all, we will see some behavioral and mental advancement. The cortical development would be a final stage of advancement. Any small advancements would be valuable. We could recalibrate and attempt the procedure again, providing us with valuable information about the microstages of advancement. We must finish our preliminary tests to see if we are moving in the right direction. If we do away with the specimen now, we will have to duplicate the tests thus far. We will lose valuable time. Any advantage you have gained will be lost."

The foggy figure of Traxoram spun away from the group. "Fine. Continue with haste."

Ethan saw the other Alorans turn back to him. He felt heat on one arm, cold on his cheek, and realized that their testing had begun again. Suddenly, from somewhere behind the group around him, the bright green light filled the room again, and he heard Kaia screaming.

His head snapped to the left and he saw, between the figures surrounding him, Kaia inside the chamber. She was suspended somewhere in the green light, her face a mask of incomprehensible pain. He reached for her with his left arm, knocking into one of the Alorans, who quickly and efficiently put him back in the darkness.

CHAPTER 23

When Ethan awoke again, he immediately sensed Kaia's presence. He turned and saw her lying beside him on the same clear, soft surface as he was. The Alorans were in the same room, but their interest was momentarily diverted to some screens off to the right.

Ethan reached for Kaia's hand and found that there was an invisible barrier between them. He watched anxiously as she began to open her eyes and breathed a sigh of relief as he saw recognition in them.

Traxoram was standing a few feet away. "Is there no way to tell for sure? The auction is only a short time away!"

"I'm sorry, Ruler. We must have more time to interpret the data."

Traxoram cursed. "We will be forced to continue with the contest. Are there other teams who may be as close as we are?"

"None, my Ruler, unless I have been deceived. I have investigated every laboratory, and I have found no evidence of progress like ours."

"We may still have some time, then. You will continue to work. I will attend the auction with these specimens, but they will be available for further testing at your direction afterward."

The creature nodded, and Traxoram spoke again. "I will go ahead. Send them with my guards." The air where he was standing began to shimmer, and he disappeared.

The Aloran to whom he'd been speaking glanced over at Ethan. When he saw Ethan's eyes open, he walked over. "Can you move?"

Ethan tried. His feet, arms, and torso all seemed to respond normally.

The Aloran keyed something into the holoscreen he was glancing at. "Can you stand?" the creature asked.

As Ethan rose, he saw Kaia being quizzed in a similar manner behind him, though the Aloran working with her seemed to be gesturing instead of talking to her. She was on her feet as well. After keying in more information, the Aloran waved a claw dismissively before walking away. "You may dress in your native clothing."

Ethan glanced toward the closet and saw the pile of clothes still inside. He was relieved that the Alorans had not gone through them. He crossed the room, and the closet door slid open for him. He entered and dressed quickly and carefully. He liked the heavy feel of the energy pistol against his chest as he exited. Kaia was standing outside the door with her back to him.

"Your turn," he said.

She went in, and he surveyed the Alorans moving about the room. When Kaia came out, the two big creatures that had brought them to the laboratory moved toward them again, and all four began transport again.

CHAPTER 24

A dazzling blue-grey hall expanded around them as they re-materialized. They were kneeling on a soft, navy circle in the middle of the hall. Tiers of Alorans rose around them, and Traxoram stood to the right of their platform. At their appearance, a deafening roar went up from the crowd.

The sheer number of Alorans stunned Ethan. He doubted he could have moved even if the shackles had been removed.

The two thuggish Alorans who had transported them raised their claws to the crowd, and then they backed away and stood on either side of Traxoram. He stepped up and raised his own claws, causing the frenzied crowd to scream in responsive cheering.

"Welcome! Welcome, my friends!" he said.

Ethan listened carefully, trying to decipher the accented words as quickly as possible.

"Every Aloran here witnesses today a historic event. We have received a shipment of the most highly adaptable creatures in the known universe."

The crowd howled, and Traxoram waited with amused pleasure for them to quiet.

"These creatures are our path to . . ." He paused, letting the crowd's anticipation of his next words build. ". . . *complete control*." The last syllable was nearly lost in the cheering, but Traxoram continued theatrically, "Imagine! Imagine unlocking the secrets to civilization class advancement. The contest has, as you all know, come to a standstill. We have run out of options with the other species we've acquired. This race gives us . . ." Another theatrical pause. ". . . new hope! The human race has advanced through the classes more quickly than any species on record! If we can capture this evolutionary power, harness it, we can force our own evolution and become the most powerful civilization ever known!"

The crowd erupted in cheers.

"We have determined that this race makes it possible for us to anticipate—within our own lifetimes, mind you!—an evolution beyond the imagination of those who have called us inferior." The crowd had settled somewhat, and Traxoram used the moment to lower his voice conspiratorially. "So, my friends, shall we get on with it? Shall I show you the stock we've received? We have 4,000 perfect breeding specimens. Males and females. Healthy, hearty animals such as these."

Traxoram gestured toward Ethan and Kaia and they felt the weights fall off of them. In fact, as they straightened at the absence of the weight, they felt themselves lifted and suspended in the air, rotating slowly under bright lights.

The Alorans went wild.

After a seeming eternity, they were lowered to the cushioned platform again. This time, they remained unshackled and stepped instinctively together, slipping their arms around each other. Traxoram went on.

"Choose carefully the best specimens you can. Remember that the Aloran who achieves class advancement first will reign with me in the new system to come! If you manipulate the genes of your specimens to advance them past their current civilization class, you become, with me, a ruler of all known civilizations!" The Alorans were at a fever pitch when Traxoram finally gave them what they wanted. "We will now begin the auction. May I remind you that you must have previously purchased accommodations in the human enclosure for any specimens on which you bid this afternoon."

A screen appeared in front of the platform upon which they stood. On it was an image of passenger 0001, a young man named Galan Sidford. He was in his stasis chamber, sleeping, unaware that his picture was being shown to thousands of aliens.

"We shall start the bidding!" Traxoram called, "at—"

"Away with this small-time auctioning!" a voice bellowed from the front row. A huge purple creature was on his feet, waving a dismissive hand. "I will take the first 200 specimens!"

Traxoram's voice was delighted. "Ahhh, Yanthaarles! You waste no time! And you have, I assume, ample accommodation for such a number?"

"You know I do! I own the entire upper sub-quadrant of the enclosure!"

Traxoram's face plates shifted into what Ethan thought might be a smile. "Very well, then, my old friend! We shall begin the bidding on the first 200 human specimens!" He consulted a small screen in front of him. "This lot includes 103 male specimens and 97 female specimens. If you want pairings for all of them, you may want to purchase more females from the random lots at the end of the auction! We will begin the bidding!"

Ethan felt his head swimming. This could not be happening. As the photographs of his passengers flashed in front of him, superimposed with the images of the gruesome creatures beyond, he felt hopeless, powerless. He saw the lots of passengers auctioned off for vast sums of Aloran currency. 300, 200, 50 passengers at a time, the screens burned their images into his brain, and he felt himself falling and crumpling to the floor.

In the darkness, he heard Kaia's voice. "What have they done to you?"

He felt her soft palm stroking his forehead and opened his eyes to find her looking anxiously into his. He felt a strange sensation of relief at his own recovery. His eyebrows drew together as he stared into Kaia's eyes.

"Oh, Ethan, I'm here. It's all right."

Ethan's senses were returning. He heard her voice again and felt a strange sensation of pain and fear.

"There are so many of them."

He reached up with one hand, brushing her lips. They had not moved when he heard her voice. As he touched them, he felt intense longing, both familiar and new.

Her voice came again as she continued stroking his hair gently. "I'm so glad we're together. I couldn't do this by myself."

He froze. Could this be possible? He looked into her eyes again and thought, very deliberately, "Kaia?"

She looked down at him. This time her lips moved as she spoke. "Yes, Ethan. I'm here." He shook his head slightly.

"Kaia, can you hear me?" he thought.

"Of course, Ethan," she said quietly into his fingers.

In the background, the Alorans' voices were muted.

"Kaia, look at my lips," he thought to her. "I'm not speaking to you. I'm thinking."

Her eyes grew wide and her thoughts fragmented. "How ... that's impossible ... you can hear me?"

He nodded.

"Now?" He saw that her lips were still and lowered his hand.

"Yes. Can you hear me?"

She nodded almost imperceptibly.

"What's happening, Ethan?"

He thought quickly. "The testing must have done something to us . . . some kind of telepathy."

He felt her fear. "Can they all hear us?"

Their attention was drawn out to the vast Aloran crowd, who went on with their horrific business with seeming disinterest in the two figures. Traxoram and his guards seemed focused on the gathering of bids and dispensing of lots.

Ethan thought Traxoram's name as he looked at the big creature. Traxoram showed no sign of recognition.

"I don't think so, but we have to be careful," he thought to Kaia. "We need to be sure, and it may be that they are just too distracted right now."

"Ethan, it's more than hearing you . . . I can feel—"

"My emotions?"

"Yes. I felt it as you realized what was happening."

"I know, I . . . feel you too."

Suddenly, powerfully, a surge of confidence and connection surged through them both. He realized that they were both feeling the same relief and affection, and the strength of their emotion was multiplied because they shared it.

Kaia was smiling at him, and he sat up, leaning against her for support. "Ethan, what if we can really read each other's thoughts?"

He was considering that possibility himself. "It could give us an advantage." He was feeling stronger, and he shifted away from her for a moment.

"We could—" Her thoughts cut off when he lost contact with her. The feeling of confidence subsided and she looked at him in a panic.

He reached for her hand. Once the connection was restored, their thoughts flowed together again.

"We have to be touching each other!" she exclaimed in her mind.

"It seems like it." The Alorans' voices faded when the mind bridge was open between Ethan and Kaia.

It was somewhere in the midst of their telepathic conversation that Traxoram's voice caught Ethan's attention.

"Thank you, my brothers, for your generosity and your commitment to our cause. You have not wasted your time nor your money." He waved graciously to the crowd. "You will be well rewarded for your efforts. We have one last lot to auction, and then our business here will be at an end. Your

Caretaker

specimens are currently in stasis, but over the next few days they will be awakened and delivered to the quarters you have purchased for them." He paused dramatically. "And now, my friends, for the final lot in the auction. This is the most valuable of the specimens: the jewel of the collection, if you will." Ethan looked at the screen, which flickered, blank, as Traxoram went on. "This specimen is a female. She is, at this moment, carrying young. This means that the Aloran who obtains her will have the unique opportunity to study more than one generation of advancement. We could learn more from these two specimens than from the entire ship."

The crowd was tense and excited. Ethan found himself on his feet, leaning toward the screen. He knew what would appear there, but something in him hoped against it.

Traxoram continued. "I make a disclaimer, however. Though there is great potential to study the offspring, we have very little knowledge of how they develop, and there is no guarantee that either of the creatures will survive genetic manipulation. The state holds no responsibility for the mortality of either specimen. Your money will not be returned, regardless of the outcome of your testing. But the potential is so fantastic that I myself will be bidding on this lot."

Ethan dropped Kaia's hand and walked directly to the screen, close enough to touch it had it been solid. Still, it flickered emptily.

The crowd was on its feet, each member ready to be the first to bid on this fantastic specimen.

"We will begin the bidding at 9 million." Traxoram thundered. "Ten!" He pointed to a flash in the back of the room. "Twelve!" As the bidding reached twenty million, the bids started to wane. Traxoram spoke between bids, whipping the crowd back into their earlier frenzy. "With this single specimen you could surpass every other competitor and win the throne!" He gave a sign and the screen jumped to life.

Ethan's eyes widened and a hoarse shout came from his throat. In front of him, innocent and vulnerable, floated an image of Aria, her pink skin perfect as ever, her mouth turned up in a slight smile, as if she were having a good dream. The sight of her overcame Ethan. He reached for the screen, and as the sound of the bids climbed in the air around him, he struck the image. The screen danced but remained.

Traxoram had not seemed to notice. His voice called over the sea of Alorans, "A pregnant specimen! A female with young! Even if they don't survive, autopsy evidence could give you all the secrets to advancement!"

At this, Ethan whirled on him. A murderous rage flashed inside Ethan. "You monster!" As the words left his lips, he felt a burst of energy leave his body as well, a shockwave that grew from his anger. It hit the screen, shorting out the image. It knocked Kaia down and threw Traxoram and his guards backwards.

The hall broke into chaos as the intensity of the wave grew, knocking Alorans down and shorting out whatever light sources hung in the heights of the hall. The huge room was plunged into darkness. Ethan was the only one standing, and he felt his own power as fury coursed through him. He strode in a flash to Kaia, scooped her up, and, sensing an exit to his right, ran through it, barely slowed by her weight.

As he fled, he heard the shouts of confusion and fear behind him. He ran up a slope and emerged into the glow of the red Aloran suns setting. As the fury began to ebb from him, his fear returned. He ran headlong through the city, trying to get as far as possible and trying to escape the images behind him. It was a long time before the energy completely drained from his body and he slipped between two huge clear buildings, collapsing to the rough rock street.

CHAPTER 25

Kaia was awake and trembling as he sat her down beside him. She cringed away from him for a moment and then seemed to lose what little strength she had, slouching against him again. They huddled together in the darkness of the alleyway. Kaia's bruised face shone purple and black in the night, and Ethan traced his fingers gently across the wounds from the shockwave.

"I'm so sorry," he whispered into her hair.

"What was that?"

"I don't know. I—I didn't mean to."

"Ethan." She was sobbing now. "How are we going to get back to the ship?"

"We'll think of something. We'll think of a way. At least now we have a chance. We had no hope of anything as long as we were their prisoners, but now . . . maybe there's a way. We've got to get out of sight. Then we'll think of something."

The dankness of the alleyway was smothering. No fresh breeze was blowing here. He listened to Kaia's ragged breathing and then heard something else. Scratching. He turned to see a little creature like the one in the cottage earlier. It was making its way down the alley toward them, carefully. He didn't give it much thought as he tried to come up with a way to get out of this, but the creature kept coming. It approached him directly, and stopped, as before, about a foot away from him.

He raised a weary hand toward it.

The little animal reached out and touched his finger. Ethan caught his breath as the contact sent a thousand new sensations into his mind. He was overwhelmed with hunger—intense, painful—and fear. Instinctively, he sent back a promise that he would not harm the creature, and the little being caught hold of his fingers with both of its hands and pulled its trembling body into his palm.

Kaia, watching, reached a weak hand forward and stroked the scales on the little animal's back. "What are you afraid of?" she asked.

A voice, strong for the creature's size, came into Ethan's mind. "The same thing you are."

"What are you?" Ethan asked aloud.

Again, the little creature communicated telepathically. "I am Tesuu, of the Zumiin race. I was taken from my planet and brought here by the same beasts I saw you with this morning."

"How long have you been here?"

Tesuu slumped. "It feels like millennia."

"Do you live in the cottage?"

"I live wherever I can find sustenance. When those like you were here before, I stole from their tables and stored up enough for a long time, but I ran out days ago. When I smelled your food today, I had to come."

Ethan's eyes were wide. "There were others like us? Humans?"

Kaia nudged him. "The people they stole from Minea. Remember? On the transmission? Flynn said his men just disappeared."

The weight of that pressed on Ethan's chest. "Are they still here?" he asked Tesuu.

The Zumiin looked up at him sorrowfully. "I'm sorry. They are not."

"What happened to them?"

"The same thing that happened to my kind. Many were taken to the labs. Of those who returned to the dwellings, some died immediately. Others grew to old age and turned to dust within days. There are none of your kind left."

"You survived," Ethan said. "Are there more of your kind still here?"

At that the little creature trembled violently and put his head in his hands. He opened his mouth to speak, but instead his head popped up and his disc-like ears twitched. A surge of horror came from him, and he leapt from Ethan's hand and raced down the alley. Ethan felt his terror as he retreated. At that moment, Ethan heard footsteps coming—the heavy steps of the Alorans. He willed himself to stand and pulled Kaia to her feet.

"If they see us, it's all over. They'll take us back. They won't fall for the same mistake again; we'll be shackled all the time and they'll do what they want with us. We've got to get out of sight." Ethan scanned the clear buildings around them. None of them would offer enough protection. His eyes fell on the rough rock streets.

Something caught his attention and he turned to see Tesuu standing in the alley. The little creature pointed at the ground below him, gesturing emphatically, and then raced toward the wall and disappeared.

"I think he's trying to tell us something," Ethan said. He focused on the rocks below him and felt a resonance, like a faraway gong. "This is crazy, but I think that there's an . . . emptiness down there. A chamber or something."

Kaia looked at the street. "Ethan, it's solid rock. How can you—It—You're right . . . something is under there." Her eyes were wide as she looked at him. "How can we know that?"

He shrugged, dropping to his knees and moving his hands frantically across the stones, trying to feel any that were loose. The ground was solid.

Suddenly, a light appeared down the street, floating in front of the small band of Alorans headed toward them.

He jumped to his feet. "They'll be on us in a second."

"Can you . . . knock them down again?"

"I don't know. I don't think so. And I don't know what it would do to you, anyway."

"What will we do?"

"We're going to have to fight. Here, take the energy pistol." He slipped it from his vest and handed it to her. "I'm going to see if I can get through this street." Ethan pulled at the rocks as he saw Kaia leveling the pistol at the approaching Alorans.

"Now's the time to use that, Kaia! Fire fast."

"Where?" she asked desperately. "Do they have hearts?"

"I don't know. Fire at their heads. That seems the most likely weakness."

"Should I—"

Before she could finish, five Alorans came around the corner, leering.

"Here you are," said the first. Ethan recognized him as one of Traxoram's guards.

Kaia opened fire. The energy beams struck the creatures on their faces and heads. They flinched back, raising their arms, but the beams glanced off their heavy armor plating and ricocheted through the clear walls of the building beside them. The energy beams bounced through the buildings like rainbows off a spinning prism, scattering into harmless diffusion somewhere beyond the walls.

Kaia kept firing, but the Alorans overcame their initial confusion and began to laugh.

"Such primitive weaponry," said the big guard. Ethan flinched as he felt the shackles overtake him. As Kaia sank to the ground, the barrel of the pistol dropped to the ground in front of them, concentrating the beam on the stone street. In a flash, the stones vaporized, leaving a crater about four feet wide yawning between the two groups. Ethan saw below the chamber he'd envisioned there, with tunnels running off on either side of it.

The Alorans looked surprised, glancing from the hole to the pistol and back. Ethan felt another surge of energy, born this time of fear, and with great effort, he threw an arm out, grasped Kaia around the waist, and fell forward into the crater. As they hit the ground, he rolled into the nearest of the tunnels, just out of sight of the Alorans.

Kaia was on her feet before he was, grabbing his hand and pulling him up and along the tunnel. He was exhausted, but they had broken the shackles. As he followed Kaia, he looked back over his shoulder and saw a huge Aloran arm reaching down through the hole, attempting to rip it larger.

He and Kaia ran on. The tunnels were black, but the strange sense of direction that had accompanied him in the darkened auction hall returned, and they navigated as if they knew where they were going. Soon the sounds of the digging Alorans faded behind them, and they slowed to a walk to catch their breath.

"Why didn't they transport down to get us?" Ethan wondered aloud.

"I don't know. Maybe the planet's rock is impenetrable."

"I thought they could control matter."

"Maybe not the planet itself. I don't know."

Kaia slowed again, and Ethan slipped his arm around her. He meant to seem comforting, but the truth was that he was quickly losing strength.

She put her arm around his waist and let him lean on her. "Do you . . ." She hesitated. ". . . feel it?"

Ethan nodded. The sense of which way to go had grown into a yearning, a physical need to continue down certain tunnels. It was as if someone were calling them, a siren song that they could not ignore.

It led them through the dark tunnels, across the uneven floor. The longer they walked, the more they found themselves stopping to lean against the cool rough walls to rest. They were on their last limping steps when they looked ahead to see a shimmering wall of light. Hesitantly, they walked toward it, clinging to each other.

The wall was made of the clearest water. Small waves undulated through it.

It looked cool and refreshing, and Ethan suddenly realized how long it had been since he'd eaten anything. He reached forward, brushing the surface of the wall with his fingertips. They came away shining with droplets. He reached his hand into the coolness of the lighted wall and drew back a handful of clean water.

Cautiously, he sipped from his cupped palm. The water was tasteless and cool.

Kaia took a sip as well.

He stepped toward the wall and looked up through its undulating surface. Above them, he saw what appeared to be the edge of a lake. Small, soft-looking plants and large red trees grew there.

He pointed up. "We're out of the city."

She nodded. "I want to go up there."

"Me too. How do you think we should . . . ?" He trailed off, looking up doubtfully.

Kaia shook back her short hair. "It's water," she said with forced bravery. "We'll swim." Ethan watched as she walked forward, holding his hand until the last second when she stepped through the wall of water and started swimming up. She smiled back at him, blowing bubbles out of her mouth as she kicked and rose.

Amazed and afraid, he stuck an arm into the wall. Squeezing his eyes shut, he plunged in the rest of the way. The cool water engulfed him. When he opened his eyes, the light above him was dazzling. He saw Kaia's kicking figure and swam hard to follow her. They quickly broke the surface. He spun in the water and saw that the other three sides were lakeshore covered with what looked like red grass and trees. Kaia was already swimming toward the nearest shore, and he followed her again.

The heat from the Aloran suns warmed them as they pulled their weary bodies out of the water and lay on the soft grass. It occurred to Ethan that they'd traveled through the tunnels all night. He lay on his back, gazing up at the sky, and listened to Kaia's sleepy breathing a few feet away.

CHAPTER 26

Gentle, musical voices reached into Ethan's consciousness. They were approaching from behind him and speaking Xardn, a clear, crisp form that put his own pronunciation to shame. He stayed still.

"Their bodies are depleted."

"They lie so vulnerably here. Perhaps they have not yet met the Others."

"I sense great fear in them. I think they have met the Others." That voice sounded very wise, somehow.

His fear easing, Ethan turned his head. The creatures hovering over him were beautiful, translucent, and shining. There were four of them. All were somewhat iridescent, but different overriding tints made them distinguishable from one another. Their faces were not human, but kind; not familiar, but safe. They peered at Ethan, and he was moved to speak to them.

"Hello," he said in Xardn, as if he had known them forever.

They smiled at his attempt. "Where have you come from?" a bright, clear blue creature asked in a chiming voice.

He pointed to the lake. "We swam up . . . from a tunnel."

They nodded to each other knowingly. "You have met the Others."

"The Alorans?" Ethan suddenly remembered Aria and the baby. He sat up frantically. "We've got to get back! We've got to save them!"

The new creatures were still looking benevolently down on him. "Those you met were not the only Alorans. We, too, are Alorans."

Ethan didn't care about semantics. He scrambled to his feet. "My family! They have my family! They are planning to experiment on them! I have to get back!" He looked over at Kaia, who still lay sleeping on the shore.

The new Alorans followed his gaze. "She is worn down. She must rest and replenish. You, too, have no hope of facing the Others without gaining strength."

Ethan felt himself stagger as he walked toward the lake. He stopped, looking over the vast expanse of water. They were right. And Kaia needed attention. Her bruising was still prominent, and he could only imagine how much pain she must be in. His own body ached, and his thoughts were foggy.

He turned back toward the creatures of light. "Can you—will you—help us?"

The four smiled in response. One drifted toward him, its shimmering form the pale blue color of wildflowers. "I am Sybillan," said the creature in a voice that reminded Ethan of church bells chiming. "She is Lassaya, he, Alzzendro, and she, Misselda." Each bowed briefly in response.

The Xardn Sybillan used was somewhat formal, and he pronounced it with a gentle twang, an accent that Ethan had never heard hypothesized. He tried to mimic it as he said, "I'm pleased to meet you." He took a deep breath. "I am Ethan Bryant. She," he pointed to Kaia, "is Kaia Reagan."

Slowly, Ethan felt himself being transported, but this time he was travelling through a tunnel of light. He felt Kaia's presence and that of the creatures. The experience was much more pleasant than the last time he had been unwillingly dragged along. He felt himself rematerialize and wondered if it was his imagination that he felt refreshed.

They were in a small, transparent cottage. The smokiness of the city was replaced by absolutely clear walls, glittering with various subtle colors, like a prism. The room felt somehow very cozy, and the furniture was familiar to Ethan. Wide couches and a tall armchair invited him. He realized that this was his father's study, just as he had last seen it. He sank into the armchair and noticed Kaia on one of the couches, still sleeping. Ethan found a table beside his armchair piled with food.

Lassaya's pale orange form drifted closer to him. "You will forgive us for drawing these things from your memories. We have very little need of such items, so we've crafted them for your comfort here. Please. Nourish yourself."

Ethan drank a hot, clear liquid that tasted like hot chocolate, then offered some to Lassaya. She raised a transparent hand to decline. "You don't eat?" he asked.

"Not the plant and animal matter that you are used to. We are sustained by drawing energy from the beings around us."

Ethan's eyebrows drew together. "You mean like parasites?"

"A parasitic relationship is beneficial to only one partner. As we draw energy from our companions, our energy also feeds them. Life energy here is not as . . . limited as it is in your species. Drawing it from another does not deplete their stores. They simultaneously gain strength through the exchange."

He took a bite of a chocolate chip cookie. "Interesting." It was strange, conversing with these creatures in such a civilized manner. After the last few days, he had begun to feel that everything unfamiliar was also unsafe. These Alorans had a calming presence, though, a deep peace about them that penetrated the entire room.

"You said . . ." He hesitated. "You said that the creatures we'd encountered were also Alorans? Why are you all so different?"

Sybillan and Lassaya glanced at each other and then nodded.

"The Others," Sybillan began, "are Alorans, but they are not considered part of our Class 15 civilization."

Ethan was stunned. "They certainly consider themselves part of it."

"Yes, well . . . they are young and still very impetuous. They have strong opinions about many things."

"So, what are they, then?"

"The Others are a subspecies of our own. For some genetic reason, they did not evolve as quickly as the rest of us. Many eons ago, we noticed this happening. Some of us began to advance in mental and physical capacities. Some did not. Over many millennia, the Others grew further and further behind. They began to be hostile and resentful. Conflicts arose which were intolerable to our society. They began to incite riots and stage attacks on those of us who had advanced. Though they posed no actual physical threat, the conflicts began to take their toll on our people's way of life. As we evolved further, they grew more and more discontent. We were forced to separate, both for our own comfort and for their safety.

"At one time, we moved freely across the whole planet. Then, with these conflicts, we were forced to isolate ourselves in the city you saw. We fortified the city against their attacks." Sybillan paused, an almost sorrowful look crossing his features. "We . . . underestimated them, as they seem to have underestimated you. They began to develop substitutes for the powers we'd developed. They encased themselves in armor impervious to the energy pulses with which we'd been able to control them. Though this made them bulky and unwieldy, it allowed them to infiltrate our city, pass the guards, and take possession of it. We fled the city and came here to dwell. We have not entered the city for many spaces of time."

Kaia spoke from where she had awakened on the sofa. "What are they saying, Ethan?"

Lassaya turned to her and spoke in English. "Hello, Kaia Reagan. I am Lassaya."

"You know our language?" Ethan asked. It had been an effort keeping up with their formal Xardn, and he was relieved to think they could communicate more easily.

"The language, too, is drawn from your memories," said Sybillan. He recounted what he had told Ethan.

"So it was not really the Alorans who have been collecting species from across the galaxy for experimentation?" Kaia asked.

Lassaya shook her head. "It was not us. The Others have long sought to force their own evolution, and over the eons they have tried many things. They began by experimenting on each other, causing great distress and death to many of their own. When those avenues were exhausted, they began to gather specimens from other planets, other galaxies. Their current ruler, Traxoram, has become frantic about finding the secrets within his own lifetime. They are finding that modifications to their bodies which they have already instituted have shortened their lifespans, and time is running out for their plans to be fulfilled." Ethan and Kaia exchanged a look.

Sybillan interjected. "They are also running out of resources. They will not be able to gather species much longer. They have only a single small vessel capable of interstellar travel."

"What?" Ethan shook his head slowly. "We understood that they could come to Earth at any time and obliterate or enslave our species."

Sybillan shook his head. "No. The Others are not technologically gifted and have not acquired the skills of building ships with instantaneous travel capabilities over large distances. The vessel they have is ours. Before we left the city, we destroyed our fleet, but were forced to flee before we could destroy the last small ship. The Others have used it to gather small numbers of specimens, but they are not capable of gathering many at one time. This limits their potential for harm."

Ethan swore softly. "They were bluffing. That's why they 'settled' for such a small number of us. They couldn't come after more." This meant that the rest of humanity was safe for the time being, no matter what happened here. But it didn't change the fact that his family was still in jeopardy.

Lassaya resumed her explanation. "The Others are growing more desperate. Traxoram has instituted a contest which promises royalty to anyone whose

Josi Russell

experimentation delivers the secrets of evolution. His people will stop at nothing to gain that place of power." Her voice filled with sorrow. "They cannot see that they will soon destroy themselves."

Ethan felt a slight jolt of hope. "How soon?"

Sybillan smiled. "Soon is a relative term. To creatures as long-lived as we are, 'soon' is many of your millennia."

Ethan was disgusted at their cavalier attitude. "Don't you see how much damage they could do in that length of time? How many civilizations they could enslave on this quest for evolution?"

Sybillan nodded. "Yes, my young friend. That is a consequence of their actions."

"Then why haven't you stopped them?"

Sybillan moved to look out the window of the little cottage at the fields surrounding them. Ethan wondered then why there were windows at all in these clear buildings. He was distracted from the question by Sybillan's voice.

"You should understand, Ethan Bryant, that not all Alorans are interested in this conflict. We few are the extremists in our society, who feel some responsibility for the Others. Most of our civilization has no interest in any of this."

"No interest? What do you mean?"

Sybillan and Lassaya exchanged a glance and then nodded in sync.

"May we take you somewhere?" Sybillan asked.

Ethan looked at Kaia. "Do you feel like travelling?" But he knew the answer before she spoke it. "No. You should rest." He turned back to the Alorans. "I'll go with you as long as you promise she'll be safe here."

"I'll stay with her," Lassaya said kindly.

Sybillan nodded, and Ethan found himself being transported. When they arrived, they were standing in a vast meadow. A cool breeze ruffled the red grass around them, and thousands of creatures like Sybillan were lounging, moving, and conversing in groups throughout the meadow.

Ethan was momentarily overwhelmed by the sheer numbers of them. He took deep gulps of the sharp, fresh air and willed his head to stop spinning.

Sybillan guided him among the Alorans. Most didn't even notice him, but some glanced in his direction and then returned to their conversations.

Ethan heard discussions about astronomy, philosophy, and the physics of Beta Alora. He heard comments on the plants and discussion about the weather. The entire meadow was full of ideas, and even though he listened, he didn't hear a single wish or a single question.

Finally, just as the strangeness of the Aloran conversations began to unnerve Ethan, Sybillan moved to the nearest Alorans and spoke, "Bellicas, Xenndrani, I have made the acquaintance of a most interesting being." He gestured. "Ethan Bryant, of Earth." The Alorans turned their beautiful faces to him and nodded.

"Pleased to meet you." Ethan used his best Xardn, trying to replicate the true Aloran pronunciation. As he looked closely at the new creatures, he was struck by the vacancy of their gaze.

"Ethan Bryant has recently escaped the city," Sybillan said. "He seeks our help to free his family from the Others."

Ethan thought he detected a hint of annoyance from the two Alorans as they glanced at Sybillan.

The one Sybillan had addressed as Bellicas responded calmly, "Be patient, Ethan Bryant. The Others will destroy themselves eventually."

Ethan stepped closer. "But we don't have time! They'll be experimenting on my people soon—maybe today. I need your help to stop them."

The creatures looked at him blankly. "Time, as even your species knows, is relative. Your passions cloud your reasoning. Calm yourself and allow the natural course of events to flow around you. You will find it liberating. When you are not tied to these petty desires you will see that all things pass away."

"So you won't help us?" Ethan said, his fists clenching.

"Our best assistance is to avoid interference."

"So you're content to lounge here in your meadow while innocent people are tortured by your cousins? When you have the power to help?"

Bellicas, finished with the human, turned away and resumed his conversation with Xenndrani. "The planet's rotation is, of course, influenced by the gravity well . . ."

Ethan threw himself at the creatures, his hands arched into claws. Suddenly, he found himself being transported. Sybillan was moving him back to the cottage.

When he felt himself standing solidly back on the ground, he whirled on Sybillan. "What kind of advanced race are you? I thought Class 15s were benevolent and wise!"

Sybillan shook his head. "There are many kinds of wisdom, Ethan Bryant. Many kinds." He drifted across the room.

Kaia reached for Ethan's arm. "What happened, Ethan?"

"They don't care. Don't care about anything! Even themselves." Their vacant stares flashed in his memory. "We won't get any help from them."

Kaia's eyes were clouded with confusion and discouragement.

He knelt beside her. "We'll just have to do it ourselves, Kaia. We're not giving up. We'll get to them. We have to." He put a hand over hers and attempted a smile.

"Your species is refreshing," Lassaya said. "It is remarkable to see such passion again. More remarkable that such passion is not aimed at destruction."

Ethan remembered his rage at Bellicas and Xenndrani and felt ashamed for a moment. "We have our share of that kind of passion, too."

"Certainly, it seems wise to strive for a balance," she responded. "We are out of balance. Because our civilization has advanced so far and has unlocked all the secrets they have encountered, they have stopped striving for . . . anything."

"But you are still so powerful," Ethan said. "You could defeat the Others."

"Only if we were to gain access to the city again, and only if we could find some tactical advantage. The city, and the Others themselves, are fortified against our powers."

"What about the tunnel under the lake? Couldn't you gain access to the city through there?"

"Unfortunately, we originally created those tunnels to drive them out. The tunnels, and every other entrance, are only passable one way. They are protected by strong energy pulses which allow for exiting the city but not entering it."

"How did they get back in, then?" Ethan asked, standing and pacing around the room.

"As I said, we underestimated them. The modifications they made to themselves shielded them from the pulses and allowed them reentry."

"But there has to be a way!" Ethan cried. "You said yourselves that your abilities are greater than theirs, that you are more powerful."

"That is correct."

"But even you have given up so easily. You *could* find a way, I'm sure."

"Bellicas was right to remind you, my young friend, that these things will work themselves out. They will be resolved in time. All things are."

Ethan scoffed. He glanced over at Kaia. As his eyes locked with hers, he heard her thoughts.

"I can't believe it. They will just sit and let people be destroyed." The strangeness of hearing her voice in his mind overwhelmed him again.

"Can you still hear me?" he asked.

"Yes." Her voice rang in his mind and she smiled.

Simultaneously, he heard the voices of Sybillan and Lassaya in his mind. "Of course."

He spoke aloud. "You can hear our thoughts?"

Sybillan nodded. "This is unexpected?"

"Very. We couldn't even hear each other's thoughts until..." He shuddered, remembering the dark scene in the auction room. "And I thought we had to be touching each other."

Kaia nodded. "We did . . . before."

"Interesting. You are gaining control of this new power at a surprisingly rapid rate. Where did this power come from?"

Sybillan's question sparked some hope in Ethan. The Alorans in the meadow didn't question anymore. Sybillan and Lassaya were different. Perhaps they could be convinced to help after all.

"I'm not sure. Do you know?" he asked Kaia. He turned and then looked at her more closely.

"Kaia, your face. It's hardly bruised anymore." He turned to their glowing hosts. "How long have we been here? Is there a time warp or something?"

Lassaya shook her head. "The time here is the same as it is in the city. You have only been here a short time."

Ethan ran a gentle finger over Kaia's face. "Our species doesn't heal this quickly. She should have had those bruises for many days."

Lassaya glanced at Sybillan again and then spoke carefully to the humans. "Would you tell us what experiences you had in the city? What you saw and what happened to you? We do not wish to bring about painful memories, but perhaps it would help us interpret your . . . unique energy signatures."

Ethan looked at her. "Our energy signatures? What do you mean?"

"Well, the two of you have very unique patterns of energy emanating from you. They seem to be in flux. Most creatures are stable, dwelling on a certain energy plane. You, however, seem to be changing . . . constantly."

"That doesn't seem good," Ethan said, not really surprised. "We went through some testing there. Traxoram ran some kind of experiments on us." He looked at Kaia. "They seem to have allowed us to read each other's thoughts."

She nodded.

"And—" He hesitated. "Could that have been why I—did what I did?"

A look of fear crossed Kaia's features for a split second, and it cut Ethan to see it.

"What did you do?" Sybillan asked.

"I'm still not sure." Ethan began, sitting down in a chair. "It's how we escaped. We were in a big auction room." He put his head in his hands as the memory came back to him. "The Alorans—the Others—were selling the passengers off our ship. They bought 4,000 of us, you know, from our government. We were on a colony ship and we were diverted here. There are many others still in the city..." His voice cracked. He took a moment to compose himself.

"During the auction I got angry," he continued. "I got very angry. I felt a power overtake me, and it lashed out, knocking everyone over. I just grabbed Kaia and ran. I don't know what it was or if it will come back. I did that to her—" He gestured to her bruises but saw that they were even more faded. Springing up, he crossed the room to her and dropped on his knees in front of where she still sat on the couch. Reaching up, he stroked her face. She didn't flinch.

"What, Ethan?" she said, confused. "Why are you looking at me like that? Is it worse?"

He shook his head. "No. It's ... better. Almost completely."

Lassaya spoke. "Do not be afraid. It is simple tissue regeneration. The girl is healing."

"So quickly?"

Lassaya responded. "This is an expected effect of evolution. The body grows increasingly adept at repairing itself." The true Alorans exchanged a concerned glance. "The Others," she said, "are getting closer."

"That seems to bother you," Ethan said straightforwardly. "What about everything happening naturally?"

"If the evidence you present to us is accurate, then there is nothing natural about the experiments they are conducting. Such genetic manipulation, if applied on a broad population, could disrupt the entire fabric of civilization." Sybillan's calm demeanor seemed only slightly ruffled. "The natural physical laws, when broken, cause vast and irreparable consequences. It threatens not only our way of life, but also our very existence."

"So," Ethan said. "Not ethical responsibility, but self-preservation will encourage you to act?"

The calm exterior had returned. "Ethics are a result of societal norms. They are not as absolute as you may think. But self-preservation is, in most species, a universal motivator."

"I suppose that's true," Ethan admitted begrudgingly. "So, where can we go from here?"

"Your description of what you experienced in the auction room intrigues me," Sybillan said. "Would you say that it compares to this?" With that, he extended a hand swiftly forward and a pulse of energy shot from it, across the room, shattering the far wall.

Ethan and Kaia stared.

With a wave of his hand, Sybillan restored the wall. "Does that seem comparable?"

"Uh . . ." Ethan floundered, trying to regain his composure. "Yeah. Yes. That seems like a much more concentrated and controlled form of what happened to me."

"Interesting. It seems you have evolved farther than Traxoram intended. You have gained some advanced abilities, Ethan. You have gained energy manipulation, regeneration, telepathy. Time can only reveal if there are more." He considered a moment. "These things, of themselves, are not enough to help us succeed in overcoming the Others. We ourselves possess these abilities and many more. However, the combination of your unique energy signatures, these abilities, and the physical characteristics inherent in your species, as well as the fact that the Others will not be expecting this kind of progress, may give us some slight advantage." Sybillan turned slowly to them. "We must meet with the few of our fellow Alorans who may consent to help and reach a consensus on how to proceed. Will you please rest here until we return?"

Ethan glanced at the door, feeling as if he were back in the cage in the city. "Can we leave if we want? Go outside? Go back to the lake?"

Sybillan seemed surprised but hurried to assure them. "You may go at any time. We, unlike the Others, do not want to keep you against your wishes." He stopped for a moment. "It should be said, too, that if you wish to leave the planet, if you wish to continue on to your destination, we have ways of allowing you to do so. You may wish to consider that possibility as well while we are away. We will discuss the matter upon our return." Without waiting for a response, the two beings shimmered and disappeared.

Ethan and Kaia were again left alone.

CHAPTER 27

Ethan sat down, reaching for a delicious-looking pastry. "Do you think this is really possible?"

"What?"

"All these new abilities, these beings that may or may not help us, the whole thing."

"I guess," she said around a bite. "We know that we can read each other's minds. We know that you did something pretty out of the ordinary back there. We know that my bruises are gone, even though they should have taken weeks to heal. Something about us has changed, and the only explanation seems to be that we've been modified. If that's true, then they're right—the Others are close enough to destroy whole civilizations. I don't think that if they begin evolving that they will be content to just rule Beta Alora. They'll spread out and eventually all organic life could be under their control. We have to do something if we can."

Ethan nodded. "But, maybe, Kaia . . ." he said haltingly. "Maybe they don't need both of us. Maybe I could help them get back in by myself . . . and we could send you on to Minea . . ." He trailed off as he saw the disbelief in her eyes. "I saw the look on your face when he said they could get us off the planet."

"Of course I want off the planet. Of course I'd go on if I could. But leave you here—" She grabbed his hand. "To face those monsters alone—no way, Ethan. We go together or we stay together."

Their minds were open to each other; the words formed internally an instant before the ears processed them. Ethan felt a strange and powerful connection with Kaia. He felt her fear, her determination, her horror at what lay in the city, and another emotion, one centered on himself, that he pushed out of his mind, back toward her. He pulled his hand away.

"Okay," he said, "we'll see what they come up with."

* * *

When Sybillan and Lassaya returned, they were joined by many more glowing creatures. The first thought Ethan had as he looked out at them was that they were beautiful. Absolutely beautiful. They were translucent, luminescent, every shade of every color that he could think of. Their presence was overwhelming. They stood outside the walls of the little cottage, waiting as Sybillan and Lassaya entered and invited them outside.

On the wide warm hillside, the Alorans greeted Ethan and Kaia. Ethan sensed an acceptance from them, a kind curiosity. He heard their voices in his mind, welcoming him, and he tried reaching back toward a few of them. He saw from their expressions that he was succeeding, however awkwardly.

Sybillan spoke in Xardn. "My new friends, we have discussed the possibility of using your unique skills to help us gain reentry into the city. My companions and I feel that it is logical to attempt this for the good of our society. We also hope to help you liberate your captive passengers. At this time, we need to meet and devise a reasonable plan of action, one which will offer us the best probability of success. We invite you to join us for planning."

Ethan searched for equally formal phrases. "We are both honored and anxious to join you." He translated quickly for Kaia.

Sybillan, Lassaya, and the other Alorans settled down on the hillside and indicated that Ethan and Kaia do so, as well. The gathering felt more like a family reunion than a war council. Ethan got the distinct feeling that though this was of more interest to these Alorans, they were still not in an intense state of concern over it.

A glowing green Aloran, who Sybillan introduced as Drammen, who sat near Ethan began to speak. "My friends," he said in a booming, gentle voice. "Through a series of events, these new friends have been brought to us. They are humans, as you have heard, and have recently been through the class advancement experiments that the Others have been working on. They are called Ethan and Kaia. These specimens have shown remarkable advancement, as you will learn should you try to unite with them in mind, though they tell us this is not usually possible for their species. Ethan, the male, has demonstrated energy control. Kaia has demonstrated advanced tissue regeneration. While these are great abilities for them, they also indicate the progress that the Others seem to be making toward forced class advancement. As we know, even their small successes in the past have had dire consequences. It may be time that we attempt to regain control of the city and put the experiments of the Others to a stop. Ethan and Kaia are desirous to reenter the city to access their ship and continue their journey. As their desires coincide with ours, we may be able to join with them to accomplish both of our goals." He looked over the crowd. "We would like you to discuss this matter amongst yourselves and join our discussion as your insights surface."

He turned back to the small group from the cottage. "We see promise," he began, "in the fact that you were able to evade the Others and find your way out of the city. Would you mind explaining how that happened?"

Ethan glanced at Kaia. "Which part?"

"Start with your initial escape, after you experienced the energy pulse that knocked the Others down."

Ethan and Kaia related their escape and then listened as the Alorans evaluated the intricacies of their story. The Alorans examined the energy pistol, affirming that the elements from Beta Alora, in their natural form, were affected by energy pulses and were able to block transport. The streets in the city were made of these natural stones, which was why the pistol had worked on the street. However, blasting their way into the city with the energy pistol wouldn't work, because the outer walls were made of resequenced elements.

The Alorans were interested to hear of the key players in the auction and the details of the experimentation. It was an offhanded comment, though, that caused the most dramatic reaction.

Ethan was explaining the strange suburbia that they'd been taken to. "It was obviously patterned from Minea," he said. "The houses, the furniture—everything looked the same except, of course, that it was all that strange transparent building material. But the oddest thing was the smoky sky. Like something was between us and the suns."

Sybillan stopped him. "That's simply the dome of the energy field that surrounds the city. But I'm sorry, did you say something about a new building material?"

Ethan wanted to talk more about the dome. "Well, it's probably not new to you."

"No, did you say the houses were transparent?"

Ethan didn't try to hide his confusion. "Yes, like all the buildings here. Only, in the city everything is smoky-looking, and here it is all very clean and clear."

"Do you mean to tell me that our buildings are transparent to you?"

Ethan felt a realization dawning. "They're not transparent to you?" he asked in awe.

"Of course not," Sybillan said. "They are built out of classanite, a mineral extracted from the planet and resequenced to suit our needs. This material is dense and opaque, even after resequencing."

Ethan's head was spinning. "Let me be clear. You mean that you can't see through the buildings?"

Sybillan shook his head. "No."

"Why would we be able to see it?"

Kaia spoke up. "Maybe we just see in a whole different spectrum than they do here. Maybe classanite allows our visible light frequencies to pass through, like our glass does at home, so our eyes can see through it in a similar way." Ethan translated and many conversations started up throughout the meadow. Groups could be seen making excited gestures as they communicated.

"Whatever the reason," Drammen interjected, "perhaps it could be an advantage."

"Is this, too, an effect of your genetic manipulation?" Lassaya asked in English.

Kaia shook her head. "No, we could see through the walls from the time we got here."

Lassaya repeated her words in Xardn and the Alorans plunged into discussion again. Their conversations had taken a much more hopeful turn.

"Why are the buildings here clear and the ones in the city are smoky?" Ethan wondered aloud.

"The only difference is the energy shielding that runs through the walls and the buildings of the city," said Sybillan in Xardn. "It connects at the city's edge to the dome, creating an effective barrier. We created it to fortify the city against the Others, but now it prevents us from entering."

"So we *see* the energy in the classanite," Ethan explained to Kaia. "It makes the walls look foggy in the city. But here, since there are no energy barriers in the walls, they are perfectly clear."

Kaia considered, then asked, "Couldn't you create goggles or something to let you see through the walls, too?"

Lassaya answered her. "We haven't used much extraneous technology in many spaces of time, but it is possible."

"We won't have time for that," Ethan said impatiently. "They could start experimenting on our people any time. We have to work with what we've got. If we can use seeing through the walls to our advantage, then we will, but if not, we have to get in there anyway. What are the weaknesses of the outer wall?"

Drammen spoke. "There are none. They are constructed of classanite. The energy field runs through them and joins seamlessly with the dome above."

"What about the portal where they brought our ship in? It must have been at the top of the dome."

"Yes," Sybillan said. "The portal can be opened by turning off the energy field directly above the statehouse. That opens a round gate in the top of the dome. Your ship is most certainly directly below that portal, in the statehouse hangar. When we were attempting to contain the Others, we made it the only way on or off the planet. Unfortunately, by gaining control of the city, they gained control of the portal as well."

"Can it be reached?"

"Not without ships. Again, we have only one left, and it is also in the statehouse hangar."

Ethan considered for a moment. "It sounds like we've got to get to the statehouse. Everything critical is there. Supposing we can breach the outer wall, how do we get to the statehouse?"

"I will attempt to send you an image of the city," Sybillan said.

Ethan blinked as a picture appeared in his mind, like a memory. He recognized immediately that it was designed from the Xardn symbol for "governing."

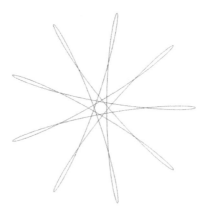

He saw the city laid out around him like a giant wheel, the statehouse and the portal at its hub. The main streets stretched from that hub out to the walls, and the force field arced above it all like a giant bubble.

His attention was drawn to nine gaps in the outer wall: gates. "If we can't get to the portals, how about the gates? Is it possible to get through them?"

"No, they are protected by one-way energy pulses, like the tunnel you came through," Sybillan said. "Without shielding, you can exit the city but not enter it."

Ethan ran a hand through his hair and stood, pacing around the little knoll. He looked off over the groups of Alorans, discussing possible options. They were Class 15 beings. If they had not been able to retake the city before, how could he hope to do it now?

"So the energy is what keeps you out?" he asked.

Lassaya nodded. "To touch it causes neural overload for us, effectively shorting out our neural impulses."

"So to get you into the city, we have to do away with the energy field?"

The Alorans nodded in agreement.

Kaia broke in. "How is the barrier maintained? Is there a power control center?"

Lassaya answered in English. "Yes, in the statehouse, but there are also substations along the nine major streets in the city that boost the power to the outer wall and the dome."

Kaia stood, too. "So if we disabled one of the substations, part of the outer wall would be passable?"

Lassaya nodded. "There are inner walls, as well, that would need to be breached, but some of them are not on the energy field grid. I assume they are guarded by the Others, but they are not protected by the energy pulses."

Ethan grabbed a stick and drew in a small patch of dirt. "So if we can get through a gate, we can start working on the substations. Would destroying substations get us into the statehouse?"

"No," Lassaya said. "The statehouse has energy shielding as well. It will have to be disabled from inside the statehouse."

So first the gates, then the inner walls, then the statehouse. At least Ethan felt like they were actively forming a plan, and every step got him closer to Aria.

When the last of the Aloran suns reached its cradle on the edge of the meadow, the Alorans dispersed, leaving in Ethan and Kaia's minds a clear understanding of the plan they'd formulated to infiltrate the city. Also in their minds was an unmistakable recognition of just how unlikely success would be.

CHAPTER 28

The wall of the city stretched as far above them as they could see. It was made of classanite, just as the Alorans had said, and it felt smooth and cold where Ethan and Kaia stood against it. On the other side, not far away, stood guards, their armor shining dully in the late afternoon sun. The guards stood with their backs to the wall, staring in toward the city and discussing the day's events.

"I've been at this post for three sunsets," said the first. His smaller claw was missing. It had been severed, and the arm above it was only a stump.

The other, whose armor was an inky green, responded, "What have you done to earn such an unfortunate assignment . . . and such a cruel punishment?" He indicated the missing claw.

The first growled back, "I was in the auction hall . . ."

The green one made a low sound. "That *is* most unfortunate."

"Only the end of the incident. The auction itself was stunning."

"Did you buy any of the specimens?"

"I did. Two specimens should be delivered soon. It is my hope that through the experiments I will find a way to replace this." He waved the stump quickly and then brought it back to his side.

"The delivery is taking longer than expected?"

"The ruler has not yet authorized the awakening of the ship's cargo. Many believe . . ." and here the creature's voice dropped conspiratorially, ". . . that if the ruler recaptures his two pets, he will retain the others still longer."

"So there is some truth to the rumors that he has already begun experiments on the humans."

"It would seem so. I believe he will keep those we purchased until he is sure that his specimens are not sufficiently changed and further experiments are still necessary."

Ethan felt a flood of relief. The passengers still slept. There might be a chance to get to them after all.

Kaia's voice entered his mind. "What are they saying?"

"Just chatting. One of them was in the auction hall. He's apparently in trouble for it."

She squeezed Ethan's arm. "He wouldn't be happy to see us, then?"

"No. They're also saying that Traxoram hasn't awakened the other passengers yet. We may still be able to get to them in time." He shot a quick smile at Kaia and then surveyed the opening between the two guards. It shimmered as the energy pulses protecting it ran back and forth between the sides. "I'm going to practice one more time."

Ethan pressed his back harder into the wall. He closed his eyes, focusing all his attention on a spot somewhere in the middle of his chest. Consciously, he flooded his mind with the images of Aria in the auction hall, of her sleeping in the hold as the first Alorans he'd ever seen crowded around like she was an oddity. He felt the anger rise, as he knew it would, and he held it in the center of his chest as Sybillan had taught him to do. As he held it, it grew. The emotions that fueled the growing power were anger and love and fear and desperation. When he felt they would overtake him, he placed his palms straight out in front of him and released the pent-up energy through them.

A small wave shot from him, destroying a rock a few inches from his foot. The fragments of rock flew back at him and Kaia and against the wall, making a small clattering sound.

The big green creature spun around, peering past the energy gate that guarded the entry. "What was that?"

The other creature shrugged. "Probably nothing. It's always nothing."

"I've never heard anything like that at this post before," the green creature said. "Perhaps I will go investigate."

"Perhaps you'll find yourself in shackles. You are aware that we are not to deactivate the energy gates for any reason until the human ship has been unloaded."

The green one nodded. "You are right, of course. Still, how much worse would it be to miss the possible reentry of—"

At that moment, Ethan stepped into his line of sight and fired the strongest energy pulse he could muster. There was time for a brief look of surprise to cross the beast's features before the pulse from Ethan hit the gate, intensifying and amplifying as it travelled past the energy waves there. The other Aloran was half-turned toward them when it hit him. Both creatures flew backwards and lay motionless on the other side of the still-pulsing gate.

Ethan and Kaia exchanged a glance. They had never expected the plan to work this far. It was encouraging to see the guards bested, but there was still a nearly insurmountable problem. They walked to the energy gate, peering through its wavy surface. It was as the Alorans had described, neatly encased in the surrounding wall, leaving no place that one could slip through. For an Aloran to touch it, Sybillan had explained, meant neural overload and paralysis for days. Though it hadn't been tested, it was reasonable to assume that for a human to touch it would be much, much worse.

Ethan turned away.

Kaia's voice came again to his mind. "We'll have to try it, Ethan."

"No. There has to be another way."

"There's not. At least not one we can find quickly enough. We don't know how long it will be before more guards are sent and our cover is blown."

"We should have through the night, at least."

"We might not."

"Kaia, it's too dangerous. What if it kills you?"

"Then you'll have to go back and formulate another way in." She moved toward the gate. "Besides, the Alorans felt it very likely that I'd be able to heal quickly if it doesn't work. We've got to try. If I can get past that gate and get to the panel on the other side, we're in!" She was standing in front of the pulsing entry now, trembling slightly. "I'm going in. You should step back a bit. We're not sure if you have any healing abilities yet."

He heard the determined sound of her thoughts, he felt her desperation to get back to the ship she knew, and he stepped back to let her try.

She reached out to the gate, then quickly stepped forward and plunged her arm into it, just as she had done with the wall of water when they had fled the city. Another flash of energy rippled the air, and Kaia's limp body flew, landing several meters away in a small heap.

Ethan flew to her side. He turned her over and saw burns covering her arms and torso. Her chest moved slightly as she took shallow breaths. Her overalls were shredded down her right side, the skin underneath protected only by the holster holding her energy pistol.

As he rolled her over, he noticed something steel and shiny on the ground underneath her. It was still surrounded by bits of fabric from her pocket. He picked it up, recognizing after a moment the attenuated laser she'd worked so hard on back at the ship. She must have been carrying it the whole time. He felt a pang—maybe homesickness—and yearned to be back on the ship, safe and unaware.

He tried to remember what to do for burns. As he peeled back the scorched grey material, he was surprised to see that the burns were not as bad as they had first looked. The angry, weeping blisters had smoothed over to crusted, tough skin. He closed his eyes in relief. She was healing.

Taking her in his arms, he lifted her gently and carried her over close to the wall. He laid her down and sat beside her, holding her head on his lap. They stayed that way for a long time.

* * *

When Kaia stirred, Ethan found himself bathed in the light of the Aloran moon.

Kaia sat up stiffly and groaned. He could see the shining smooth scars where the overalls hung away from her skin.

She followed his gaze and turned, running her hand up her side. He felt her horror. She met his eyes. "Well. I do heal," she whispered aloud.

"I'm sorry, Kaia."

"It's okay. I should be glad to be alive . . ." Her eyes dropped to the ground and he saw them widen. "Ethan!" She scrambled forward and snatched up the laser razor. "What if we can use this?"

"Is that possible?"

"I'm not sure. I don't know anything about the minerals this wall is made of. It's not impossible . . ."

She pointed the laser at a rock near her foot and activated the beam. Nothing happened. The dot of light wavered harmlessly on the rock. Kaia switched it off and tinkered with the settings, and then she tried again. On the fifth try, Ethan saw a hint of smoke from the rock.

"There! There! That's doing something."

Kaia turned up the intensity and cut a small circle cleanly in the rock. They beamed at each other. Turning to the clear wall, Kaia aimed the laser at it and activated it. The beam hit the wall and its light dispersed through the energy barrier in its transparent surface, making the wall light up. Quickly she switched it off.

She turned to Ethan with wide eyes. "I hope they didn't see that!"

He shook his head. "The walls are opaque to them, remember? They won't be able to see the light."

She nodded and set to work attuning the laser. After several tries, the laser cut through the wall and left a small, neat hole for them to climb through. Ethan hugged Kaia hard and they scrambled into the city.

It was dark inside. Kaia moved to the panel beside the gate and pried it open. Ethan checked the two unconscious guards and then joined her. Shortly, Kaia shut down the energy pulses that made up the gate. Their shimmering waves disappeared abruptly, leaving a gaping dark hole in the wall. Ethan held the image of it in his mind, trying to send it to Sybillan, who was waiting with the true Alorans beyond the crest of a hill directly outside the gate.

Before Ethan knew what was happening, a huge contingent of true Alorans appeared at the gate and entered the city.

Hopeful, even jubilant waves of emotion flowed from the Alorans as they moved silently through the darkened and deserted nighttime streets. The group got smaller as contingents branched off and worked toward the substations. Ethan thought again how much easier it would be if they could simply teleport around the city, as the Others did, but without the bulky armor plates the true Alorans would be vulnerable to the neural overload caused by the energy field in anything they tried to teleport through. Ethan and Kaia walked close together, unable to shake their fear as they caught sight of the huge, smoky skyscrapers.

Sybillan's clear voice came into their heads. "We must get to the statehouse. We will need your help once again in order to infiltrate it."

Ethan and Kaia nodded in unison. They knew what the next stage of the plan would bring. He didn't balk at the thought, though it would most surely mean losing his freedom again.

CHAPTER 29

Ethan felt Kaia's hand in his; small and strong, she squeezed his fingers fiercely. He tried smiling to reassure to her. As he did so, he caught her eye and the fear he saw there gripped him harder than his own.

"It's going to be okay," he thought to her.

Her thoughts were shielded from his own, but he felt her squeeze his hand again.

Suddenly, he felt agitation in the Alorans around them. He looked up. Ahead of them, the street was filling with the bulky shapes of the Others.

"You must go," Sybillan thought to him. "Continue on and we will meet as soon as possible. You must get to the statehouse."

The Alorans swarmed around the two humans, hiding them from the view of the Others coming toward them.

"GO!" Sybillan's thoughts had an intensity that Ethan had never heard in them before. Perhaps this mission meant more to the Aloran than he had admitted.

Ethan and Kaia ducked down an alley between two of the large buildings. They wove up and down the streets and alleys for several minutes until the din of the conflict behind them faded.

After what seemed an hour of walking, they slipped down another alley. It was dark here, even more so than it had been outside the outer wall. Inside the translucent buildings beside them were more labs, similar to the lab where they'd been experimented on. Ethan noticed the strange phenomena of being able to see through the buildings. Inside, he saw the interiors of the labs lit up, but the light didn't penetrate into the alley.

He saw, in one lab, the corpse of a lovely fishlike alien being, flayed open and lying on a table. Three of the hulking Others stood around it, arguing and poking at it. Ethan looked away quickly, feeling sick.

Kaia slipped closer to him, up under his arm. He felt her warmth beside him and longed, briefly, to be laying with her again on the wide leather couch in the Caretaker's hold. He ran a hand up her side, feeling the soft skin where her overalls fell away. She held him tighter, and their steps slowed.

They reached a lab that was dark inside except for a few blue lights far back in the room, and he felt his eyes relax. He could see slightly more clearly in the dark alley without the competing light from inside, and he glanced down to see the pale sheen of Kaia's dark hair and the soft glow of her skin.

"Kaia," he said softly, stopping and pulling her to him, "I want you to know that nobody else could have gotten us this far." He leaned against the wall and felt her in his arms.

She smiled up at him. "Turning soft, Ethan?"

"Maybe." He slid his hands down her back, pulling her close and feeling her breathing against him. They stood quietly, the press of their great responsibility held at bay while they held each other. "I—I lied to you."

She tucked herself closer into his chest. "When?"

"When we talked on the ship. I do—I do love you, Kaia." He hated himself for saying it, but hated more the feeling he was lying to her. "I don't want you thinking that I don't care for you if—if something happens."

"I know, Ethan. I know how you feel. I've seen into your mind, remember? You love me, but you will always belong to Aria. She was loyal to you, and you'll be loyal to her. I know you won't betray her. I've seen exactly how you feel."

This time, when she kissed him, he kissed her back. He let himself, for one moment, feel her surrounding him.

And then he heard the sound. The low, guttural grunt that could only mean they'd been discovered. Turning, he saw a huge hulking creature shuffling toward them down the alley.

"Taking a break?" the monster growled in Xardn.

Ethan put himself between the creature and Kaia. "Don't come any closer."

The creature continued to advance. "The ruler has put a nice price on your heads," he growled. "Bringing you to him will win me much favor."

"You don't look like a soldier," Ethan said.

"I am no soldier." The creature sounded disgusted. His claws clicked agitatedly. "I simply work in the labs, cleaning up all the waste from the experiments. I was not considered clever or strong enough to join the ranks of the leader's elite. But perhaps your capture will force them to see me differently."

Perhaps, Ethan thought, only the soldiers possessed the ability to use the mind shackles. Surely by now they would have been immobilized if this creature had such a power. Before he could think, he was testing his hypothesis: "What makes them so elite? So much better than you?"

The monster snorted. "So many things. They can bend others to their will." He stopped his awkward shuffling toward them and shifted the plates of armor across his shoulders, as if working out a kink in his neck. "All others must bow to them. If you cannot make others bow, then you will be the one on the floor."

"So they treat you cruelly?"

The creature's eyes twitched. "You are trying to trick me. You think you can learn secrets from me. You think I will help you." He snorted again, and then, without warning, he lunged forward, claws snapping.

Ethan felt Kaia jerk away from the creature. He stepped back with her but caught her hand and held her from going any farther.

"Ethan, we've got to get out of here," she said softly.

Ethan nodded slowly. "He doesn't seem to be armed. He can't immobilize us. I think we can outrun him."

"Okay," she said, her voice trembling slightly. She stood still but let go of his hand as she tensed to flee.

"One," Ethan counted, turning slightly toward Kaia, "two."

"Stop mumbling," the creature said impatiently. "Even if I am inferior to the leader and his soldiers, I am far superior to you. I will take you to him."

"Three!" Ethan spun and he and Kaia began running down the alleyway.

Behind them, the creature bellowed his frustration, anger, and surprise before starting his pursuit. His heavy steps followed them, the armor on his heels clanging against the stone street. Ethan knew he was getting closer.

"We've got to run, Kaia!" Ethan shouted. "Faster!" Something inside him snapped, and he found himself racing to the end of the alley. Suddenly, he knew he had gone too fast for her. As he reached the main road, he glanced back to see her small form clasped in the arms of the Other.

Ethan whirled back towards them and sprinted. The translucent walls around him blurred as he braced for impact and threw himself at the creature. He realized too late that though the creature did not have the ability to shackle them, he did have the ability to transport.

Ethan saw them fade as his momentum carried him through the space they had occupied and slammed him onto the cold stone floor of the alley. Pain shot through him as he hit, and so did the sickening realization that Kaia was gone.

CHAPTER 30

Ethan scrambled to his feet. Frantically, he paced from one side of the alley to the other, looking for a clue as to where she might have gone. He knew, though. The monster had taken her to the statehouse, to Traxoram.

Ethan tried to block out what they might do to her. They would probably keep her alive, at least as long as they thought she might be useful. They would try to get information from her, he was sure, and he knew Kaia well enough to know that she wouldn't give it to them.

Unless . . .

Ethan knew the creatures would not mind torturing her to get what they wanted. He had to get to her before that happened.

He strode down the alley to the main road. Checking carefully for Others, he slipped along beside the big buildings. There was no foot traffic on the street. The Others preferred to remain inside, working in their labs. He remembered the pictures of the city Sybillan had planted in his head and looked down the long street toward the center of the city: the statehouse at the hub of the wheel. If he could get through the city to the series of walls surrounding the statehouse, he might have a chance at getting to Traxoram. And to Kaia.

Her absence was like a ragged hole. As he moved stealthily, pausing, ducking behind garbage bins or into doorways, he felt the weight of her loss. He knew he couldn't have stopped the creature from transporting, but somehow, he felt that if he had been quicker, more focused, more careful, he could have kept her with him.

The city was still and quiet. Above him, through the red lens of the force field, he could see the lesser Aloran moon, ragged and sharp in the sky. It glowed bloody above him.

He was nearly halfway to the statehouse now. He could see, far down the street, a bright orange glow that he assumed to be the outer wall of Traxoram's estate. It seemed so easy to simply dash down the long, straight street and end the skulking through back alleys, but Sybillan had told him to take a more or less spiral route through the city, avoiding being on any one street for long.

Still, he could make a lot of progress if he took the main street for just a few more blocks. He was wild to get to Kaia before something happened, something he couldn't undo. So he peered as carefully as he could down the red-washed street and cut directly for the orange glow. He made it several blocks before he realized his mistake.

He heard the clicking sounds before he saw them: the Others patrolling the tops of two major buildings along the thoroughfare. He realized that they were stationed on the main street sides of the buildings, so if he had stuck to Sybillan's route they would have been unlikely to see him.

Their excited clicking grew in intensity as he started to run down the nearest alley. Others began to appear around him, and he knew it would be only seconds before he felt the shackles.

And then he heard another sound, a small sound, like singing. As another of the Others appeared directly in his path, he stopped his headlong dash and looked frantically for the source of the singing.

Without thinking, without understanding, he rushed to the side of the alley and stood in front of a garbage bin. The singing was coming from above him. He looked up and saw a window in the building open just enough for him to dive through into the room beyond.

He stood and instinctively fled from the great mass of Others who were appearing outside the transparent wall. Already they were clawing at the opening he had gone through. Ethan ran out of the room, through a hallway, and into a cavernous inner room. He slammed the door behind him and then turned and saw the singer that had saved him from the Others.

Its black eyes blinked back at him from a table in the center of the great room. Its iridescent scales caught what little light emanated from a single tiny lantern on the table. It was Tesuu. The little Zumiin held out a fragile paw.

Ethan walked cautiously towards him. He reached forward, watching the animal's catlike eyes focus on him. As its tiny fingers reached out, it made contact with Ethan's hand. Both froze.

Ethan was overwhelmed with images and thoughts flowing from the little being. Another place, a vast grassland. Another creature like this one, beloved. The Others. And death. So, so much death. He tried to pull away, but the little animal caught hold of his hand with both of its hands and pulled its body into his palm.

"You helped me," it said in a language Ethan was sure he had never studied but that he knew nonetheless. It wasn't simply telepathy, as it had been before when he'd met Tesuu. His linguistic ability seemed to be enhanced as well.

He opened his mouth to speak, and the Zumiin words were clear in his mind. "You just helped me, too," he replied, surprised at the easy way in which his mouth formed the syllables of the alien language.

"They will come here," the little creature said. "We must go below and wait." He gestured toward a row of cabinets that sat on the floor at the back of the room. "Hurry."

Ethan carried him back to the cabinets and followed his directions to the third one from the right. He pulled it open and the little animal jumped inside, scurrying off to the right inside the row of cabinets. Ethan cautiously leaned inside, curling his shoulders inward in order to fit through the hole. Behind him he heard the voices of the Others growing closer in the corridor outside. He pulled himself inward with some effort and closed the cabinet door behind him.

"Come this way."

He heard the small voice ahead of him in the darkness and followed it, crawling on his elbows. A pang of regret hit him as he realized how alike this was to the tunnels on the ship where he'd followed Kaia.

Before he knew it, the bottom of the cabinet gave way and he felt himself falling. Sliding, more accurately, down a long slope. As he cleared what he now realized was a trapdoor, the bottom of the cabinet sprang closed again above him and latched with a click as he continued to slide. A light grew brighter ahead, and he fell out at the bottom of the slope into a cozy room lit all around with tiny lanterns, some perched on a pile of rubble where the opposite side of the room had caved in.

A table near the rubble was heaped high with food that Ethan recognized from the cottage. He sat up and turned to look at the little being who had led him here.

"Your name, please," Tesuu said apologetically.

"Ethan Bryant." He took in the details of the little room, feeling somehow secure here. "What is this place?"

"A refuge. I believe it was created by one of the races brought to this planet for experiments. There are many such rooms, but most are in ruins. And those who built them are all gone." The creature looked away, and deep sorrow radiated from him.

"What about your race?" Ethan asked and was immediately sorry.

"Gone. All that came here with me. We do not belong here, either. We are of a different world, called Entewn One."

Involuntarily, Ethan leaned closer. He sensed the story to come was a terrible one, and he tried to send support to Tesuu, who trembled as he spoke.

"We came, as you did, as prisoners. The beasts brought us here and imprisoned us in a network of warrens below the ground where the dwellings I first met you in now stand."

"Warrens?"

"Tunnels. Chambers. Much smaller than this room. Just large enough for us. They were homes like we had back on Entewn One. They were all connected. The beasts constructed them to be identical to the burrows we lived in on our home planet. But as you've seen, they were not like home."

"You're right. There is something wrong about the cottages they built for us, too."

"Perhaps because they are built on a graveyard," Tesuu spit vehemently.

"A graveyard?"

"All my fellow prisoners are buried below your cottages."

Ethan felt a wave of horror. "What?"

Tesuu slumped into his scales, leaning back and closing his eyes. His small, fine face was a mask of pain. "When we came, the beasts began their experiments. They started at one end of the warren and took those who were unfortunate enough to be housed there to the labs. My mate and I were in the far end, and she grieved as she learned how few were coming back from the labs. The beasts were discovering that our race did not serve their purpose. She was so afraid that she would never see our children again back on Entewn One. We had hidden them with relatives when the beasts came to take us, and she hoped to return to them. We both did.

"And then they came to our home. They took us to the labs." He stopped, and Ethan saw that he was not trembling. He was deathly still and silent. His silence stretched on.

Ethan knew that pain. He shifted his gaze to the dirt-covered floor and waited. His eyes had adjusted to the lantern light, and he watched a flame dance until he heard the little creature's voice again.

"Their experiments endowed me with some unique abilities," Tesuu said.

"Now I can slip in and out of almost anywhere in the city, though I cannot seem to go farther than the city walls."

"Why didn't you escape the warren?" Ethan asked gently.

"I couldn't leave. My mate was not as fortunate as I. She could not escape. She was crippled by the experiments and stayed in the warren day and night. Every night I slipped out of the warren and found things to cheer her. Bright rocks, leaves, whatever I thought would bring her some small joy. She decorated our burrow with them, exclaiming over each one and taking delight in that one bright thing amidst all the horror."

Tesuu's voice grew fainter, and he closed his eyes again. "But the Zumiin were not what the beasts were looking for. We did not respond to the experiments as they had hoped." Tesuu drew in a ragged breath, and a tremor ran through him. He did not open his eyes as he continued. "And then one night, while I was out collecting stones, the beasts came and sealed up the warren. They—" The little creature was crying quietly. "Filled it with poison gas. Everyone gone. But me."

"I'm sorry, Tesuu." It was all Ethan could think of to say.

Tesuu opened his eyes, and understanding passed between them. He shook himself, his scales making a soft hushing sound as they slid across one another. "I'm sorry for you, too, Ethan Bryant." He grimaced. "I've seen your kind massacred too. After the Zumiin were lost, I hid myself and watched as the beasts created the dwellings for your kind, and I saw the first humans come and die in the labs. But apparently there was more promise in your race, because they continued to bring specimens, and they very much want you back."

For a moment, Ethan became afraid that his trust in this little being was misplaced. Might Tesuu turn him in? But one look at the yellow eyes, brimming with compassion and pain, reassured him.

"How did you get here?" Ethan asked.

"I found a tiny glitch in the electronic field around the dwelling area, and I made my way into the city. I explored the vast tunnels under the city and burrowed through where I thought I could create a sanctuary. I found this old room and made my home here. I slipped in and out of the dwellings and stole food from the tables of the other humans, and I stored it here as long as I could. I have refilled my supply from your table. I hope you'll forgive me and that you'll eat, too, while you're here."

"Nothing to forgive," Ethan said, taking a hunk of bread from the table and biting into it. "You can have it all. I don't plan on going back."

Tesuu looked at him. "Don't you? Where else will you go? A creature my size may survive in the city for a while, but not a creature so easily seen as you."

Ethan nodded and swallowed. "I'm getting off the planet."

"How? There are no ships."

"I have a ship," Ethan said.

Tesuu brightened. "Can I come with you? Can you take me home?"

Ethan's eyebrows drew together. "You can come with me and we'll find a way for you to get home. But I can't take you to your planet in my ship."

"Why not?" Tesuu's ears drooped slightly.

"Because it's a stasis ship. It has to go directly to its destination in order to keep all the passengers safe."

"I understand. I'll go with you. I must get off of this planet."

Ethan ate a piece of cheese. "You said this room connects to the tunnels. Can I take the tunnels to Traxoram's estate?"

Tesuu shook his head. "I'm afraid not. Most of the tunnels have collapsed inward. There are none remaining that go to the estate. I can get you closer through the tunnels, but then you'll have to go above ground."

Ethan slumped and breathed in the musty smell of the little room. Tesuu's story, the impenetrability of the tunnels between him and the statehouse, and the cool darkness of the underground made him doubt that this could work. The last he'd seen of the true Alorans had not been good. They were being overtaken even as he and Kaia ran away. Who knew if they had made it to their goals?

There were six strategic points throughout the city. The Alorans had told Ethan that if they made it to those points, the outside of the statehouse would be secured. The Others would most likely flee back into the large estate that surrounded the statehouse at the center of the circular city. Once inside, they could defend the statehouse indefinitely, as it was also protected by one-way pulse circuits.

That's where Ethan and Kaia came in. If they could breach the walls of the estate and make an entrance for the Alorans, there might be a chance.

But now Kaia was gone, and so was her laser. He had no idea how he was ever going to breach the exterior wall of the estate now. He ate slowly, his earlier agitation gone. It was replaced with a deep discouragement that seemed to seep into his very soul. What was the point? Why should he bother standing and going out into the street to be captured again? He pondered briefly the possibility of living here with Tesuu.

The little creature's mind touched his. "It would never work, my friend," Tesuu thought softly. "I am small and well acquainted with tight spaces. Some I've been forced into have been too tight even for my comfort. There is no way you could escape them forever. This is only a resting place in your journey."

Ethan shifted. "Okay then," he said aloud, still unnerved by the feeling of hearing someone else's thoughts in his own mind. "What do you think I should do?" His voice was hostile, he knew, but what point was there in all this?

Tesuu switched tactics. "Tell me about her," he said. "Tell me about the one you are trying so desperately to get to."

Ethan's eyes closed involuntarily, and he leaned his head back against the dirt wall. A picture of Aria formed in his mind. Not as he'd seen her last, but as he had known her before. Smiling, laughing, sleeping.

"I miss most the way she made me feel," he said quietly, "like we were on some grand adventure together. Whether we were going to the store or . . . or going to another planet, everything was new and fun when she was around. I miss the moments of complete contentment: reading the morning screens together over breakfast, fixing our leaky old heating reactor, sitting together in a hovercab on our way home. Just being there with her, knowing that she would be next to me. I miss that. I miss having her input on things. I'd ask her what she would do, and she'd tell me something I never thought of myself. I miss fighting with her and loving her and planning all our days ahead. I miss the baby and what it means for our future together."

A wave of empathy washed through his mind and he knew that Tesuu's loss was as great as his. Greater.

Ethan sat up. "I'm sorry, Tesuu. You—you—" He couldn't think what to say that wouldn't bring more grief to his friend.

"I know how you feel," Tesuu said softly. "It's all right." He twitched his long tail. "But I'll tell you—if I could go back, if I could get to the warren that night, I would waste no time feeling sorry for myself."

Ethan knew he was right. As Tesuu's words sunk in, he felt ashamed and desperate. "I need to go." He stood, his head barely clearing the low ceiling of the place.

"We need to go," Tesuu said decisively. "Follow me." And he set off at a quick pace through a gap in the caved-in rubble.

Ethan wedged himself into the gap and wriggled through it. On the other side, the tunnel stretched ahead, and he heard Tesuu's feet scratching along.

He followed the sound. Ethan felt his way along the tunnel wall. He learned to step high and anticipate an uneven path under his feet. The smooth dirt sides of the wall were broken by very few roots, and he wondered if anything living grew above.

Soon, the scratching in front of him halted, and he caught up to Tesuu standing in the pale glow of his little lantern. The tunnel ended abruptly in another massive pile of rubble. This was the end of the underground route.

Tesuu pointed upwards. There, a cleft in the ceiling showed the ragged moon outside, remarkably larger than it had been before. Ethan realized that night was fleeing. He would have to move quickly to get into the estate before daybreak.

He reached up to the hole. It was not big enough for him to squeeze through, but the edges came away with some digging. He began to pull the crumbling earth away, feeling it rain down on his face and arms. When he had moved enough of it, Tesuu scampered up the wall and through the hole, and he stood waiting on the other side. Ethan reached through the hole, took hold of some of the street stones beside it, and then pulled himself up and out.

The feeling of the city stretching around him was doubly unnerving after coming from the coziness of the tunnels. It seemed that every shadow, every corner, held danger. He kept low. They were in an alley, different from the others in that the buildings around them were all dark. Not even blinking lights broke the black forms. A quick glance above showed none of the Others atop the buildings.

"What's this? Where are we?" Ethan asked, feeling a chill in his spine.

Tesuu nodded. "This is the only way to get near the estate. These three blocks are deserted."

"What? Why?"

A strange look crossed the little Zumiin's face. "The testing here. It went wrong. Some of the byproducts leaked. They caused mutations and lameness in the beasts, so they barricaded this area and refuse to set foot here again. They are, in their ways, very superstitious."

"Is it dangerous to other species?"

Tesuu shrugged. "I don't know. It's never affected me, but we should probably keep moving unless you'd like to find out."

Ethan nodded grimly, and they set off through the eerily deserted streets. The outer wall of the statehouse loomed before them, its translucence making the grounds beyond seem wavy and ethereal. A wide lawn stretched away from them, dark red like all the vegetation here, making the grounds look like they were bathed in blood. Ethan tried not to think of what might be happening to Kaia, forcing himself to focus on the obstacle of the statehouse wall as each step drew him closer to her.

Finally, they reached the wall. Shadowy figures moved through the grounds on the other side. The waviness of the wall made it hard to be sure exactly how far away they were. He crouched next to Tesuu, extending his hand. Tesuu reached back, and as their hands touched, Ethan felt in his mind the presence of the little creature.

"What now?" he thought.

"I can slip in through a chink in the wall down there," Tesuu responded. He gestured with a small paw. "But you can't get in that way." He surveyed the wall.

"Go," Ethan thought to him. He wanted someone to be with Kaia as soon as possible to make sure she was okay. So she wasn't alone. "I'll find a way in. I'll meet you at the statehouse. On the side away from the moonlight, where it is darkest."

Tesuu hesitated, then, feeling Ethan's urgency, consented and nodded before scampering away.

As he disappeared, Ethan caught a whisper. "Good luck, Caretaker."

CHAPTER 31

The night was quiet in this part of the city. No glowing labs or clanking machinery, just the high silent wall and the faint sound of movement inside.

Ethan remembered Sybillan's description of the estate. The one good thing about the estate was that its wall was not shielded by the energy pulses of the city's outer wall. Inside it lay a wide expanse of manicured lawns and fountains. There would be little cover except for a few small groves of trees. He wasn't sure where they were in relation to where he was now, but he had to try to find one. They were his only chance at getting close to the statehouse without being seen.

He pressed close to the wall and crept along slowly, listening. He needed to know where the guards were stationed. At this time of night, he could only hope that they were chatting in order to keep themselves awake.

He smiled slightly as he heard rough voices on the other side of the wall.

"I was on the main gate when they brought them in."

"When will it happen?"

"Daybreak. The next guard should get here just in time for us to get over there to see it."

The second guard laughed, a grating rumble that hurt Ethan's ears.

He moved on. As the voices began to fade behind him, he glanced up to see the branches of a tree just grazing the top of the wall. This was his chance. Reaching high, he grasped the edge of the wall and pulled himself up and over. He felt so vulnerable atop the wall that he scrambled down and fell harder than he meant to. The thump was loud enough to stop the faint voices off to his left . . . and, he realized, to his right. He must be close to the next guard post.

The guards were moving toward him rapidly. He was briefly grateful that the Others moved so noisily as he slipped between the trees and ran toward the statehouse.

He heard them crashing behind him. "Someone was here!" They were spreading out, calling for reinforcements.

He kept running. Behind him, voices and lights were approaching. He looked around frantically. Off to his right was a dense bush. He thought he saw, inside it, a hint of space. He dove for it. He felt the limbs rake his arms and face, but he landed in a small opening near the roots, and the limbs sprang back to cover his entrance. All his weight was on his right elbow, but he didn't dare move as the creatures crashed into view outside his hiding spot.

"I heard something over here," one growled, and Ethan saw the elephantine feet stop just an arm's length from where he lay.

He tried to ease his feet a little closer to his body, hardly daring to breathe. He focused his attention on shielding his mind, allowing no stray thought to escape and give him away.

There were several creatures now, some pushing roughly through the bushes and some just standing still, listening. Ethan's heartbeats ebbed in his ears. It was only a matter of time. Perhaps he should just walk out now and give himself up. That was, he supposed, one way to get to Traxoram. But they would have him in shackles then, and he would lose the element of surprise, which was key to the success of the mission. If he could not penetrate the defenses of the statehouse without the Others knowing, the true Alorans would have little hope of getting in. Still, it was beginning to look like he may not have a choice. They would find him any moment.

The dull ache in his elbow had grown to a sharp pain, and he had to shift again.

"Hey," one of the creatures growled, "I heard something over here." He was peering at the bush, his pig-like eyes squinting as he leaned closer. Ethan froze.

Suddenly, a crashing came from the bushes off to Ethan's right. A loud crashing. Ethan didn't dare move to see what was there, but all the creatures straightened and took off in pursuit. He heard them yelling, "Over here!"

"This way!"

"I see something!"

"Catch it!"

They were gone, and Ethan took the opportunity to slip out and run from the cover of the bushes. He climbed a small hill and ducked against a guard tower. He heard one of the creatures inside, pacing restlessly.

Ethan slipped around to the side of the tower that faced the statehouse and looked around. From the top of the hill, he could see that the hill he was on wasn't a natural rise in the land. Another fortification, it encircled the dark shape of the statehouse, forcing any intruders to crest the ring of the hill on their approach, leaving them exposed. The other side of the hill sloped down to a central courtyard, where a huge crowd was gathered.

Just as day broke, Ethan saw why.

CHAPTER 32

Many of the Others were gathered below in a central courtyard. A line of the big creatures were kneeling, arms outstretched, as three Others stood spaced out in front of them. Something seemed odd about those three, but Ethan couldn't put his finger on it.

Before he figured it out, a fourth began to speak. This one also stood in front of the line of kneeling monsters, and he addressed both them and the crowd gathered behind them.

"The special rank of guard is accompanied by grave responsibility. Each of you has failed in that responsibility. In your failures, be they in the auction house, in the streets, or in the tunnels below the city, each of you has disappointed the ruler and let down your brothers. By allowing the escape of the humans, you have cost the ruler—and all of us—a great deal. For this, you will be punished."

Ethan's eyes widened as the three standing creatures advanced on the line of those kneeling. They raised their own arms, and, with a dark flashing, struck the arms of their kneeling captives just above the smaller claw. Bursts of black light shot from the severed limbs, and the kneeling creatures crumbled and screamed. The crowd roared.

The screaming was a horrible, strangled sound, and Ethan felt his stomach twist. He watched, horrified and fascinated, as claw severed claw all the way down the line. By the time the punishers had reached the end of the line, those at the beginning were staggering back into their kneeling position, their severed claws littering the ground in front of them.

Ethan shook his head to clear the dark scene. He knew he needed to move while that crowd was distracted. It would only take one stray glance up here at the tower and he'd be discovered. Once the crowd dispersed, he knew he would never be able to get past the clearing. He took a deep breath and ran, keeping as low as he could, toward the inner wall of the statehouse.

He remembered the statehouse from his first day on Beta Alora. It towered over him, and as he looked up, he saw the balconies and remembered transporting out of here with Traxoram what felt like a lifetime ago. The harsh light from the suns left Ethan no hope of blending into the wall. As he shrank against its smooth surface, he saw, for the first time, a pile of crates next to an inconspicuous door in the wall. Ethan ducked behind them just as he caught a flash of movement on the other side of the wall and the door flew open.

"They're bringing them in through this service door. Keep an eye on it," he heard a huge dusty orange creature say. The creature crossed the threshold of the door, the plates over his eyes sliding down as the sunlight hit him.

"What do we want with corpses in the statehouse?" the other, a sickly greenish one, replied.

Ethan kept an eye on the door. They left it open but stopped too close for him to slip in behind them.

"How would I know?" said the first. "I am sickened by the weakness of them. These so-called guards who expire at the loss of a mere claw."

So some of the Others who were punished had never risen from the courtyard. Ethan felt sick.

"It seems our race grows weaker even as the experiments promise such strength." The words had barely left the mouth of the green creature when the orange one spun on him, raising his huge claw threateningly.

"How dare you say such a thing?" he growled. "Our race grows ever more powerful until our moment of triumph!" He cuffed the smaller creature roughly, sending him staggering backwards toward the door. The green one caught himself on the doorjamb, glowered at his companion, and then launched himself forward and grappled with the orange creature. Claws locked, they staggered back and forth, roaring with rage.

Ethan waited a heartbeat, two, then shifted in anticipation of running for the still-open door. Just as he moved to spring, the two twisted, losing their balance and crashing into the crates in front of him, cursing and kicking their way back to their feet. Ethan froze. They were feet away from him. One wrong breath and he'd be caught.

Suddenly, four other Alorans appeared, dragging a sledge with the shells of the dismembered and dishonored creatures from the courtyard. The fighters scrambled to attention. In front of the sledge strode Nakthre, sneering derisively at the two door guards.

"What is this foolishness?" he barked. "Has there not been enough punishment for one day? Are you asking for more?"

Both shook their enormous heads.

"Have you any idea how easy it is to slip past guards who are more interested in their own petty squabbles than they are in the good of their society?"

The guards mumbled apologies.

"Statehouse Guards should hold themselves to a higher standard," Nakthre chided. "Now, you are to bear these bodies to the sixth level immediately. They are to be examined to see if their encounters with the energy pulses weakened them to the point that they could not withstand their punishment."

"Yes, Nakthre." The guards took over and pulled the sledge toward the door. On it were four or five dead creatures, piled unceremoniously atop each other, with arms and legs dragging in the red dirt. Ethan assumed that they were very heavy since the two burly creatures strained to move the sledge.

One of the creatures with Nakthre stepped forward. "Perhaps I could help you transport them the rest of the way," he said.

Nakthre laughed. "Idiot!" he said. "How long have you been commissioned?"

The creature cringed slightly. "Only a few weeks, sir."

"Ah. That explains it. Only Statehouse Guards are allowed inside. You're a Grounds Guard. You'll stay out here where you belong."

Without speaking, the red creature stepped back to his comrades, nodding.

"Get that to the sixth level immediately," Nakthre growled. Then he motioned to his contingent and stalked away. The three Grounds Guards followed him silently.

Ethan watched them shrink into the distance and then disappear into the crowd far across the wide lawn. He turned his attention back to the door.

The Statehouse Guards continued to struggle toward the door with the sledge. As they strained, one blade of the sledge caught on a rock, and the whole thing tipped sideways. The largest of the dead creatures rolled off the heap and smashed the front crate inches from where Ethan was concealed. Ethan felt the tremor as it hit the ground. The guards swore and disentangled themselves from the yoke of the sledge. They began to struggle with the hulking carcass, grunting as they attempted to lift it back onto the pile. Ethan cringed at the screeching, grating sound of their plates scraping against those of the dead guard. He closed his eyes briefly against it.

Suddenly, he heard a sharp crack. His eyes flew open just in time to see the dusty orange creature stagger back, the head of his dead comrade in his claws. He winced, dropping it and stepping involuntarily backwards.

"What have you done?" the green creature snapped.

"It just came off! His armor is brittle. Perhaps because of the blast?" The orange creature made a sound of disgust and then nudged the head with one blunt foot. "I hope we're not going to have to pick up pieces of them all the way up to the sixth level." He scooped up the head and tossed it onto the sledge, where it rested in the crook of another corpse's arm, and then he moved back to help the other guard. But before they had time to try lifting the body, a frantic contingent of Grounds Guards loped up to them.

"What luck! You're Statehouse Guards!" one creature said excitedly.

"What luck for whom?" the orange creature growled.

"We have been sent from the watchtower to convey this prisoner to the Statehouse Guard." Ethan craned his neck but couldn't quite see past the two Statehouse Guards.

"Find someone else. We already have a job."

"This prisoner is to be taken directly to the High Stateroom," the Grounds Guard said with a tantalizing note in his voice.

At this, the Statehouse Guards exchanged a glance. "The High Stateroom?"

"Traxoram himself would thank you for your service."

"Well, perhaps we could do that first and then come back for these," said the green Statehouse Guard.

"I think that would be a wise career move."

"Let's have a look at this prisoner," the orange Statehouse Guard growled. A Grounds Guard stepped forward, and Ethan stiffened as he saw the prisoner.

Tesuu dangled limply from the beast's claw.

CHAPTER 33

Ethan was frozen for several minutes after the door closed behind the Statehouse Guards and Tesuu. He realized now that it was Tesuu that had created the commotion when he was cornered in the bushes, Tesuu that had drawn the guards away from him.

If he wanted to help his little friend, he had to get to the High Stateroom, and to do that he had to get inside.

Ethan glanced around. The Grounds Guards had gone back over the hill after transferring Tesuu to the Statehouse Guards, so he was alone, but he had heard the energy shield switch on around the door as they'd passed through, so he knew it wasn't worth the risk of being seen to try to breach it. He put his fingers to his temples. Without the attenuated grooming laser, there was no hope of going through the wall, and an energy pulse would have the Others on him in seconds.

He stared at the load of dead creatures that lay baking in the sun in front of him. They gave off a sharp metallic smell. His eyes lighted on the huge beast still lying on the ground.

And then he saw it. The emptiness inside the shell. The neck hole was easily two feet in diameter, and beyond, where he had expected to see gore, he saw the smooth shining interior of a hollow shell. He quickly calculated how much of that space his body would take up.

Cautiously, he slipped out from behind the crates and crept toward the fallen leviathan. Without another thought, he plunged his head inside the beast and worked his shoulders through the opening. Slipping his hips and knees in, he crawled to the very bottom of the beast's torso. It was tight, but when he pulled his knees to his chest there was still space enough behind him that he thought he might avoid detection.

The stench inside the dead beast was overpowering, and the suns beating down on the shell had sweat dripping off Ethan in minutes. But this was his only chance, so he waited.

At last the beasts returned, grumbling about their cursory meeting with Traxoram, and heaved the carcass with Ethan in it back onto the sledge. He heard them grunting as they strained to get their cargo moving.

"It would take seconds to transport this garbage to the sixth level," the orange creature complained.

"And seconds more to end up on the floor with them. Transporting in the statehouse is forbidden until the city is secured again. The ruler will take no chances of being surprised."

The orange one swore as they continued to struggle with the weight. "It would almost be worth it."

Ethan had to brace against the inside of the shell to keep from sliding out, and by the time they reached the sixth level, he was as exhausted from that effort as they sounded from theirs.

When the sledge came to a stop, Ethan heard the green creature wheezing for breath. "At least this is our last duty of the day. I'm ready for the shift to be over." He laughed derisively. "For such an important delivery, I would have expected the researchers to at least be here to receive it."

"They probably don't even know we're coming. Everything is top priority to Nakthre. Let's leave them and get back to the High Stateroom. I want to see what becomes of that Zumiin. Traxoram seemed anxious to find out how it had survived this long."

"We can't get back in without official business."

"Katarem is on duty. He'll let us slip into the balcony."

There was a pause and then a grunt. "It's worth a try."

He heard their heavy tread as they crossed the room and Ethan waited. One long breath. Two. At five he reached for the gaping hole that was this creature's neck and slipped his hands out. Grabbing the shell, he pulled and slid his head out. The height and breadth of the room, compared with the cramped inside of the shell, made him reel for a moment, and he sucked in the cool air greedily.

This was a lab room, with tables and diagnostic machines along the wall. Vicious-looking instruments gleamed back at him from the cabinets.

Ethan shuddered to think what the researchers would do if they found him here. He pulled himself the rest of the way out of the shell and clambered down the pile of bodies, then he crouched a moment on the floor, listening.

The voices of the Statehouse Guards who had brought him in were fading outside the high, arched doorway. On impulse, Ethan moved after them.

As he slipped along the long hallways and up the transparent stairs, following the sounds of the creatures' grumbling, Ethan noted that the statehouse looked just as he remembered it. Vast and dizzying, the rooms stretched around, above, and under him. He kept his eyes on the immediate hallway, not wanting to run into any other beasts. Twice he had to duck into doorways to avoid oncoming creatures, but he made his way to the High Stateroom behind the Others who had gotten him in.

Ethan had lost count of the corners they'd turned and the floors they'd climbed when he heard the volume level in front of him increase. Instead of just the two voices of his guards, he heard multiple voices clamoring. He pressed close to the wall and slid forward.

Peering around the corner, Ethan saw a pair of huge doors wide open. Through the doors flowed a crowd of Others, paying no attention to the few Statehouse Guards stationed there who were trying to stop them.

"You cannot enter!" one of the guards bellowed as he was jostled aside by the throng.

"I am a senator," a creature in the crowd shouted back, cuffing the guard as he passed. "I will enter the High Stateroom at my whim. And I will see these proceedings."

More of the Others were pouring in from what looked like two main concourses emptying into the vestibule in front of the huge doors.

"I've got to get in there," Ethan said under his breath. Tapestries hung along the vestibule walls, and without thinking, Ethan darted to the nearest one and slipped behind it. There was a slight space here, just enough for him to lean against the wall and slide along sideways without touching the tapestry in front of him.

It smelled dusty behind the tapestries. The smell reminded him of waking up on the lakeshore outside the city. Part of him wished he were back there now.

He made it to the doors, and as he peered out, he saw that the desperate guards were beginning to pull them closed. In an instant, Ethan slid out behind the last beast to squeeze through the doors, and he slipped in as the smooth door thudded behind him.

He was totally exposed, but his back was pressed to the now-closed door, and all the creatures around him were straining to see what lay ahead in the center of the High Stateroom. A hush fell on them as Traxoram's voice filled the room. Even though Ethan's view was blocked by the broad backs of the creatures around him, he heard and felt Traxoram's anger. Waves of animosity flowed from the ruler of the Others.

"You will not talk, eh? You think we have no ways of finding out what we want to know? Perhaps this will encourage you to talk." Traxoram was quiet for an instant, and then a strangled scream echoed through the room.

Was that the cry of Tesuu? Ethan fought waves of nausea.

"Now will you tell me?" Traxoram asked. "I know now how you escaped, but you must tell me how you got back in. I am surprised at how far into the city you were able to come. How is it that you made it as far as you did?" Traxoram waited for an answer.

Every being in the room was quiet but the prisoner. A small choking, weeping sound filled the silence.

"And what of your mate?"

Ethan shook his head slightly in confusion. Tesuu's mate was dead. Why didn't he just tell the ruler that? There were no more Zumiin left on the planet. Why torture Tesuu for such an insignificant detail?

And then, in one horrible instant, Ethan knew why. As Traxoram focused his energy once more and the anguished cry reverberated again through the chamber, Ethan knew the prisoner Traxoram was torturing wasn't Tesuu, and he couldn't avoid crying out himself.

"Kaia!"

As the beasts in front of him turned shocked masks toward him, he threw himself forward, clawing through the crowd as Traxoram's cruel laughter filled the room. He scrambled out of the mass of creatures to see the small, dark figure of Kaia Reagan crouched on the floor under the weight of the Others' shackles. Beside her, in a small heap, lay Tesuu. Ethan could detect no movement in the little being, not even the rise and fall of his breath.

Almost immediately, Ethan was immobilized. He felt his body overtaken by the paralyzing weight of the shackles. Traxoram's anger multiplied the intensity of the bonds, and Ethan felt the weight of that anger crushing the breath out of him. He knelt, folded over, without the ability to even lift his head to look at Kaia.

"So, you've returned for your cargo," Traxoram hissed. "We knew you would. Your tricks at the auction were of little consequence. We anticipated your return, though I admit your turning up in my High Stateroom is a bit of a surprise. But your cunning did you no good in the face of your emotions, did it? If I had known her pain would bring you rushing into the open, I would have held my interrogation sessions on the balcony, where you could have heard her screams throughout the city. Perhaps that would have brought you more quickly and saved her some of the pain."

Traxoram sighed, a grim, self-satisfied sound. "Ah, well. Now that we have you both here, perhaps answers will be more forthcoming. You will tell me how you made it so far into the city."

The weight of the shackles eased slightly. Ethan drew in a breath and raised his head enough to take in the scene around him, but he said nothing.

Traxoram walked closer. "Perhaps you've been conversing with our cousins?" He sneered. "How are they? Have they told you all about our inferiority? Did they mention how far beyond us they'd evolved and how weak and pathetic we are compared to them?"

"Actually—" Ethan began.

"Did they also recount to you the horrors of the day we, with all our inferiority, forced them from their fortified city? Did they tell you how many of them we destroyed on the day we bested them with *our* might and intelligence?" Traxoram laughed. It was obvious he felt no threat from the true Alorans. Here, surrounded by so many of the Others, with their coldness and cruelty, Ethan began to believe the creature was right to feel that way. What could the ethereal energy beings do against such powerful, armored monsters?

"I've received reports that our cousins are being done away with as we speak, which indicates that we shall soon be able to refocus on our work. So we are back at the beginning, with you and your mate." Traxoram gestured to Kaia. "Wonderful. Though I've been reading your writings, and I have discovered that you are a fortunate creature indeed."

Ethan's heart stopped.

"You have another . . ." Traxoram waved a claw and a screen appeared. Aria, still sleeping, shone on the screen.

Ethan looked away.

"This one is yours, too, isn't she? Which explains your emotional outburst at the auction."

Ethan clenched his jaw and remained silent. He longed to look at Aria, to assure himself that she was still all right, but he didn't dare. He had no idea how much control he actually had of his power, and with Kaia in her weakened state and the hundreds of Others surrounding them, another energy surge was likely to hurt her and unlikely to injure enough of the Others to do any good.

But the chance to take out Traxoram was tempting.

Painfully, Ethan turned his head slightly to glance at Kaia. She was still shackled, but her piteous cries had ceased, and she turned her head to meet his gaze almost as if she knew he was looking at her. He heard her voice in his head almost instantly.

"Ethan."

Ethan blinked in recognition and then looked away from her at Traxoram and the creatures standing behind him. He knew he couldn't answer her. Not yet. The ruler was still gazing at the picture of Aria on the screen, seemingly unaware of Kaia's communication. Still, the Others could be listening without revealing their understanding. The ability could give the humans an advantage, but if they took it for granted, it could also be their downfall.

Traxoram turned from the screen. "Ethan Bryant, your tricks on auction day were very upsetting to us. After our many kindnesses to you, you should not have treated us so shabbily." Traxoram moved closer. "However, you are young, and you seem to have acquired some new abilities, which perhaps you do not know how to control. We have had many disappointments in our experiments, and we did not expect this course of tests to be any different. We now know better. You apparently gained, for some time at least, the ability to control energy. Tell me, is this power still with you?" The shackles eased again, as if Traxoram was trying to be friendly.

"I don't know," Ethan said. One part of him hoped that they'd let him try it, but he knew better.

The shackles bit into him with force. "Don't lie to us, Ethan Bryant. Two guards were found at the Fourth Entrance. They had been neutralized by an energy pulse, much like several of my guards were many eons ago when our cousins tried to reenter the city. However, this time there was also a crude hole in the outer wall, one forged by some sort of primitive cutting tool."

Suddenly a force hovered over Kaia. It drew from her pocket, as if by magnetism, the attenuated laser.

"Ahh, yes. Like this." Traxoram gestured and the tool clattered to the floor. "Such primitive technology, but effective. Also very traceable. The hole indicated that perhaps you, rather than our cousins, were behind the breach." Traxoram chuckled. "Your limited minds are somewhat creative. But the tool is of little consequence when compared with the power you used to disable my guards." He turned back to Ethan. "Now, I would like to know if you are still able to perform this act of energy control. Remember, you are only alive because of the slim possibility that you can provide me with information about my testing. I have no use for you if you have no information. Can you still do it?"

Ethan gritted his teeth. "Only when I'm very angry," he growled.

Traxoram seemed pleased. "Very good. Perhaps there is not such a difference between our two species after all." Traxoram moved to Kaia. "It's a pity, though. This one seems largely unchanged." He prodded her with a claw. "Any new powers, young female?"

"None," Kaia said aloud, her voice weak but defiant. "Except my ability to avoid tearing your heart out. Get your claws off me."

Ethan drew in a breath in surprise.

Traxoram prodded her again. "None but the ability to interpret what I am saying to you."

Kaia's eyes widened and she glanced quickly over at Ethan.

"You can understand me, can't you?" Traxoram said, placing his claw under her chin and forcing her to look into his face.

"Yes," she said boldly.

"And I can understand you. Both of you have much improved linguistic abilities. This could be encouraging, or it could be simply a fluke. More extensive testing must be done with a more diverse experimental population." He turned, still holding Kaia's chin, and looked at the screen. "Perhaps, we will begin with another human female. Perhaps with that one."

Ethan bit his lip. Somehow he had managed to put both of them in danger.

Suddenly, shouting echoed through the room, and Ethan heard the big doors swinging open behind him. The crowd pressed forward and several Statehouse Guards came clattering in. "Ruler, our cousins are in the statehouse as we speak."

A look of surprise and rage crossed Traxoram's features. He threw Kaia to the ground in disgust, and Ethan heard her crash against the stone floor. Traxoram struck out with a huge claw at the messenger, slashing across his chest. The same dark flash they'd seen in the courtyard sprung from the slice in the creature's armor and he crumpled, hitting the ground just inches from Ethan.

Traxoram turned his anger back to his prisoners. "You have allowed our enemies entrance into the city."

The shackles pressed Ethan down until he was prone on the clear, cold floor. It was if Traxoram were stepping on his back, crushing him.

"You should not have involved them. You and your females could have lived here in luxury as our special guests. In moments we'll be at war with our enemies again, and before they come I will kill you myself. When we've vanquished them once more, we will learn what we can from your corpse."

Ethan struggled to breathe. He felt his consciousness slipping away as the weight on his back increased. Around him, he heard the sounds of conflict. He dimly registered that the room was beginning to fill with shining Alorans; an intense battle was taking place. He felt two sharp pops in his chest and realized that his ribs were breaking. As a circle of darkness began to twist around the outer edges of his vision, he registered the sight of Aria on the screen and heard, simultaneously, an agonized cry from Kaia somewhere behind him. At least, he thought, they would be his last thoughts.

But something else entered his thoughts, eased its way in around the blackness. It was another presence. Sybillan was nearby, and his mind was merging with Ethan's. Ethan felt the Aloran's quiet confidence, felt his deep empathy for his lesser cousins. When these emotions mingled with Ethan's own fear and loathing of the creatures, Ethan found himself confused. How could Sybillan not hate them as he did?

Another consciousness was also creeping its way into his. It was full of dark hatred and disgust. He recognized it as Traxoram's mind, and the intensity of it made him convulse. He pushed it away as best he could while concentrating on the tranquil light of Sybillan in his mind. The crushing weight on his body gradually began to ease as Traxoram's attention was divided.

Sybillan drew closer.

As Ethan's breath came again, his senses began to return with more clarity. He heard Traxoram growling, low and menacing, and began to make out words.

"You've come again, my cousin. But this time, you will not be allowed to leave."

And Sybillan, in a musical voice, responded from somewhere behind Ethan. "Traxoram, your time is over. You must not fight against the natural course of things any longer."

The shackles had eased considerably, and Ethan scrambled to his knees. His stomach dropped as he realized that Kaia lay unmoving on the cold floor. He searched for her in his mind, but felt nothing of her consciousness. He tried to move toward her. Not having her there left him more afraid than he'd anticipated.

He fixed his eyes on her, willing her to get up. She lay small and vulnerable in the shadow of the huge beasts around her. Suddenly, Ethan recognized Nakthre breaking away from the crowd and moving toward Kaia's still form.

"No!" he shouted. "Get away from her!"

Nakthre glanced at him and then reached down to poke her with a claw. He looked deliberately at Ethan and did it again.

In the midst of the battle around him, Ethan focused only on Nakthre. He felt his anger rising, felt a surge of energy building, but as it crested Nakthre sneered and twisted his head sideways, his eyes still locked with Ethan's. Ethan felt pain rip through him, beginning at his chest, where the heat of the energy surge turned back inside him and raced through his arms and legs and face. Nakthre laughed as Ethan's body convulsed from the power of the surge.

Dimly, Ethan registered Kaia's form on the floor beside Nakthre. She was moving, or, more appropriately, being moved. She slid as if being pushed across the smooth floor.

No, not pushed, Ethan realized from inside his pain. Dragged. She was being slowly dragged across the floor toward an open side door by a small shelled being. Tesuu.

Ethan almost smiled as the pain began to ebb. He tried to build another energy surge, but nothing but relief welled inside him.

As Kaia disappeared through the doorway, Nakthre was set upon by two Alorans, and Sybillan's voice turned Ethan back to the faceoff between the two rulers.

"I'm sorry for what I must do," Sybillan said soothingly to Traxoram.

Ethan wondered briefly why Sybillan was speaking rather than thinking to Traxoram. The thought was fleeting, though, as another intense emotion swept over Ethan. Traxoram was enraged, and the intensity of his anger nearly forced Ethan back to the floor. He managed to stay on his knees, and with great effort he turned to take in rest of the scene around him.

Sybillan approached from his left about a hundred yards away. Traxoram's attention was fixed on his approaching cousin, and he had come closer to Ethan. Ethan could almost touch him, could hear the scraping of his armor plates as the creature towered above him.

Around the great hall, similar scenes were playing out. Alorans faced the Others, approaching them slowly but with confidence. The Others stood their ground, all bent forward as if ready to spring upon the intruders, though Ethan doubted that physical combat would have much effect on the bright beings.

Suddenly, though, he realized that he was wrong. Across the hall, one pair of opponents was grappling. He saw one of the Others spring upon the Aloran and grasp its neck with the larger of the two claws. The claw lit up in a dazzling crystalline display of light. The beast's whole exoskeleton began to glow. Ethan realized with horror that the Aloran's energy was being sucked out of it.

Traxoram noticed, too, and Ethan felt the creature laugh. "Our latest modification works!" Traxoram thought. He flexed his big claw in anticipation.

Ethan glanced at Sybillan, whose empathy for his cousin had grown. He was sorrowing already over what he saw as the impending, unavoidable death of the monster. He was focused on it, seemingly oblivious to all that was happening around him.

Behind him, the Alorans were falling. The Others who'd defeated them glowed like coals in the crowd as they drank in the energy of their cousins.

Ethan tried to warn Sybillan. "Don't let him touch you!" he thought frantically as Sybillan advanced. "They've developed a way to capture your life force!"

But Sybillan was transfixed on Traxoram. He continued forward. His sorrow was all-consuming, all-encompassing. Ethan realized that this was true of all the Alorans. Their empathy was killing them. As each focused on his or her potential victim, they were unable to process what was happening around them.

Traxoram noticed it, too. Some of his fear dispersed, and his confidence and his disgust for the Alorans grew. "They are truly the weaker strain," he thought. "Today they will be eliminated, as is proper. We will continue to rule here and will soon rule all that lies beyond!"

As his anticipation for the victory increased, Traxoram's grip on Ethan grew weaker. Ethan tried again to warn Sybillan, but the Aloran simply continued the stream of sorrowful and comforting words directed at Traxoram and continued to move towards the ruler.

Ethan felt Traxoram's growing desire for killing as Sybillan drew closer. The beast had almost forgotten Ethan's presence completely in his desire to destroy his cousin.

Suddenly, Ethan's eyes fell upon the laser razor next to Traxoram's feet. It was close enough that if he leaned he could reach it. He leaned toward it slowly. Traxoram didn't seem to notice. Ethan's fingers closed around the cold metal. He eased back into his kneeling position and focused his attention on it. What had Kaia said? The two dials adjusted for the density and chemical composition of the material. He thought of the wall they had last cut. Guessing, he assumed it was less dense than Traxoram's armor. He spun the density dial toward the right. The chemical composition was impossible to guess, but he remembered that the armor was somehow organic, that the Others had made it an actual part of them. He remembered the setting for hair cutting and spun the dial back to that.

Pointing the tool at the dead messenger in front of him, and keeping an eye on Traxoram, he carefully flipped the switch. The light hovered on the dead creature, but nothing seemed to happen. Moving slowly, Ethan spun the dials slowly, noting the effect on the creature. He began to see a small plume of smoke where the light hit the exoskeleton, and a surge of hope shot through him.

Sybillan was still advancing, only ten yards away now. Ethan had to hurry.

Just as Sybillan reached the corpse, Ethan's experimentation paid off. The beam of light split the armor of the dead creature, leaving a wide, clean slice. Ethan simultaneously felt Traxoram's overwhelming bloodlust and saw him raising his claw, extending it toward the approaching Aloran. Sybillan's mind sang a slow, sad song, replaying his regret over and over. He, too, leaned toward his cousin, as if they were drawn together by an unseen force.

An instant before Ethan anticipated it, Traxoram leapt forward. His claw lit up. Sybillan's thoughts stopped abruptly, and Ethan knew there was no time to spare.

He was on his feet instantly, forcing back the remainder of the shackling force. He scrambled onto the chest of the dead monster and stood, raising his head to shoulder-level with Traxoram. Ethan pointed his weapon at the huge claw that held Sybillan. As he flipped the switch, the beam shot out and caught Traxoram's arm just below the shoulder. The air filled with a short burst of darkness. Traxoram screamed and whirled, pulling Sybillan with him like a rag doll. The ruler lashed out with his other, smaller claw towards Ethan.

Just as it hit him, Ethan moved the razor across it and heard Traxoram's scream as the severed claw dropped to the ground. Ethan fell backwards off the body of the messenger. The razor flew from his hand.

He hit the floor hard and lost his breath, but he struggled back to his feet and fought back toward Traxoram. The creature was screaming in pain and anger but still clutched his hapless cousin with great intensity.

As Ethan ran, he scooped up the razor and hit the switch, pointing it toward the back of Traxoram's head. Instead of the usual silent beam of light, however, the tool emitted a high-pitched sound and then went cold in Ethan's hand. His steps stalled, and he flipped the switch several times to no avail. He felt Sybillan's consciousness slipping and Traxoram's power growing. There was no time.

He threw himself at the creature, catching Traxoram around the waist and tearing at the edges of his plates of armor. The sharp edges sliced Ethan's hands, and he pulled them back just as Traxoram knocked him down with the stump of his smaller arm. Again Ethan hit the floor. This time, though, he landed on the sharp edge of Traxoram's severed claw. He felt his flesh tear around it and rolled off in pain and surprise.

The scene he'd witnessed in the courtyard hours ago sprang to his mind. Suddenly, he knew the only chance he had at penetrating Traxoram's armor. He grasped the blunt end of the severed claw and leapt to his feet, the pain in his back and hands forgotten. He moved in dangerously close to Traxoram. Raising the claw, he brought it down with all his strength on the joint above the claw in which Sybillan was trapped. The force of the blow knocked Ethan backward, and he saw Sybillan drift away, hovering cloudlike, as Ethan heard the anguished, enraged cries of Traxoram.

Ethan staggered again to his feet and saw Traxoram reeling in pain and fright. The ruler turned on Ethan, staggering toward him with his useless, truncated arms raised. Ethan felt the crushing weight of the shackles begin to overtake him. Traxoram was having to expend much more effort to apply the shackles this time, and it was taking longer, but Ethan felt the power behind it and knew that in seconds he would be immobilized. With one last, long cry, he rushed toward the monster, the claw raised, and plunged it toward Traxoram's chest. As the point of the claw plunged through the armor, Traxoram fell forward, impaling himself still further. A cloud of the dark, shimmering light enveloped Ethan as he used his last strength to throw himself sideways, out of the path of the falling creature.

CHAPTER 34

Ethan lay on the cold floor, watching the battle scene play out around him. His body was heavy, and he felt Sybillan's consciousness slowly returning in his mind. As he recovered, the Aloran whirled and began firing instructions to the other Alorans. Ethan heard them in his mind, felt the intensity with which Sybillan was transmitting them. There was still sorrow and regret interlaced in Sybillan's cries, but there was also a new urgency as he saw his fellow Alorans in the grips of the Others. He called to them, in his wordless way, a warning about the new modification. Ethan saw the Alorans gain a new awareness and come out of their trancelike state. They began to send energy pulses toward their opponents before the Others could trap them.

But many were still immobilized by the Others. Ruthlessly, Sybillan tore a claw from the dead guard and rushed forward, severing claws and freeing his comrades with fury. He called instructions to the other Alorans, and they fell upon the Others while defending against new attacks. Ethan realized that their victory was eminent, and the pain in his body returned. He turned his eyes away from the carnage and laid his cheek against the cool floor. Blackness overtook him.

* * *

Ethan's consciousness returned slowly. He heard voices in his mind as he opened his eyes. He felt the familiarity of the Caretaker's hold around him and was overcome with relief that he was back on the ship. As he opened his eyes, he saw several Alorans around the room, investigating the ship. Their calming presence permeated the atmosphere. As he opened his eyes, they turned to him, smiling kindly. He recognized Lassaya as she came toward him.

He stood up. "Where is Kaia?" he asked immediately.

"She is safe. She's making needed alterations to your ship. We will inform her that you are awake—"

Just then, Kaia burst into the room. "Ethan!" She threw herself into his arms. "Ethan! We did it! We really did it! We get to leave!"

Ethan hugged her. "How are the passengers?"

"They're fine, just fine. They're all still in stasis and the computer reports all readings as normal."

Ethan's brow furrowed. "The computer! I forgot it was misprogrammed. What are we going to—"

Kaia interrupted. "I'm returning the whole ship to specs right now. I've already disconnected the tertiary nav system and put new flight plans back in. I've had a lot of help from the Alorans, entering beginning coordinates and charting the way to Minea."

For the first time in days, Ethan felt his face break into a smile. "Really?"

The Alorans' calming presence still pervaded the room. Ethan felt safe and hopeful. Then he remembered the carnage in the statehouse. He turned to Lassaya.

"How is Sybillan? How are the rest?"

Lassaya's face was serene but sorrowful. "We lost many. Sybillan is here." She motioned across the room, and the pale blue Aloran that Ethan had come to love moved gracefully toward them.

"Those of our kind who survived are weakened, but healing nicely under the ministrations of our skilled healers," Lassaya continued. "Life energy is difficult to regain, but not impossible. Perhaps some will heal in time to see you off on your journey."

"Have the Others been defeated? Completely, I mean?"

Lassaya nodded. "Few are left. The toll on their population was great. Most refused to surrender and insisted instead on fighting to the death. Those who are left are of a different mindset. They were the least vehement of the Others. We are currently holding individual trials for each of them. It is our hope that after much discussion and education, peace on the planet can still be achieved."

Ethan was doubtful. "And if not?"

Now Sybillan showed some sorrow. "Their time as a subspecies is short anyway. Because they devoted their lives to battle and domination, neglecting the natural life cycle, there are no young with their altered genetics. When those of this generation reach the end of their shortened life spans, the Others will be but a dark memory. If no compromise can be reached, we must simply contain those individuals who are left until the end of their lives. It is our hope that this will not have to be."

"Where is Tesuu? Is he alive?"

"Alive, yes." Sybillan's voice was gentle. "But wounded. He rests here on your ship." The Aloran's fluid gesture indicated the far wall of the hold, and Ethan saw one of the panels ajar.

Ethan rose carefully and crossed the room, reaching down to remove the panel. Inside he saw Tesuu curled into a ball, his armadillo-like scales shutting out the world. He stirred and slowly uncurled. Then he caught Ethan's eye and painfully crawled out of the panel.

Ethan felt tears sting his eyes as he knelt in front of the little creature and extended his hand. Tesuu climbed into it and gazed up at him.

"I don't—" Ethan's voice failed, and he tried again, gazing into Tesuu's bright eyes. "Thank you. I don't know what would have happened if you hadn't been there."

"I take great joy in the fact that we defeated them in the end."

"We did."

Ethan felt how anxious the little Zumiin was as the question formed in his mind. "You'll take me with you, won't you, Ethan Bryant?"

The thought of Tesuu's company on the ship delighted Ethan, and he saw Tesuu's joyous reaction the moment the feeling crossed their bridged minds. "Of course."

"We will go to your new planet and then you will get me home?" Tesuu's hope was overwhelming. "To my children?"

Ethan knew that hope, knew what it was to long for the ones you loved to be in your arms again. He nodded.

"I'm sorry, my friends, that cannot be," Sybillan said from behind them. Ethan felt a shadow of regret in the Aloran's mind. "Your species, Tesuu, does not live as long as the humans. For you to travel to Minea in their ship would take many of your lifetimes, and they do not have the means there to return you to Entewn One."

Ethan felt an old frustration rising in him. He felt again the fury at the immensity and indifference of space.

Tesuu's furry brows drew together. "On our planet," he said thoughtfully, "we lived many cycles. Here, though, our lives were . . . not so long."

Lassaya and Sibillan exchanged a glance.

"We owe you a great debt," Lassaya said. "There is a way for you to return."

Ethan stood, raising Tesuu to Lassaya's height.

"We have but one small ship remaining of our fleet. We will take you home."

Tesuu turned to Ethan. "Could you take my friends to their homes as well?"

Ethan's heart soared. Perhaps the sacrifice he'd been steeling himself for would not be required after all. He felt discouragement from Kaia, though, and looked in her direction as Lassaya spoke, her voice apologetic.

"I'm sorry, but there are many complications that make this vessel the best choice for the humans." A wave of empathy travelled from her. "Though I understand it means a great sacrifice for the Caretaker."

"What complications?" Tesuu prodded.

Ethan admired that he would not give up so easily.

Kaia spoke up. "Our passengers, Tesuu, would all have to be awakened. Their stasis capsules cannot be transported on the Aloran's ship. Our technology and theirs is just too far apart to make it work. Even if we awakened them all, very few could travel at a time, and the forces of FTL travel would pose dangerous risks so soon after their time in stasis. The Alorans and I have done some experiments, and even I am too recently awakened to travel in the ship. Even with my new abilities, a fraction of the forces caused me excruciating pain and damage. I would not risk that with our passengers."

Ethan shook his head to clear his disappointment. A part of him had been clinging to the hope that there would be a quick and easy way to Minea ever since they'd formed the attack plan with the Alorans.

Tesuu spoke again. "Then you, my friend? You could be free of the ship and spend your life on your new planet."

Ethan shook his head. "My heart is here, Tesuu. My life is here."

Tesuu bowed his head as Lassaya moved forward to take him from Ethan. "I hope we'll meet again, Ethan Bryant—under more favorable circumstances."

"Me too, Tesuu." Ethan watched as they left the hold and murmured after them, "Thank you."

Kaia was watching Ethan closely. "How are you feeling? They said you were amazing. And that you were injured."

Ethan turned toward her and ran his hands down his torso. "Well, I know that my ribs were broken, but they seem to have healed. Looks like you're not the only one who can regenerate." He smiled at her. "In fact, I'm tired, but I'm not even sore. How long did I sleep?"

"You've been on the ship for four days. For a while, I wasn't sure you'd wake up." She looked down, and he put a reassuring arm around her shoulders and squeezed. Her mind was open to him, and he sensed the fear and pain of the last few days hovering as a shadow behind newfound relief and happiness.

Ethan felt her affection, too. He felt her tenderness toward him. He knew that his own feelings were as transparent to her. It seemed so natural now, after all they'd been through, that they would have this bond. Still, another emotion called to him. He withdrew his arm gently from her shoulder.

"I—I want to check out the ship." He averted his eyes from hers and started for the door.

He felt her understanding and also a twinge of pain. "I'll be back in the nav rooms. We're within a day of being able to leave," she said, following him.

When they reached the hallway, they walked in opposite directions, their minds still intertwined.

CHAPTER 35

The passenger hold was quiet except for the whirring of machinery. As he approached Aria's chamber, Ethan nearly broke into a run.

There she was, sleeping before him. Without thinking, he threw his arms wide around the chamber and rested his forehead against the glass. He felt like weeping, or shouting, but instead he just held the chamber and let relief wash over him. Her smile, her voice, her expressions danced in his mind. Their dreams of building a life in their little blue cottage on Minea seemed so distant now. He knew now that he'd be an old man by the time he touched her pink skin again, but after all that had happened, it was enough. He knew now that he could live the rest of his life on the ship, as long as he was secure in the knowledge that she and the baby would someday walk as free people under the Minean sun.

He saw her stir in her sleep, just slightly, and he imagined that she knew he was there. "It's all right, Sweetheart," he said softly, putting his hand against the glass near her face. "We'll be on our way soon, and you'll be safe."

His eyes caught movement in her abdomen, and he looked down to see the baby stirring as well. A slow bulge moved across her belly as the little one rolled inside. He thought of it there and envisioned them both wrapped in his protection. He had to get them to Minea, no matter the personal cost.

"I'll come and see you both every day," he promised. His lingering fingers drew reluctantly away from the glass, and he headed for the nav rooms.

* * *

The navigation rooms were sealed when he got there, and the interior airlock had been engaged. As he waited for it to open, he felt anxious. Why would the airlock be engaged? Had there been some damage to the outer shell? Even if there had, they were still on the planet's surface and there should be no problem with decompression.

As the airlock slid open, Ethan was taken off guard as he floated upward. The artificial gravity was turned off inside, and as he headed, arms flailing, for the ceiling, he saw why. Kaia was clinging to the ceiling, working inside a panel there. Sweat clung to her forehead as she worked to loosen a set of wires.

"How's it going?" He swam awkwardly toward her through the air.

"Fine. Much better since I got this panel off." She glanced over at him and a smile broke over her features. "For a guy who's spent five years in space, you're not very good in zero g."

"Hey, for the first three of those years, I had no idea how to turn off the gravity. After I figured it out, it made me so sick I didn't have much desire to do it often. This—" He gestured at what she was doing. "—seems to be the only reasonable use for it."

"This from the bravest man on Beta Alora?"

Ethan's face colored. "I don't know about that."

"I heard what you did. Did you really calibrate the laser and chop off Traxoram's claws?"

Ethan shuddered involuntarily. "Yes." He spent a moment remembering and then amended, "I only cut off one claw with the laser. It was a good thing you taught me how to work it."

Kaia nodded. "I heard how you got the other claw off." She shook her head. "How did you know it would work?"

"I didn't. I just knew that the Others in the courtyard had used their bare claws to cut through the armor. I figured of all the options I had, it was the most likely to work." He paused, grasping a handle on the ceiling to steady himself near her, and watched her work for a moment. "Still," he said quietly, "it wasn't how I thought it would be."

She stopped and peered at him. "What do you mean?"

He shifted uncomfortably. "When I stabbed him, at the end, his—I guess the Alorans would call it his Life Energy, rushed out, and I was . . ." He hesitated, not wanting to reveal too much. "I felt this horrible sense of loss."

Her eyes showed him that she didn't understand.

Hastily he added, "You know, it's probably because the Alorans were there, and they were sorry about it from the beginning. I mean, they didn't want to kill Traxoram at all . . ." He trailed off, realizing that some things would take more sorting out in his own mind before he could share them, even with Kaia. But that may take too long. She'd have to return to stasis soon, and he may not have enough clarity by then to share what he'd gone through—

"I'm not going back into stasis."

He glanced up, staring into her eyes. "Of course you are."

"Of course I'm not," she retorted, pushing away from the panel and throwing her head back defiantly.

"Kaia, we can't both stay awake. There's still one stasis chamber."

"*Your* stasis chamber."

"*A* stasis chamber."

"Ethan, I'm not going to live my life on Minea. There's nothing for me there." Her voice was hollow.

"You don't know that."

"David's gone—"

His voice was firm. "Yes, David's gone, but as rough as it sounds, you have no idea what other happiness you might find there."

Her jaw was set stubbornly. "Ethan, you have a real reason to make it to Minea. I'm not destroying that for some vague hope of my own happiness." She turned back to the panel and began to work again.

He glimpsed a fleeting thought, and he tried to chase it into her mind, but she quickly shielded it from him. He felt her drawing away, not just physically but mentally. It felt like she was closing a door between them, and he sensed that the distance she was putting between them would continue to grow.

He began to speak, but she kept her back to him, and he knew they would get nowhere arguing about it now. He pushed off for the floor, aiming back toward the airlock. He'd talk some sense into her when they were back on their way.

"Don't count on it," she said aloud, shooting him a grim smile.

CHAPTER 36

The shining Alorans filled the ship on the day of its departure. Ethan and Kaia greeted them on the observation deck and bid them farewell. Their goodbyes were more poignant than either of them had anticipated. Something about the openness of their minds, the entanglement of their emotions with those of the Alorans, made them vulnerable to the finality of their parting.

They felt joy and relief, too, both their own and that of the Alorans. Both had had their freedom and their lives restored, and they celebrated those things even as they grieved that they wouldn't see each other again.

The ship made its way back into space without incident. Though it had been built in space and not made to land on or take off from a planet, the Alorans lifted it through their atmosphere and on its way as smoothly as a feather on a gust of wind.

Both Kaia and Ethan waited tensely to see if the navigation systems would function properly with their new coordinates, but they needn't have worried. The ship was once again bound for Minea.

The first day was tense as they watched the star charts. Kaia avoided him as much as she could, keeping to one side of the nav room and shielding all but her most trivial thoughts from him. Even when he tried reaching out to her or teasing her, she remained cold and aloof.

That evening, they found themselves back in the Caretaker's hold, eating their favorite Earth meals and letting relief over their escape finally permeate their thoughts.

"I don't think any food has ever tasted so good," Ethan said, taking a long drink of soda.

"Agreed." Kaia talked around a mouthful of cheeseburger.

"So if I read the instruments correctly, it seems that we won't be too late getting there, right?"

"Amazingly, no. Thanks to that little boost from the Alorans, we're only a few days behind schedule, as impossible as that seems."

Ethan was relieved. Aria wouldn't suffer any ill effects of the catastrophic events of the last few days. She'd never know they'd happened, in fact, until the press on Minea got hold of the story. He still wondered briefly if they should relate their ordeal.

Kaia answered as if he'd spoken the question. "Of course we should! People need to know exactly what value the government places upon their lives and their freedom. Something has to be done to ensure that this doesn't happen again."

"You're right, of course. I guess I'm just not looking forward to reliving it all again."

Kaia shuddered. "Me neither." She paused. "Those testimonials from the Alorans should help, though."

"True." Ethan shifted uncomfortably. It was now or never. "Kaia," he started.

She looked at him, her eyes smoldering, and he knew she could tell what was coming.

He rushed on, "We need to get you back in stasis."

"Ethan—" she began, but he talked over her.

"It's fine if you want to stay awake a few more days. I'd like that, in fact, but we need to set a date and get you back in there."

She put down her burger, sighing. "Ethan, we've been through this."

"I'm not going into stasis, Kaia."

"Ethan, it's ridiculous for us to consider anything else. You have to go back into stasis. It's the only logical choice." She seemed more subdued this time, more solemn.

He didn't look at her, just continued eating. "Kaia, there's no question." He knew he had to be firm with her if he ever hoped to win this fight.

She was quiet a long time, long enough to make him glance at her. There were silent tears slipping down her cheeks.

He softened a little. "Kaia, you have to go," he begged.

She continued to weep. "She'll wake up alone, Ethan. She won't—" She choked and stopped for a breath. "She won't know what happened."

"I'll be there to tell her. I'll be old, but I'll still be me. Besides, I'm not letting you sacrifice your life to this ship."

Kaia reached over and took his hand. "Don't make her go through losing the man she loves, your dreams together, your child . . ." She trailed off. "I couldn't stand knowing that you'd caused her that pain just for me."

He shifted his eyes from hers. "Kaia, it's—it's not just that. It's more selfish than that." He paused, searching for words. "I've got to watch over this ship. After the last few days, after what I've seen, after what I've learned about evil, I—I can't trust anyone else to do it."

Kaia pulled her hand away, sensing his resolution. "Not even me?"

He shook his head slightly and reached for her mind with his. The wall she'd raised still stood between them, though, and he retreated, standing to take the rest of his lunch to the recycler. A sense of finality settled over the hold, and a few more tears rolled down Kaia's cheeks.

CHAPTER 37

The next few days slipped away from them. Ethan and Kaia watched old Earth movies, ate every good thing they could remember, and ran through the halls of the ship like children. Ethan couldn't bear to think of the long years ahead, the silence that would fill the ship after she was asleep, the pain of losing her to stasis.

Kaia seemed to avoid thoughts of their parting. He only got glimpses of her shielded mind in moments of distraction or intensity when their thoughts still intertwined. Then he saw briefly why—she knew that her own sorrow over losing him would only make his pain worse.

Each day he slipped away and visited Aria, keeping his promise to her and keeping his resolve strong. He wanted to protect her, wanted to know that she'd be all right, and he felt a resurgence of his sense of responsibility every time he stood in the pink light of her chamber and watched her sleep.

He and Kaia had agreed on one last week together. On the eighth day, she was to enter stasis. Every day it was becoming harder to keep his distance, to avoid pulling her into his arms. Every day he felt his resolve to send her back into stasis wavering. Worse, every day his longing to be with Aria again grew. Every time he stood in front of her chamber, he longed to step into his own stasis chamber and sleep until all that had happened was decades behind him. Sending Kaia back into stasis would settle all of it.

The day finally came.

Ethan opened his eyes with feelings of dread and relief. He heard Kaia breathing softly on the couch. He'd taken to sleeping on the crooked massage table again, the short leg propped up with a book, so that they didn't have to miss one moment of their last few days together. He sat, thinking, on the edge of the table.

She stirred and then her dark hair popped up over the back of the couch.

She turned to look at him and he saw that her eyes were red.

"I guess we'd better head down to the hold," he said as gently as he could. He tried to sense how she was feeling about it, but she kept her thoughts carefully veiled from him.

She nodded, and they made their way through the ship for the last time together.

The stasis chamber stood ready, its door closed, awaiting their final goodbye. They stood in front of it awkwardly, trying not to look at each other.

"I can't hear all your thoughts," he said softly to break the silence.

"I just—I just don't want you to feel how hard this is for me. I—" Suddenly she spun, throwing herself into his arms, sobbing. "I'm just going to miss you so much, Ethan."

He stroked her hair, and the ache of those first five years on the ship, when all he heard was its mechanical sounds and the voice of the computer, rushed back to him. He held her tightly, pushing away his dread at the years of emptiness ahead, feeling his own face wet with tears.

She began to draw back from him, a steely resolve in her eyes. "I have to go now, or I won't be able to do it." She reached up, brushing the tears from his face, and kissed him gently on the cheek.

"I will always love you, Ethan." She let go of his hand and stepped to the door of the chamber.

He watched her struggle with the handle, trying to pull hard enough to break the inner seal. She was still weeping, and he saw that she couldn't open it alone. Stepping close behind her, he reached around her and put his hands over hers. Together, they pulled the door open. He heard the hiss of the seal breaking and felt the whoosh of cool air from inside. They stood for a moment in front of the open door, his cheek next to hers, his arms still around her. He felt her relax against him, and he leaned into the embrace.

In an instant, Kaia tensed, wrapping her hands around his right arm. She pulled, catching him off guard and tipping him off balance. He spun around her and then stumbled backwards as he tried to catch himself. Ethan fell backwards into the chamber, and with a feeling of dawning horror, he saw Kaia throw her shoulder against the door and slam it closed as he scrambled to his feet. Her deft fingers punched a sequence of keys on the keypad, and the chamber began to fill with sweet-smelling gas.

He pounded on the glass. "No, Kaia, no!"

She pressed her palms on the outside of the door. "We'll be there before you know it, Ethan."

His fists slowed as the gas began to take effect. "Kaia, you can't. Kaia, let me out." He knew that it was futile. The stasis sequence had been initiated, and even if she did let him out, her chance at stasis was gone.

He pressed his own palms against the glass. "Kaia, Kaia." His mind was fogging over, and he slouched back against the soft foam backing in the chamber. His hands slipped down the glass and came to rest at his side. He wanted to chide her for such a foolhardy move, he wanted to thank her for it, but her image grew fuzzy in his mind and his eyelids dropped closed as he felt the wax coating his skin and heard the chamber filling with liquid.

CHAPTER 38

Ethan's breath came deep and slow. His foggy mind fought the heaviness of sleep. He tried to roll over and then realized that he was standing, leaning against the soft back of the chamber. He opened his eyes, blinking away the fluid that blurred his vision. Frantically, he searched the world beyond the curved glass door for any sight of Kaia. But no, she wouldn't be there. She would be overseeing the final details of the awakening.

His body was still numb from its long sleep, but with some effort he was able to roll his head to the side to look for Aria. Her chamber was empty and open. She would be with the other passengers, preparing for reorientation.

He felt a cool gust of air as the final awakening compound was vented into the chamber. Feeling crept back into his limbs.

A man in a green lab coat appeared, studying the vital signs on the panel outside his door. He was not a man from the ship, and it was a shock to see the strange lines of an unfamiliar human face.

The man finally looked up at Ethan and punched a code into the panel. The seal on the door hissed, and as it opened, Ethan saw Aria standing behind the man in the green coat.

She was beaming.

He scrambled around the technician, ignoring his offer of support, and fell into Aria's arms. He crushed her to him, feeling her breathing against his neck, her soft hair on his cheek, her stomach between them. He laid a hand on the side of it, pulled her face close with his other hand, and kissed the lips he'd longed for.

"Ethan, Ethan, we're here!" she said excitedly. "We're orbiting Minea. It was just like you said. I went to sleep and woke up on the brink of a whole new world! I feel like I've hardly been asleep a moment—" She stopped abruptly, her eyes searching his face.

"Are you all right?" he asked. "Do you feel all right?"

She smiled. "I'm fine, honey. Just fine."

He ran his eyes over her again, drinking in the sight of her, the feel of his arm wrapped around her body.

The technician also smiled. "Both of you check out. You're as fit as you were the day you entered stasis." He glanced at a portable screen he was carrying, and his eyebrows drew together slightly. "You," he gestured at Ethan, "more so." He looked at the screen a little longer and then nodded slightly. "Anyway, if you'd please both accompany me to the reorientation room . . ."

He was already walking away down the long row of empty chambers. Ethan drew Aria closer, and they followed him together.

Ethan knew what to expect. He'd watched the reorientation video at least ten times and had almost memorized the cheery narration. "Section One: How You Got Here and What to Expect after Stasis. Section Two: Your New Home." He'd always liked the stunning views of Minea in the video, and he looked forward to a little time to zone out and collect his thoughts while it played.

They left the ship by the lower hold doors, entering a hallway lined with elevators. The technician led them into the nearest open one. As they dropped from the spaceport down to the Minean receiving center, Ethan wondered about Kaia. Was she still on the ship or awaiting them below?

The elevator doors slid open to reveal the elaborate receiving center. As they passed the statues of Minea's founders that lined the hallway from the elevator to the reorientation room, Ethan was overtaken by a short burst of landsickness, for which they had to stop their progression. Aria watched him with a concerned expression, and the technician tapped something on his screen. Ethan was relieved when the sickness passed and he was able to move down the corridor and into a vast hall filled with people. The technician seated them and wished them luck in their new life before disappearing into the sea of green coats at the back of the room.

"Look at all these people!" Aria's voice was still high with excitement. "Can you believe there were this many on our ship?"

Ethan's eyes scanned the room as she went on. He felt disoriented, surrounded by the people who he'd watched over in their sleep, seeing them moving, laughing, talking. It seemed surreal.

He realized that Aria was watching him. As he met her puzzled eyes, the lights in the big hall dimmed, and the crowd quieted. Aria turned reluctantly to look at an enormous screen at the front of the room. The first images of the reorientation video began to flash.

A mellow male voice began to speak. "For centuries men dreamed of finding paths through the stars to new worlds. Today, you are the fulfillment of those dreams." Stars streaked by on the screen, superimposed with a map of the route from Earth to Minea. The image faded into a video clip of a greater erleckt, a large, heron-like bird, standing knee-deep in a pristine Minean lake. "Today, you will see with your own eyes a new world." Instrumental music swelled. "*Your* new world. Minea. Your new home." Shots of Minea's woodlands, plants, and animals, interspersed with images of the cottages and people of the Minean colonies, accompanied the narration.

Ethan tried to focus, tried to avoid thinking about what he should do when the movie ended.

"Over the next thirty minutes," said the video. "You will learn what to expect—from yourself and from Minea. You may be feeling afraid, apprehensive, or confused about how little time seems to have passed. As we discuss what you can expect to find in your new home, you will soon find any negative feelings transforming into excitement and confidence. When you leave the reorientation hall today, you will do so armed with all the knowledge you need to understand life on Minea."

Ethan glanced again at the people surrounding him. Suddenly, he registered a change in the familiar video. He looked up to see, on the screen in front of him, a familiar face.

Kaia.

"Armed with all the knowledge you need," she repeated.

Ethan looked around again. No one else seemed to have noticed the abrupt change in the video. Of course, they wouldn't notice. They'd never seen it before.

Kaia went on, "Your journey here should have been peaceful. You should have—" Here the original movie came back in, and the male narrator's voice continued the original narration.

"—slept peacefully for what seemed only hours while your ship was guided smoothly on its course through the stars to this world. Your Caretaker saw to every detail, though the ship did all the work. As you know, you were brought in a state of suspended animation called stasis across vast empty stretches of space to awaken here on Minea—"

Kaia appeared again. "Only space wasn't that empty, and you were not intended to wake up here on Minea." Suddenly, images began to flash across the screen; images that made Ethan's skin crawl and forced shocked gasps from the crowd around him.

Traxoram. The clear cottages on Beta Alora. The auction house. The Others. The images flashed, and all the while Ethan trembled, remembering.

Video from the secret meetings of the Earth delegation. David McNeal falling.

Suddenly, it was his own face on the screen. Kaia told the story of Beta Alora, how he'd defeated Traxoram, how he'd saved them all.

Aria was staring at him, wide-eyed.

The video transitioned back to images of Minea, but Kaia's voice continued. "You deserve to know what happened while you slept. You deserve to know what your government did and who really got you safely to this new world. It's up to you to make sure it never happens again." An image of Ethan lingered a moment more, and then the screen went blank.

The hall was quiet, still, waiting. Then, seemingly all at once, the passengers began to speak, to cry, to shout. They clamored for answers, for reasons. They pulled their families to them, the images of the horrible creatures still flashing in their minds.

Ethan reached for his wife. She clung to him. Her voice was small and hoarse. "Is it true?"

He nodded.

Just then, the man next to him grabbed his shoulder. "Hey! You're the guy from the film! You saved us!"

Ethan sputtered to answer, but someone in the next row had heard the man and reached out to grab Ethan as well. Within seconds, he was being propelled to the front of the now cheering crowd.

They laid their hands on his arms, shook his hands, and slapped him on the back. He knew them as he passed each one, knew where they'd come from, knew which of the other smiling faces they belonged with.

Standing in front of them, he drew a deep breath.

Out of the corner of his eye he detected a quick movement. As he turned towards it, he felt two men grab him by the arms. They rushed him out of the hall.

Looking over his shoulder, Ethan's last glimpse was of Aria's pale face in the clamoring crowd.

CHAPTER 39

Ethan was rushed to a glassed-in room. The men departed without a word.

Within minutes, a man in a dark blue uniform appeared in the hallway. The man entered the room and sat down, gesturing at one of the empty chairs. He looked oddly familiar to Ethan.

"Sit down, son."

The sound of his voice brought recognition. The man was General Reagan, Kaia's father.

Ethan sat across from him.

"You're a rather remarkable young man," he began.

"General, I want to be with my wife."

"I'd think so," he replied. "As soon as we're done visiting, we'll get you right back to her. For now, though, don't worry. She's resting in the infirmary. She's fine and just as anxious to see you as you are to see her."

"What do you want from me?" Ethan hated the feeling of being a prisoner again.

"Well, you can imagine that the little video in there has got people pretty riled up."

Ethan nodded coldly.

"It's nothing compared to what happened when the news hit Earth, though. Kaia sent broadcasts back to them and forward to Minea. She told the whole story, and apparently set off quite a storm."

Ethan almost smiled. "I'm not surprised."

"Me, neither. That's just what she should have done."

"So the news preceded us, then?"

The general nodded. "The whole government was tossed out and reorganized. I've only been here a little while, but it seems we're a lot better off. You probably know that I didn't agree with the way things were being run before."

Ethan thought for a moment. "You've retained your rank, I see."

Reagan nodded. "Advanced in rank, actually. Kaia made a point to illustrate my dissent. I've gotten more credit than I deserve. I hate that I was ever a part of it at all." His eyes held a faraway look.

"So it sounds like everything's fine," Ethan said. "Why am I here at all?"

"I wanted to prepare you. You're something of a celebrity on the planet. They're going to be making all kinds of offers. Don't be surprised if they want you to be president."

"You're joking."

Reagan shook his head. "And there's something else. I brought you here to ask you a question." Reagan's eyes suddenly shifted and he fixed his gaze on the table. His shoulders slumped a bit.

"What is it, general?"

Reagan took a deep breath. "Do you know where my daughter is?"

The question hit Ethan like a punch in the stomach. "What do you mean?"

"There's no sign of her."

Ethan felt sick. He put his spinning head in his hands for a moment.

Suddenly, the air around them exploded with sound. Ethan whirled toward the wall of windows that faced the hallway. There, pounding on the glass with both fists, was Aria.

"Let me in!" she shouted. Her face was red and her chest was heaving. She'd obviously run here.

Behind her stood two helpless-looking soldiers, obviously seeking direction from the general inside the room.

"I want to talk to my husband!" Aria shouted. "Open the door!"

The general stood. "I guess she's not resting." He nodded at the soldiers and they keyed a code into the door.

The plate of glass slid open and Aria threw herself into the room and into Ethan's arms. "They told me I had to rest. They said I couldn't leave, that I'd never find you anyway. I said 'Watch me.'"

In spite of himself, Ethan smiled. "I'll bet you did."

Aria pulled away and looked him in the eye. "What is going on? Is all that stuff in the video true?"

He nodded.

"So you really saved us all?"

Ethan shrugged and drew her close to him. "I was only thinking about saving you."

Her eyes searched his for a moment, then she looked questioningly at General Reagan.

He smiled and extended his hand. "I'm Phillip Reagan. Your husband is a hero, young lady."

She smiled at him. "I'm Aria."

Ethan leaned on his wife, feeling very tired. "Are you sure she's not here?"

The general shook his head, and Ethan saw a great sadness in his eyes. "We've looked everywhere."

Suddenly Aria flinched almost imperceptibly under Ethan's arm. His attention was immediately drawn to her.

"Are you all right?"

She began to answer, but her face contorted with pain, and she bent over.

Reagan stepped forward swiftly and steadied them both, pulling a chair around for her with his free hand. She relaxed a bit as she sat down, and he looked at the young couple for a moment.

"We should get you both to your home. Our business can wait till you've rested a while."

Ethan looked at him and then back to his wife. He nodded. "Let me get her home."

When Aria seemed steady, the two men helped her out of the chair and down the long corridor outside the glass room. They turned out of the corridor into a wide lobby, where the walls were hung with burgundy tapestries. It was filled with people. When they saw Ethan, they turned toward him. A cheer went up, and they moved forward as one.

General Reagan stepped up. "People, please," he said loudly, "Mr. Bryant and his wife are tired. She needs to rest. We are taking them to their new home now, but we'll arrange for Mr. Bryant to speak to you all when he's had some rest. Please."

The people, smiling and waving at Ethan, stepped back respectfully. As he passed, they patted his back, touched his arms and hair, and spoke gentle words of appreciation.

The ride in the hover car was a blur. Before they knew it, the hover car stopped and Ethan saw, for the first time, the little blue cottages from the brochures.

"Ethan," Aria said softly, "they're beautiful!"

Ethan felt a subtle apprehension as he looked at them. Each had a small yard with a garden in front. Each had a lovely little rounded door with a window set in it. The general helped them carefully into the house, and Ethan felt a rush of relief when he saw that the interior was unlike the prison houses on Beta Alora. Where those had been cold and clear, these were warm and homey. They felt like new construction, but they also had subtle flaws that lent a distinct air of humanness to the structures.

The men laid Aria down in the master bedroom and closed the door softly.

Before he left, Reagan gave Ethan his communicator code and shook his hand. "Thank you for what you did, son. You saved them when I couldn't."

Ethan nodded. "About Kaia—"

Reagan stopped him. "Call me when you've had some rest. I'm going now to keep looking."

Ethan's head felt foggy as he watched the general go. Kaia. Missing. The thought of the many years that separated them made him feel dizzy. Where could she be?

And Aria. The memory of her flinching in pain drew him to her. He opened the door softly and found her asleep, the covers pulled over her. As he looked around the room, Ethan fought a wave of panic. It was so similar to the cottages on Beta Alora. He forced himself to see the differences. Here, the chair, the dresser, the floors, all felt warm and imperfect and cozy. On the dresser were the boxes containing their belongings from Earth. He crossed and opened them, pulling out the letters and photos, the baseball glove and Aria's wheat.

Ethan sat heavily on the bed next to her. She looked so much like she had for all these years, sleeping, unaware of his turmoil. Yet nothing separated them now. Nothing ever could again. He reached out and touched her cheek. Her green eyes opened and fell on the sheaf of wheat in his hand.

"It made it! All these years! Is the hermetically sealed sample still in there, too?"

Ethan nodded. "All safe."

She reached out and took his hand. "You kept us safe."

He glanced away, not knowing how to feel, and felt her squeeze his hand.

"It's amazing, Ethan," she said softly.

"It sure is." Suddenly, he leaned down and kissed Aria, fiercely. She pulled him close and kissed him back, then pulled him into an embrace.

"We are here, honey," she said, "and we're okay."

CHAPTER 40

The windows were dark when Ethan began to awaken. He knew where he was, knew what was happening, but he still couldn't make sense of something. A stray, upsetting thought pulled at the corner of his consciousness.

Aria slept softly beside him. He put an arm over her and pulled himself close to her. As he was drifting back to sleep, the thought hit him with powerful clarity.

Quickly, he rose and slipped out into the chilly night. He oriented himself by looking for the tall, straight shafts that he knew connected the receiving center with the spaceport above and headed down the street toward them.

No one else was up this early. He crossed a wide meadow and three more streets before seeing a hover cab on the curb. Gratefully, he caught it and rode to the receiving center in silence.

Once there, he walked into the lobby. The crowds were gone, and only a sleepy staff member manned the wide desk there.

"Mr. Bryant," he said, surprised. "How can I help you?"

"I need to get back to my ship."

"Yes, sir." The attendant keyed in some information. "Just in time. They finished up with it last night and were going to undock it first thing this morning. You should have a couple hours or so before they get here, though. It's on elevator seventeen."

Ethan, with a renewed energy, sprinted to the elevator. All the way up, images of Kaia's face as she said good-bye flashed in his mind. Getting out at the spaceport, he ran down the long hall and up the ramp into the hold.

The doors to the main part of the ship were closed, and impatiently he barked the order for them to open. He breathed a sigh of relief that his clearance still worked as they slid open and the computer gave him an update on the state of the ship: Docked. Empty.

Ethan wasn't so sure. He broke into a run. In the secondary nav room, Ethan dropped to his knees. The panel came easily away under his hand, and he pulled himself quickly through the hole.

And there she was. Kaia. His Kaia. Sleeping curled in the corner of the tertiary nav room. The sight of her took his breath away.

Her face, in sleep, was soft. The deep wrinkles around her eyes lay still. Her hair, once the color of the night sky, had faded to the color of the stars, but it was still short, and she still retained that ethereal grace. He found himself touching her face, softly, and she opened her eyes.

A smile touched her lips. "Ethan."

He tried to speak, but felt his voice stop on her name and simply pulled her frail body into his arms. They sat, holding each other.

When he finally spoke, he was weeping. "Why? Why, why?" The single word was all he could say.

She was weeping, too, but she responded in a stronger voice. "You know why, Ethan." She pulled back and her fingers traced his face. "We made it. We made it."

His eyes moved back and forth across her features. She was so familiar to him but so different. "But your life, Kaia. Your *whole* life!"

She looked down then, and her fingers moved to her own face. "Yes."

Ethan knew then that he would carry the weight of her sacrifice with him for the rest of his life. He saw himself at her age and knew that even then he would still love her for it.

She smiled, and he felt a thought reaching its warm way into his mind. Their minds were still bridged, and he saw a few glimpses of her life on the ship as he'd slept. He knew, without asking, how those years had been for her.

They embraced once more.

Moments passed, and then he asked, "Why are you in here?"

She drew away from him and seemed unsure for a moment. She looked, then, like the old woman that she was. "I—I don't know what to expect. I don't—I haven't seen anyone, talked to anyone, since you. I—I don't know how to walk back into the world." She wrapped her arms around herself. "I'm scared, Ethan."

Ethan straightened his shoulders. "Me, too, a little. Come on." He held out a hand toward her. "Let's go together."

Timidly, she reached toward him, letting him help her out through the panel. Together they walked down the long corridor toward the new world.

* * *

Ethan heard the crowds before the elevator doors opened. They were even louder than yesterday, and he expected to see the lobby packed again with people. When they finally reached the tapestried room, however, it was nearly empty. He glanced at the front desk attendant, who peered guiltily back at him.

"I'm sorry, sir," the attendant said sheepishly. "I only messaged a couple of friends that you were here."

Ethan looked out the wide glass door and saw a huge crowd. Darkness surrounded them, but they were bathed in the bright lights at the front of the spaceport. They held signs and banners with his and Kaia's names on them. They cheered even louder when they saw the pair reach the door.

The doors opened and he held tightly to Kaia's hand. He had explained to her what he knew as they'd made their way from the ship, but he hadn't expected this. He glanced tentatively at her and found that she was smiling broadly. As he looked back at the faces in the crowd, he saw why. Most of these people were *their* passengers.

As they stepped to the top of the wide stairs that separated them, the cheers were deafening. People climbed to meet them, and they embraced their fellow passengers. These were no strangers, but the people whose lives had hung in the balance as Ethan and Kaia had fought the battles on Beta Alora so many years ago.

Over and over the passengers thanked them, hugged them, kissed their cheeks. They wept, cheered, and thanked them again.

The two were caught up in the joy of seeing their charges and didn't notice at first the quiet figure that pushed his way through the shadows to the front of the crowd and stood watching them. Ethan was the first to see him. He gently laid a hand on Kaia's shoulder and turned her toward her father.

For a moment, the two stood quietly looking at each other. The crowd stilled instinctively and respectfully. General Reagan's eyes were fixed on his daughter. Suddenly, she crossed the distance between them and threw her arms around his neck. Tears slipped out of the general's closed eyes and ran down his cheeks. His lips were moving, but at first Ethan couldn't hear what he was saying. Then it registered. "I'm sorry. I'm so sorry."

Then Ethan heard Kaia's voice, one word, gentle as a bird. "Daddy."

Reagan pulled back, keeping the frail old woman in his arms. "I'm sorry, sweetheart," he said again.

"I know. It's all right."

Reagan shook his head sharply. "It's not. You can be angry at this whole mess. I know what you wanted. You and David. You wanted a life. You wanted a family–"

Unexpectedly, Kaia smiled. She turned and gestured at the crowd. "But look around, Daddy. These are my passengers." Taking her father's hand, she led him to the Karthans, a young family whose four-year-old boy was watching them with wide brown eyes. "This is Alexander. He loves to draw and he wants to be a teacher just like his dad when he grows up."

The little boy smiled widely. "And I want to go out in space again."

"Oh," Kaia said. "That wasn't in your profile. That's new, huh?"

Little Alexander nodded.

"Well, I'm sure you'll get to." Kaia pulled her father gently to a couple standing quietly. "These two travelled together all the way across the sky just so they could get married on Minea and begin their new life together here." The couple smiled at her as she pulled him on to others. After several quick introductions, she turned back to her father. She swept her free hand in an arc, encompassing the throng. "See, I've had a life. I have a family."

CHAPTER 41

In the pre-dawn chill, Ethan, Kaia, and the general stepped out of the hover cab in front of Ethan's little blue cottage. At the window, Ethan saw the outline of his wife against the yellow light of their kitchen window. He almost ran up the path to the door. They were in each other's arms immediately, and they turned together as Kaia and the general entered.

Ethan pulled his wife forward and introduced her.

"Kaia, this is Aria."

Kaia smiled. "I know."

Suddenly, Aria moved forward and threw her arms around Kaia. "Thank you for helping him. Thank you for getting him safely back to me."

Kaia put a hand on Aria's shoulder. "You're welcome. How are you feeling?"

"More pains today. But they're not regular yet."

Ethan felt Kaia's concern before she spoke it. "Sit down. You should rest."

It was then that he noticed how weary Kaia herself looked. "You, too," he said to her.

"I was just thinking so myself." She turned to the general. "We should go." He nodded as Kaia hugged Aria warmly and then put her arms around Ethan. "You two take care of each other."

Ethan felt his breath catch. "But Kaia, I can't let you—how will you—"

"I'll be fine, Ethan. I've gotten along on my own for nearly fifty years, remember?" She smiled. "I'm ready for a little rest, too." Ethan nodded, and Kaia took Reagan's arm. Tears stung Ethan's eyes briefly as another door closed between them.

Ethan turned to see Aria's eyes shining with tears. He laid a hand on her shoulder, and she held his eyes with hers.

"Aria," he said softly, wiping the corners of his eyes. "Here. Sit down."

She shook her head. "Ethan, I've realized something."

He had dreaded this moment since he'd first seen Kaia. He steeled himself as Aria went on.

"You've seen things I can't even imagine. You're different, Ethan. But I'm not. You might be very, very different."

He ached to tell her he wasn't, that he was the same as when they'd left Earth, but it wasn't true, and she'd never allowed him to deceive himself.

He spoke quietly. "I am different. In a hundred ways, Aria. Does that change things?"

Aria grabbed his hands and stared into his eyes with new intensity. She was searching for words. "No, Ethan. I love you still. I love you the same as I did the day before yesterday, back on Earth. I can love the new you. But I'm scared that the new you . . . might not be so excited . . . about the old me." She paused, playing with his fingers, not looking at him. Her voice got softer. "You've shared so much with her. I see how you feel about her. I see what she sacrificed. I'm glad she was with you—that you didn't have to go through it all alone. I love her for that, and I love you. But I don't know . . . how it changes *us*. I just feel like this was supposed to be our adventure, and you've already *had* your adventure. I—I slept through the whole thing."

He loved her for saying it, for opening the door so they could talk about it. He loved that she knew him well enough to know that he was not the same. He loved that he didn't have to pretend to be.

He took a deep breath and then laid a hand on her stomach. "Aria, *this* is our adventure. Everything I did—everything she did—we did to get me to this moment." He leaned forward, asking permission with his eyes. She hesitated and then kissed him carefully. As they pulled apart, the baby under his hand kicked. Ethan smiled, knowing, finally, that he had brought his family safely through the stars. And they could begin again here, in this small, safe place.

Aria stepped back. "It will be an adventure. There's a whole new planet out there waiting for us."

Ethan nodded. "Do you want to take a walk?" he asked, feeling a cool breeze calling to him from the open window of their bedroom. Through it, he could see the tall trees of Minea as morning began to break.

She shook her head. "If I went along, you'd have to roll me down the trail. And I don't want to start those contractions up again. You go, and bring me back some leaves to look at. I've got to get started figuring out the plant life here."

"I will," he said, heading for the door. On his way out he grabbed his journal and glyphtol. The Alorans had presented them to him with some reverence before the ship had left Minea. They had been pleased at his use of Xardn. He smiled, remembering what Lassaya had said as she'd returned the journal to him.

"You use the language well," she'd said. "Your writings show the wisdom of the ancients blended with the unique emotion of your species."

Ethan found a small path through the trees behind the cottage and followed it, taking long strides and deep breaths. This world felt solid and real under his feet. The trees surrounding him were beautiful in their imperfections, the sky lovely in its arcing grandeur. The path inclined, and he rose with it, higher and higher until his lungs burned. By the time he reached the top of the hill, he felt strong and invigorated. Below him, the cottages slept. He crossed the crest of the hill and saw, on its other side, a wide lake stretching away from him. Facing the lake, he sat down with his back against a tree, snapped a leaf off a nearby bush, and opened the journal, sliding the leaf into the front cover.

He turned the pages, reading through the entries up to the day of their capture. Reading his thoughts again brought back the sound of Traxoram's voice in the throne room. Traxoram had described love as "the most fleeting and ridiculous of emotions." Ethan thought about that as he sketched several Xardn symbols:

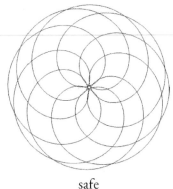

safe

Josi Russell

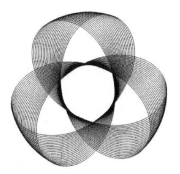

fear

family

home

anger and

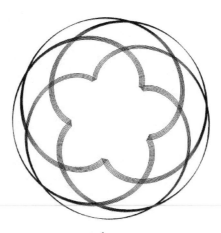

love

He drew the last symbol slowly, thoughtfully. There was nothing ridiculous about the emotion that had moved Kaia to push him into the stasis chamber, nothing fleeting about the place she held—and would always hold—in his heart. And it was his love for Aria that had brought out the incredible powers that his mind and body were capable of. It was his love for her that had gotten him through five years of loneliness, had given him the courage to face monsters, had given him the strength to turn away from Kaia, had driven him across the stars to bring them safely here.

The most fleeting and ridiculous of emotions? It seemed to him that the truth was just the opposite. He had found, through his journey, that everything else changed: anger was momentary. Hatred passed. Fear eventually moved into memory. Love, it seemed to him, was perhaps the only emotion that endured.

He stood and looked up from the journal to see the sky lightening. The rippling lake caught the light and reflected it back to the sky, making the surrounding forest seem darker by comparison. Out of that dark wall of trees, Ethan watched two calterleks emerge carefully. He'd seen them in photos before: large hairy creatures whose bearlike heads belied their gentle, flighty nature. He watched them standing motionless in the last shadows at the lake's edge. Though they were unfamiliar and strange, he felt a kinship to them as he, too, stood anxious and eager at the brink of the coming day.

ALSO BY JOSI RUSSELL

We appreciate your purchase of this book. We hope you enjoyed it, we had a lot of fun making it! To help us keep telling great stories, we'd love it if you could take a few minutes to leave us an honest review. Thank you in advance!

If you love Caretaker, then you might also like Josi Russell's other books.

Caretaker Chronicles

Caretaker

Guardians

Sentinel

Stasis Dreams
A Short Story

ABOUT THE AUTHOR

Josi Russell teaches creative writing and fiction courses as an associate professor of English for Utah State University Eastern. She lives in the alien landscape of the high desert American Southwest with her family and a giant tortoise named Caesar. Josi is captivated by the fields of linguistics, mathematics, and medicine, by the vast unknown beyond our atmosphere, and by the whole adventure of being human.

Connect with Josi Russell:
http://www.josirussellwriting.com
http://facebook.com/authorjosirussell
http://twitter.com/josi_russell

GET IN TOUCH

Interested in having Josi Russell come visit your school? Have a question about the series or want to talk with the Future House Publishing team?

We'd love to hear from you! Follow us on social media, visit our website, or send us an email.

For more information visit us online at www.futurehousepublishing.com or contact us: books@futurehousepublishing.com

Please join our mailing list for new releases, exclusive offers, and our best deals. You can join by visiting www.futurehousepublishing.com!

Printed in Great Britain
by Amazon

22185069R00148